The men and women around the table nodded. Scillia was not a great favorite at the moment, being a cranky thirteen-year-old. But she *was* the heir and no one doubted her strength of purpose, or her mind, which was quick. Or her heart.

Carum continued, speaking to the window. "The Garum heir is—as I now understand—already fifteen and as hard and unyielding as his father, Kras. This younger one is of a tender disposition. And he has formed an attachment to Corrie. They are already like brothers."

"Squabbling, you mean," Piet said.

"Not at all," Jenna put in. "He looks up to Corrie. He calls him 'Killer of Cats'—a slight exaggeration."

A ripple of laughter ran around the table.

"He can be molded." Carum turned and looked directly at Piet as he spoke.

Piet unflinchingly returned that gaze. "So can young Jemson."

Jenna shivered. *That* had been in her mind from the first.

By Jane Yolen published by Tom Doherty Associates

The Books of Great Alta
(comprising *Sister Light, Sister Dark*, and *White Jenna*)
Briar Rose

Edited by Jane Yolen
Xanadu
Xanadu 2
Xanadu 3

With Music of the Dales
by Adam Stemple

Jane Yolen

A Tom Doherty Associates Book
New York

THE ONE-ARMED QUEEN

A Tor Book
Published by Tom Doherty Associates, LLC
175 Fifth Avenue
New York, NY 10010

www.tor.com

ISBN: 0-812-56479-0
Library of Congress Card Catalog Number: 98-23525

First edition: November 1998
First mass market edition: August 1999

Printed in the United States of America

0 9 8 7 6 5 4 3 2 1

For Elizabeth Harding
and Louisa Glenn—
They know why

One to make it,
Two to break it,
Three to carry it away.

—An old prophecy

one

Rivals

THE MYTH:

Then Great Alta took the warrior, the girl with one arm, and set her in the palm of Her hand.

"There is none like you, daughter," quoth Great Alta. "Not on the earth nor in its shadow. So I shall make you a mate that you might be happy."

"And why must I have a mate to be happy?" asked the one-armed girl. "Do you, Great Mother, have a mate? And are you not happy? Perhaps I could be your blanket companion."

"To reach too high is to fall too far," Great Alta replied.

THE LEGEND:

When the White Queen Jenna was still alive, she brought her three children to the town of New-Melting-by-the-Sea where she still, herself, had cousins.

The children were twin boys and a girl whose short cropped hair and leather trousers led her to be mistaken for a third boy.

The queen planted a rowan by the old Town Hall, the boys each planted a birch. But that night, the girl sneaked out from the encampment and broke off the tops of her brothers' saplings, leaving only the rowan standing whole.

In the morning she confessed her crime and was whipped in front of her mother by the head of the royal guards with switches from those same damaged trees.

But lo! After the queen's entourage left the town, the rowan tree died. However, the birches grew round and about one another, twisted and twined.

You can see them there still by the tumbled wall. They are old and weathered, their trunks supported by metal poles. They are so grown together, they are often mistaken for a single tree.

THE STORY:

The queen's party had passed by the Old Hanging Man early in the day, but the weather was so foul, nothing of the rocks could be seen. Jem and Corrie had been fighting since dawn, the sort of squabbling that seemed to be made up of endless name-calling. Even the queen's good captain Marek could not keep them separated for long.

"Is it the weather?" the queen asked, peering into the gloom. "Or the nature of this place?"

"It is the nature of the boys, Jenna," Marek said, his long friendship with the queen allowing him such familiarity.

"It is the nature of *all* boys," Scillia complained.

Her mother shot her a sharp glance.

"Well, it *is*," Scillia muttered. The stump of her left arm ached, which was odd. It was not an old wound that could be expected to pain her in rain or cold. She had been born without the arm and for her to be one-armed was as normal as for her brothers to have two. But somehow today, riding next to her mother on the endless track, her brothers quarrelsome as pups, she felt an ache there as if she had but recently lost the limb. Reaching up with her right hand, she massaged the shoulder and partway down the stump.

"I will rub oil into your shoulder when we rest, child," the queen said. Scillia did not like the servants to touch her.

"I am fine, mother," Scillia answered. "If only the boys would be silent."

But they would not. Or could not. Calling one another

"Catch-pole" and "Woodworm," "Gar-head" and "Toad," they had settled into a rhythm of slander, beating the names back and forth between them till it got to be a game that eventually had them both laughing.

Scillia only scowled the more.

"It is a boy's nature to make games of troubles," Marek remarked to the queen. "And a girl's nature to disapprove of game-playing."

Jenna sighed deeply and ran a hand through the fringe of her white hair, "I thought, my dear old friend, that we fought a war not thirteen winters past over such gross statements: A boy does this, a girl does that. It does not become you to speak this way."

He smiled wryly at her. "Don't we say in the Dales: *A snake sheds an old skin but still he does not go skinless*."

She had the grace to laugh back at him. Shaking her head, she added, "Then I will expect to have to skin you now and again. Just for old time's sake."

"As you wish, my queen." He saluted and kicked his horse into a trot till he had caught up with the boys. By riding between them and telling them some of his old war stories, he managed to turn their attentions elsewhere and the game of calumny was ended.

"Why do you put up with him, mother?" Scillia asked when Marek was too far away to hear. "Why do you just make light of such things? Why do you . . ."

Jenna turned to her daughter. "Do you remember the old saying, *Before you make a friend, eat dirt with him?*"

Scillia shook her head. "I always thought that a particularly dim bit of wisdom."

"Not if you had eaten the dust of travel and the clods of battle with him. Not if you had buried dear ones and had him weep silently by your side."

"Battles and wars. It is all you ever talk about."

Jenna's face went first red, then white. "I talk peace and pacts, child. I talk of rebuilding lives."

"When I was young you talked of that. Now it is all rumbling about war. The war that was, the war that will come." Scillia's voice was high and harsh.

The queen's white horse seemed to take exception to the tone of the girl's voice and shied from it as if from a serpent on the ground. It took Jenna a moment to calm the mare down. When the horse had at last returned to its good ground-eating walk, she looked at her daughter with as mild an expression as she could muster. "You are still young and therefore I forgive you."

"I am thirteen. And the boys are nine and ten. Old enough, mother."

"Old indeed," her mother said. Then, fearful of saying more, she kicked her horse into a canter, passing Scillia, the boys, Marek, and the small bodyguard with ease.

•

THE BALLAD:

THE TWO KINGS

There were two kings upon the throne,
Lonely, oh lonely, the queen rides down.
There were two kings upon the throne,
When one was gone, one ruled alone,
The queen rides in the valley-o.

The one ruled East, the one ruled West,
Lonely, oh lonely, the queen rides down.
The one ruled East, the one ruled West,
And neither ruled the kingdom best,
The queen rides in the valley-o.

Ill fares the land where two are king,
Lonely, oh lonely, the queen rides down.
Ill fares the land where two are king,
For names and swords and bells do ring,
And blood flows down the valley-o.

THE STORY:

Lunch was a dismal affair, as they ate at a local farmhouse. Eating with the villagers—usually the lowest of villagers at that—was one of the things the queen always insisted upon. She would never eat at a Village Hall under the watchful eye of some magistrate or other. She considered it the mark of her reign that she cared for the poorest folk first. And she always paid for what food they ate. Unfortunately, that was no guarantee of the cook's skill.

Scillia toyed with the stew on her plate. It had not been a good winter; two months of deep frost had frozen even the deepest of root cellars. The vegetables in the stew were tasteless, the chicken clearly had starved to death. And the farm wife, a matronly woman with a half-cast in her right eye, had never been taught the use of strong spice. Scillia thought of the castle's kitchen with longing.

The boys ate it all uncomplaining. They even asked for seconds. The farm wife gave it to them cheerfully, chucking each of them familiarly on the cheek. She was unaware that it was sheer bulk they were after.

The pudding was a swollen, pasty thing. Jenna smiled as she ate it, and the boys shared Scillia's helping after she refused it. Marek ate his without complaint, used to such fare himself since a boy. The bodyguard had their supper of trail rations outside and when the farm wife brought them what was left over from the queen's table, they were grateful for every bit.

Once the farm wife disappeared outside with the scraps, Jenna turned to her daughter. "You *must* learn to disguise what you feel."

"Why?" Scillia toyed with one of her braids. "Don't you always tell me to be honest?"

"There is honesty—and brutal honesty," Jenna said. "Something I have learned these last years on the throne. Villagers have quite enough of honest weather and honest frost. But if they believe you believe in them, they will follow anywhere a queen leads."

"I will never be queen, so what does it matter," Scillia said. "I am not deaf; I have heard the talk. I am not your true daughter. I was the daughter of some warrior killed in the war. Jemson will be king." Her face was bleak and there was the beginning of a line settling between her eyebrows, drawn in by anger or sorrow.

Jenna was furious. "Who dared tell you that?"

"Well, is it true?"

Her mother was silent.

"True, Queen Jenna. Without disguising what you feel. I am no farm wife to be cozened."

"Where did you hear such a thing?" Marek asked gently, seeing that Jenna was too stunned to reply.

For once the boys remained silent, staring down at their bowls. Jem twiddled with his spoon, as if he could not will his fingers to be still, but young Corrie sat like a stone. When he dared look over at his sister, her face was white and hard.

"Where?" Marek asked again, only not so gently this time.

"Everywhere," Scillia said. She shrugged but it was no casual gesture. "There is even a rhyme about it."

"A *rhyme* about it?" Jenna's voice was barely a whisper.

Jem's voice sang out:

"Jenna's girl is nowt a queen,
Hair is black and eyes are green,
Only one arm to be seen,
And she's got no father!"

Corrie kicked him under the table and the last word ended on a scream.

"Toad!" Jem cried. "Stupid, sucking toad."

"Marek, take the boys outside," Jenna said, and when no one moved, she added imperiously, "Now!"

Marek stood, his eyes like flint, and ushered the boys out, though it was clear that neither one of them wanted to go. Jem even opened his mouth to protest, and Marek clipped him on the back of the head. That Marek would do such a thing to one of the princes so startled Jem, whatever he had been going to say was forgotten. He put his hand to the back of his head and escaped through the door like a hare through its bolthole.

Jenna waited until the door closed behind them, then took a deep breath, and faced her daughter. Scillia's eyes were clouded with tears, but there were no tears on her cheeks.

"You *are* my daughter," Jenna began.

"The truth, mother," Scillia whispered hoarsely.

"That *is* the truth," Jenna said. "Someone else gave birth to you, a fine warrior, murdered in the Gender Wars. You were strapped to her back. I took you from her and slew the man who had killed her. And from that moment on, you were *mine*."

"And what was my name?" One tear had started out of Scillia's left eye and ran straight down her cheek. She did not bother to wipe it away.

"Your name then—and now—Scillia." Jenna did not move. The light coming in from the window lay across her shoulders like a shawl. She would have welcomed its warmth, but it seemed cold. So cold for a spring day. She shuddered with the chill.

Only then did Scillia scrub at her face with her fist, leaving a dark smear where the tear had traveled. "Why was I not told?"

"What was I to tell you?" Jenna asked. "You are my daughter. My only daughter. Nothing anyone says can change that."

Scillia's shoulders trembled visibly.

"Perhaps I should have said something. Your father wanted you to know. And Skada."

"Your dark sister and father agreeing on something?" That almost brought a smile from the girl.

Jenna took that almost-smile and gave it back to her. "When it is about something I have left undone, they *always* agree," she said. "Oh, my darling child, I would not harm you for the world." She stood shakily and went over to Scillia. Kneeling beside her, Jenna encircled her daughter's small waist with her arms.

It took almost a minute before Scillia trusted herself to reach down and begin stroking her mother's long white hair. It was stiff and wiry to the touch.

They sat that way, not speaking, till the light from the windows dimmed and the cottage was dark with shadows.

"Come, Mother," Scillia whispered at last, "time to have the farm wife light the fire. You can tell Skada all."

"I am sure she knows it already," Jenna said with a sigh. Then almost as an afterthought, she murmured, "And will never let me forget it."

"Neither will I," said Scillia.

Jenna could not tell if that was a promise or a threat.

THE HISTORY:

Memo: Dalian Historical Society

For a biography of my late father, who was a past member of the Society and two-term General Secretary, I am seeking anecdotal material as well as letters concerning his lifelong quarrel with certain individuals in the Society on the subject of the true history of the Dales.

As you are all aware, he felt that history should remain uncorrupted by legend, myth, balladry, and folklore, considering them "cultural lies." And while his own lens may have been somewhat shortsighted, I am not so sure that he was otherwise incorrect in his assessment of matters concerning the indigenous populations of the Dales.

Because of his untimely and tragic death, I have taken on the task of organizing his papers and publishing what will be both a critical and yet loving book about his work, as only a daughter—and fellow historian—can.

Thanking you in advance,

THE STORY:

The farm wife came back into the house to light the fire. Then bowing her way out again, she left Jenna and Scillia together.

Once the fire had caught well enough to throw shadows across the grate, there was a low chuckle from the chair next to Jenna's.

"Sister, too late by half and too short for a whole," Skada said.

"And too cryptic by far for me to understand," Jenna retorted. She pushed her fingers once again through the fringe of hair on her forehead and Skada imitated her. "I hate that kind of talk."

"She means, mother, that you should have told me years ago and you have not told me all of it now."

"She's always been the brightest of your children," Skada said. "Though Corrie's a love."

"Don't push me." Jenna turned angrily to her dark sister.

"I only say what you will not." Skada glowered back at her. "And Jem . . ." Jenna's face was suddenly drawn in on itself, like an apple left out all winter. Skada stopped whatever it was she'd been about to say.

"Jem is going off to the Continent when we are back from this trip. A little less family and a little more schooling is all he needs," Jenna said steadily.

"Then I am *not* to be queen," Scillia interrupted. "*Nowt a queen.*" Her voice was eerily like Jem's. "He'll learn about ruling with a hard hand there. I could never do such a thing."

"Of course you are to be queen," Jenna said. "You are the oldest, and that's all there is to it. Your brothers will make you excellent counselors."

"If they ever give up squabbling," Skada added.

"We never have," Jenna said.

She rose and Skada rose with her. They matched pace for pace to the door. Jenna turned suddenly, but not too quick for Skada. Their faces held the same concern as they gazed back at Scillia.

"When I die . . ." Jenna began. "And your father as well. *You* will . . ."

"*If* you die, mother. You are a hero. You are a legend. Such people do not die. They just . . . are no longer physically in the Dales. But they aren't dead." Scillia's face in the shadow looked much older, as if a mask of age had suddenly slipped down over it. "They are always with us."

"Definitely the brightest!" Skada said.

Jenna turned on her heel and flung open the farmhouse

door. The afternoon light slanted down to outline her in the doorway. When she stepped outside, no one was by her side.

"Mother!" Scillia called. There was pain in her voice but little hope. "Mother . . ."

"We ride," Jenna cried out. And without thanking the farm wife, she got onto her horse, kicking it hard enough to surprise it into a canter, leaving Marek to organize the children and guard to follow.

They rode till past supper and into the dusk. As there was no moon to call Skada forth, Jenna rode at the forefront alone.

She was tired. Thirteen years as a queen had exhausted her. She had long found the throne a troubling seat and missed being able to spend weeks off in the deep woods. On the other hand, Carum reveled in the details of the royal work: the sums and substitutions of a kingdom's finance, the niggling judgments, the exacting language of the law. But Jenna hated it, escaping whenever Carum could spare her.

This time he had let her out of a meeting with the mayors and aldermen of the northwest Dales. She had taken both the boys and Scillia with her, promising Carum that they would all stay with the guard. That promise was dragged from her, but she argued more from form than need. Both Jenna and Carum knew she needed the trip and they hoped it would be good for the children as well.

"I will go back to Selden Hame," Jenna had said. "Scillia has never been inside. It has been years since I've gone myself. Once we are safe within, the boys and the guard can stay in the village."

"I know how much you have missed Pynt and the women," Carum had answered. The years sat more lightly on his brow than on Jenna's, though his hair was now as white as hers. "And I know all the letters back and forth between you and

Pynt have still not salved the wound of parting. You were friends long before I found you. Selfishly I took you from her. But it was for the kingdom. The people needed their Anna, their White One."

She had waited, not smiling, but knowing that he would say the words which, as ever, she could not resist.

"As do I, sweet Jen. As do I."

"I will not stay at the Hame, Carum. I will return. I am like the old tale, the girl who could not stray from home." She had smiled then, putting her hand on his.

"But which is your home, I wonder?"

She knew he asked the question to himself and so did not return him an answer.

As they rode, Jenna remembered the scene with some sorrow. She bit her lip, guessing how Skada would have played it out. "But I am *not* my dark sister," she whispered to herself, knowing full well that she had talked to Carum about the trip in the palace garden in daylight just so Skada could not intrude her sharp wit into their conversation. Just as Jenna always lay with Carum in the full dark of their room, the great wine-colored drapes pulled tight across the oriel windows and the fire burned down to embers. Skada might be her shadow, her other self, but there were some things Jenna preferred to do without her.

She remembered suddenly the birth of her first son. Jem had arrived with difficulty, laboring thirty hours to creep from her womb. He had tried to make up for it ever since: walking early, talking early, fighting early, always at odds with both his brother and his sister, the uneasy in-between. She loved him the more for it, her difficult first-born.

Skada had insisted on sharing the second birth and, as she predicted, the birth had been easier therefore. But then Corrie had always been an easy child. Easy and stubborn at once. Jenna could not sort it out.

But of the three, Scillia was the child of Jenna's heart, and she had always hoped that, woman-to-woman, they would live into old age together. More like sisters than mother and daughter; they were not, after all, that many years apart. And so it had been, until this last year when Scillia had changed beyond reckoning: critical, unhappy, listless—and always angry. Jenna could not remember having herself gone through such a change.

"You spent your change-time fighting a war," Skada reminded her. "With me by your side. Who had time for such drama when people were dying? Who had time for selfishness when there was blood being spilt?"

But that did not explain it. Not at all.

They entered the town of Selden in the dark. The Hanging Man hostel had been forewarned of their coming, and had warm food waiting.

"Scillia and I will go on to the Hame," Jenna told Marek. "We will not stop here with you."

"The guard will ride with you to the walls," Marek said.

"They will not." Jenna yanked on the reins and her mare half rose on her hind legs, whinnying annoyance. "I am not a child to need a nurse."

"You are the queen and need safe passage," Marek said, but found he was speaking to her back.

Shaking her head, Scillia kicked her gelding into a canter. She caught up with her mother a half mile up the road.

They went along in less-than-companionable silence until they came to a bridge where they paused.

"The water is not yet in flood," Jenna remarked dryly, hoping to cut through the uncomfortable tension between them.

"Unlike your temper," Scillia said.

"A *woman's mouth is like a spring flood?* That is a Garunian adage," Jenna said. "I would not have you speaking so."

"Then why are you sending Jem across the sea to the Garuns? That is the very sort of thing he will learn there, and he will be the worse for the getting of such wisdom." Scillia's voice broke in the middle, anger and sadness competing in it.

"I send him for the peace," Jenna said, "which you have so recently accused me of forgetting. And we are taking one of their princes into our court in his stead. It is a kind of exchange to guarantee amity between our lands. Besides, Jem is excited about it."

"What kind of peace is it, Mother, that takes little boys to hold it?"

"I thought you didn't like Jemmie."

The wind had begun puzzling through the trees. Jenna remembered that particular sound, such a part of her childhood in the Hame: trees, river, and the mountainside changing the tone.

"He is my brother and I love him. Even when I cannot abide him."

"He is my son, Scillia, and though I cannot stand the thought of sending him away, it is what is best for our land. Once the Dales had little girls fighting a war. Surely a little boy can be charged with the peace." She kicked the mare into a trot across the bridge and her voice threaded back through the clatter of hooves. "I am tired of talking."

But Scillia would not let it go, and she chattered for another mile up the winding mountain path before the thick, close dark finally stopped her.

When Scillia finally quieted, Jenna relaxed into memory. Even though the forest had changed somewhat in the plus twenty years since she had wandered it alone—fourteen years as queen, the several years of war, the five years under the hill with Great Alta—by squinting she could still see the place as it had been. It was a palimpsest forest, with enough of the old growth left, the old turnings of the road, to remind her.

But she could not get back the child she had been, who had played the Game of Memory so well, who could sort out the scratchings of coon and cat and bear with a single glance.

She sighed, a sound well lost in the mix of pounding hooves. But the sigh reverberated inside. It was Scillia's youth and her lack of passion *for* rather than passion *against* that irritated Jenna. She remembered herself at age thirteen, and Scillia was no mirror of that girl. Skada's answer that it had been a war that made the difference between them was not answer enough.

Perhaps, Scillia will find that child at the Hame, she thought. But she did not dare finish that thought: that perhaps she might find the child she had been there as well.

THE HISTORY:

From a letter to the editor, Nature and History, Vol. 45:

Sirs:

Your recent article on "The Last Goodly Hame—A Look at the Walls of Selden" by that eccentric scholar, Lowentrout, makes much of the folk history of the area. But to state, as he does, that Selden Hame remained a center of culture and learning for women of Alta and their dark sisters, merely perpetuates the myth that the Dale females were able to call up some mysterious Other Self. I thought we had long ago dismissed such maunderings as mere fairy stories.

It is clear from the stones that have been examined by careful scientists, that the walls that stand on the site are but several hundred years old, not a thousand. The wall construction is typical of the Middle Period, not the Old Dales. Lowentrout's assumption that there had been new buildings built exactly over the bones of the old, because of stories of ghosts or some such, merely flies in the face of science and technology.

As long as we repeat the old legends and folk tales as something more than simple imaginative stories, using them to reconstruct a historical base, we will continue to make the same old mistakes in our archeology. There were no dark sisters; the great Queen Jenna was but a jumped-up folk hero, more legend than real. And as for those beliefs that state she and her consort still sleep Under the Hills till the Dales shall need them again . . . well, really! That's a folk motif that can be traced all around the world and is typical of hero tales in most primitive lands.

THE STORY:

As they approached a seemingly impenetrable rock face, Jenna waved her hand oddly at it. The trail twisted abruptly to the right and up and the mare followed it without urging. Scillia's gelding plodded placidly along behind.

"Was that some kind of signal?" Scillia asked.

"Yes."

"Wouldn't they have changed the sign after so many years?" Scillia's voice held a measure of amusement.

"I do not even know if they still use watchers at the turnings," Jenna said. "But the hand has its own memory. I could no more have gone past here without signalling than . . . Wait!"

They both reined in their horses, for a light of some kind seemed to be coming down the mountainside toward them. When the light came closer, they saw it was not a single light, but two torches—held aloft by a pair of women.

"Hail, Jenna," the watchers said together. "Hail, Scillia, daughter of women."

As the torchlight touched her horse's back, Jenna felt the familiar warmth of Skada behind her.

"And what do you return to them?" Skada whispered into her ear.

"Hail, sisters," Jenna said. And all her anger and troubled thoughts slipped away with the words.

They rode slowly along the path, following the torchbearers. The light only occasionally fell upon Jenna and so Skada flickered in and out of hearing. But whenever she was there, comfortably behind Jenna on the mare's broad back, she continued to comment on everything along the way.

At last Jenna held up her hand for silence. "Enough! You are worse than a jay."

"I *would* prefer conversation," Skada said. "But who is to supply it? Scillia is all but asleep on her horse and the two up ahead are paying us no heed. As for your sulking presence . . ."

"I am remembering, not sulking."

"With you the two are often the same," Skada said.

"And with you . . ." But whatever it was Jenna was about to answer was never spoken aloud, for just then the great wooden gates of Selden Hame were pushed open by the torchbearers and light blazed forth in welcome.

The doorway of the main house was crowded with women, all in pairs, except for one small woman at the front who was singularly alone. Her black hair was worn long in a warrior's braid but curled like a crown atop her head. It added little to her height. So fine-boned, she seemed almost a girl but for the great strength of purpose that shone in her face.

"Pynt!" Jenna cried out, leaping from her horse. She held out her hands to the small woman.

"I am called Marga now," the woman said sharply. "Or as the M'dorans among us say, *Marget*. No one but you knows me by that old name." She touched hands with Jenna, then Skada, then turned to help Scillia down. "And this, of course, is the M'doran child."

"My child," Jenna said.

Scillia held out her one hand to the small woman but did not say anything, being slightly overwhelmed by fatigue and the fact that the woman—Marga—had challenged her mother. No one—except maybe Skada and her father, Carum, and old Marek—*no one* spoke like that to Jenna. As much as her mother liked to believe she was of the people, Scillia knew they held her in too much awe, as both a legend and their queen, to talk back to her.

"Her womb mother was Iluna. You have raised her in a hero's place."

"Pynt, she is *my* child in all but birth. How can you, above all people, say other?" Jenna's face was no longer shining with pleasure, but beginning to darken. Skada's face was glowering even more.

Marga pulled Scillia close to her and with the light on them for a moment—just a moment—they looked like a pair of dark and light sisters. "I am True Speaker for the M'dorans, Jenna. I say what must be said. I do not say it in anger or in chastisement. But it must be spoken for truth's sake." She turned a moment and whispered something to a woman near her, then turned back. "But come, we have a light meal for you. It is never good to sleep on an empty stomach, worse to sleep right after too great a meal." She smiled briefly and drew Scillia into Selden Hame, forcing Jenna and Skada to follow.

THE SONG:

Pynt's Lullaby

Sleep, my child, wrapped up in a dream,
The stars looking down where you lie.
The stars have no words to tell of your past
And neither, my child, have I.

Sleep, my child, for the past is a dream,
And women do weep that it's gone.
But we shall not weep anymore for the past
For after each sleep comes the dawn.

Sleep, my child, into dawn's eager light
And wake to the song of the dove.
Forget all the dreams of the past, for the past
Is present in all of my love.

THE STORY:

Scillia had no memory of that first meal at the Hame. It was hazed with candlelight, firelight, sleep.

And dreams.

She had dreamed and woken and dreamed again. All that she remembered of those dreams was that someone had been singing to her, and it had not been her mother.

Rising, Scillia got dressed in what clothes had been placed at the bedfoot for her. Not her riding clothes, the leathers stained and smelling of horse, but a soft, white shift with an overdress of linen the green of late autumn. There was a pair of hose in the same green. The boots alone were her own, brown, heeled, scuffed-toed, and comfortingly familiar.

Whoever had left the clothes had also opened the curtains and she could heard mountain doves coo-coo-rooing from the trees outside. It was a homey sound, not so different from that of the birds that littered the hedges and ledges back at the castle.

She went over to the window and looked out. After days of foul weather—spitting rain and a wind that had found every crack in her clothing—the sky had finally turned a slatey blue and there was not even a cloud to mar it.

Something moved in the trees closest to her window.

Scillia thought at first it was one of the doves till she glimpsed a stockinged foot and heard a laugh.

"Mother!"

She was shocked beyond measure that her mother should be climbing trees like some young, hoydenish villager, and was preparing to say so when Jenna's face poked through the leaves.

"Awake then, lie-abed?"

"What are you doing out there?"

Jenna laughed again. "Rediscovering my childhood."

Scillia's lips drew down into a thin, disapproving line. "Mother! You are the queen."

"Then I am rediscovering the queen's childhood," Jenna answered placidly, unwilling to be drawn into an argument. "And it included climbing many a tree."

Scillia turned away from the window abruptly and went back to the bed, flinging herself face down upon it. She covered her head with the pillow. *Why*, she wondered. *Why? Why? Why? Why?* She had no idea what it was she was questioning.

She felt a hand on her back and slowly lifted the pillow from her head. Turning over, she expected to see her mother.

It was Marga.

"Brush your hair, child, and come down to breakfast. This first day you will have no chores. We give guests—even royal guests—a day of rest before we work them. Then . . ."

"What do you mean *even* royal ones?" Scillia asked. "I cannot think you have had many."

"Royal guests we work the harder," Marga said. "Though . . ." and here she laughed, "we have had *none* before you."

"As it should be," Jenna said, swinging in through the window. "That you work royal guests the harder, I mean. Does it not say: *The king should be servant to the State*."

"I have never heard that bit of wisdom before," Scillia said.

Marga smiled. "Your mother has spent the morning reading *The Book of Light.*"

"My mother has spent the morning climbing trees," Scillia muttered.

"In many ways it is the same thing," Jenna said. "Come. Let us go down to the kitchen. I am starving."

Marga put her arm around Jenna's waist, as comfortable as any old friend. "You sounded just like Skada then."

"I *am* Skada. Or Skada is me. It is just that sometimes I forget that when the crown sits too heavily upon my head." Jenna draped her arm over Marga's shoulder, and they walked out of the room together.

Scillia would have lingered longer to show her displeasure, her anger, her dismay. But she was suddenly much too hungry for such displays. Without even tidying her hair, she ran after them.

At breakfast Jenna seemed absolutely transformed and Scillia could not get over it. The mother who had been so distracted with matters of state, so distant with worry, so often quick to judge or to correct, was gone. In her place was some stranger who told jokes and laughed loudly, who recounted incidents in which she was as often the villain of the adventure as the hero, and who broke into snatches of old songs.

Scillia was embarrassed beyond telling, and though she had thought herself starving, she suddenly found she could not eat a bite.

She excused herself and left the kitchen, going out the door they had come in, turning right, and quickly getting lost in the maze of halls. At one last turning, she found herself in a room that was steamy and moist.

"Baths!" she breathed, her word almost forming in the hot, wet air. No one had mentioned baths last night, when she had been filthy and aching from the long riding. And though one part of her remembered that she had fallen asleep at the dinner table, the other part counted the lack of mention as a rough snubbing. She turned and walked out of the room, but her clothes were a moist reminder.

"Probably cold water anyway," she muttered, though the steam had certainly argued against that. But she was feeling too put out to let logic get in the way of her anger. With a few more turns, she thankfully found herself outside.

She walked through a courtyard where several straw targets leaned against the stone wall. Three hens clucked at her, but she ignored them. There was an open gate, and she slipped past it.

Clearly it was not the main gate, for there was a meadow on the left, not a forest, and the path that skirted the meadow was not the worn road they had ridden up in the night.

She started down the path, expecting at any minute to be summoned to return to the Hame. She even set her back stiffly, ready to refuse the call.

But no call came.

The path went down steeply at first, then crested over a small rise. At the top of the rise she could see into a great natural amphitheater. Some sort of rough stone altar was at the center of the circle, flanked by three old rowans.

She tried to remember the stories she had heard of the dark and light sisters who had lived in the Hames. A few of the stories her mother had told her, casually, and in an off-handed manner, and only when pressed. Others Skada had recounted, with a great deal more vigor. But Skada's tales were always vigorous in a way scarcely to be relied upon. Most of what Scillia knew about the Hames—Selden being the only one left of them—came from her old nurse. Nana had spoken much about the sisters, and not all of it complimentary.

"Your royal mother, the Anna, being the exception, my cherub . . ." was how many of Nana's stories began.

She could not remember any stories about sacrifice, however, so she wondered what the altar was for.

She must have spoken the question aloud, because suddenly there was an answer from behind her.

"For Mother Alta to sit and rule."

Scillia spun around. One of the sisters of Selden was standing, hands clasped in front of her, smiling. Scillia did not know her name.

"Our last Mother was not a happy woman. She was hard and not always fair. But she was ours and so we loved her. She's dead now, almost ten years. Best to remember only the good of her. *The Book of Light* says: *One can never repay one's debts to one's mother.*"

"Especially," Scillia replied under her breath, "if one's mother is the queen." She went around the woman and back up the path toward the Hame.

THE TALE:

There was once a king who had three daughters, each one more beautiful than the last. But though he loved his daughters well, he loved the golden bird in his garden more.

One day the golden bird disappeared. All that was left was a single feather. The king took the feather and held it to his breast, crying:

> *"Oh, me, oh my, oh me, oh my,*
> *Without the golden bird I shall surely die."*

And he lay down on his bed and was indeed seen to be dying.

The youngest daughter wept and wept until her eyes were red with weeping.

The middle sister threw herself on the floor and thrashed and moaned till she was quite black with dirt.

But the oldest daughter said, "Father, do not die. I shall find your golden bird."

She left the palace and rode and rode until she came to a place where the road forked. There was an old woman, dressed in rags and looking quite pitiful. The princess got down off her horse.

"Old woman, may I help you?"

"Some food and water would be nice," said the old woman.

So the princess gave her food and water and her own crimson cloak besides.

"As you have given something to me, so I will give something to you," said the old woman.

"But you are poor and have nothing to give," the princess said.

"I have something I can give away and yet still keep," said the old woman.

"And what is that?" asked the princess.

"Advice," the old woman replied.

"I am listening," said the princess.

"I can tell you where the golden bird nests or I can tell you where your own fate lies. I cannot tell you both."

The princess shook her head. "My father's fate and mine are intertwined," she said. "Tell me where the golden bird nests and I will get it for my father so that he will not die."

So the old woman told her that, but not where her own fate lay, which was actually quite a different thing altogether, and might have been better for the kingdom than saving a cranky, self-devoted monarch from death.

Do you think the princess made the right choice?

THE STORY:

If Scillia had expected lunch to be different, she was soon disabused of the notion. Her mother acted neither like a mother nor a queen, but some stranger telling tales about other strangers who played at something called the Game and something else called Wands.

"What are those?" Scillia whispered to a woman by her side, a woman whose mouth seemed overfull of teeth.

The woman turned and stared at her. "What? Jenna's daughter has never heard of Wands?" She grinned and the entire range of teeth seemed to conspire at some joke. She turned back to the table and spoke to Jenna. "A child of yours knows not of Wands? Then we must show her."

"I don't want . . ." Scillia began. But the toothy woman already had her by the hand, dragging her up from the table and over to the hearth where a small group of women—including her mother—formed a rough circle.

Marga took a long leather cylinder from the mantel and another woman, a blonde with hair cropped like a man's, took down a small hand drum. As Marga untied the cylinder's top with much ceremony, the women began to chant a slow singsong, accompanied by the steady beat of the drum.

Round the circle, round the ring,
The Wands of Alta now we fling.
Praise Alta's name, all blessings flow,
As round the ring the willows go.

Finally the cylinder's knots were undone and Marga poured a set of twelve ivory-colored willow wands into her left hand. Plucking two wands from the set, she flung them with quick flicks of her right hand one after another into the circle.

One wand was caught by the toothy woman next to Scillia, one by Jenna who was on the other side of the ring from them.

Slip-slap.

They flung the wands underhanded across to one another,

the passage in midair making a strange *shushing* sound. The toothy woman caught hers smoothly, but Jenna had to make a second quick grab for her wand, an awkward recovery.

"You are out of practice, my queen," called Marga as the wands went back again.

Slip-slap.

"With wands," Jenna replied, but she was smiling.

"She is soft," someone else called out.

"A wand is not a sword," Jenna replied, but she was grinning as she flipped the wand swiftly across to the speaker.

Slip-slap.

The wands were traveling more quickly now, end over end, with a fine, sharp rhythm. Then, just as Scillia was getting used to the sound of them, Marga called out "Two!" and set another pair of wands flying.

Now the game became considerably more complex, as four willow wands cartwheeled through the air.

Slip-slap.

Slip-slap.

"Two!" Marga called again, adding a third pair to the ring.

Several more women left the table to enter the circle and soon Scillia lost count of the number of wands whizzing past.

"Two!" Marga called again. And again, "Two!"

"You catch one, child," the toothy woman whispered to her. "Go on. We like to say, *A girl is never too young for the game*."

"I can't," Scillia said, turning her head and gesturing with her hand, as if to remind the woman she had but one. As she turned, a wand smacked into her hand.

Slip-

But the satisfying echo of *slap* did not follow as the wand fell, clattering to the floor.

No one seemed to mind. One woman simply leaned down and picked up the wand and the game continued.

But Scillia minded. "It is a stupid game for old women to be playing at," she said, walking out of the circle and heading toward the door. Her palm tingled where the wand had slapped it. "And stupider still for a cripple."

Somehow Marga was by her side and with a hand on Scillia's arm, stayed her. "Women with one hand have played before," she said. "Do you think you are the only such one in the world?"

"I think I am the only such one to find it a silly game."

"That is the second wrong thing you have said," Marga told her. "It is not *just* a game. It is practice as well."

"Practice for what?"

"For swords."

"These women are past fighting prime," Scillia said witheringly. "Besides, they are cooks and farmers and carders of wool. I doubt any of them could hold a sword in battle."

"Then you would be wrong a third time," Marga said. "Most of them fought by your mother's side in the great battles of the War, or fought with their backs to the walls for the life of their own Hames. And they are hardly old. Except, perhaps, to one of your age."

Scillia shrugged and turned her hand up to a window's light. There was a bright red mark in the center of her palm from the wand.

"We call that 'Alta's Wound,' " Marga said. "You are one of Hers."

"I am not one of Hers or anyone else's," retorted the girl. "I am my own."

She turned and walked out the door and after several wrong turnings, found her way to the stairs that led up to her room.

Jenna showed up moments later. "You were rude," she said. "And you were unkind. Queens do not have leave to be either."

"I am not the queen, mother," Scillia said. "You are."

Jenna sat down on the bed and looked away from Scillia toward the window where the sky was darkened for a moment by a rush of-flying crows. "I know how to be a queen. But it seems I no longer know how to be a mother. You *try* me, my child."

"I am not a child anymore. I am thirteen. And I am not *your* daughter, though it seems I cannot get out of the habit of calling you mother."

"Is that what this is all about?" Jenna turned to look at her. "Is that what all this tasking has been about?"

"I want to know her name at the very least. And what she was like."

Jenna sighed. "She was . . ."

"Besides being brave and being murdered, I mean," Scillia warned.

"Come, sit by me and I will tell you all." Jenna patted a place by her on the bed.

"Are you ordering me as my queen?"

"I am asking you as your mother."

"I prefer to stand."

Jenna sighed again. "Her name was Iluna and she was one of the few who ever saw that I was a woman, not a myth. I liked her for that."

Scillia sat on the bed, as if her legs would suddenly no longer hold her up, but not too close to Jenna. She left enough space between them that another woman might sit there.

"Iluna." Scillia made the sound of the name last a long time.

"She lived atop a rock with her sisters."

Scillia leaned toward her mother. "A rock? What do you mean?"

"There was a Hame called M'dorah carved into a great

cliff. And there Iluna lived with her sisters. They did not have a Mother Alta, a priestess, to lead them, as did all the other Hames. Instead they had someone called a True Speaker who . . ." Jenna's voice trailed off. "My little Scillia, do you really want me to tell you all of this? What does it matter now? I have forgotten so much."

Scillia pulled back from her, sitting up straight. "It matters to *me*. She was my real mother. I want to hear it all."

"The True Speaker told us that they had broken with the other Hames and worshipped the real Alta who waits in the green hall where no one stands highest when all stand together."

"And what does *that* mean?"

Jenna stood and walked over to the window. "If you interrupt me, the tale will never be done."

"Done? You want it *done*? I want to hear it now. This moment. And tomorrow. And the next day after that. I want you to repeat it to me till the parts you have forgotten come back to you. This is my life, oh queen, that you have purposely kept from me. *Yes*—I want to hear it all!" Scillia's body shook with her anger.

"Then listen. At that place, M'dorah, where I had gone to enlist more warriors to our cause, there were many women. But the very first to volunteer to fight was Iluna. She said—and this I will never forget—she said 'I will go though no one else goes with me.' Though of course *you* had to go with her, tied as you were to her back by cradle strings."

"I was tied to her by more than that. By flesh. By blood."

"Not by flesh. Not by blood."

Scillia stood and went over to stand so close to Jenna, their shadows were one on the rush floor behind them. "What do you mean?"

"The M'dorans got their daughters from the New Steading folk. They took those the countrymen left out, neglected, ill-treated, or threw away. Iluna told me that is where she found you."

"But Marga said Iluna was my womb mother." Scillia unconsciously began to rub the shoulder of the stunted arm. If she was unaware of the gesture, Jenna was not. She reached out and gently pulled the unresisting girl to her.

"Marga did not know Iluna. I let the story stand."

Scillia spoke, her words partly muffled in Jenna's shirt. "Was I thrown away because . . . I was not whole?"

Jenna stroked her hair. "I was whole, my darling, and yet I, too, was thrown away as a babe. Girls were of such little value in those days. It is a custom your father and I have worked hard—and fought hard—to change. No children—boys or girls—should ever again be lost that way."

They stood, breast to breast, mother to child, until the darkness beginning in the sky was neither crows nor clouds but simply day's end. They did not cry for they were past crying with one another. But they did not speak either, until night rushed in around them.

Then Jenna said, "Do you want to hear more?"

Scillia shook her head imperceptibly, adding aloud, "In time, mother. In time."

THE HISTORY:

Memo: Dalian Historical Society (First Draft)

The materials you have sent over so far included one of Magon's infamous challenges to my late father's scholarship, specifically Magon's insistence that the empty leather cylinders found at the Sigel and Salmon digs—which he labeled "wand carriers"—was further proof of the dark sisterhood in the Hames. It is yet another quarrelsome piece in the war of words my father had with this ~~insufferable~~ man. I hesitate to use the word "scholar" in his case.

Is it not laughable that, so many years after their conflict,

Magon's words still have the power to wound me. Of course, his work is now mainly discredited and the dark sister thesis, which he held on to so tenaciously, is hardly even referred to in scholarly circles any more. But it is fascinating to see how he tries to bend or warp every Dalian artifact to prove his ludicrous point. Metaphysical claptrap it was then, and metaphysical claptrap it remains.

But what else can we expect from a man who spent his final years in front of one of the excavated mirrors trying ~~in vain~~ to call up his own Dark Brother? If his ending had not been so pitiful, it would have been amusing. I have actually considered writing a screenplay based on his life.

This brings me to the core of this memo. To whom must I apply for permission to print the unpublished memoirs and memoranda from Magon? I am sure that if Magon's entire correspondence with my father and other members of the Society were made available to the general public, my father would finally be ~~avenged~~ given the credit he deserves.

THE LEGEND:

It was in the town of New Teding, at the yearly Lammas Fair, that a certain Mrs. Morrison saw the one-armed child. A baby it was, unwrapped and sleeping, lying in a cradle of rushes near the Clamat River.

Thinking the child's mother was nearby, Mrs. Morrison did naught but cluck at its poor missing arm, and cover it up with the blanket. Then she went on to the Lammas Fair with her pies.

On returning, she saw the basket still out in the open air. And thinking that was surely a long time to leave a child on its own, she went over to check on the puir wee thing.

This time there was nothing in the cradle but a figure of sticks, one branch of which was broken off at the crossing. It was a tinker's sign.

Mrs. Morrison thought nothing more of this, till the following year when she was once again going home from the Lammas Fair, and she once again took the shortcut past the river.

There was the rush cradle again, lying on the river bank, close by the water.

Being a good soul, though a bit nosy if truth be told, Mrs. Morrison went over to peek in. There was nought lying in the rushes but the figure of sticks with the blanket snugged up under its broken-off arm.

The next year Mrs. Morrison took a different route home. Best to take care. There is no knowing what the tinkers—the Greenmen—will do if you meddle too often with their things.

THE STORY:

That evening, before dinner, the women of the Hame gathered in the amphitheater. It was in the lee-time of the moon, and so but half the sisters stood silent in the meadow. Once the torches around the inner bowl were lit, the number of women was immediately doubled. Only Marga and Scillia were without a dark twin.

Standing next to Marga, her cape pulled tight against the cold, Scillia asked, "Why of all these women are you alone?"

"A long story, child. But in the short: It was my own choice." She moved away before she had quite finished speaking, the word *choice* floating back to the girl like the train of a bridal dress.

Mounting the steps to the altar, Marga looked neither right nor left till she reached the stone. She put her hand on it, turned, and only then surveyed the women below whose faces were silvered in the flickering torchlight.

"Who bears the child?" she asked.

"Mother, we do." The speakers were Jenna and Skada. They moved to stand by Scillia.

"What are you doing?" Scillia asked.

"Something Jenna should have done thirteen years ago," Skada said. "No one ever said she was quick about things. Though in the old days we did these rites in the summer time, and not on an achingly cold early-spring night."

Jenna took Scillia's hand in hers. Skada covered them both.

"Is this some sort of . . ." Scillia began.

"Hush!" Jenna and Skada said together, pulling her up onto the first of the steps.

"And who bore the child?" Marga asked.

"A woman of New Steading," Jenna said.

"And she gave her away," added Skada.

They pulled the now rigid Scillia to the second step.

"And who bleeds for the child?" Marga asked.

"Iluna, a warrior of M'dorah bled for her," said Skada.

"And now we bleed for her as well," Jenna said.

"Don't *do* this, mother." Scillia's voice was a harsh rasp.

They yanked her onto the third step and Marga leaned forward, holding out a hand.

Scillia was trapped between. Ignoring Marga's hand, she pulled away from Jenna and Skada. "You could have *asked* me."

Marga whispered. "There is no precedent for asking. This is done to a baby. A baby has nothing to say in the ritual. We thought it best therefore . . ."

"Best for who?"

"For you," said Jenna.

"For *whom*!" Skada said at the same time, a hint of laughter in her voice.

"We haven't done one of these ceremonies in years," Marga explained.

"Well, don't start again on my account."

"I told you it was a bad idea," Skada said to Jenna.

"You said it was better now than never."

"I did not."

"Indeed you did."

"Jenna, you have ears like the Garunian cat, the one who hears wind passing but knows not the weather."

Jenna's voice was nearly breaking. "I just wanted Scillia to understand that we had ties, too, greater than old blood. I wanted her to know she is as much mine as Iluna's. And more certainly mine than the poor fool who . . ." Her voice trailed off.

". . . who threw me away?"

It was as though they had forgotten Scillia was even with them. Both Jenna and Skada turned, startled by the girl's remark. But even as they were turning, Scillia pulled loose of them, running down the few steps and past the assembled sisters, going so quickly the tail of her cape fluttered as if there were a strong wind.

"I knew I should never have allowed this," Marga said. "Jenna, you still have the power to talk me into mischief."

For once Jenna and Skada were both silent.

Leaning forward, Marga whispered to them. "Things have changed greatly in the years, my dear friends, though we here at Selden have changed least of all. We do not do these old ceremonies anymore for a reason. There are no more girl children for us to take in, and that is a good thing you have done for the Dales, Jenna. You should have trusted in your legacy. Selden is a Hame for old women now, not girls." She straightened and said in a voice that carried to all: "Let us go back inside. It is too cold to stand about here in the meadow. And the child refuses the rite. We have many chores still, and the infirmarer needs no one sick with a spring chill." She descended the stairs, followed by the still silent Jenna and Skada.

There were whispers as they walked past the rows, but Skada was wise enough not to comment back until they reached the Hame. Then all she said to Jenna was "I did not!"

It was enough.

Jenna returned no answer, but left the well-lit dining hall

at once and went into her bedroom where she guttered the torch against the metal brackets so she might be alone.

Her thoughts were jumbled, water over stone, and though she lay down at last in her bed, she did not fall asleep until dawn.

THE BALLAD:

Song of the Three Mothers

One is the mother who bore me,
In bright red rivers of blood.
Two is the mother who wore me,
Through fire and fever and flood.

Three is the mother who carried me
Year after year after year.
And she is the mother who married me
To my faults and fancies and fear.

One to make me,
Two to take me,
Three to carry me away.

One is the mother who bred me,
A moment of passion and heat.
Two is the mother who fed me
Her blood and milk and meat.

Three is the mother who led me
Through love and pain and war.
She is the mother who's wed me
To all that is worth living for.

One to make me,
Two to take me,
Three to carry me away.

THE STORY:

"Jenna, wake up! You must get up! She is gone!"

Sunlight puddled on the floor near the window, too far from the bed to wake a really deep sleeper. But Marga's insistent voice pulled Jenna out of her dreams at once.

"Who is gone?" she asked sleepily.

"Scillia. She did not come to dinner, but then neither did you. But her bed was not slept in which we found when we went to call her for breakfast. We have searched the Hame for her. She is not here."

Jenna sat up in an instant. "Why did you not call me sooner?"

"We thought she was just hiding. Or sulking. We are not so old that we have forgotten what it is like to be thirteen. And many of the women here were part of the old cullings, adopted into Hames by second mothers. They are not unsympathetic to the child." Marga handed Jenna her leathers.

"Have you forgotten my own history?" Jenna growled. "I had three mothers, just as Scillia had. But worse, there was the scandal of my last mothers, dark and light, who quarreled over me which led directly to their deaths. Surely you recall it?"

Marga did not answer her question, but said only, "Her horse is gone as well."

Jenna pulled on trousers and tunic, then bound up her long braid with a thick ribband. She vowed to herself not to say a word more to Marga about the past. *Only the present.* Finding her boots, she pulled them on with two quick tugs. "Did Scillia take any food as if for a long trip?"

"Not that we could tell."

"Then she was being stupid. She is not trained for the woods as we were, Pynt."

"Perhaps," Marga said slowly. "But perhaps she only means to be gone for a little. To frighten you."

"She *has* frightened me," Jenna said. "And probably frightened herself as well by now. Are there still cats in the woods?" She walked out of the room without waiting for Marga's answer.

Marga followed quickly behind. "They are mostly gone." She almost had to run to keep up with Jenna's long strides. "But it was very cold last night."

"A little discomfort and a little cold should bring her to her senses," Jenna said cooly, but the speed of her steps belied the coolness of her voice.

"It never brought you to yours," Marga replied.

In the kitchen Jenna grabbed up half a loaf of bread and filled a skin with water. "You check the woods close by here," she said to Marga. "I am going on to the village. She may have slept the night with her brothers."

"Send us word."

Jenna was already out the door and heading toward the stable. "I will," she called back.

Only the final word, *will*, floated back to Marga. *Will*. She whispered to herself, "There is already too much *will* in that family." Then she abruptly turned to organize a further search for the girl.

Scillia had left directly from the aborted ceremony, wandering about in the dark woods for hours. Only luck kept her from a rough trail that ended up in a cat's cave. Only luck kept her from a rock slide into an icy stream. She paid little attention to where her feet led her, her anger keeping her warm.

Never, she thought, *have I been so humiliated.* It wasn't true, of course. But truth has little to do with anger. She forgot in her anger the time her brother Jem had tugged so hard at her skirt for attention, the bands on the material had split and he'd fallen backwards, the entire skirt bunched in his little hand. She forgot as well the day in her first year of riding, when the horse had thrown her off and she had landed at the feet of her father who'd been boasting of her skill to a visiting delegation of Garunians. She forgot the hundred of other slights and mishaps that befall a growing girl, even a growing girl who is a princess.

But the more she rubbed this particular wound, the sorer it became.

There was no moon, but the sky was clear and the stars shown brightly. Luck brought her to the road, luck and those stars hanging comfortably overhead. She knew them all from her lessons: the Huntress, the Great Hound, Alta's Braid, and the rest. They showed her the road back to the Hame where in the mid of night she quietly saddled her horse and rode him back down into the village.

The hostel's lanterns were still lit, illuminating the sign. The Hanging Man looked extremely jolly for someone swinging on a gibbet. Scillia shuddered, as much from the gruesome sign as from the cold.

She dismounted and led her horse around back to the inn's stable, giving the horse over to a sleepy stable boy. Then she went around to the front and entered the hostel without even hammering upon the door.

The heat of the place hit her at once. Her eyes teared up and her nose began to run. Quickly swiping her hand across her face, she found the source of the heat: a great open hearth on the north side of the common room. Without so much as a greeting to the innkeeper, she went over to the fire, shrugged off her cape, and held out her hand to the flame.

"There are other ways to get warm, sweetheart."

She turned abruptly and stared at the speaker, a man in his late twenties, a wide gap between his two front teeth, and laugh lines about his eyes like deep scars. At the same time she was taking in his face, he noticed the sleeve of her blouse tucked up to cover the missing arm. Something in his eyes went a bit dead.

"There is a saying in my house," Scillia said coldly. "*Do not roll up your trousers before you get to the stream.*"

The man threw his head back and roared.

Scillia blushed. She had meant to wound him, to make him go away. She had no idea why he was laughing.

"I like women with fire," he said. "As we say in my house: *The sharper the thorn, the sweeter the rose.*"

"And as we say . . ." came a dark voice behind him, "*Do not speak to a man's girlchild lest you come bearing a wedding ring.*" A heavy hand on his shoulder spun the laughing man around.

The laughing man continued to smile, but he put both his hands up. "Peace, traveler, peace. I was just having a bit of fun. I did not know she was your daughter."

"She is a child," Marek said.

"Leave him, Marek," Scillia ordered. "He meant me no harm. Not after he saw my arm, at any rate." She blushed again saying it.

Marek withdrew his hand from the man's shoulder, but only as far as the hilt of his own sword.

"I did not know her for a child," the laughing man continued, his voice remaining calm and even. "I saw only a lovely woman who was all alone at the hour of bedding. And I am always ready to give a compliment where it is due."

Scillia picked up her cape and flung it across both her shoulders.

"One arm or two does not change true beauty," the laughing man added. "Surely you know that." He sketched her a quick bow, saluted Marek, and walked to a back table, far from the hearth.

Scillia watched him go, then turned to Marek. "Why did you say I was your child?" she asked quietly.

"Would you have me tell him—and the world—that you are the queen's daughter? That the queen's two sons lie abed in back with but a small guard to keep them safe? We would be issuing an invitation to every clodpate and dissident to make a run at us. As your father knew. As your mother *should* have known." Marek's face was red with the effort of controlling his anger.

"The people love my father and mother," Scillia said. "Surely we are safe in our own land."

"The people *should* love them," Marek said, "after all they have sacrificed. But it is far easier to love a hero than a king when the small harvest is in and the taxes handed over."

Scillia thought about that for a long moment, looking down at the wooden floor strewn with old rushes. When she looked up again, her eye caught the eye of the laughing man. He winked at her and it made her blush once more.

"And why are you here, child? And come through the dark without an escort of any kind?" Marek asked.

"I could not stand another moment with all those old women. It seemed . . . unnatural."

"Old?"

"Old enough," Scillia replied. And then, to put the knife further in, she added, "Ancient even."

"Your mother gave you leave?" he asked, as she knew he would. He was not called Jenna's Lapdog behind his back for nothing.

"What do you think?" she asked, then added quickly. "I am starving, Marek. I came away without dinner. Is there something in this hostelry to eat?"

Marek turned and went into the kitchen and was back

quickly with a bowl of stew and a mug of cider. "Come, sit and eat it by the fire. The cider is still hot, and the stew is remarkable."

"I would eat by myself," Scillia said in her queen's child's voice.

Marek nodded and took a seat at another table, but pointedly between Scillia and the laughing man.

She ate the stew slowly, savoring it. It was, in its own way, as good as any she had ever got from the castle's cook, savory with sprigs of thyme and marjoram. The cider was a common variety, but spiced with a cinnamon stick. She could feel it go right to her head. Suddenly she was overwhelmingly sleepy.

"I will tuck in with the boys," she said. "No need to fuss, Marek." It stopped him from organizing another room and thereby ruining her plans. "Just show me where they are sleeping."

He took her down the long corridor and indicated with a nod a room to the right. When she went in, closing the door carefully behind her, the familiar smells of her two brothers and their light little snores made her smile for the first time that night.

She lay down on the edge of the bed next to Corrie, wrapped herself in her cape, and was asleep almost at once. She was too tired to dream.

She awoke four hours later with a start when Corrie, in turning over, pushed her off the bed onto the floor. It was still dark out, but through the window she could see the sky was already beginning to lighten along the horizon.

"Pssssst," she hissed at the boys. When neither one wakened, she poked them, then quickly put her hand over Jem's mouth, knowing he'd be the first to complain. "Hush."

"What are you doing here, Sil?" Corrie whispered. "Is something wrong with mother?"

"Nothing is wrong. But we are going off on an adventure." She kept her hand over Jem's mouth just in case. She could always convince Corrie to go along; Jem was another matter altogether.

"An adventure?" Corrie sat up. "What will Marek say?"

"How can it be an adventure if Marek is along?" Scillia whispered back.

Jem eeled away from her grasp. "You just mean he doesn't know . . ."

"Of course he doesn't know," Corrie said sensibly. He was entirely on Scillia's side already. "Where are we going?"

"That would be telling," Scillia said.

"She doesn't know," Jem added acidly.

"I have spent the night exploring the forest between here and the Hame," Scillia said. "I know enough."

"It's cold out," Jem reminded them.

"When you go on an adventure," Corrie said, "cold is part of it." His voice was withering, and Jem gave into it at last, pulling on his clothes quickly so as to be ready first.

"The hardest part will be sneaking out of here without the guard knowing," Scillia said.

"No, that's the easy part." Jem grinned and pointed dramatically to the window. "Marek complained about it but there was no better room for us. Look."

Right outside the window was an apple tree, gnarled and ancient. The boys skinned down the tree with no trouble at all. It was a bit more difficult for Scillia, but she'd been all her life with just one arm. She managed, though not with any grace.

The boys waited at the tree foot and gave her what help they could at the end of her descent; then they held a hurried conference.

"Do we take horses?"

"They will hear."

"Is this an adventure—or an escape?"

"Escape from what?"

"A little bit of both?"

"It is *perishing* cold."

"It is almost spring. What would you have done in winter?"

"Stayed abed."

"Toad, toad, stuck in the mud."

"We're going to freeze."

"Mother says: *Dogs bark, but the caravan goes on*."

"I don't know what *that* means."

"Hush."

They hushed, listened, heard nothing, and as if some kind of agreement had suddenly been reached, turned away from the stables and headed toward the trees behind the hostel. They became shadows and, once in the tree shadows, all but invisible from the inn.

The three remained quiet until the dark of the forest enclosed them. Then Jem began his litany of complaints again.

"It is cold," he said. "And dark."

Scillia made a noise of contempt and added, "Tell us something we don't know."

"Well, it is."

"See, Jem, it will be warm and light soon," Corrie said. "That's why we are in the forest now. To get as far as we can from the hostel before the warmth and the light."

"That doesn't make any sense, you know," Jem answered.

"That's what makes it an adventure," Corrie said.

"Hush," Scillia hissed. "Do you hear something?"

But though they all strained to listen, there was nothing more to be heard.

As they groped their way deeper into the forest, the boys began to enjoy themselves. And as the forest lightened and birds began to decorate the air with song, they started their familiar bantering. But Scillia's mood got lower and lower, for she alone suddenly realized the foolishness of her plan.

"Which is no plan at all," she muttered to herself. She had thought that by running away, she would force her mother to understand how deeply unhappy she was. Her brothers were a kind of insurance that someone—anyone—would come looking for her. Now she was worried that something awful would happen to one of the boys and she, alone, would be to blame. If there was one thing she could not stand, it was to be found wrong in a matter concerning her brothers.

"This is silly," she said aloud when they reached a small clearing.

"What is?" Jem asked.

"This." She gestured around them.

"It's not silly. It's fun!" Corrie said. "No grownups and no . . ."

"No food," Jem finished for him.

"Mother lived in the woods during the war," Corrie said. "She ate mushrooms and nuts and berries and . . ." Here memory failed him. "And stuff."

"I don't want to eat *stuff*." Jem turned to Scillia. "Do you want to eat *stuff*?"

"I think," Scillia said slowly, "that we ought to go back."

"Go back?" Corrie sounded stunned. "We've just got here."

"Which way is back?" asked Jem sensibly.

"That way," Scillia said, pointing. It was clear which way they had come for the trail was marked by broken branches and scuffed earth.

They plunged into the undergrowth, only this time Corrie did the complaining, not Jem. It took them about fifteen minutes to realize that they were thoroughly lost.

"At least it's daylight now," Jem said. "And we can yell." He proceeded to do so, calling out "Help! Help!" loudly until Scillia slapped him.

"Hey!" he cried. "What's that for?"

"Now listen carefully," Scillia said quickly. "It is one thing to be on an adventure. It is another to let every . . . every . . . clodpate and dissident know the queen's children are lost and available for kidnap and ransom."

"Kidnap?" both the boys breathed as one.

"Ransom?" Jem added.

Miserably, Scillia nodded her head.

"So why did we come out here alone in the first place?" Jem asked.

"Because . . ." Scillia was suddenly too embarrassed to say anything more.

Loyal Corrie came to her rescue. "Because she thought we'd have fun." And when Scillia broke into tears, he put his arm around her.

Making a sound of disgust, Jem turned away from them and started off on his own.

"Wait!" Scillia called out, her voice still thick with emotion. "Jem, we *have* to stick together now."

It was such a sensible thing to say that even Jem had to acknowledge it, and he came back.

"All right," he said. "But you have made such a hash of things, I am going to get us back. I *am* the oldest boy, after all. *And* the king's true son." He said it on purpose, knowing how it would hurt Scillia, and smiled when her face took on a stricken look. Then, glancing around, he added, "No one move. We will have to be careful not to make any more new trails."

They stood still and tried to unravel the proper direction to take, but it was quite beyond them all.

Finally Jem said, "I *think* this is the way," and started toward an opening between the trees with such authority, Scillia and Corrie followed at once.

When they came at last to a stream tumbling around

enormous boulders in its spring spate, Scillia sat down grumpily on the bank. "We did *not* pass a stream before."

Jem nodded miserably, his failure too obvious for excuses. But he made one anyway. "I was not the one who got us lost first."

"Never mind," Corrie said, "we could all use a drink." He kneeled down at the water's edge and proceeded to lap at the icy water.

There was no warning growl as the great cat leaped from an overhanging branch, landing on Corrie's back, and tumbling him into the river. Corrie screamed with pain and shock and Jem, on the bank, screamed back in fright. But Scillia tore off her cape, grabbed up a fallen tree limb, and waded into the water. She began to whack hysterically at the floundering cat, and occasionally landed a blow.

The cat was flustered by the attack, hampered by the rushing water. It backed away, snarling, then was caught by a heavy undertow and swept downstream a hundred yards. When it emerged, it was on the other side of the river and too far away to mount a second attack. It shook itself angrily, growled once in the direction of the children, then turned and trotted off to find easier prey.

"Are you hurt?" Scillia cried, pulling the sodden Corrie onto the bank where he stood shakily, staring into space.

"What a stupid question," Jem said, his voice still high with fright. "His neck's bleeding."

"Where?" Scillia turned Corrie around. His eyes were cloudy with shock and his teeth chattered. Two deep holes on the left side of his neck bled profusely now that the cold water was no longer staunching them. "Does it hurt, Corrie?"

"Hurt?" The word was ghostlike, breathy, full of pain. He began to tremble. "Hurt?"

Scillia put her arm around his waist.

"Of course it hurts." Jem was in charge once more. "We have to get him some help."

"Help?" Corrie seemed incapable of more than one word at a time. He looked as if he were about to fall down.

"Jem, we will have to carry him."

"Carry him? He weighs more than I do."

"If we hold our hands together, hand over wrist, we can make him a seat," Scillia said.

"Seat?" Corrie was breathing funny; his face had lost all color.

"The first thing you had better do," a sensible voice, a bit out of breath, said behind them, "is to get him out of those wet clothes and see how bad the bites are."

Scillia turned so suddenly, she nearly let go of Corrie. The speaker was the laughing man, though he was not laughing now. He took Corrie from her and laid him down on the ground. Stripping off the boy's wet jacket and shirt, the man rolled him gently onto his right side.

"Deep punctures but no tears," he said. "Good news—and bad." He swabbed at the bleeding wounds, then held Corrie's wet shirt hard against the punctures. "We need to get you a good salve, my lad. And dry clothes."

"He can have my cape," Scillia said.

"Give me your jacket, boy," the man said to Jem, ignoring Scillia's offer.

"Wouldn't Scillia's cape be better?"

"You young snot! She was in the water herself after that cat, and you still wetting your pants on shore."

"I never!" Jem said. But he handed over his jacket quickly. Then he asked, his voice suddenly sly, "If you were close enough to see all that, why weren't you in the river, too?"

Scillia stared at the man, her face full of the same question.

He shrugged. "I had my bow out and an arrow nocked, boy. I was waiting for a shot that wouldn't hit your brother. But then your sister waded in with her cudgel and the cat was gone downstream before I could let it fly. You can go back and pick up my gear. I dropped it and came at a run." He gestured back along the river bank with his head. "I was out hoping for some deer meat. I didn't expect to be carting home such a young buck!" He laughed. "Up you come, my lad." He picked up Corrie easily in his arms and walked along the river side.

Scillia trotted next to him, holding on to Corrie's hand.

After a moment's hesitation, Jem ran back, found the bow and arrows on the trail, gathered them up, then followed quickly after.

THE TALE:

Cat was sleeping in a tree by the river when he heard a call for help. Looking down, he saw Boy being swept along by the water.

"Whatever are you doing?" asked Cat, arching his back and walking to the end of the limb.

"I am drowning," Boy cried. "Pray give me a hand."

"As I am a cat, I have no hands, only paws," said Cat. "And how do I know you will thank me for what I do? Besides, water is not my element, and the river is much too cold this time of year. And . . ."

But by the time Cat's excuses were counted, Boy had drowned.

Moral from the South Dales: Help first, chat later.

Moral from the Northern Provinces: If you cannot swim, do not go near the water.

Garunian adage: Never trust a cat to do a dog's job.

THE STORY:

They met one of Marek's men halfway back to the inn.

"What goes?" he cried out the moment he spotted them, then came at a crashing run.

"A tussle with a mountain cat," the laughing man said.

"And a plunge into the river. But he's a tough lad. He'll have scars to show his mam."

"His . . . mam . . ." the guard spluttered, and Scillia had to cover her mouth with her hand to keep from giggling aloud.

"My mother is . . ." Jem began, drawing himself up proudly.

"Jem!" Scillia cautioned, but it was too late.

"My mother is Queen Jenna," Jem announced. But if he thought this news would devastate the man who had so recently been calling him names, he was mistaken.

"I know," the laughing man said. "We all know around here. But if the Anna wishes to see her old mates, and do it in private, we can all turn a blind eye."

Scillia rounded on him. "You knew when you . . . you . . . you . . ." Her blush deepened.

"I did not know who you were till the captain claimed you," he said. "So the compliment stands, lass."

Scillia thought he must have known when he had seen her empty sleeve, and she couldn't decide which was worse, his knowing or his not knowing.

Just then Marek himself appeared on the trail. "By Alta's Hairs!" he called and ran toward them. "Is he hurt? Is it bad?"

By then even Corrie was willing to attempt conversation. "I'll have scars," he said, an obvious pride in his voice. "A mountain cat. It was an adventure."

"Adventure, my ass!" Marek exploded.

Scillia began to giggle in earnest then, and her laughter rose precipitously toward hysteria. "I'm sorry," she gasped. "I am sorry, Marek."

"*Sorry puts no coins in the purse*," the laughing man quoted.

Marek took off his cloak and wrapped it around Corrie. "Give me the boy."

"Gladly," the laughing man said. "He's no small burden."

"And tell me your name that we might reward you."

"As for my name, it is Kerrec. But reward the girl. It was she drove off the cat and pulled her brother from the river."

Jem pulled a long face at that. "It was Sil's fault he was in the river to begin with. She . . ."

"Kerrec's right," Corrie interrupted. "Sil saved me. But my neck hurts something fierce. Is it all right if I cry now?" His voice was hoarse and there was a bit of a whimper in it, though he tried valiantly to hide it.

"Cry on, lad," Kerrec told him. "If it had been me, I would have been out-howling that cat long since."

The men took turns carrying Corrie, quick-marching him to the hostel.

But all the way back, Scillia could not help but agree with Jem's assessment. It *was* her fault that Corrie had been in the water and under the cat's claws. She knew she would never forgive herself for it.

THE HISTORY:

Memo: Journal of International Folklore

In your Volume #372/4, you published an article by the late professor of history, L. M. Magon, entitled "Cat's Cradle: A Study of Feline References in Dalian Lore."

Magon postulates in this article that a great cat, somewhat between puma and African lion in size, roamed the Dales in the period just before and after the Gender Wars. He makes this incredible claim though no fossil evidence for any such animal have been found in the Dales past the Late Pleistocene. He cites ballads like the famed "Lullaby to the Cat's Babe" and widely-disseminated folktales such as "The Cat and the Drowning Boy" (Folk Motif #763, Long Excuses) to support his hypothesis, but nothing at all in the way of fossil history.

As you no doubt know, the cat family can be traced through fossil records about forty million years into the Lower Oligocene. They were recognizable as cats even back that far while most other modern mammal types looked scarcely the same creatures as today. However, cat distribution in the Dales was always spotty after the land mass broke away from the mainland, about one million years ago. This information in short form is available to anyone with an encyclopedia, though for a more in-depth look, see Dr. M. J. Piatt's remarkable book The Catastrophe of Cats *(Pasden University Press). Therefore I am puzzled as to why you let such a piece of pseudoscientific maundering into your otherwise fine scholarly journal.*

It is certainly true that Dalian folklore is liberally sprinkled with references to cats. I have no quarrel with that. Adages such as "Better the cat under your heels than at your throat"; *songs like the above named ballads; the ever-popular* Cat Cycle *of stories; and even the famous* March Tapestry *in which Great Alta is pictured with a cat's head and one cat's paw peeking out from beneath the folds of her dress. But there is no way a careful scholar can connect these references to a hitherto unknown species of large wild cat roaming the Dales. Not if that scholar has paid attention to the well-documented studies of the family Felidae published both here and on the Continent.*

I uncovered this travesty of scholarship while researching my father's life. He was a man who spent years battling the false notions and absurd allegations put forth by "Magic" Magon.

Therefore I hope that you will run my letter in your regular letter column and answer it—if you can.

THE STORY:

Jenna was at the inn when they arrived back. She gathered Corrie up and saw to his doctoring without recriminations of any kind.

Scillia thought that her mother's attitude seemed careless, but Jenna was being rigorous in her even-handedness. She was afraid that if she started to scream—at Scillia for casually leading the boys off into danger, at the boys for being so stupidly biddable, at Marek and his men for their damnable inattentiveness—she would not be able to stop screaming. Mostly she was afraid to task Scillia for running away because of the answers she might get back from her. Jenna felt the weight of guilt descending on her, a guilt she had been feeling more and more of late. Before, it had been guilt about the kingdom, about how she and Carum were managing the ever-increasing burden of it. Guilt about taxes, about short crops and long winters, guilt about the threat of invasions from the Continent. That she would now have to add guilt concerning her children to that litany made her afraid.

She had grown used to the guilt.

She was not used to the fear.

The Hame's infirmarer, a stern-faced woman with a large jaw, was providentially with Jenna's party, not still out searching the woods with others from the Hame. Even more providentially, she carried a vulnerary in her leather kit.

"Lay the boy down by the fire," she said. "I will do what is necessary." She made him comfortable, got him into dry clothes. And as he dozed by the fire, worn out from fear, shock, and blood loss, she made a poultice out of HealAll and bandaged his neck.

"Soup when he wakes," the infirmarer said, "and wine for the strengthening. He is not to be moved from here or agitated for a full week."

"Boys are boys. He will be up and complaining in a day," Kerrec whispered to Marek who nodded his agreement. But neither of them said it aloud.

Jenna shook her head. "But we were planning to leave sooner than that."

"*You* may leave," the infirmarer told her as though she were the queen and Jenna a mere subject. "The boy must remain."

"I will stay with him," Marek said.

"And I," Kerrec added. "He will come to no harm here." He grinned suddenly, the laugh lines around his eyes deepening. "No *further* harm, that is."

The infirmarer turned to the two men, patently ignoring Jenna who was all abristle with guilt. "The boy's wound does not touch the great muscles and he will not lose the use of the arm. But boys being boys, he *will* need to be encouraged in the use of it later in the week or it will go stiff from his fear of moving it."

"I understand," Marek said, his face reddening.

The laughing man just grinned.

"And I will leave the vulnerary. The poultice should be changed beneath the bandage four times daily."

"I have some knowledge of that," Kerrec said.

"Good." The infirmarer's large jaw seemed to chew on the word. Then she turned to Jenna. "Now, you see, there is no need for you to stay. I will myself return daily to check on the boy as well."

"No need," Jenna said aloud, adding only to herself, *except the need of the heart.* She sat down next to Corrie and ran her fingers through his fair hair. He did not even stir.

He has, she thought, *his father's face. The same long lashes fanning and shadowing his cheeks*. She sighed. *He is so young.* Fighting back the tears, she thought: *I have been so stupid in this. These children are not just mine. They belong to the Dales. I must preserve them.*

She turned to Marek. "We go back this very day. You will remain here with Corrie and I charge you not to move him till he is fully recovered. The rest of us go home for I promised the king not to be overlong."

"May I stay, mother?" Scillia asked quietly. "May I help nurse Corrie?" If she could do this one thing, she thought, there might be a bit of atonement in it for her.

"You are the throne's heir," Jenna said. Her voice showed her exhaustion. It was uncharacteristically distant. "You will not mope about here trying to assuage your guilt. You will act like a queen and return with me. It is past time you learned what it is to rule."

"Me, too?" Jem asked. "Me, too?"

"Of course you will come, too," Jenna said. But there was only crankiness in her sentence and Jem's eager face turned wary. They both knew that he was soon—too soon—to be shipped off to the Continent, a hostage to the fate of the Dales. To tell him with good grace that he was coming home when it was not to be for long and certainly not to rule, would have broken even Jenna's resolve.

Turning, she signaled the guard. "Be ready to ride before the noon meal. We will eat along the road." Then she was gone back to Selden Hame to gather up her things and Scillia's for the long trail home.

THE MYTH:

Great Alta took the girl child in her hand and turned her this way and that.

In the sun of Alta's gaze, the upper half of the girl turned dark, as if baked by the sun. But her lower half remained light.

Then Great Alta broke the girl in half, as if she were a cake fresh from the oast, holding a piece in each hand.

"So you shall be broken by history, by family, by love," quoth Great Alta. "And when you are repaired, you shall be greater than before."

two

Hostages

THE MYTH:

Then Great Alta took the boychild to place him in the oast of her gaze. But the boychild twisted and turned and managed to slip from her grasp. He ran across a great bridge that spanned an ocean and was gone from sight.

"The farther you run, the nearer you stay," quoth Great Alta.

THE LEGEND:

Jess Hamesford of New Moulting has an iron figure that has been in his family for generations. The figure is in the shape of a gingerbread boy. The top half is painted a light color, the bottom dark.

It is said by the Hamesford family that the figure was one of twenty handed to the men—ten Garuns and ten from the Dales—who accompanied the Two Princes when they were exchanged at the port of Berike. The captains of each accompanying force got the same, but their figurines were made of pure gold.

THE STORY:

The day the princes were exchanged was one of those cold, grey days in late winter when there was a skim of ice on the ponds, and both horses and humans breathed out a moist mist.

King Carum had insisted the family have red robes lined in ermine for going down to the dock, ostentatious for the Dales but necessary for the occasion. *And warm*, he reminded himself as a sop to his conscience. Their inside wear was just as ornate. Jem and Corrie wore green and gold cottas, and stockings of green embroidered with gold leaves. Jenna and Scillia were in dresses of the Garun courtly style—low in the bosom and high in the waist, with ribbands below the bodice bound round to the back and tied in a false bow. They looked beautiful and uncomfortable in equal measure.

Jenna did not complain but held her head in a manner that suggested—to those who knew her well—pain and distance. It looked to outsiders like royal disdain.

However Scillia voiced her dis-ease and unhappiness at every opportunity.

"Papa," she told Carum, "they are all staring at me."

He knew she meant that people were staring at the one empty sleeve, so apparent in the formal dress.

"They see me next to mother and know I am not . . ."

Not whole. He knew that was the bald statement beneath her plaint. *Not entirely whole*. So he did what any father would have done: he wrapped his arms around her, no matter the councillors gaped at it, and whispered, "You are the loveliest girl in the room. Lovelier even than your mother."

The last was too blatant a lie for Scillia to stomach. "Oh, papa—not you, too!" She pulled away from him and would have fled the room except that the first of the Garuns chose that moment to arrive in full regalia and with trumpets—*trumpets!*—blaring.

Carum looked over at Jenna and for the first time she raised an eyebrow at the proceedings. Holding out his hand, he said: "Come. We will see their trumpets and raise them."

Jenna, who did no gaming, looked slightly puzzled, but took his hand anyway. He led her away from the children to the twin thrones on the raised dais. *A dais just new-made for the occasion*, he reminded himself, careful not to move awkwardly as he took the high step up. He held Jenna's hand firmly to keep her from turning around too soon, their backs to the Garunian delegation almost—but not quite—an insult. Then just short of the full snub, he turned them both in place and slowly he sat onto his throne.

Jenna sat on her throne at the same time, holding herself upright, aloof. Partially—Carum suspected—to keep from weeping at the prospect of letting her son go across the ocean. But partially because the low bodice of her dress embarrassed her.

Their three children stood slightly to the right of the platform, backs to their parents, all in a line. The privy council—three men and two women—stood slightly to the left. It made an imposing picture.

There were no candles or torches ablaze near the thrones. Carum had been quite specific about that. He would rather be in the half-shadows than have Jenna's dark sister Skada with her brutally honest tongue mixing in the final negotiations. Honesty had its place, but Carum knew its place was neither in horse trading nor treaty talks. *This*, he thought with sudden bitterness, *is a bit of both.*

For all that he disliked the Garuns—a silly, contentious people—Carum had his son's welfare to consider. He had no illusions about his children, though he loved all three with equal fervor. Corrie was a go-along, content to follow anyone else's lead, but with a sense of humor that made him a good companion. Scillia was a moody questioner, never content with easy answers, especially for herself. And Jem was an occasional bully and a frequent blusterer. But he had a core of fire. *Like my own brothers*, Carum thought. Still he was only a boy.

But he was also a prince. Carum knew that it was imperative that the Garuns be reminded that all the Dales held the child—son of the Anna—in the highest esteem.

He sighed, a sound so quiet he thought that no one had noticed. Just a soft expiration into a noisy chamber. But Jenna, always alert to such changes in him, reached for his hand. *He is my son*, Carum thought angrily, *and all I can think of is esteem*. His anger was all turned inward and for once Jenna's touch did not help.

The actual words of the exchange treaty had been worked out months before between councillors on both sides. Carum and Jenna had held themselves apart from the meetings, as had the Garunian king, Kras. But nevertheless, they knew every word of the pact.

As if they were burned into my heart, Carum thought.

Today was to be the public reading of the document and the exchange of tokens: bejeweled figures of the two boys made by craftsmen from both sides of the waters. Carum shook his head at the waste of labor, at the expense. The figurines were pretty baubles, but he would rather have spent the money on the farmers in the Maulten District who had had too little rain in the spring and torrents of it in the fall.

Tomorrow on the tide, both boys would set sail from their homes, Jem in a Garun ship and Kras' son Gadwess in a ship from the Dales. Somewhere midsea the ships would pass, flags would be lowered, then raised again. A silly bit of business when smooth sailing and a stiff wind were all that were wanted or needed. But Kras had insisted on it, and it had given them another bargaining chip with the Garuns. Carum hoped he could use it wisely.

Glancing over at Jem, Carum wondered if the boy had any misgivings about leaving home and family. If he did, he hid them well. His color was high and his eyes sparkled. Carum suspected that Jem, who liked being the center of attention, would play The Prince to the hilt. *I should have said to Scillia that no one would be looking at her or any of the rest of us today, that it was all Jem's moment*. But it was already too late to salve that particular wound.

"Papa," Jem said, without turning to look at Carum, as if

he feared he might miss something, "Why don't *we* have any trumpets?"

"Because," Jenna said before Carum could answer, "they separate the kings from the people. We do not do that in the Dales."

Jem muttered, "I *like* trumpets."

"You would!" Scillia spat at him.

Only Corrie looked sad and a bit uncertain. He tugged at the back of his cotta.

"Stand straight, Corrie," Carum warned quietly.

Corrie stopped fiddling with his cotta but his fingers still twitched, as if he did not know quite where to put them.

At that moment the Garunian delegation stepped forward and bowed, a long, slow, elegant, and—Carum thought—somewhat mocking bow to the royal family. It was certainly a grander bow than any used in the Dales court. Full leg extended, a flowing hand movement that went down to the ankle of the extended leg then seemed to flutter and flow back up to the waist.

Jem clapped his hands in delight and the chief Garun, a man with a moustache that waterfalled on either side of his mouth and ended in twin points, smiled indulgently.

Nodding briefly at the bowing delegation, Carum signalled them with a pronouncedly languid hand to come closer. Only the man with the moustache left the protection of the group, walking toward them as if he were sailing through the space. When he arrived at the foot of the dais, standing so that his left shoulder nearly touched Jem's, he bowed again, if anything more extravagantly than before.

"Enough!" Jenna muttered, sounding like Skada in the explosion of that one word.

"Your Majesties," the Garun said, still bowing. "My name is Sir Rodergo Malfas."

"Rise, Sir Malfas," Carum commanded, and the man straightened up smoothly.

"My bonfis," he said, handing Carum a scroll.

"Thank you," Carum answered, keeping his voice low and controlled. "I am sure they are in order." But he glanced at the scroll anyway. *It is my son, after all,* he told himself. *I should know something of the man he sails with.*

The scroll was an ancestor-line, males writ in large, gaudy, gilt-lined letters, the females in a smaller but still precise hand. Carum glanced at it quickly. Malfas was well-connected; Carum recognized many of the names. There was even a line, on the sinister side, that went directly to the king.

"I am impressed," Carum said in his still-careful voice, though he was not impressed at all. He measured a man by his actions, not his ancestors. Still he knew the Garuns counted a man differently. *And a woman not at all!* "Your bonfis . . ." he used Malfas' own pronunciation: *bon'fees.* "Your bonfis are sterling indeed. You seem remarkably close to the throne." He guessed that mentioning the bastard line would be both a compliment and an insult, and meant it to be.

"Too kind," Malfas responded, a bit coldly.

A hit! Carum thought, feeling the bite of it. He wondered suddenly if that indulgence had done his little boy any good. He promised himself to be more careful.

Jenna had remained absolutely still throughout their exchange. If she had any desire to look at the scroll or talk to Sir Malfas she did not communicate it by the slightest movement. Carum knew her dislike for the Garuns exceeded his own, but he also knew that the exchange of princes was a necessary evil for continued peace between their two countries, a peace hard-won scarce thirteen years earlier. *Perhaps,* he thought, *perhaps her silence will not be read as anger or sorrow or hatred, all of which he was sure she was feeling. Perhaps the*

Garuns would read it through their own lenses as the silence of a woman who knows her place. No sooner had he thought this, than he regretted the thought.

"Sir Malfas," Carum said, "may I present Queen Jenna, called The Anna by our people. And these are our children—Scillia, Jemson, and Corrine." He was taking a chance naming Jenna that way, though the Garuns knew they shared the throne in equal rule. He had not mentioned that Scillia was heir to the throne. This, too, the Garunians surely already knew and disapproved of. But it was simply not tactful to rub the fact in. Not here. Not now. There was much to diplomacy that irked Carum beyond measure; he knew it bothered Jenna even more.

Sir Malfas bowed again, to each of them in turn, but it was to Jem that he held his bow the longest.

Jem grinned, squaring his shoulders.

"And now," Carum intruded on the last and longest bow, "please join us for a feast, Sir Malfas. I have put you between Jemson and myself, that we may all get to know one another."

"*Know* one another?" Sir Malfas' voice held a disapproving note.

"In the Dales," Jenna said suddenly, her own voice distant and cold, "we prize that kind of intimate knowledge."

"Then, madame," Malfas said carefully, not calling her either Highness or Majesty, "as I am in the Dales, I shall endeavor to know you as well." But it was clear he was referring to Jemson and Carum, not Jenna.

Jem giggled and only with an effort kept from clapping his hands.

Carum led the way with Jenna a reluctant step behind. They came off the dais, passed between Malfas and the children, split the Garunian delegation in two, and went through the door into the great dining hall where a feast, indeed, awaited them.

THE SONG:

Feast Song

Bring in the pheasant, so pleasant to eat,
Bring in the grouse and the lamb.
Bring in the capons and salmon and geese,
Bring in the sucklings and ham.

Bring in the butter and cheese and the beans,
The porridge, the barley, and oats.
Bring in the ale and the red wines and white,
Bring in the milk from the goats.

Fast day to feast day to fast day again,
We feed down from castle to cottage.
One week we're ample with courses to spare,
Next week we dine upon pottage.

Bring in the black breads, the brown breads, the gold,
Bring in the honey-sweet beer.
Bring in the onions and garlic and cloves,
Bring in the cup of good cheer.

Bring in the berries, red, purple, and black,
Bring in the caramelized candy.
Bring in the fruit pies, the cakes, and the tarts,
Bring in the possets and brandy.

Fast day to feast day to fast day again,
We feed down from castle to cottage.

One week we're ample with courses to spare,
Dining on venison, wild pig, and bear,
Finishing off with both apple and pear.
Next week we dine upon pottage.

THE LEGEND:

There is a stone at the entrance to Berike Harbor called "Prince's Landing." It is a large grey boulder with a foot-shaped hollow in the top.

The men of Berike say that stone was the site of the Prince Gadween's first step on to Dalian land.

The women say rather it was the last place the Anna's son Jemuel stood before embarking for the Continent. Further, say the women, the hollow is always filled with salt water. It is not salt from the sea but from the tears the Anna shed at her son's leaving. When Jemuel returned a man, he was changed beyond all measure. And so, the women of Berike say, the hollow holds her tears to this day.

THE STORY:

The dinner was a long drawn-out affair, with too many courses and toasts to both sides of the ocean. Never any good at such festivities, and tongue-tied when it came to making toasts, Jenna longed to excuse herself, to take Jem out for a walk under the familiar stars.

She had so much she wanted to tell him before he left, so much to remind him of. Stories of his birth, his first steps, his first word—which had been "crown." She wanted to tell him again about how she and his father had met, parted, met again in the midst of battle. She wanted to warn him about the Garunians' softness toward warfare, their hard-heartedness toward women. It would be her last chance to talk face-to-face with Jem for many years to come. She did not doubt that her letters to him would be routinely censored, or read first by the stone eyes of Kras and Malfas and their like.

She had given Jem a small satchel of gifts she had put together, but privately, not in view of the Garunian delegation. They would certainly have made mock of her offerings. A packet of his favorite dried blackberries, so delicious on porridge, like a burst of late summer on the tongue. A leather-bound copy of Blessum's *Book of Wisdoms*, with her own favorite sayings underlined in red ink. A book marker woven of marsh-rush and dyed purple with madder, with his name and a crown embroidered with gold thread; Scillia's handiwork, all the more to be prized because it was so difficult for her to do. A pillow potpourri with rose petals from the castle garden, as well as lavender, orris root, and other spices from an old receipt she had found in the archives. If he slipped it under his bed linen, the bed would keep fresh for days on end. A ginger chewing ball in case he had more problems with his back teeth. And his old stuffed bear, resewn and rehatted by her own fingers. Jem had put the bear away only last year, but she thought that a boy in a new place would want to be surrounded by some of his familiar things.

She remembered when she had traveled away from Selden Hame her first time. She'd been older than Jem, but had lived a much more restricted life, a life that was both more sheltered and yet harder than her own children's upbringing. Four girls—she and Pynt and two others—had been sent off together on their year's mission, parting at the confluence of two rivers. She—like Pynt—had carried a corn dollie in her pack. It had meant a great deal to her at the time.

Jem's bear—Brownie—could serve as his blanket companion in the foreign court. *If*, Jenna thought suddenly, *the Garuns let him keep it.* He had certainly seemed pleased enough with the things in the satchel, giving her a little hug and a half smile as he looked at every item.

"Jenna!" It was Carum, calling on her for the next toast.

She raised her glass reluctantly and looked around the long table, at Carum at the far end, his face slightly flushed with the wine. She looked at the Garun, Sir Malfas, who was so like one of her old enemies, she had trouble focusing on him. Then she looked at Jem beside him, his little face bright with the watered wine and the excitement, rather more the second than the first, she imagined. Then her eyes strayed to Corrie next to his brother, in whose mien pleasure and sorrow were mixed together. She let her eyes track widdershins around the banquet feasters until they rested, at last, on Scillia to her own right.

Scillia was staring down at her plate.

Jenna stood. She stood very straight, lifting her chin and looking as regal as she could. And looking as well—if she had but known it—like the goddess the country people thought her. She willed her voice to betray nothing.

"I give you—my son," she said, deliberate in the play on words. Then knowing she would have to say more, added, "We have a saying here in the Dales: *What you give away with love, you keep*." She lifted the glass to her lips and drank the wine down quickly. There was little left in the bottom of the goblet anyway, and what remained was warm and slightly sour.

"Jemson!" Corrie cried, leaping to his feet and holding his own cup aloft. "To the great adventure!"

All around the table the feasters likewise rose. A few had clearly been refilling their cups to the brim for each toast. Marek seemed to have the most trouble getting up.

Scillia, though, was a beat behind them all. "Mother," she whispered and Jenna heard the strain in her voice even though the dining hall was noisy with the sound of chairs shifting against the floor. "Mother, you can still stop this. Do not let him go. It will be the worse for him."

Privately Jenna agreed. But she knew she could not stop the exchange now—not without dire consequences to the Dales. She feared the tide of history that could drown them all.

"Be still," she whispered back, as much to her own traitor heart as her daughter.

Jem rose last of all. Raising his own glass, he said "I have something to say, too." He hesitated a moment, then turned to Carum. "May I, father? May I say it?"

At Jem's hesitation, at the childishness of the request, Jenna's eyes filled with tears.

Carum nodded.

Jem grinned broadly. "Today," he said in his high, unbroken voice, "today I am a boy. Tomorrow I will be a man, taking a man's journey, going as my country's pledge to the land of the Garuns."

Carum mouthed the words with him. It was clearly a rehearsed speech, none the less charming for being rehearsed. Jenna had no idea when they had thought it up or had time to practice.

Then Jem added, and this was certainly his own addition, "When I return, you will all know I am a man."

Involuntarily, Jenna shivered. There was too much of a threat in his little boy's voice. She thought of the bear in the satchel. Brownie. *Perhaps*, she thought, *I should have taken off the bow*.

"I thought it went well," Carum said, taking off the gold-lined jacket. The collar of his silk shirt was grey with sweat. He sat down on their great bed to slip off his stockings. As he bent over, Jenna saw how thin his hair had gotten on top.

I never noticed, she thought. She was standing in the dark corner of the room, her back against the wall. Neither moonlight nor candlelight illumined her. *Being king has aged him so*.

Then she made a small grimace. *We have both grown older. He is just too kind to say anything. Or to notice.* She sighed.

"You did not think so?" Carum asked, sitting up straight.

"My son is going from me in the morning, perhaps forever, and you ask if things went well?" She had not meant to snap at him.

"He is my son, too, Jenna. And we long ago agreed that this exchange was our only guarantee of peace."

"It is easy to agree when the day is far off."

It was Carum's turn to make a face. "You knew this day would come eventually."

"I am like the prisoner waiting the executioner. As long as the blade is not on my neck, I do not think of the morrow."

"You are sounding remarkably like Skada."

"I *am* Skada," Jenna said, moving out into the arc of the candlelight. "And on occasion she is me."

"Only on difficult occasions," Skada said, suddenly standing by Jenna's side. Dark sister and light, they mirrored their sorrow.

This time it was Carum who sighed.

"Jem is only a child," Jenna said.

"A boy," agreed Skada.

"And will be a man," Carum said. "Even he recognizes this fact. Why can't you?"

"I would he become a man of the Dales," Jenna answered.

"As he is and will always be," Carum countered.

"He will be what *they* make of him," said Skada.

Carum stood up, and the one stocking he was still wearing slid down around his ankle, giving him a slightly comic look. But his face held anything but amusement. "*We* had the making of him for ten years. *That* making will prove true."

Jenna moved toward him till she was close enough to be touched. He did not reach for her, nor for Skada who stood just as near.

Jenna's eyes searched his and he did not flinch from her gaze, but Skada snorted. "Remember what the farmers in the South say: *Better a calf of one's own than a cow owned by another.*"

All three of them burst into laughter at that, more from the relief of tension than good humor.

"I don't know what that means," Jenna said.

"You will," Skada answered.

Only then did Carum put his hand out to draw Jenna to him and Skada, of course, came too.

"Put out the light, Carum," whispered Jenna.

Skada laughed.

In a swift, practiced movement, Carum turned and blew out the candle on the washstand. Then he lay back on the bed, and pulled Jenna, alone, to him.

THE TALE:

There was once a widow with three sons: Carum, Jerum, and little Jeroo. They lived in a hut in the middle of a dark and tangled wood. Their lives were hard and their days were long and there was precious little laughter in them.

"Do not go to the north of here," said the widow to her three. "For under the hill and under the dale lives the King of the Fey. He will steal you from me as he stole your father and that will make our lives harder than before."

For years the boys listened to their mam. And though they went east, and though they went west, and though they went south to pick blackberries and nuts, to gather windfalls and storm-blowns, they never—not even once—went north.

One day, when they were all but men, Carum strayed into a path that was lined with bluets and set about with bay. He was so mazed by it, that twisty, windy path, that he walked a night and a day going due north and straight away was stolen by the fairies.

When he did not come home, his mam wept and wailed and threw her apron up over her head. She knew then that what she had feared most had come at last. So she made the other two, who were still left at home with her, promise faithfully that they would never stray.

Still, one day Jerum, too, found the twisty, windy path. Only this time it was lined with currants and set about with pine. He was so mazed by it, he walked a night and a day going true north and then he, too, was stolen by the fairies.

"Oh, my dear little Jeroo," said his mam. "Do not dare the fate of your brothers. Stay at home east and stay at home west and stay at home best with me."

Now little Jeroo was a good boy and he did as he was told. He stayed at home and took care of his old mam. But when he was an ancient himself, and his mam dead lo! that many a year, he went out into the forest one day to gather firewood.

And even though he was not looking for it, he found the path the others had taken. Long did he stand upon it, looking due, true north past woodbine, bluets, bayberry, and thorn; past gorse, currant, yarrow, and pine. He thought he saw figures dancing in the distance—young men he could almost remember, their heads crowned with garlands, singing and drinking and being merry.

Then he turned his back on them, the young and ever fair. He went home, lay down on his old, cold bed, turned his face to the wall, and died.

THE STORY:

Jenna did not have time to do more than shove her feet into boots and tie a fresh belt around her tunic. Her long braid had hundreds of escaping wisps, as if mice had been at it. But the tide was an early one and she had overslept, wine and weariness combining. No one had dared wake her until the sun, full on her face as she lay in her bed, reminded her that it was the day.

The Day.

She had rushed through her dressing and managed to get down the stairs in time, but just.

Now she stood on the shore with the others, watching as Jem—looking small and terribly alone in the midst of the Garunian oarsmen—waved at them from the front of the boat, the satchel she had given him snugged under one arm.

The sailors were a rough lot, Jenna had thought, despite their grand red-and-gold outfits. Black might have better suited them. Then they would have been as funereal as the day. She did not move until the rowboat had reached the ship, and the ship had cleared the breakwaters to sail out to sea.

The ship's bright red sails filled with the breeze. But the color only served to remind Jenna of blood. It was an inapt figure, but Jenna was too much mother and too little queen at the moment to care. She willed herself not to cry, but her face was a desolation.

Corrie came over to slip his hand in hers. "I shall have to be two sons for you now," he said.

She looked down at him. "Did your father tell you to say that?" she asked, and when he looked hurt, she hugged him. "You do not have to be any more than just Corrie," she said. But the damage was already done and she knew it. So she held his hand as they marched back to the palace the long way, through the winding streets of the harbor town crowded with well-wishers. She hoped that her hand, strong on his, would tell him what she could not.

Part way through Berick, Corrie slipped her hand like a dog off a leash, running away to join some boys playing mumbles in front of the WindCap hostelry without so much as a faretheewell. Which, Jenna thought, was just as well. There had already been too many farewells that day. Farewell to Jem and farewell to her own innocence.

No, she thought suddenly, *that had gone the day she'd agreed to exchange him for a Garun prince*.

For the first time she began to wonder what young Gadwess would be like. Would he be one of those boastful, self-satisfied princelings who looked down on the common folk? And what would his mother be feeling. *Any less than I*, Jenna wondered, *because she is a Garun woman and not supposed to feel any pain?* She scolded herself aloud for such an ungenerous thought. "How could I . . ."

"For the people, Anna. For all of us." The speaker was an old woman, her face scarred badly, the right cheek almost quilted with lines.

"I'm sorry . . ." Jenna began, realizing the woman had misunderstood her.

"Ye had to let him go for us," the old woman said. "For the ending of wars. It says so."

Jenna stared, recognizing her for a fisherwoman by the striped petticoat and the black skirt kilted up over the wide leather belt. "What says so?"

"The prophecy. Dinna ye know the prophecy?"

"I am done with prophecies," Jenna said. "Done these thirteen years."

"Aye," the old woman said, lifting up a hand as scarred as her face. "But are they done wi' ye?"

Jenna reached into her pocket and drew out a coin. "Take this and forget the prophecy, old one. Buy yourself a tot of rum and toast my baby over the sea."

But the old woman had already begun in a singsong voice:

> *"Babby over the water,*
> *Babby under the ring,*

Babby brings a sword and stone
To come and crown a king."

"That is no prophecy," Jenna said, dropping the coin on the ground before the old woman. "That is a children's song. I sang it with my own when I dandled them on my knee."

She turned and walked away quickly, but the old woman kept singing the song over and over, even after she had picked up the coin from the dirt.

THE HISTORY:

The exchange of princes as hostages between formerly warring nations as a pledge of peace was not new when the first prince of the Dales set sail to the Continent. But his ten-year exile in the land of the G'runs was marked at home by a stunning surge of poetry and songs about "the prince over the sea." Not a few of the poems—and the entire flowering of the First Romantic Movement—can be laid at the feet of the G'runian hostage who brought with him a fresh, poetic voice and a wealth of Continental song traditions.

Until that time, the few extant Dalian tunes had been modal and without much instrumentation. The tembala—a stringed instrument of the guitar family with five melody strings and two drones—was the exception. For centuries musicologists thought it the only native Dale instrument. However three other instruments have recently been discovered from the early Altan period, instruments that have Continental counterparts but seem wholly of Dale manufacture.

The first of these is the barsoom, *which is a small hand-held skin drum, with copper bangles around the rim. The fragment of drumhead is goatskin. The bangles have slight indentations on their edges, which lends them a variety of tones.*

Secondly, there is the temmon, *an early flute with five holes and a range of two modal "octaves." There were two different flutes found in the dig, both with lateral mouth holes. One was made from a local ash, one from a black wood which never grew outside the Dales.*

The third instrument is the fidoon, *a highly arched fiddle-like instrument which is played with a bow on the underside of the strings.*

All three kinds of instruments were found in the Berike Barrow, a dig of utmost importance to musicologists as it has been reliably dated to the early Altan period. We already knew that during the years of the hostage exchange, Dale songs had been marked by particular solo instrumental parts, but until the time of the Berike Barrow excavation, no corresponding instruments had been found. A few of the sophisticated Continental instruments, like the viol and shawm, were used instead by people playing Early Music concerts, for they seeming closest to the range demanded. Also as a further clue, there was still, on display in Baron Fuchweil's collection on the Continent, "The Prince's Consort"—a viol and a shawm said to have been brought over with the G'run prince, then returned home with him. But the Berike Dig was the first in which actual instruments of Dale manufacture of that period were found.

Furthermore, the ten piece song-cycle collectively known as the "O'er the Sea Suite," with its intricate rhyme schemes and surprisingly salacious (for that period) plays on words like "Jemmie went o'ering, went oaring, went whoring . . ." all pointed to a new and unprecedented influence from the G'runs.

The "O'er the Sea" songs are also remarkable for their three-part texture which had long been a feature of G'runian secular songs but not previously found in the Dales. The practice of having one or more parts whose only—or principal—function is to complete the harmony was entirely a G'runian invention. However the G'run choirs, being male only, had a built-in limitation on the range of voices. When the three-part songs became integrated into the Dales, the voices included sopranos and contraltos which allowed for a greater variety in the vocal lines. This marked out the

"O'er the Sea Suite" and made it such an interesting puzzle for musicologists.

—*Cat Eldridge*, The Dale Musician's Handbook

THE STORY:

The boat bearing the Garun prince sailed into the harbor the following morning, but Jenna did not go down to meet it. Carum and she had decided that he and Corrie, along with a guard of twenty men led by Marek, would do the honors. She preferred the task of overseeing the reappointment of Jem's room for the Garun prince. Though it was a task that any of the servers could have completed without her, Jenna was determined to put things right for the young hostage on her own.

"What I do for him, perhaps his mother will do for Jem," she told Carum in Jem's bedroom when he asked her a final time whether she wanted to accompany them to the harbor.

"His mother will not have seen Gadwess except at formal occasions for the past six years," Carum reminded her. "Lest she unman him. Lest she make a woman of him."

"A woman of him!" Jenna's voice shook. "Do they forget that it was a Dale woman who bested them at war?"

"Dale women *and* men together bested the Garuns," Carum said acidly.

For a moment they glared at one another, till Carum looked down. "Lips," he said.

"Knives," Jenna answered, sitting down on the unmade bed.

It was their private code, a way of remembering the old saying: *If your mouth turns into a knife, it will cut off your lips*. It was their way of making sure they did no lasting harm through arguing.

"Whatever is done for Jem or not done, I must still do

what I can for Gadwess. He will be wretched from the journey, and frightened. He will be alone in a new land."

"He is a Garun," Carum said. "Which means he will never show his wretchedness or fear."

"He is still a boy," Jenna countered. "So I will make him his own room. And freshen the bedding. *Let a new wind blow through an old place.*" It was a line from a song they both loved.

"Then I will go along with just Corrie and the guards."

"Best that way," Jenna said. "Carum . . ."

He looked at her face and its familiar grief.

"I need more time."

He nodded, leaned over, kissed her on the brow, and left.

But Scillia, coming into the room on the heels of her father's departure, cried out in dismay. "Mother! What are you doing? Do you wish all reminders of Jem gone before his boat has even reached the Garun shore?"

Jenna turned her full fury on her daughter. "Wretched girl, how dare you say that. I carry him here, still, under the breastbone, where I carried you all."

"You never carried *me* there," Scillia said, leaving as explosively as she had come.

There were three servers, two men and a woman, standing in the hallway, ready to enter the room, and they did not move as Scillia stormed away. They were rigid with embarrassment for both the queen and her daughter. Jenna saw them, but said nothing directly about the incident. Her renewed fury, which was but a displacement of her sorrow, had nowhere to go but inward. She would never castigate her serving people when the fault was her own. So she grabbed up the bedding and began beating it with her hands until the air was filled with dust and bits of down.

"Take this away," she said between slaps to the bedding,

"and bring me a new coverlet. And move this bed to there." She pointed to the window and the servers came in to the room at last, but tentatively.

"No—move it there." She pointed to the far wall. "It is still too cold to sleep so far from the fire."

The two men picked up the heavy wooden bedstead and carried it where she commanded. Under the bed, where brooms had never fully reached, was the dirt of a long winter, a wooden ball from the Peg-in-the-Ring Jem had so loved the last summer, three game cards, and his bear still wearing its jaunty red bow.

"Brownie!" Jenna sobbed. Then she turned and raced out of the room so that none of the servers could see her cry.

Once in her own bedroom, Jenna closed the curtains to make a night of the morning light. She lit the hearthfire and crowded close to it. When the logs had fully engaged the flame, throwing out a rosy light, Skada appeared beside her.

"So," Skada said, "the Gender Wars continue to wound us all."

"I am not dead of them."

"Not yet. But something will die if you continue on this way."

Jenna turned on her dark sister. "What do you mean?"

"You know exactly what I mean."

"Say it."

"Love will die. Family. All that you hold dear."

"A prophecy, sister? You think less of them than I do."

"Not a prophecy. A prediction."

"Am I that awful a force?" Jenna held her hand out and twined her fingers in Skada's.

"You are the Anna, the White One, the Girl With Three Mothers, the Queen."

"You know I am only Jenna. You have seen me bleed." She gave a half-cozening smile.

"I have seen you shit in the woods." Skada gave the half smile back, only on her mouth it was fully ironic. "But what you and I know makes no matter. The people believe. And Belief trumps all."

"You think this but a game, sister?" Jenna asked.

"It is Alta's game, sister," Skada answered. "And we are but players on the board. You are the White Queen, and I the Black."

"Thank you for that reminder," Jenna said. She rose and walked out of the room into the day-lit hall, alone.

Carum stood at the water's edge straining to see the incoming ship while Corrie sat atop a grey stone that humped out of the water. He was dropping shells onto the stone, making splashes in the rainwater that had been caught in a deep hollow on the boulder's surface. The water splashed onto Corrie's trews, staining them.

A strong wind blew from behind them and out into the harbor, making white-topped waves that looked like many little knives. The wind whistling by their ears caused Corrie to shiver.

"There'll be a hard landing today," Marek commented.

"They won't sail her in, but use the oars," Carum said, putting a hand up to shade his eyes. "Provided they get past the Skellies."

"They will, sir, don't you fear," said one of the guards, whose eyes were bluer than the water. "My brother's on that ship. No finer sailor in the Dales."

"No finer sailors—all of them," Marek amended quickly. "They are not about to lose *that* ship."

"Or *that* prince!" added Carum.

"Father," Corrie said suddenly, looking up from the grey stone, "what of Jem?" No one had been paying any attention to Corrie, but though he'd been playing with the shells, he'd been all ears for their conversation.

Carum was silent, as if weighing his answer, but Marek did not hesitate "Now, boy, don't we say: *Storm in Berick, sun in Bewick?*"

"You mean Jemmie will have good weather there if we have . . ."

"Just so, young master." It was another guard, his cheeks scoured to the color of early wine by his days out in the wind and sun.

"I hope so. Jemmie's never been good in a boat."

"Corrie!" Carum's voice was steel.

Just then one of the men cried out, "I see it! I see the ship." He pointed to a speck on the horizon.

"Where? Where?" Corrie leaped to his feet, scattering shells over the top of the boulder. Treading carelessly on them, he placed both hands up to shade his eyes. "Where?" One leg slipped on the crushed shells, his hat fell over the rock's edge, and he started to slide after it into the ocean.

Marek was quickest into the water, and knee-deep, caught the boy before he fell in. "Sometimes," Marek whispered to him, "you are too much bother." He waded back and deposited Corrie on the shore.

Corrie twisted out of Marek's grasp and ran over to his father. "Where is it?"

Putting his left hand on his son's shoulders, Carum showed him. "There. Follow my finger."

"That? That speck?"

"That speck."

"But it is so small."

"It will grow sooner than you, little master," said the red-cheeked man, laughing.

The others passed the joke around and the laughter tracked all the way through the guard.

Corrie's cheeks burned with embarrassment. He was not so young that he did not know *that.* He had meant that the boat was actually small. Smaller than the one that had taken Jem away. Four masts to the Garun's eight. But anything he said now would only make the men laugh the harder.

Marek stopped the laughter soon enough. "Look smart!" he scolded them. "Or do you want to bring shame on our king and queen and all the Dales in that young Garun's eyes?" He did not mention Corrie, but he had not missed the brands on the boy's cheeks.

"Aught will shame us for laughing," called out one man, but he quickly found his place in the proper formation with the others.

The speck was now visible as a ship, sails down and long oars out. But before it had completely cleared the Skellies, that double line of dangerous rocks that cupped the harbor entrance like two hands almost at prayer, a cold rain began. At first it was a sputtering, spitting sort of rain, and then it came down in hard, heavy drops.

Carum, Marek, and the guards were all wearing hats, but Corrie's had fallen off in his mishap on the rock and was even now floating out of reach.

"Corrie, go back to the inn and wait for us there," Carum said.

"But Father, I want to see the Garun prince."

"You will have plenty of time to see him. Almost a lifetime. However, if you stay out here without your cap, you will catch your death. And then I will be without *any* sons."

The red-cheeked guard broke ranks and came over to Carum. "Never mind, sir. I've got an extra tam in my pocket. If it's all right for the young prince to wear it."

"Give it here," Marek said, holding out his hand. "And what are you doing with it in your pocket?"

"These damned helmets don't keep out the cold when we are on duty," the man said. "My wife knit it for me."

"Humph." Marek took the tam and gave it to Corrie who immediately tugged it down over his already-sodden hair. The tam was big enough to cover his ears and go partway down his neck.

"Can I stay now, father?" he begged.

Carum pulled a long face at the boy, but his eyes were smiling. Only Marek noticed.

"Please . . ."

"It you are quiet about it," Marek said in a gruff voice, "and are as good as a soldier, never complaining, not even once, of the chill, the king will most likely let you stay."

"I never . . ." Corrie began. When he saw Marek's finger up to his lips, he did not finish the sentence but stood at attention next to his father until the ship was safely moored.

It took another hour for the ship's mooring to be completed, the waves now furious with the storm. And another half hour after that for the small boat it carried to be let down and rowed through the angry lashings to shore. Corrie did not, of course, last at attention all that time, but he made no more complaints. Indeed, he said nothing at all but watched the whole maneuver with a rapt look.

Carum himself waded out to the little boat as it began to beach, his red cloak black with the rain. He picked up the whey-faced, thin-lipped Garunian prince and carried him onto the shingle. Jem was not the only poor sailor on the sea that day.

They wrapped Gadwess in Carum's cloak. Though his teeth were chattering, he did not moan about it.

"Nor did he on board," the captain said to Marek, away

from the boy's hearing. "Though he was sick over the side of the ship more times than I could count."

"I do not like his color," Marek said.

"You'd best get boiled water into him, and soon. Before we leave the shore. Then a bit of twice-oasted bread and thin soup next."

Marek nodded. "Not what a prince might fancy for his first meal ashore."

"Trust me, he is less prince than sick boy at the moment. He won't keep down anything more than that." The captain wiped his own wet forehead with a neck cloth that was too damp itself to make a difference. "But a good night's sleep by a warm hearth and plenty of liquids, and he'll be all right. The young recover faster than you or I. Still, I've not seen one quite so sick and quite so uncomplaining."

"He's a Garun," Marek said. "And a prince."

"Which is all that needs saying," said the captain.

Gadwess was too weak to walk, but he refused to be carried. Marek sent the red-cheeked guard up ahead to commandeer a horse from the inn and a skin of weak sweet tea.

Marek offered the skin to the prince, but it was not until Carum as king insisted he drink ten sips before they could move, that Gadwess drank. Then with a guard on either side—more to catch the boy should he start to slip from the saddle than as an honor escort—they went quickly up the road toward the castle.

Sodden but undaunted, Corrie capered at his father's side.

The tam had proved useless against the wet and cold, and Corrie was put to bed the same time as the Garunian prince. Both had hearthfires blazing through the night to ward off chill, and cups of steaming broth were brought to them both at intervals from the kitchen.

Jenna ignored young Gadwess in favor of her own sickling. She reasoned that the castle infirmarer, an old man with older ways, was certainly competent enough to treat the prince's condition. No one died of seasickness, not on shore. But it was her guilt, not her reason, that drove Jenna to stay in Corrie's room.

Nose streaming, Corrie was silent in her company. He was alternately shivering and feverish, but he pushed her hand away when she tried to feed him the soup. He ignored Skada completely.

"I'm too old to be fed," he said, sitting up in bed. But when he tried to feed himself, his hands shook and he managed to spill the broth down the front of his nightshirt.

Jenna helped him change it.

"See," she said, paying no heed to Skada's cautioning look, "you are never too old for your mother."

Corrie turned over in the bed, putting his back to her. "Let Sil feed me," he said, his voice muffled by the pillow. He would not turn back again and, reluctantly, Jenna called for her daughter, sending a server to find her.

They waited near an hour for Scillia to come, while Corrie alternately shivered, dozed, and awoke to shiver again. At last Jenna and Skada went down the great torch-lit stairs, shouting "Where is she? Where is Scillia?" their voices rising and falling together. In this one thing, at least, they were united.

Carum met them halfway. "My love, she is gone," he said quietly.

"What do you mean—gone?" Jenna asked.

"Gone where?" Skada added.

"Into the storm. Hours ago. A kitchener packed her saddle packs with several days' provisions. She rode off. West, according to one of the guards."

"Provisions? And no one thought to tell me?"

"Why should they?" Carum asked. "Jenna, you do it all the time."

"But I am a grown woman."

"You are the queen."

"This is not a family or a kingdom," said Skada. "This is an anarchy."

"Shut up, Skada!" Carum and Jenna said together.

Wisely Skada was silent.

"Where will she go?" Jenna asked.

"Where did you go at her age?" Carum answered question with question.

"On a mission. But I was prepared. I knew the woods. I was trained in weapons and woodcraft and . . . By Alta! How can she do this again, stupid, wretched girl. She'll get *herself* mauled this time." Jenna's voice shook with fury.

"May I speak now?" Skada asked quietly.

"No!" Jenna said.

"Why?" Carum asked at the same time.

Skada looked at them both for a long moment. "Because I believe I knew where she has gone."

"Where?" They stared back at her.

"To the Hame."

"Selden Hame? But she hated it there," Jenna said.

"To her mother's old Hame: *high towered where eagles dare not rest.*"

"M'dorah?" Jenna said. "But it is only an inaccessible cliff. There is nothing to see. No women. Nothing. We fired the buildings when we left. Even the eagles shun it."

"Still, where else would she go, Jenna? Think. Think! One brother gone, her mother fostering another in his place. The other brother so excited to meet the new, he'd rather stand out in the rain and make himself sick than be with his sister. What is there left for Scillia to do but go look for her first family?"

Carum was thoughtful. "First she will have to find M'dorah. It is not an easy or accessible spot."

"She is her mother's daughter," Skada said. "The Anna's daughter. In all but blood. She can find it. She *will* find it."

"Send Marek to shadow her," Jenna said. "There are more dangers than cats for a girl her age out alone."

Skada added, "He knows most of the way already."

Carum smiled grimly. "I had thought of that, of course. Leave Marek to me. You go tend to those boys."

Corrie was asleep again and so Jenna and Skada covered him gently with the down comforter. Then they turned as one and went to the door that connected the boys' rooms. Just as Jenna's hand touched the latch, with Skada's beside hers, they heard an odd sound.

The Garunian prince was weeping quietly.

"He is only a boy after all," Jenna said, pushing the door open.

"But still a Garun," Skada reminded her.

The fire had burned too low to throw much light so Skada never made it further than the threshold before disappearing. Jenna went over to the boy's bed alone.

"How can I help?" Jenna said to the lump under the coverlet.

There was a quiet snuffle, and then a head emerged from the bed linens. "I need no woman's help," the boy said, his eyes dark as new bruises.

"Some broth will settle your stomach," Jenna said. "And if you have been sweating with a chill, I can get you a new nightshirt to put on."

"Out!" the prince said. "I can take care of myself."

The coverlet had slipped further, and his shoulders and arms showed. Even in the room's twilight Jenna could see enough to know the child was even younger than Corrie. And painfully thin.

"You do not even know where things are in this room," she said sensibly. "I do. It would be faster if . . ."

"Send in a man to serve me." He pulled the covers back up to his chin and his lower lip quivered just a bit.

"*You*," Jenna said, "are in the Dales now. Where men and women serve equally."

His eyes suddenly had a liquid shine to them, like a deer in the moonlight. And then—to her heartbreak and his shame—he began to weep in front of her.

Jenna sat down at once on the bed and pulled him to her. For a moment he resisted, then gave in because his sobs had already so unmanned him. His body shook with his sobs.

"There, there," she said. "No one shall ever know you cried."

He pulled back from her, shivering. "You will know. And you will tell. Servants always tell."

For a second she did not reply, and then she laughed. It was a laugh compounded of relief and delight.

"Woman!" Gadwess said, looking as stern as an eight-year-old can. "Why do you laugh at me? In my country a servant who laughs at a prince can have her lips sewn together."

"I have no doubt of that, my young prince," Jenna said, making her own face look as stern, "But if you wish to do such a thing to me, you will need a very long needle and golden thread."

Unprepared for such a reaction, the little prince blinked once, twice, then a third time, his mouth wide open.

"You look like a fish caught on a hook," said Jenna.

"You . . . you will look worse," the boy said, his lower lip beginning to quiver once again, "when I tell the king."

"The king will laugh as well, I am afraid," Jenna said, "for I am no servant. I am the queen."

"The queen? Queen Jenna? But I thought that . . ."

"That Queen Jenna has teeth with terrible points to eat the small parts of young boys for dinner? Oh, I have heard those scurrilous Garunian rhymes, even here across the sea. *Gena's tooth be very long . . .*" She smiled at him.

He shivered again.

"Now get under those covers before I do bite you. I shall bring you some fresh soup, hot from the fire. And some bread from the kitchen. Myself. Like a servant. I would not subject any server in my castle to your temper yet." As she stood, her foot kicked something by the bedside. She glanced down and picked it up. "But till I return, this bear shall keep you company. His name is Brownie." Quickly she untied the red ribbon, crumpling it in her hand.

"A girl's toy," the boy said, some of his arrogance returning.

"Not in this country. Here it is a boy's blanket companion. To tell his secrets to. And, like the queen, the bear keeps secrets well." She smiled at him as she put the bear by his pillow, then pointed to her teeth. "See—no points. Believe me when I tell you, I vastly prefer boar and venison to small boys when it comes to meat."

She left before he could return comment, but she felt far better than she had in weeks which was odd, she thought, given that she had a son hostage in a far-off land and a daughter lost in the woods.

THE RHYMES:

Gena's tooth be very long,
Very long, very long,
Gena's tooth be very long,
And she gonna bite ya.

—Jump rope rhyme, Bewick-on-Sea

Jenna bite de head off,
Jenna bite de neck off,

Jenna bite de shoulder off,
Jenna bite de arm off . . .
—*Baby teaching rhyme, Krasstown*

Sleep baby, byanby,
Sleep baby, byanby,
Sleep baby, byanby
Or de jenger's goin' ter getcha.
—*Patois lullaby collected from the G'run Penal Colony of Calabas*

THE STORY:

Corrie woke slowly, the sun streaming through his window and the fire in the hearth but a bed of cold ashes. For a moment he thought there was something he should be remembering, something about the night just past. But then he sneezed three times in a row which gave him no more time for thought.

"Lord Cres keep you."

Corrie sat bolt upright in bed. There, at the bedfoot, was a small, thin boy at least a year or two younger than he was, with hair the color of soot and periwinkle-blue eyes.

"I could have slit your throat a hundred times and you not even aware. You are soft, Dales boy."

"Why would you want to do that?" asked Corrie, then sneezed again.

"Do what?"

"Slit my throat."

"I don't *want* to. But I *could* have," the boy explained.

"Well, we don't do that sort of thing here," said Corrie, suddenly realizing who the boy was. The head cold was making him slow.

"Why not?"

"Because it's . . . it's . . ." Corrie tried to find the right word though the fuzz in his head, and finally gave up. "Because it's stupid!"

"What's stupid?"

"Slitting throats is stupid. And threatening to do it is stupid. And . . . and . . . *you* are stupid!" Corrie said passionately, and then sneezed three more times, which rather spoiled the moment. Before he knew what was happening, the boy leaped on him and had him around the throat with incredibly strong hands for such a small boy. Then, just as suddenly, the boy unaccountably let go.

"Say—what's that on your neck?"

"Where?"

"There." He pointed at Corrie's neck with an imperious finger. "Are they scars?"

"Oh, that." Corrie shrugged. "I got bitten by a big mountain cat."

"You did?" The boy looked impressed.

"He jumped me from an overhanging branch and we tumbled into the river and . . ."

"Can I look close?"

"Sure."

Gadwess leaned over and put his two forefingers on the scars. "Did you kill it?"

"No. It got away. Downstream."

"Did you cry?"

Corrie considered the question for a minute, then opted for the truth. "Yes. It hurt something fierce."

The Garunian prince put his head to one side. "If that had happened to me, and I cried out, I would have gotten hit for crying."

"Really?" Corrie was appalled.

"Only girls cry, you see."

"Really?"

Gadwess took a deep breath. "And sometimes . . . sometimes *little* boys cry. But only sometimes. And not for long."

"Well this happened only a few months ago and I cried good and proper. But only right after. And not when the infirmarer fixed the wound."

Gadwess' eyes were wide. "Not then?"

"Not at all."

"That's all right then," Gadwess said. He leaned back and surveyed the bedroom. "My room is bigger."

"Some," Corrie admitted.

"That's good."

"It doesn't matter. This room is plenty big enough," Corrie said. "And I've got the south light." He wasn't really sure why that should be important, but Skada had told him that once, when he and Jemmie were quarreling. It seemed a good thing to point out.

"It's important, you see, that I have the biggest room, because of who I am," Gadwess said.

Personally Corrie thought the statement was as stupid as threatening to slit someone's throat. But he preferred the peace he had just won so he didn't answer, only wiped his nose with the sleeve of his nightshirt.

"So—when does a fellow get something to eat around here?" Gadwess asked abruptly. "I haven't eaten much for two days because . . . well I haven't. And I am starving."

Corrie stood. He was pleased to see that, despite an exceptionally runny nose, he no longer felt feverish or dizzy. It was the fever he'd been trying to remember. That and the fact that he thought he had heard crying in the night.

"I'm starving," Gadwess said again. This time it sounded like an order.

"Then put on some clothes and I'll take you downstairs to the kitchen."

"Put them on *myself?*"

Corrie didn't understand. "Who else?"

"A servant, of course. I am, after all, a prince."

"We don't do that here. We dress ourselves. And we don't say *servant*. We say server."

"Why?"

"Because to say servant," Corrie explained in a schoolmasterish voice, "is demeaning."

"Servants," Gadwess answered, "are meant to be demeaned. Like women."

"Better not let my mother hear you say that," Corrie countered quickly.

"Your mother?"

"Queen Jenna," said Corrie and was quite satisfied to see the Garunian prince go suddenly white. *Like a fish belly*, Corrie thought.

"I . . . I . . ." Gadwess took a deep breath. "I thought you had been sent across the sea. Hostage to my hostage." Suddenly he looked very young and very frightened.

"That was my older brother, Jemson."

"Oh." Some color returned to his cheeks. "I didn't know there were two of you."

"That's all right," Corrie said. "I thought you were supposed to be older."

Gadwess looked down. "My older brother could not be sent because he is the heir. Why did they send yours?"

"He is *not* the heir to the throne. Scillia is."

"Who is Scillia?"

"My sister."

The idea was so foreign to Gadwess that his mouth dropped open.

"You look like a fish caught on a hook," Corrie said.

"Do you all speak of fish, like mongers?"

"All?"

Gadwess shut his mouth and his eyelids dropped halfway as if—Corrie decided—he was desperately trying to keep a secret. Corrie had, himself, often been in the same situation: the youngest trying to hold on to a bit of dignity. And then Corrie had a wonderful revelation: *He* was no longer the youngest prince in the Dales. He was so pleased about this, he decided to let Gadwess think he had been fooled. "Come on," Corrie said, "let's get dressed."

Gadwess jumped down from the bed, relief writ large on his face. "If I have trouble with the clasps, will you help me?"

Seizing the moment. Corrie answered, "Not as your servant."

"As what?"

"As a friend," Corrie said adamantly.

The Garunian boy nodded and quickly ran back through the door that connected their rooms.

The council chamber was in an uproar. The long-bearded head of the army had leaped to his feet, shouting almost incoherently. "Tricked us, by damn. Tricked us. Alta's braids! Shouldn't have trusted them damned Garuns. Too soon."

"Sit down, Piet, and think. Think!" Carum said calmly. "Is thirteen years too soon? Trust must begin again or we are at war once more. I do not think this poor country could stand it."

Still standing, Piet shouted again. "The army is ready, sire."

"The army may be ready to fight. But no one is ever ready to die," Jenna replied. She stood as well to make her point, staring across the council table at her old friend.

"Pah! You sound more like your dark sister every day," Piet said, finally settling back in his chair, but not without a great deal of purposely loud fussing.

"A hero no more, Piet? The Anna no more?" Jenna replied.

There was a muttering around the chamber, but it was an old argument between the two of them, though suddenly inside-out. No one wanted to get in the middle of it.

"I would die for you, Anna. And that you know," Piet said, pounding his fist on the table.

"Then live—and listen to Carum. He has more to tell," Jenna replied, sitting down again.

Piet started to sputter once more, but was interrupted by the man next to him with a strange croak of a voice. "Shut up, Piet. You were always better with your fists than your brain."

"And you," Piet growled back, "were best when that collar choked off your voice, Jareth." But it was said for form. Old comrades from the Gender Wars, they were like quarrelsome brothers and never easy in the council chamber.

Once the room was finally quiet, Carum stood. "It is true we were tricked. Or at least misled. But why should we have assumed they were sending their eldest, their heir? We did not send ours." He stepped away from the table, turning his back to them and staring out the window where a sullen rain was falling.

"Only because she is a girl, and unacceptable . . ." Piet said.

"To them," Jenna added quickly. "To them."

The men and women around the table nodded. Scillia was not a great favorite at the moment, being a cranky, moody thirteen-year-old. But she *was* the heir and no one doubted her strength of purpose, or her mind, which was quick. Or her heart.

Carum continued, speaking to the window. "The Garun heir is—as I now understand—already fifteen and as hard and unyielding as his father, Kras. This younger one is of a tenderer disposition. And he has formed an attachment to Corrie. They are already like brothers."

"Squabbling, you mean," Piet said.

"Not at all," Jenna put in. "He looks up to Corrie. He calls him 'Killer of Cats'—a slight exaggeration."

A ripple of laughter ran around the table.

"He can be molded." Carum turned and looked directly at Piet as he spoke.

Piet unflinchingly returned that gaze. "So can young Jemson."

Jenna shivered. *That* had been in her mind from the first.

At dinner in their bedchamber, the hearth fully aflame, Jenna sat on the big bed and toyed with her knife. A light supper of fish pie in Nillum white wine and a cress salad was on the table. It was one of her favorite meals, but she had not eaten more than a few bites.

"You have been silent, my love, for half the dinner at least," commented Carum.

"*To speak is to sow,*" Skada said, her fingers on her own knife.

"*. . . and to listen is to reap,*" Jenna finished for her. "I do not like what I have harvested, Piet is quite right."

"About what?" Carum asked.

"About Jemmie."

Carum sighed. "We have been over and over the same ground, Jenna."

"But we have never dug up the true dirt," she countered.

There was a long silence in which the only observations came from the fire which snapped noisily. Finally Carum stood, brushing off the front of his shirt. He walked over to the fire and with a poker settled the logs into a better, quieter confirmation. Turning his back to the fire, he said, "And what is in that dirt?"

Jenna did not answer directly, but fired a series of questions at him. "Is Jemson a good son of the Dales? Does he honor women? Does he love his sister? Does he think too much of himself? Does he lie? Does he bluster? Is he susceptible to flattery? Does he bend the knee to blood?"

"In Alta's name," Carum said, "stop." He turned back to the fire. "Do you not like our son, Jenna, that you think so little of him?" But he said it softly because he had had many of those thoughts about Jem only days before.

"I love him," Jenna said. But she knew that was not the same thing. Not the same at all.

Unusually silent throughout the exchange, Skada stared into the fire from her place by Jenna's side. Before the last flames disappeared, calling her back to her own dark world, she spoke. "Trust Alta," she said, "to see us through the end of this turning." And then she was gone.

"And what," Carum said, facing Jenna once again, "do you suppose she meant by that?"

"I have long ago told you about Alta's turnings." She held out her hand to him and he sat down by her where the moment before Skada had been.

"You told me a fairy story, my love. About the Green Folk and an Alta who is a woman hundreds of years old and yet not a god. Also something about a paring. I took it to be a parable."

"*Core to rind,*" Jenna said, almost as if reciting a child's verse. "*Rind to core, paring the world. One apple on a vast tree. One tree in a vast grove. One grove in . . .*"

". . . a vast green." Carum's voice was full of sudden anger. "Riddles! Once you hated them. Once you found them tiring. Have you changed so much, Jenna?"

"I have grown old," Jenna said wearily.

"How could you not, my love? We all do."

"In Alta's grove no one grows old," Jenna said.

"A story for children," he reminded her. "Only a story."

"And my children are all grown."

"At thirteen and ten and nine? Not yet."

"I feel them grown away. They are not babies."

He put his arms around her. "Not grown away. Just growing up. It is the world's way. The *real* world, Jenna. Not the world of story, where heroes are ever young and beautiful and unmarked by time." He smiled at her, anger abated, and took her long white braid in his hands. "As I recall, you never much liked being a hero anyway."

She shook her head vigorously, snapping the braid from between his hands. "I must follow Scillia," she said. "I must show her the way to her mother root."

"No, my love, she must find that way herself. Else it is your way, not hers."

"But the way is long. And hard. She could be hurt."

"So she could. But if I can trust her to Alta, so can you." He flexed his hands and the fingers creaked like a rocking chair. "You see—you are not the only old one in this room."

She smiled crookedly at him. "You are still as young as when we met."

"Not so young, I hope," he said. "*Ich crie merci*, Sister of Alta."

At the memory his appeal evoked, when he had first crouched mud-stained, weary, and frightened at her feet, thinking her an illiterate savage, she laughed. Then, as sudden, she was serious again. "But I killed a man to save you then. And I was Scillia's age."

"The woods are no longer filled with marauding Garuns. Women are no longer prey to such villains. We have done some good these thirteen years, Jenna, though we are no longer heroes in everyone's eyes." He stood and moved the table away from the bed. "If you come to bed with me, though, I shall prove that in some things at least, age and experience are the better."

THE HISTORY:

Mother root (mah' ther root) [OD moder rood]

1. *The female genealogy, i.e. the mother's side of the family.*
2. *One's native country.*
3. *A plant of the yam family,* tuberisis genetica.

—Shorter Dictionary of the Dales, *Vol. II Mark-Zygoz*

From a letter to the editor, Nature and History

Sirs:

I have recently discovered in my father's unpublished papers the notes toward an answer to Dr. Magon's article "The Rood to Recovery" in your issue #41.

It is Dr. Magon's odd contention that the ancient Dalians, who were a matriarchal society, had actually discovered that using tuberisis genetica *in an herbal douche guaranteed female babies. We know this is scientific nonsense. My father's notes clearly show that he consulted the heads of three major teaching hospitals and a half-dozen directors of family clinics, all of whom confessed grave doubts that any such thing was possible.*

Magon's thesis about the douche is based on folklore and a totally bizarre reading of a line in the only extant—though water-damaged and stained—copy of Langbrow's Book of Battles: *"Moder rood is my way and my rite."*

In the BOB *that phrase is used one warrior to another, though because of the staining, one cannot read the gender of either warrior involved. The paragraphs before and after the exchange are totally illegible. Still, Dr. Magon has chosen to ignore the other possible (and more probable) readings to offer your subscribers his preposterous herbal trifle.*

My father's more moderated and sensible readings of that line are threefold:

1. *The phrase may be referring to a particular food preference,* *or religious dietary law ("rite"). We know such practices certainly existed in the army. For example, soldiers from the southern parts of the Dales often made a savory cat-tail stew which they served only on the eve of their sabbath. And soldiers from the Galanza area ate raw roots of the yam family the eve before a battle, to purge the body's evil.*

2. *Alternately, the phrase may be referring to the ritual known as "Taking the Mother," a form of self-flagellation with a large stick ("rood") known as The Mother. This ritual, brought over by the first of the conquering G'runs, had only a small following. But, especially the day preceding an expected battle, those who were believers whipped themselves into a frenzy till—as has been noted in Doyle's early work—"The Mother ran red with the blood of would-be heroes."*

3. *A third alternative is that the phrase may be a reference to the great central road that once ran through the Dales, known to some as Alta's Way and to others as The Mother Road.*

Without knowing the exact context of the phrase—even with laser technology the stains have remained unparsable—we have only educated guesses. But surely my father's three suggestions are at least as viable as Dr. Magon's. I feel—and I hope you do, too—that they deserve publication so that your readers might make up their own minds.

I would be happy to send on a copy of my father's notes. Or even happier to write them more fully in a complete paper. I am not only executor of my father's estate, I am a scholar myself, holding a doctorate in Dalian studies under Dr. Cowan at Pasden University.

Yours,

THE STORY:

Scillia had ridden out into the storm but had been wise in dressing for the weather. Her waterproof cloak and great traveler's hat kept the rain off her clothes and head, and her boots were equally waterproof and warm. She had been as smart about her food, her saddlebag packed with enough provisions for five days, and some journeycake for beyond that. And for protection, as well as for further provisioning, she had taken two knives from the kitchen—a short knife with a blade that was finger-length, and a larger knife that had a blade as long as her forearm. It was useless for her to take a bow; that was not something that could be used one-handed, so she had never learned how to shoot. But she *had* taken her father's short sword, still wrapped in its ceremonial cloth. Though she had only actually seen it once before—when he had shown them all the watering on its blade and told them stories about the Gender Wars because Jem had asked—she knew where it was kept. They *all* knew where it was kept: in the great wooden cupboard in her parents' bedchamber.

She did not think that taking the sword constituted theft. After all, her father never used the thing and therefore would not miss it. She would get it back to him long before he even knew it was gone. But carrying it tucked beneath her leg, against the saddle, she felt invulnerable. That sword had killed its share of men in the Wars, and the blood grained into the steel would keep her safe. She did not just *know* this, she believed it utterly.

She thought about her brother Jemmie, now well on his way to the Garunian shore. She did not miss him, not the real Jem, who was a whiner and an occasional liar, and who always made himself out to be the hero of any tale. But she missed the brother he *could* be, her good right hand when she was queen.

"*If* I become queen," she reminded herself. Being the daughter, or the adopted daughter, of a queen did not routinely mean queenship. Not in the Dales where the people had already, in her lifetime, rid themselves of a hated king.

But Scillia hoped that this adventure would prove her worthy. To herself, above all others. "And," she whispered into the rain and wind, "at the same to find my mother root."

She did not remember when she had first heard the phrase. But long before she had learned about the warrior woman of M'dorah she'd known it. There was a story, a fairy tale really, that her old nurse used to tell. About the little woodcutter's child who went to seek her lost mam, going along the "mother rood," the mother road, and finding not one but ten mothers awaiting her. It was an odd tale, not one of Scillia's favorites. But her old nurse had a lot of stories that were odd to a Southern sensibility. She was from some mountain village in the back of beyond, brought home by a soldier as wife, and then widowed in the Wars. In the South, everyone seemed to say "mother root" when they meant simply the mother who bore you.

"And that's not Mother Jenna!" Scillia said aloud, renewing her anger which had gotten soft under the lulling rain.

The horse flicked its ears back and forth as if agreeing, and Scillia leaned forward to pat its neck. Then she urged it off the road and under a tree. Her stomach had just reminded her it was well past time for eating.

The rain continued all day and by early evening Scillia was too tired to ride any longer. There was no town in sight, and so she unsaddled the horse and tied it loosely by one leg to a tree so that it would not wander off in the night. Then, remembering her mother's stories about her time in the woods, she climbed the same tree, but with little grace, and settled into the main crotch to sleep. She was not about to chance a wolf at her throat. As as for cats—she kept the large knife unsheathed in her lap.

Sometime in the middle of the night the rain stopped. Startled out of sleep by the horse's night-time grunting,

Scillia looked up and saw stars overhead through the interlaced branches. She spoke the patterns aloud as if by naming them she could regain a familiar sense of comfort. "The Hound," she said, outlining one figure with her finger. "Alta's Braid."

As she shifted about in the tree to see all the stars, the knife fell from her lap and clattered to the ground. The horse shied from it, giving a frightened snort, but the rope around its leg held fast.

Scillia thought about climbing down in the dark to find the knife, but was suddenly too afraid to attempt it. Instead, she took the smaller knife from her belt and, holding that, finally fell back to sleep.

The morning was cold and grey, but clear. When Scillia woke, the first thing she saw was her own breath pluming out. Her legs were cramped and when she stretched them, she realized that the little knife was no longer in her lap. Looking down, she saw it resting, blade on blade, atop the larger one, not far from where the horse was contentedly cropping a patch of old grass.

She managed to get down the tree with even less grace than she had gotten up, only to discover that some small animals had been at her pack.

"What a ninny!" she scolded herself aloud. She should have carried the pack up the tree. A wolf or a bear would have made quick work of it on the ground. But with only one arm, climbing the tree was difficult enough. How could she bring the pack up as well? In her teeth? It was much too heavy. She would have to figure that out before another nightfall.

However, although the animals—probably wood mice, she thought—had nibbled a bit of the journeycake and burrowed well into the loaf of bread, they had left the rest of her food alone. She had been lucky this time. She would not chance it again.

She ate enough to be comfortably full and drank several long swallows from her waterskin. Then she saddled the horse. She'd long practice in that, at least. Setting the two knives well into her belt, she mounted the horse and urged it along.

She was soon too warm in the cloak and hat, skinning out of them both without dismounting and tucking them into the left saddle pack. The woods were alive with animals, but none that she could see. There were tracks crisscrossing the path, especially at the narrower points. But nothing that looked big like bear, or as threatening. She was glad of that.

She yawned loudly and the horse pricked its ears up at the sound, but did not otherwise change its plodding pace. She fell into a half sleep as the horse picked out its own way, following the easiest route.

By noon the road had straightened and ran alongside the woods instead of through them. It was hard-packed and rutted, as if wagons had been pulled frequently along the track. Scillia's naps had finally ceased and she was able to watch the road and forest beside her with equal parts interest and wariness.

She did not recognize where she was; there were no landmarks she could name. But she knew where she was going: past Selden Hame and on to M'dorah. Wherever that was! She planned to ask for information at the first inn but only enough—she warned herself—to go one stop farther on. She did not want to be tracked by either her mother or father, which was why she had not gotten directions from the kitcheners or from the one guard who had seen her leave. If it took longer this way, then it would take longer. She was, after all, not in any great hurry. M'dorah would still be there whether she got there in one day or ten.

She could have been farther already had she left directly north from the castle. But to fool the guard—who would undoubtedly tell her parents which way she'd gone—she had left by the west gate and ridden straight until she was well out of sight. Only then had she made a great quarter-circle turn to the north.

She smiled. Being tricksy was not in her nature.

"So they will never guess," she whispered, knowing she had made a good go of it.

A small bird flew out before her and she took that as a kind of sign. Kicking the horse into a gallop, she halloed lustily, grinning as the wind whistled past her ears.

She was off. Alone. On her own.

It was enough.

Slowing at last to rest the horse, Scillia twisted in the saddle to look around. Now there were signs of habitation: a well-kept stone wall ran for many lengths along the road between her and a field that spoke of summer tillage. There was even a tattered scarecrow in the field, its stick arms poking through the sleeves of an old cotta.

She thought about sleeping in a tree another night, decided against it.

"Save that for when I must," she told herself. She would pay the farmer for what food she ate, what bed she used.

"No!" she scolded aloud. "Work for it!" If she worked, she would be one with her people. She liked that idea much better.

Kicking the horse again into a rough trot, she rose up for a moment in the leather stirrups. There was a farmhouse on the rise just ahead, its front face an invitation. Strangely, though, there was no smoke issuing from the chimney. That was one puzzle. The other was that no dog came down the road to clamor at horse and rider. Surely a farmhouse so far from a village would have need of both fire and alarm.

When she got closer, though, she saw why. Only a front wall and half roof was still standing facing the road, but the side and back walls had mostly tumbled in. There would be no bed there for the night.

She left the horse tied by the gate and wandered through the ruin. When they had come this way before, on their visit to Selden Hame, there had been no ruined house. Of that she was certain. Her mother would have made a fuss about it, searching out the farmer and his family and offering them help. Besides, the stone walls held in a field that had been recently farmed; the scarecrow was standing guard over the winter fallow.

Shaking her head, Scillia poked about the four ruined rooms, finding nothing of value and nothing, either, to inform her what had happened, except a great quantity of ash and char which bespoke a devastating fire.

"Did anyone come through this alive?" she wondered aloud. In her mind's eye she saw flames, heard screams. Then she shook her head for such havering. Her mother always said: *Do not measure a shroud before there is a corpse*. For the first time she understood what that meant.

At least she could sleep by the wall under the partial roof. That was marginally more comfortable than crouched in a crotch of a tree. Though perhaps not any safer.

She took the packs from the horse and hung them on a hook high on the wall, proud at how well she was learning to cope on her own. Then she unsaddled the horse, hobbled it, found some grain in a covered wooden tub the mice had not yet tunneled into. There was an unfouled well outside, and she drew up fresh water for them both, a difficult task with just one arm, but do-able.

Laying out her blanket under the partial roof, she sat on

it a while, just thinking. Thinking about the road ahead, the road behind, and what it felt like being somewhere in-between. Not a comfortable feeling, but not entirely uncomfortable either. She smiled ruefully then shivered. It was cold and damp and she badly needed a fire. So she got up again and found some pieces of wood lying against the front wall, sheltered from the rain. With them she built a small fire in the old stone hearth, the only part of the back wall still standing. When the fire began to crackle merrily, she sat down to let the warmth soak into her bones.

She thought of Skada, and suddenly found herself wishing she could have had a dark companion of her own. Father always said something about a friend shortening the road. But no one called up the dark sisters anymore. That magic—like most of the old ways—had been ended with the dissolution of the Hames.

Probably, she thought, *no one even knows how to do it any more. Except the old women at Selden*. For a moment she was bitter. *There's lots I haven't been taught. But*, she added, *I will learn it all nonetheless*.

She tried to remember how in the old stories women called their dark sisters out. Something about moonlight and water and mirrors. A chant. "Come to me . . ." or some such.

She said the words aloud several times, feeling silly all the while. She even thought about seeing if she could try speaking the chant while leaning over the well. Then suddenly she was much too tired to think of it any longer. Before she could stand and get over to her blanket under the overhang, she fell asleep, still sitting by the fire.

When she woke at dawn, she was lying on her back, far from the roof, and the rain was spitting callously into her upturned face.

THE SONG:

The Dark Sister's Lullaby

Come to me, sister, for long is the night,
And dreams cannot keep body warm.
I'll cradle you carefully, darkness to light,
I'll keep you quite safely from harm.

Come to me, sister, the night will be deep,
And sleep comes not easily soon.
I'll cradle you closely, my promises keep,
My night for the light of your moon.

Come to me, sister, the stars all take flight,
Come kiss me this once ere I go.
I'll cradle you carefully night after night
As I did in the dark long ago.

THE STORY:

"What do you mean," Jenna said savagely to Marek, "that you could not find her trail?"

"We cast both west and north for two days, Jenna," he answered, his calm voice giving the lie to two days worth of stomach cramps, two days worth of heartache. "West because the guard saw her ride that way and north because that is the road to Selden Hame and then M'dorah, where *you* said she would be heading."

Jenna turned her back on him, trembling with fury and fear, and cursing under her breath.

"Then we must try south and east," Carum said sensibly. "There are only four directions, after all. Scillia is unused to the woods and a novice at concealing a trail. Though she is but one girl on one horse, she will no doubt leave a swath as wide as a legion's."

"So one would think," Jenna said, turning slowly back to face them both. "So any *competent* woodsman would think."

"I am as good in the woods as you, Jenna," Marek said, looking grim.

"Never. You were but a ferryman's boy when we met. I was trained to be a hunter."

"That was eighteen years ago and more, Jenna. A man can learn something in that time."

"Not all men have the capacity for learning," Jenna said. Then speaking to Carum only, added, "I will go south first."

Carum put a hand on her wrist. "You wound an old friend with a new sword, Jenna. And he has ridden off sick and come home sicker. Look at his grey face."

Jenna looked instead into Carum's eyes for a long moment, then sighed. "You are right as always. Marek—go first to my own infirmarer. And if she says you are fit, ride east. But pray, before even you have the infirmarer's ear, send men to scout again the territory you already rode. Though . . ." she said looking down at her feet, "if you did not find the trail, it is probably not to be found."

"I could have missed something, Anna."

She went over to him and took his hands in hers. "Salve for your wound, old friend. You miss nothing." Her eyes searched his face. "Lest . . . lest in your illness . . ."

He nodded and she turned and left the room at a run, mounted the stone steps to her chamber two at a time, and in minutes had traded her skirts for pants and her slippers for heavy riding boots.

In the kitchen they were provisioned for a week's riding. Jenna herself put journeycake into her saddle packs. Then in the stables, she apologized to Marek once again.

"My heart bids my mouth speak faster than my head. I did not stop to think."

"It is already forgotten, my queen," Marek said. "But what if one of the men finds her—what should they do?"

"Just keep watch. Keep her safe. She needs to be on this trip alone, or at least she must believe she is on the trip alone. Now get you to the infirmarer."

"I will when I return, Anna," he said. "I am feeling better by the minute."

"You are greyer by the minute," said Carum. "But I expect your mind is made up."

"We must waste no more time," Marek said as confirmation.

Carum put his arms around Jenna. "I would come with you. She is my daughter, too."

"Now as ever the kingdom needs its king," said Jenna.

"And its queen," he countered.

"You know I find the throne a troubling seat. I will not miss it nor it me while I am gone." She gave him a weak smile, kissed him lightly on the mouth.

He hugged her to him and whispered, "Find her, Jen."

"You know I will, though others mount the search as well."

They both knew the truth of that.

Scillia had managed to get into her waterproof cloak and hat just before the rain had soaked her through, but only just. She could not get the fire going again for there was no more dry tinder to hand, and at last she left off trying. Instead she saddled the horse who, it turned out, was as cranky as she. When she mounted up, her father's sword fell out of its wrappings, clattering to the ground. She was so angry with it and with herself, she nearly just left the thing in the foreyard.

In the end, of course, she dismounted and picked up

the sword, shoving it savagely between the saddle pack and the horse with such roughness, the horse reared, nearly tearing her arm from the socket in the process. Her hat fell off and when the horse came down again on all fours, his front hooves ground the hat into the dirt.

"Lord Cres himself must have sent you to me, horse!" Scillia cried. Tears of pain and frustration streamed from her eyes, but by then her face was already so wet from the rain, no one could have told she had been crying. But her eyes hurt from crying, and her heart seemed to be beating erratically.

She tied the horse to the front-door latch and picked up the hat which she tucked into her belt. Then she went around the side of the standing wall and stood for a while under the bit of roof. The pattering of the rain on the wooden laths had a calming effect and at last her heart started to beat normally again.

"If I lose my temper *and* my horse," she scolded herself aloud, "I will have a long, cold walk home." *And*, she thought, *a lifetime in which to be embarrassed*. It was the thought of the embarrassment more than than the length of the walk or the cold that settled her.

Drawing a deep breath, she walked around to the front again, hat in hand. It was much too filthy to put back on her head.

"Now, horse," she said, walking up to it quietly, "we must have a talk." She placed her hand on its nose and rubbed it softly. "You must be a sweetling. You *are* a sweetling." Then in cozening tones she added, "And you are much too stupid to know that I mean not a word of it as long as I speak to you nicely."

She got out some journeycake from the saddle pack and held it out to the horse. Quickly softened by the mizzle of rain, the journeycake made an excellent pacifier. The horse lipped it eagerly. "Sweets for a sweetling," Scillia said, though the cake was actually rather salty.

While the horse was still savoring its bits of the cake, Scillia untied it and mounted once again.

"At least," she said, leaning toward the horse's flicking ears, "no one saw that performance, or we should both be mortified."

The rain continued and, seeing no hope of its ending soon, Scillia finally took her hat from her belt and shoved it on her head. Dirty or not, at least it would keep her head dry.

THE TALE:

Once Horse lived in a beautiful green meadow by himself and was happy with his lot.

Then one day Deer came to be his neighbor.

Now Deer did not eat as Horse did but trampled all the grass beneath his sharp little hooves and stripped the leaves of the trees bare.

Soon Horse was fed up with Deer's uncouth ways and took himself off to town. There he knocked on the door of the house.

Boy came out and saw Horse. "What can I do for you, Four Legs?"

"Stop Deer from trampling my green meadow, Two Legs."

So Boy took his bow and arrow and slew Deer and had a winter of venison in the bargain. And for a time both Horse and Boy were happy.

But a new and bigger Deer came to be Horse's neighbor and once again the meadow was trampled beneath sharp little hooves and the leaves of the trees were stripped bare.

Horse went back to town and knocked again on the door of the house.

This time Man came out and saw Horse. "What can I do for you, Four Legs?"

"Stop Deer from trampling my green meadow, Two Legs."

So Man took his sword and spear and slew Deer and had a winter and a spring of venison in the bargain. And for a time Horse and Man were happy.

But a new and even bigger Deer came to be Horse's neighbor and once again the meadow was trampled beneath sharp hooves and the leaves of the trees were stripped bare.

Horse went back to town and knocked on the door of the house.

This time Woman came out. She knew what Horse wanted. But she also knew better than Man and Boy. "Twice we have done as you have required," she said. "Now you must do something for us in return."

"As long as it is within my power, Two Legs," said Horse.

So Woman held out a halter of leather which she had made from the tanned skin of Deer. "What we want is ever so simple. Just put this on your head," she said.

So Horse did.

Man and Boy killed Deer and, under the direction of Woman, fenced in the meadow. And from that day till this, Horse has worn a halter and served Two Legs within fences. And Deer has roamed without, often hungry, often cold, and most often in Two Legs' pot.

THE STORY:

With more luck than logic, Jenna found her daughter's trail by the second day. She had gone south first, without much hope, knowing that the soaking rains would have washed away all signs of riding. Still she had kept at it, admitting only to Skada at the fire the first night that she feared for the girl's safety.

"She is a sturdy child," Skada said. "Several nights in the wet and cold will not kill her."

"But there has been unrest in the South," Jenna said.

"I know."

"A farmhouse here, a travelers' inn there." Jenna sighed. "Little enough, I know."

"Except for the folk burned out. And the girls taken."

"Except for them."

They were silent, attending the fire, for a long while. Then Jenna reached in with Skada's help and snatched out the coney on its stick from the center of the blaze.

"And what will she eat?"

Skada laughed. "Journeycake and cold meat if she must. The kitchener said she took enough with her for an army, and she was never a girl for large meals. It's Corrie who would starve from the second day on."

At that Jenna laughed, too, tearing off a bit of meat, the blackened part that Skada preferred, and handed it to her sister.

As they chewed, once again in silence, Jenna thought about the trail. She was close to asking her dark sister, when Skada blurted out an answer.

"I do not think we have lost ground coming south. But another day of this and we'd best turn west."

Jenna nodded, knowing that she would have to do the daylight riding on her own.

They slept side by side till the fire damped out and Skada was gone. Jenna was sleeping so deeply, she never noticed when Skada disappeared. But then, she never did.

It was at a burned-out farm, the fields quietly wintering over and watched by a scarebird of little craft, that Jenna found the signs. First a scumbling of hoofprints in the foreyard, the imprint of some sort of struggle. The overhanging eaves of the house had kept the telltale prints from disappearing in the rain.

Jenna's throat closed and her heart thudded loudly in her breast until she read them more closely.

One set of bootprints, the maker's print in the heel clear enough.

One horse. The characteristic twist of the castle blacksmith's iron shoes easy to remark.

"And one arm to do the saddling, the bridling, the mounting. Good girl!" Jenna said aloud. "That you got here safely on your own. Good indeed."

In the shambles of the farmhouse she found proof of a single sleeper near the hearth. The house had burned down well before that, and while Jenna could not be happy for the farmers, at least the ash and char under the roof gave her a definite impression of her daughter's night. For that she had to be grateful.

"She is not far from here," Jenna said to her white horse. The horse, so long her companion, whinnied back as if in answer. "If Alta's luck goes with us," Jenna added, "we will find her before morning."

She did not, even once, question that the signs might not be her daughter's passage. True, it could have been another solitary traveler, sheltering in the burned-out house, fighting an obstinate mount. But not with the mark of those boots, those hooves. She was as certain of Scillia as if she had been there with her on her solitary trek.

"Full moon tonight," Jenna said to the horse. "If the clouds favor us, Skada and I will follow my child all the way to the place where she now sleeps."

In fact, the moon kept appearing and disappearing, making conversation with Skada difficult, and reading the road more difficult still.

"Why is she heading due south?" Jenna asked, as much to herself as to her dark sister.

When the moon slipped away from the clouds, Skada answered, "Either you are following a Garun, or . . ." and once more she was gone as the moon hid again behind a large cloud.

"Or more likely," Jenna finished for her, "Scillia has little sense of direction and no sunrise or sunset in the day's mizzle to guide her. I *should* have taken time to teach her more about reading the woods. But there is always so much to do in the kingdom. And whenever I can stand the nattering of councillors no more . . ."

The moon shone suddenly bright on the path and Skada, behind her, laughed. "Then you run off into the woods on your own."

"Not on my own, sister," Jenna countered. "There is always you with me."

"And is that so bad, sister?"

"On occasion." Jenna turned around in the saddle to speak to Skada, but once again the moon was gone and Skada with it.

Afraid to miss something each time the moon hid behind the clouds, Jenna made slow passage in the night. However, it soon became clear that the rider—Scillia she was sure—was not one to leave the road and strike off into the darker woods. Or even, when the road passed a wide expanse of meadow, to gallop across the brown wintered grass.

So at last Jenna settled the mare into a steady walk until about an hour past midnight, when the horse stopped dead in the track. No amount of urging on Jenna's part would move the animal forward.

"Tired?" Jenna asked, already knowing the answer. She unsaddled the horse and let it find its own poor grazing while she climbed a tree. Settling with the ease of long practice into the crotch, she closed her eyes. It was much too dark beneath the sheltering upper limbs for the moon to reach her so Skada did not appear. That was just as well. There was not enough room there for the two of them.

She slept alone till the first false dawn.

Scillia's clothes were still damp. Her hair, loose from the plaitings, was in dirty knots. Her teeth had a scummy feel and she could still taste the last three meals of old meat and journeycake. Every bit of her ached: her arm where the horse had pulled away from her; her thighs from riding three days; her back from sleeping rough; her hand from gathering firewood and pulling aside brush. The only thing that did not hurt her was the stump of her missing arm. And that was very odd, indeed.

And yet she felt good.

Felt great!

In fact, she felt . . . free.

For the first time she understood why her mother so frequently went woods-trekking on her own. Scillia had always resented the times Jenna had left them for days to the care of nursemaids and tutors; had always wondered how her father stood Jenna's frequent absences from court. But now, the third day out, when fear was no longer a constant companion and she knew herself a competent traveler, Scillia felt a comradeship with her mother.

"I see, mother," she whispered. "At last I see."

Ahead there was a particularly difficult place in the road. A large ash tree had fallen straight across the path and only a narrow passage remained at the root end. She got off her horse and led it around, pushing with her back against the brush so the horse could get by. She was wondering why a tree still so alive should have come down when she heard a voice.

"Girl!"

Looking past her horse, she saw three men in the road ahead—two fairly young and one much older, with grey interleaving his scraggly beard. The older man's hair, the color of old bowstring, was long, hanging well past his shoulders. They were a rather unsavory crew, but she did not let her unease show in her face. Instead she started to greet them companionably.

But the older man spoke first. "Stand, girl. We will have what is in your packs."

For a moment she thought to reveal herself to them, to tell them she was the king's own. In the same instant, she realized how foolish that would be, and reached instead to the knives in her belt. She drew the long one and stood still, the knife upraised. *If worst comes to worst*, she thought, *I will let them have the horse and packs*.

"Come no closer," she said.

The older man laughed. "A kitchen wench with a kitchen knife! Think that will win you some time?"

The two younger men laughed at his wit, the taller revealing a gap between his teeth.

"Knife or no, we will have your packs, girl," said the older man.

"And you after," Gap-tooth added.

"There is nothing in my pack but journeycake and old meat," Scillia said, lowering the knife a bit to show good faith.

"But there is new meat in your counte," Gap-tooth said, bringing his hand down to his privates and laughing. His companion laughed again with him.

The old man came forward, though remaining a cautious distance from her knife, just in case. "And what of your horse, girl? It's a fine-looking gelding. And what of that thing behind your saddle, shaped like a sword and wrapped in fine cloth? A present from your master? I doubt it. You have the look of a thief."

"Like you? I think not," Scillia said. But for a moment she turned her head toward the horse, remembering her father's sword with regret. And in that instant, the old man moved in and grabbed the knife from her. He reached at the same time for her other arm in order to immobilize it.

"One-armed, by Cres! Not even a whole woman to share," he shouted to the others. "But no doubt she'll do."

"Do *what?*" The voice was soft, but with the full authority of a warrior behind it. Scillia knew that voice well though she had never heard it quite so throaty and stern.

For once she was silent.

Standing by her white horse, the sun behind her shining full in the villains' eyes, Jenna was haloed by light. She had a sword in one hand, a wicked long knife in the other. "This is the Dales. We do not treat women so. By Alta, you shall pay the blood price!"

"It is the Anna!" cried Gap-tooth. "See how she shines."

"Pah! It is just another poxy woman with the sun at her back," said the old man. "Do not be unmanned by stories. There are three of us to her one."

"Two!" cried Scillia, wrenching from the older man and diving toward the horse which, for once, did not take fright but stood till Scillia had pulled the sword from behind the pack. Then it shied, sidestepping between the two younger men and splitting them apart.

In that moment, Scillia had unwrapped the sword by the simple expedient of twirling it with her hand so that the cloth fell to the ground. The sword was heavier than she recalled, and it took an effort to keep it raised. Nevertheless she held it steadily, backing away from the men to stand by her mother's side.

"Get on my horse and ride from here," Jenna said under her breath. "I will follow after."

"I will not leave you, mother," Scillia whispered back.

"You will be no help in a fight. And there are but three. I have handled more in the Wars."

"You are no longer a young warrior," Scillia said. "How many years has it been since you fought in earnest?"

"Do not remind me," Jenna said.

And then with no warning, she charged the three men. A quick downward stroke to the leg put the gap-toothed man out of commission. He fell screaming.

The second young man had been knocked too far by Scillia's horse for any such quick disabling stroke. He backed away further and to Jenna's left.

It was the older man who proved the fighter. He parried Jenna's first two thrusts and then struck back. She missed stopping his stroke, and the tip of his sword sliced through her leggings, running a long, bloody line down her right thigh.

"Ouf!" Jenna cried, more in surprise than pain. With a quick upswing of her own sword, she caught his blade and sent it high in the air, sailing back behind the fallen tree.

But the old man was fast. He drew a small knife from his boot top and flung it at her. She had but a second to raise her sword like a narrow shield, but it was enough. The knife clanged against the handguard and glanced aside. Still the force of his throw was so great that she could feel the sting of it in her hand for moments after.

And then the younger man was behind her, his arm around her neck, choking her. She tried to flip him, but she did not have the strength. And just as she despaired of getting rid of him, he suddenly went limp, sliding to the ground behind her. She coughed twice, experimentally, then saw that the older man had chosen this moment to run. He was scrambling over the fallen tree.

She flung her sword at his back and it hit him, point squarely between the shoulder blades. He lay, pinned to the tree, and did not move.

Jenna turned to see what had happened to the one who had tried to choke her and had so nearly succeeded. He, too, lay still, face down in the path, a familiar-looking sword in the back of his neck. Scillia was standing over him, stunned, staring down.

"Oh my sweetling," Jenna said, going over to her. "My brave child."

Scillia looked up slowly. "It felt like a knife through venison, mother."

"So it should," Jenna agreed, "for are we not also meat?" She did not put her arms around Scillia because suddenly her arms were so tired she could not raise them.

"Then I shall never eat meat more," Scillia said clearly, before turning her face away and being noisily sick.

Only Gap-tooth was still alive. For a moment Jenna thought about finishing him with a knife stroke. But his eyes were frightened, beginning to glaze over with pain. Indeed he looked more like venison than man.

"Know," she said going over to him, "that the Anna spares you this time." She thought he heard her, though it was not easy to tell.

Then she turned back to her daughter. "Enough killing," she said. "We will leave him to bury his mates and follow on, if he can. He is nothing on his own." Taking a kerchief from her pack, her hands shaking with the effort, she poured a bit of water from her waterskin and wiped Scillia's face as tenderly as if Scillia were still a small child, the old adage running through her mind—*Kill once, mourn ever*. She did not say it aloud.

"Do you get used to it, mother?"

"Get used to what?"

"The killing."

"You saved my life, child," Jenna said. "And your own. If any killing is worth the doing, it is for that."

Scillia stared at her. Then, remembering the feel of the sword through flesh, she was sick all over again.

THE SONG:

The Warrior's Song

Going our way on the warrior track,
Shoulder to shoulder and belly to back,
Riding one horse, a quite notable hack.
We will win through to the morning.

Swords are now red that were shiny and new,
Arms that were white are now blackened and blue;
Still we are sisters and always are true,
And we will win through to the morning.

You kill the man who is fast on our track.
I kill the man who has you on your back.
We parry and thrust and we sever and hack,
We always win though to the morning.

But when we grow old and our hands lose their guile,
And we cannot kill with a casual smile,
Pray turn on me straight with your usual style
And I'll run you through, too, in the morning.

THE STORY:

Jenna's leg wound proved to be but a deep scratch, though by the moonless evening her leg ached enough to make climbing up a tree uncomfortable. So she sent Scillia up the tree alone, settling herself below with a horse hobbled on either side to serve as an early warning of any intruders.

But the horses kept silent watch all night, and Jenna slept through until dawn like one dead. In the morning she awoke to the smell of a new fire and journeycake heating.

Neither one of them spoke until they had eaten the warmed-up cake, washing it down with fresh water Scillia had drawn from a nearby stream. Then Jenna asked, in as casual a manner as she could, "Why have you been traveling south?"

Scillia stared moodily into the fire a moment before answering. "Because I did not know the way, obviously."

"If your way is to M'dorah, then you should be going north. We will be many days getting there."

"We?" Scillia's voice held the same forced casual tone.

"You will not find it on your own."

"And you would go with me?"

"I am your mother. And a goodly part of your mother road. *Moder rood ist lang.*"

"What if I do not want you along?" Scillia asked quietly.

Jenna was silent for a minute before answering. "Then I shall make you a map and send you on your way."

"Without trailing after me? You swear it?" Scillia looked straight on her.

"I swear it," Jenna said, putting out her hand to seal the oath. It was not an easy thing to swear, and her jaw ached saying the words.

Scillia did not take the offered hand. "Company . . ." she said slowly, "would be nice. If you will be dark sister to my light, and *not* my mother. After all, I killed the man at your back. You owe me."

"I owe you," Jenna said. "And I will try."

Scillia grasped her hand then, though she did not add: *I*

shall try, too. But the phrase hung there, unspoken, between them like an apple ripe for the plucking.

What does it mean to be dark sister to her light? Jenna asked herself as they rode along. My *dark sister speaks hard, uncomfortable truths to me and holds my back against the foe*. For all that Scillia had just killed an enemy at her back, Jenna did not know if her daughter wanted that kind of relationship. Any truth told her would still be coming from her mother's mouth. Thirteen is not a year for listening.

So Jenna said nothing, and the day stretched like a border between two countries, she on the one side and Scillia on the other, aware of possible incursions while crying all the while "Peace! Peace!" It was as if they were hostages to one another's good intentions.

Hostages! She thought at once of the two boys, her own Jem and young Gadwess, alone in foreign lands and at the will of masters who would try to mold them. She and Scillia were never such.

And thinking this, Jenna turned in her saddle to speak to her daughter, now for the sake of a quiet journey her sister. "Can you let an old woman rest?" she asked. "My leg is hurting."

It was a lie when she spoke it, and a truth when they dismounted. She walked out the pain, and then walked longer than she intended because she saw in her daughter's face relief, anger, and love mixed in equal measure. They shared a bit of cold journeycake and water.

When they remounted, they rode on until evening and the road declared a real peace between them.

A wide turning brought an inn to view, and Scillia said: "I need a bath and something sweet to wash out the taste of blood."

Skada would have spit back, "That is a taste that no amount of washing takes away." But Jenna did not have the heart to tell Scillia such dark truths so early on her life's journey; she herself had had many a nightmare about the first man she'd ever slain, a man who would have murdered Carum, then taken his rough pleasure with Jenna and Pynt. She had regrets about killing, but none about killing *him*. Instead, she said, "I could use a bath, too. Do we give them money here or work off our stay? It is not so rich a place as to refuse even small coin."

"I have money," Scillia said. "For *this* time." She did not thank her mother for letting her make the decision alone. And as Jenna knew Scillia would have an easier time complaining than offering up thanks, she let it be.

The inn was not only rundown, it was all but empty except for the keeper, his wife, and a daughter who looked quite simple and appeared to do all the hard work. Still, Jenna counted that to the good. She knew the roughness of the place meant she and Scillia would not have to explain the state of their clothes or their relationship to nosy travelers at dinner.

"A room, a bath, a meal, in that order," Scillia said, with such authority, it sounded as though she had a long acquaintance with such inns.

The innkeeper was a sallow-faced man with lips that seemed permanently puckered, as if he had been raised on lemons or had a sour disposition. Or both. If he guessed who they were, he did not say. His wife and daughter were too obviously cowed by him to bother them with questions.

The room they were shown was none too clean, but the bath water in the tin tub was kept hot by frequent infusions of heated rain water. The simple daughter was the one to do the carrying. She was more like a domesticated animal than a human, and Jenna felt sorry for her, and grateful, too.

Scillia took the first bath, a long soaking, and Jenna

helped soap her hair, afterward pouring fresh water over her to rinse it out. She did not ask Scillia's permission, though it was clearly a mothering sort of thing to do. But Scillia did not complain of it.

In turn, Scillia did the same for her, clucking over the long, reddened leg wound.

"Does it hurt?"

"It stings."

"Can you ride on?"

"If you wish it."

Their conversations, Jenna thought, were more like Garunian fight songs: short, pithy, and full of unspoken antagonisms. But at least they were speaking.

Scillia refused the beef pie at dinner, asking instead for a bowl of steamed vegetables which the innkeeper served grudgingly. Jenna did not show, even by so much as a conspiratorial shrug to the man, that she was aware it was an odd request. She ate her own hearty meal without comment, surprised at how good it was. If Scillia wished to give up meat because of killing a villain with a sword, then her hunger would be her own. Jenna knew there would be days on end when they would have no meat on their long riding. Or even any food at all. The rind end of winter could be a hard time to travel in the forest. But she did not say a word about it.

I am trying, she thought. *I will try*.

They shared a bed, of course. They had not the money to waste on two rooms, and besides the warmth was welcome. But Scillia had never been a quiet sleeper, always claiming more than her half of any pallet. Even as a small child, she would travel about the mattress, forcing Jenna or Carum to get up and seek a bed elsewhere. In those early days there had been no nursemaids, no tutors, no one else to take charge of a child at night but the parents.

Lying by Scillia's unquiet body, Jenna remembered those times with an uncommon longing. How easy it had been to be a mother to a child who adored her unconditionally. And—she thought almost bitterly—queen to a kingdom full of people who felt the same.

Enough! she told herself fiercely, grabbing back part of the coverlet from Scillia who had somehow managed to twist the entire thing around herself without ever waking. *Stretch your feet according to your blanket.* Jenna snorted at the thought; it so particularly suited the situation.

She did not have an easy night, all things considered, with dark dreams, old feet, aching leg, and a daughter who did not lie easy. On waking, Jenna was as tired as if she had not slept at all.

They took the long way around, through small villages, skirting the edge of the deep and unmapped western woods. They could have ridden the great King's Road that ran north and south, but Jenna knew instinctively that would not have suited Scillia's need for a hard and long search. So she told Scillia nothing about the route, talking instead of woodcraft each time they slowed or stopped.

She showed Scillia the kinds of wintered-over plants that could still be used for food, like wake robin which, boiled down till the acrid taste was gone, served a nutritious if bland turnip meal. Like the hard fruit of trees—butternut and chestnut, "That is," she cautioned, "if the squirrels have spared any."

And she showed Scillia how to read the tracks that crisscrossed the path: the difference between wood rat and squirrel, the long lope of wolf, the longer of hunting cat, the deep scratches on trees that bespoke bear.

Scillia listened like a child with a beloved tutor, storing away information for hours on end. Occasionally she asked

Jenna to repeat something just explained, or pointed with pride to tracks or fruit or roots she could now name. She seemed to forget nothing.

She proved an apt pupil in the Eye-Mind game as well, remembering much of what she had seen hours later. Long lists of things she recalled with ease. Jenna knew that kind of recall was now beyond her own reckoning.

Only once did Scillia complain, and it was to say baldly, "I should have been taught this before."

"I had hoped," Jenna answered simply, "that you would never need it."

"You hoped, rather, to keep your time in the woods for yourself," Scillia answered.

Jenna had no response. Indeed, she greatly feared that Scillia might be right.

They stopped at another inn, this one filled with a wedding party and many cheerily drunk soldiers. The captain of the men recognized Jenna at once. He made her a deep bow and she shook her head at him, a warning that she wished to remain unremarked. But once Scillia was abed, all the covers twisted around her, Jenna went downstairs and called the captain to her with a quiet nod.

When he came over, she said quietly, "I have a message for the king."

"I will take it myself, Anna," he said.

"There is nothing written. I give this to you mouth to ear, and so it must be delivered. Tell him that Jenna and Sil are well and on the mother road together. He will pay you handsomely for that one sentence."

"My queen, I do it for the honor alone." He bowed his head. "Do you need a guard?"

"Have I ever?"

"You look . . ." he hesitated, ". . . well-traveled."

She laughed. "Like the scruff of a mongrel, you mean?"

"Never that, Anna," he said, but joined in her laughter, adding, "I have seen you worse."

"And that was . . . ?"

"At Bear's Run," he said, naming the great battle at which so many of Jenna's troops had fallen, yet was a victory nonetheless. "You know, of course, it is but an hour's ride from here."

So close, Jenna thought. "You must have been a mere boy there," she said.

"And you a mere girl," he added graciously.

"War is a great ager," Jenna said. "And kingship worse yet. Good night, good captain." She started to leave, then turned back. "There is one other thing you can do for me."

"Name it, my queen."

"A man lies on the road by a great line of elder pine in the southern woods, two days ride from here. He will be by an ash that has been struck down across the road. The tree may have been pushed off by now, to let carts go by; the man has a deep sword slash in his right leg and will not have moved on his own. He may even be dead of blood loss. Bury him if he is there, else bring him to the king. He laid hands on the king's daughter and would have done worse than that."

The captain nodded, his face dark and disturbed. "Were there others?"

"There are always *others*," Jenna said. "Two of them. They are dead. If he has not put them in the ground, take a moment to do so."

"My lady, I ask again: Do you need a guard?"

"Did I at the ash tree?"

"You walk with a slight limp."

"But I walk. You cannot say the same for the men I left there. My daughter and I would ride alone."

"I will go at once, Anna."

"The dead have a long patience," she answered him. "Go

in the morning." She turned and went up the unlit stairs, not looking back. She was glad she was far enough from firelight and candlelight that Skada had not appeared. At the moment, her dark sister's wit would have been too much to bear.

The door to her room creaked when she opened it, but Scillia lay too deep in sleep to waken. Jenna lay down on the bit of bed left her and, even without a blanket for warmth, she was almost instantly asleep.

The trip to M'dorah took longer than Jenna had anticipated, for when at the morning meal she casually mentioned that they were close to the site of the Battle of Bear's Run, Scillia—all unaccountably—wanted to see it. Jenna had not been back to the site since the battle thirteen years earlier, and when they came to the field she was shocked to see how small a place it was.

"I had remembered a vast plain," she said quietly. "And the bodies . . . and all the blood." She shivered.

"Father often told us of the battle," Scillia said.

Surprised, Jenna turned to look at her. "What did he say of it?"

"He said many good men and women died here."

Jenna did not say anything more, but dismounted and walked toward a stand of trees, their branches so overhanging they brushed the withered grass. A cold wind puzzled through the clearing, delivering a sharp shock between the shoulder blades. Jenna shivered again. Suddenly she recalled Alta's words to her in the grove so long ago: *Remembering is what you must do most of all.*

And she had spent the last fifteen years trying to forget.

"Forgive me, Alta," Jenna whispered, staring into the shadows behind the trembling branches and seeing figures that were not there.

"Mother."

She thought she heard the grunting cough of an old bear.

"Mother!"

She thought she heard the scream of a woman warrior riding into battle.

"Mother, please!"

She thought she heard the thin, mewling cry of a child.

"Mother, you are frightening me. What is it?"

Jenna shook her head and turned. Smiling ruefully, she said, "Ghosts."

Scillia held out her hand. "There is nothing there but some trees. And an overgrown field."

Jenna took the hand. "There are ghosts here all right. And one of them is you."

"Now you are *really* frightening me. I am very much alive, mother. How can I be a ghost?"

Jenna pulled her around the trees. Behind them were two high mounds covered with coarse wintered-over grass. "Those are the common graves," she said. "One for the men—boys, really—and women who fought with us. And the other for the Garuns and their allies who fought against us."

"Which is which, mother?"

"I no longer know," Jenna admitted. "Is that not a horrid epitaph? I no longer know." She sighed. "But if you look between those two mounds, you will find something more."

"What will I find? Scillia asked.

"Go—and then come back and tell me what is there."

"Not ghosts, mother."

Jenna smiled at her. "Not for you, perhaps. Now go. I cannot."

"Cannot?"

"Cannot. Will not. It is the same."

Scillia raised an eyebrow at that and when no more admission was forthcoming, turned and disappeared between the mounds.

Jenna looked away, staring instead at the sky where an eagle was hunting on set wings, gliding over the meadow without a sound. She was glad it was not yet winter's end. She didn't think she could have borne visiting the place with spring running riotously green and dozens of birds singing from the branches.

"Mother." Scillia was standing not three feet away, a puzzled expression on her face.

"And what did you find?"

"Two graves with markers. One of them has a crown on it and Gorum's name. That was father's brother. Why have we never come here before?"

Jenna stared at the ground as if she might discover answers there. "Because of the ghosts. And because we wanted you to be children of the peace, not inheritors of the war. Though your father does manage to come once a year, in the fall. He is always especially solemn afterwards."

"Who is in the other grave? The one marked with a goddess sign."

"Iluna. This is where she fell, under this tree. I killed the man who killed her, and took you from her back."

Scillia put her hand on Jenna's. "So it is her ghost you cannot face."

"And Gorum's and all the men and women, boys and girls who died here."

"But you said *my* ghost was here, too. What did you mean?"

"Because here died your old life. I took you from dead Iluna and strapped you on my own back. I can hear you crying still."

Scillia drew her hand away. "We have further to go. And probably more ghosts to meet. Are you willing?." She started toward the horses.

"You will not find the woman who abandoned you."

"I know that." Scillia's voice floated back to her in the cold air. "But I will sit atop M'dorah and see the world as Iluna saw it. Perhaps then I will be ready to go back home."

Jenna sighed. She thought she'd done it quietly, but Scillia heard and turned.

"You do not have to come along."

"I am your dark sister," Jenna said, smiling a little. "I must go where you go."

"Mother!"

"Besides, how can I not go when I know what you will find there?"

"And what do you think I will find?"

"Nothing. You will find nothing. It all burned down over thirteen years ago."

It was Scillia's turn to sigh. She brushed a stray hair from her face. "Even ash is something, mother, as you have found tracking me."

Jenna smiled and did not point out that there would hardly be ash left after years of scouring winds and rain. "How smart you have become in one short journey."

"It is because I finally had a teacher worthy of the lesson," Scillia said, smiling back.

Jenna's face flushed with embarrassment, and she opened her arms. Scillia rushed in and they embraced mother to daughter, sister to sister, almost—Jenna thought—friend to friend.

They foraged for lunch. Jenna showed Scillia an odd grey mass, like a mushroom, that grew on a dead tree. With a bit of added journeycake crumbles, it cooked up to a bland porridge. And she pointed out which green roots to boil for a gingery tea.

"Quite filling," Jenna said when they had finished.

"Makes up in bulk what it lacks in taste," Scillia said. But she did not say it with anger or even as a complaint. It was, Jenna thought with relief, merely an observation.

They sat for a while in companionable silence while a green finch serenaded them from one of the trees.

"Mother," Scillia said at last. "I have been thinking."

Jenna did not mean to, but she set her shoulders, waiting for an outburst. "About . . . ?"

"About having a dark sister. I mean—a *real* dark sister."

"Not a mother as a dark sister, you mean."

"Yes."

"Do you want one?"

"I am not certain."

"Once gotten, never given away."

"That is why I am not certain. You and Skada do not always . . ."

"Always?"

"Agree."

"No more than you and your brothers."

"That is different."

"Yes. Different. But the same."

Scillia sighed.

"I am not even certain I could tell you how to call up a dark sister, now that the hames are gone. There is a period of training, you know. An entire ritual, involving special breathing, prayers. And the help of the hame sisters around you." She did not mention that she had called up Skada at a time of tragedy and despair, when she was alone and surrounded by the dead.

Scillia looked at her sharply. "There is still Selden Hame."

"But as you pointed out, only old women live there now. One can only call up a dark sister as a girl newly turned woman. They may not remember all the parts of the ritual. You saw how badly we stumbled on the Bearing ceremony."

Scillia got a sour look on her face.

"And not all who call are answered."

"I thought . . ."

"Then you thought wrong." Jenna stood. "There was a girl at Selden Hame when I was a girl who tried and failed." She paused, remembering. "It was awful."

"But if I really want to try?"

Jenna reached a hand to Scillia and pulled her up. "Then I will help you, of course. After all, I am your mother."

They stayed the night at the battlefield, building a large campfire next to one of the mounds. They ate what was nearly the last of their provisions and made a thin soup slightly flavored with winter roots.

Scillia sat a long time by Iluna's grave, but Jenna remained close to the fire, not for the warmth but for Skada's companionship. Skada, however, was notably silent, so much so that Jenna was forced, at last, to comment on it.

"No words of wisdom, sister?" she asked. "No bitter commentary?"

"For once you have done everything right," said Skada.

"To have come so far for such small praise."

"Far indeed," Skada said. "But will you know when it is far enough?"

"Far enough for what?"

"Far enough to cut the leading strings."

Jenna shook her head, "She has cut them herself."

Skada shook her head at the same time. "And tied them up again, more firmly than before. The knots may be different, but the string pulls the same."

"And would you have had me let her fight three men, be raped, sliced open, and die unshriven?"

"Those are not the strings I am talking about, and well you know . . ." but the fire burned low and Skada was gone.

". . . it," Jenna said, finishing her dark sister's sentence.

She did not get up to stoke the coals again until just before laying down next to her sleeping daughter. Then she turned her back to the flames so as not to have to see Skada again, though she could feel her close behind.

They left camp at first light and Jenna, at least, did not look back at the field. She knew that they still had a few good hours' ride to the forests near M'dorah. And then they would have to leave the horses and pack in through a tangle before coming to the M'doran plain.

Weather luck was with them at least. Though they were now well in the north and west, signs of spring—early and welcome—were everywhere. Jenna pointed out small, curling ferns shoving through the earth by the roots of some of the larger trees. And a green finch sang to its mate from the branch of an oak. Above them the sky was still the bleached bone color of late winter, but the ground held a different promise. Jenna always believed earth before sky.

As they rode along, Jenna thought about what Skada had said at the campfire. *Have I pulled the string tighter?* she wondered. *Have I encouraged Scillia to knot it up again?* Surely she had given Scillia plenty of leeway to go on alone. *Alta's wounds! I even offered to make her a map*. And they had been getting along beautifully until Skada's thoughtless words had set this trap between them. *Now*, Jenna thought angrily, *I shall have to watch every word and every gesture*.

She was still fretting when they reached a fork in the road, and she knew it to be the turning to M'dorah. Dismounting and leading the horses off the path, Jenna hid them in a small copse, hobbling them loosely. Then she showed Scillia how to take what they would need for rest of the day.

"And blankets for warmth."

"It is coming spring, mother. I saw the ferns. And heard the bird singing."

"That was a green finch," Jenna said. "All early signs. Don't you remember:

> *"When you hear the green finch sing,*
> *Heralding the first of spring,*
> *Do not shed your heavy cotte,*
> *Winter's reign is over—"*

"NOT!" Scillia filled in the final line. "I thought that was but a nursery rhyme."

"Some of those rhymes began in the farmyard and field; they were only later brought into the nursery," said Jenna. "Do not be too quick to dismiss what you hear growing up. In the Hame we had many such rhymes to memorize. Besides, M'dorah is a high place and so it will be colder than down here."

"Where eagles dare not rest?"

Jenna smiled. "Not quite that high, perhaps. But there is nothing at the top to stop the wind now."

Jenna had not remembered the woods being such a tangle of beech and oak, whitethorn and larch. Still, thirteen years more undergrowth certainly made walking difficult, and the sharp ascent of the trail soon had them both puffing badly.

Luckily the higher they got, the sparser the trees and bushes. Pretty soon they could see clear space ahead.

"At last," Jenna said.

"M'dorah?"

"At least the M'doran plain."

As the path crested over the last rise, Scillia could see what Jenna meant. Before them was a wide, treeless plateau that was covered with gigantic, towering rocks rising like teeth from the ground. Some of the rocks were needle points, others huge towers of stone.

The sight, even a second time, was so stunning that for a moment Jenna could not speak.

Breaking the silence at last, Scillia asked, "But which one is M'dorah?"

Jenna pointed to the far side of the plain. "That one, the broad crowned rock there. Once it had a wooden hame atop, an aerie even eagles envied."

Scillia squinted. "How did they get up there?"

"By a hinged ladder of rope and wood."

"I mean the *first* M'dorans."

Jenna laughed. "Arguing first causes like a child learning of Great Alta?"

"But . . ."

"How do *you* think they got up?"

Scillia shrugged. "Surely there are steps carved in the stone. Or handholds and footholds."

Jenna shook her head.

"Or a slope around the back?"

Again Jenna shook her head, and without a word more began walking across the plain. Still speaking, Scillia had to run to catch up.

"A kite! They made a kite of sticks and cloth. A *huge* kite, and flew someone to the top."

Jenna did not stop her strides. "Now that is one method I had not considered. I had no kites as a child."

"But then how . . ."

"Wait till we get there to ask. Save your breath for the walk. We want to be there before dark."

They walked for well over an hour before reaching the foot of M'dorah's rock. It was a grey granite, sheer for ten feet, then bowing out, muffin-like, before rising again in another sheer cliff face for thirty or forty feet. There were half a dozen ladders hanging over the sides, disappearing at the top of the rounded surface.

"Look, we can still climb up," Scillia cried.

"Perhaps," Jenna said. "But remember how old these ladders are, how many years they have weathered here. They are but rope and wood. Consider this well—are they still safe?"

Scillia looked both chastened and angry. "But to have come so far . . ."

"Far enough," Jenna said, suddenly recalling Skada's words.

"Do you mean me to fail after all?" Scillia asked, her voice holding a tone of accusation that had been missing since the ash tree.

"I do not mean you to *fall*," Jenna said. "Caution is but the first part of any adventure."

"So says *The Book of Light*?"

"So says the Book of Jenna," Jenna replied patiently.

Scillia ignored her and went to the nearest rope ladder. She gave it a strong one-handed tug. "See, Mother, it's . . ." But whatever else she was going to say about the ladder ended when the pieces of rope near the top end gave way, sending a dozen wooden rungs showering down on her. "Ow . . . ow . . . ow!"

Jenna bit her lip to keep from laughing.

All of the rope ladders proved as flimsy, rotted away by the years of weather.

"Never mind," Jenna said, "we have yet to check the opposite side."

"Will any ropes there be stronger?" asked Scillia wearily. "Would sun and rain be less harsh around back?"

"It is," Jenna pointed out, "the south-facing side. Stranger things have been known to happen."

So they made their way around the rock, finding a half

dozen more rope ladders, none of them strong enough to bear their weight.

In the end, they could not find a way up without constructing an entire scaffolding. And that—as Jenna pointed out—was something two women and *four* hands could not manage. "We would need a whole crew of willing workers."

"Then I have failed," Scillia said.

"Failed in what?"

"To find my mother root." Scillia looked up to the top of the rock which was now barely visible in the fading light.

"You found the grave of the one who first bore you in her arms. And you have ridden far with the mother who has loved you for thirteen years. What else are you seeking, child?" Jenna could not keep the exasperation from her voice.

Still staring at the top of the rock, Scillia said, "More than ash, Mother. More than grave dirt. Probably more than there is to find."

"I found my birth mother," Jenna said suddenly. "Or at least I found out who she was."

"You never said . . ."

"Because it made no difference. She had given me birth all right, but she was not my mother where and when it mattered. Blood counts a great deal less than love."

"At least you knew," Scillia said. "My birth mother could be a farm wife or a beer maid." She looked once more up to the top of M'dorah.

"Or she could be dead," Jenna said. "Mine was."

"I only hope she *is* dead," Scillia said. "Else I would hate her for giving me up."

"I expect that whoever she is—or was—farmwife or beer maid or princess, for that matter, you will know who she is when you are queen."

"Why do you say that?" The sun was dropping fast and shadows played around Scillia's face, making her suddenly look far older than her years, making her look—Jenna thought—like a stranger.

"Because when a one-armed queen is on the throne, anyone who ever gave away a one-armed daughter will come forward to claim you," said Skada. There was only a sliver of moonlight, but it was enough for Skada to appear since there was not a cloud in the sky. "And blood counts most when there is coinage at stake. And a crown."

"Skada!" both Jenna and Scillia cried together.

"Now are we going to stand around this forsaken plain till we freeze to death, or are we going to pull those blankets around us and jog-trot back to our horses? I am ready for a good bed and home."

THE MYTH:

Great Alta took the girl child and set her on the eagle's nest. "Fly!" quoth Great Alta, "And I shall be the wind beneath your wings."

Then Great Alta set the girl on the ground. "Crawl. And I shall be the ground below your belly."

At last Great Alta set the girl on the throne. "But sit. And I shall be the shadow behind you that all but you shall be able to see."

three

Turnings and Returnings

THE MYTH:

Then Great Alta took the boy and turned him ten times around. "Now," quoth she, "you are a man."

The new man took his first steps and fell down, crying, "How can I be a man when I still walk like a boy?"

"Take smaller steps," quoth Great Alta.

THE LEGEND:

In the town of South Berike there is a ghost of a drowned boy who wanders the harbor on the fourth day of spring. Some say he is a fisher lad, part of a six-man skimmer that overturned in a storm off the Skerry Light.

Some say he was the cabin boy on the Ginger Pye, *the factory ship lost in the Great Storm of '37, one of seventeen bodies that washed ashore in two days.*

But some say he is the lost prince Jemuel, drowned in a rough crossing, come home at last and no one left to welcome him ashore, so he wanders the strand forever.

THE STORY:

It was thirteen years before Jemson came home, in the late springtide, sailing under an oyster-colored sky that tumbled out rain for the disembarking.

His father had turned fifty in the fall and was failing quickly, or so it was said by the Garuns, though that was not the real reason Jemson had returned. Thirteen years had been the term set by the hostage agreement. It was time that both boys sailed for home. Jemson would have stayed if he could, but he knew where duty lay, unpleasant though it might be.

Was Carum indeed failing? Jemson could not tell. His father seemed as tall as ever, a mighty oak under whose branches saplings did not thrive.

Well, Jemson knew that was not strictly true. Corrie had turned into a big, fleshy man with cheeks like polished apples. If not an oak, at least an ash. And an ass, too! He laughed silently at his own rough joke, but without any real humor.

And I, first born, am the short one in the family. Even my mother is taller. That Scillia was taller than he did not count. She was not of his blood really, and blood—he knew well—was the coinage of royalty. Besides, she was only a girl. And a homely girl at that. Hardly worth flattering.

He had landed in Berick Harbor with less fanfare than he had left. Only a small bustle of townfolk was there to greet him, people he supposed he should have recalled well but did not.

There had been a greying woman, Petra, at the head of the bustle who claimed she was his mother's dear friend. "Do you not remember me, Jemmie? I'm the one who can always make your mother laugh."

"A talent, madam, I never had," he said, bowing his head to her. But there was no warmth in his greeting, no pretense at intimacy.

Her husband, Jareth, was equally familiar in his address, calling him "Young Jem," and speaking of his youthful antics, all of which made Jemson sound like an absolute jackass of a child. Jemson did not remember any such child and, besides, a royal should never be remembered as less than perfect.

"My title, sir, is Prince Jemson, and I prefer you address me that way." Better to begin as he intended to go on. Old Faulk, his Garunian tutor, would have given him grudging, grunting approval for the way he handled that. It pleased him enormously that Jareth flushed from the reproval and his wife's eyes got like hard pebbles. Satisfied that the lesson had gone home, Jemson turned away to look at the troop waiting for him.

There were seven guardsmen under the command of a sloppy veteran who would have to be reprimanded later, for his jacket buttons were not properly shined and he should never have led out an uneven number of men on such an assignment. Six or eight would have been proper. Twenty or thirty would have been better. A hundred would not have been amiss. Jemson ground his teeth in anger, a sound he no longer heard, but one that set the grey woman to shaking her head.

The return of the eldest son and heir to such a greeting! Jemson could scarce credit it. Neither his father nor mother—nor yet his brother nor sister—had bestirred themselves to meet his ship, though of course the ship was five hours early and the weather drear. He knew that Gadwess, for all that he was not the Garunian heir, was to be hailed on his return with a parade of hundreds and a great banquet whatever the time, whatever the kind of day. Crown Prince Malwess had included Jemson in on the planning. There were to be minstrels and jugglers and an indoor archery shoot which Malwess would no doubt win. He was a wonderful shot, especially when there was no wind to contest his aim.

And no Dales prince to pace him! Jemson thought with a small, knowing smile. He was himself a better shot than Malwess, especially outdoors, especially with a moving target. But he would not be there to pull for the prize. *Damn the hostage agreement anyway!*

No matter that the excuse in the Dales was that it had been a hard winter and the farmers had few extra supplies to spare for any feast, great or small. The winter had been just as severe on the Continent, the snow up to the eaves of lowland houses, and wolves in packs chasing after sledges. Jemson bit his lip and ground his teeth again. The Garunian farmers had complained as well, of course. It was the nature of farmers to complain: about wind, about rain, about sun, about everything. But a royal homecoming deserved some sacrifice. The Garunian people understood this. But not—it seemed—the people of the Dales.

Jemson was not at all happy.

The later, intimate dinner held in his honor for the family and a few of his parents' closest friends only added to the insult. The food was unimaginative, the talk as stolid as farmers' conversation, the wine just this side of vinegar. His mother kept wanting to touch him—on the hand, on the cheek, as if to excuse herself for not being at the harbor. Her real excuse—that she had been out riding and had not known of the early landing of his ship—was unacceptable. Jemson told them what he thought, straight out, without bothering to couch it in courtly terms. They deserved no face-saving.

His return was not a success.

"He went away a small boy," Scillia complained, "and he returned a large one." She did not say this to her mother, who had problems enough with her father's winter-long cough, but to Corrie. "And our loss is doubled with Gad gone, back to that awful place."

Corrie smiled at her, in that blurry way he had. "Jem's just arrived home, Sil. Give him time."

She was not soothed. "He was bad enough before he left, don't you remember? But he is all Garun now, and the worst kind. Wants to be called *Prince* Jemson by the family's friends, and *sir* by the guards."

Corrie shrugged. "That is his right, you know. I wonder . . . would they call me *Prince* Corrine?"

Sil was not amused. "He called me girl. *Girl!* And I three

years his senior. As well as the kingdom's heir. Which, by the way, he refuses to acknowledge." She flung herself into the cushioned chair by Corrie's hearth where a small fire kept a kettle boiling.

"That's what really gripes him, of course," Corrie said. "You know what the Garuns think about a woman on the throne. Give him time to become one of us again, Scillia."

"I shall be 101 before I get to rule anyway," Scillia said. "Father may not look well, may Alta hold him. But mother will go on forever."

Corrie took the kettle from the metal arm over the fire and spilled a bit of boiling water into the earth-colored teapot. He sloshed it around, then emptied it into the corner of the hearth where it made a comfortable hissing. "The trouble with ruling," he said wryly, "is that by the time you get to sit on the throne, your bones are too brittle for the seat."

Sil stared at him for a moment, then broke into laughter which completely changed her face. One minute she was a rather ordinary-looking young woman and then, with the smile, a striking one, the planes of her face shifting with her merriment. "Oh, Cor, you do amuse me." For all his outer softness, she knew, her brother had a hard, fascinating center, like the jester in one of the old fairy stories.

"My goal, actually," he said, as he continued making the tea, tipping out just enough leaves from the caddy into the pot. Tea was a disastrously pricy commodity but one of the few that even their mother thought worth the expense.

Scillia stuck her tongue out at him. Then she turned serious, the planes of her face shifting back to ordinary again. "I do not want the throne if it means mother or father dying."

"No one thinks you do," Corrie said as he poured the hot water into the pot. "Especially not mother or father. But they will die, nonetheless. *Even a highest tree . . .*"

She finished the adage for him. It was one of Petra's favorites, or at least one that she quoted most frequently. ". . . *has an axe at its foot*." She sighed.

"Which is why," Corrie reminded her, putting the kettle back on the flame, "Mother had you tutored in history and governship, taught higher sums, and made to learn the diplomatics of the Continent. Thank Alta it was you, not I, who had those extra hours in the classroom. And it is why she has been having you sit in on all the Realty Sessions and helping form the judgment of the court these past five years. And the Farmers Council and the Market Fairs Meetings and . . ."

Scillia sighed again. "It is dreadfully boring stuff, actually. I can understand why she takes off for the woods whenever father can spare her."

"Boring, but necessary. Like eating."

"Like making babies."

"Like learning scales."

It was an old game between them, and they both enjoyed it.

"Of course it is necessary," Scillia said. She leaped up, nearly turning over the small table on which the pot sat brewing its musky tea. She walked over to the hearth and set her back to the fire, less for warmth—it was early spring after all—than to glare at her brother. "Only there needn't be half so many meetings. Or councils. Or sessions. Why can't the people just do what is right on their own?"

"You are so like mother, you know," Corrie said suddenly.

"I am certainly not like her at all," Sil said, "being dark and short and one-armed."

Corrie smiled again, a grin which dimpled on both sides. "And she is tall and fair and two-armed. And you, of course, share no blood. I see. No resemblance at all." He handed her one of the mugs and poured the tea. "Except that inside, dear sister, which is the only place that counts, you are as much like Queen Jenna as her own dark twin."

"I have a slower tongue."

"And lighter hair."

"And . . ." they both said together, "one less arm than Skada."

"I give up," Scillia said. "You are the one who should be next on the throne, Corrie. You are smarter and dearer and . . ."

"Too smart to want to be king and too dear for the kingdom," Corrie said laughing. His one failing, they both knew, was a love of rich, flamboyant clothes and ear-bobs. The embroidered caftan he wore now, with its swirls of red and gold leaves, its jeweled bucklers, was but a minor player in the cast of dozens in his dressing closet. He and Gadwess had loved to dress up outrageously, even as boys, calling one another Sister Light and Sister Dark, and riding out in their flowing robes on full moon eves to frighten cows in the meadow and—once—stampeding the entire herd of army horses. Gadwess' share of their clothes had not gone with him back to the Continent but remained in Corrie's room, waiting his return.

At the thought of Gadwess, Scillia's thoughts turned soft and sad. She loved him equally as she loved Corrie.

"What do you suppose," Scillia said, "that they will make of Gad at home?"

"They will try and make a man of him," Corrie answered.

"Like Jemmie."

"Jemson."

"*Prince* Jemson," Scillia said.

"And fail," Corrie added. "Because their idea of a man is not Gad's. Not any longer."

"Poor Gad." Scillia sighed.

"Poor Garuns," Corrie countered. "He shall mock them to the end. And then, perhaps, he will come back to the ones who know and love him best." He said it with neither conviction nor hope.

"Us." Scillia put the cup down. "Thanks for the tea, little brother."

"As always, big sister," he said. It was an old joke between them, begun when he had gotten his first rangy growth and put a full hand's span of height between them in less than a year.

"He is appalling," Skada said as she and Jenna huddled by the fire. Carum had had a bad night, coughing until blood flecked his lips, and neither of them had slept. "Jemmie is worse than a Garun now. He has adopted their creed barrel, stave, and bung, and like any convert works harder at being correct."

"He is my son," Jenna said quietly. There was little conviction in her voice.

"He is pompous, overbearing, full of ill-considered brags. He is . . ."

". . . my son," Jenna said, but this time her voice cracked. "I am tired of repeating it."

"That you gave birth to him in no way excuses him," Skada pointed out. "Have you heard what he said to Scillia? To Petra? Have you heard what he says about you? About me?"

"He talks too much. As you do," Jenna said wearily. "It is no wonder when given the chance, Scillia declined to call up a dark sister. She knew you all too well." She stood up and walked away from the fire, crossing to the great bed. There were no candles there; the dark was to encourage Carum to sleep, a sleep prompted by the infirmarer's poppy drought. Without candlelight, Skada could not follow.

Jenna sat on the bed and smoothed back Carum's hair from his broad forehead. *Made even broader*, she thought, *by the years*. In sleep he looked peaceful, vulnerable, even young. Jenna smiled down on him. She loved the way the dark lashes fanned out on his cheeks. *He needs to be shaved*, she thought.

Suddenly fear, like a sharp spear in the side, made her gasp aloud. Carum was going to die. Not this moment. Not this day. Likely not for some months yet. His lungs were bad, yet it was a slow disease. But for the first time ever she actually thought about life without him, considered the world without his presence.

It is not bearable, she thought. *I cannot be here without him. I cannot go into the woods knowing that when I come out he will not be there, waiting.*

She went back to the hearth to weep where Skada, at least, could comfort her.

It was not only the lack of formality that Jemson hated, it was the stinginess of the court. He had grown up in Continental opulence and now took it for granted that a royal family should live differently—and on the backs of—the people it governed. The Garun king and his relations dressed in silks and changed clothing for every meal. *Why*, he thought, trembling with indignation, *there is not even room enough in my chamber here for storing away all my shoes. Most are still in the trunks they were packed in for the sailing.* Here King Carum and Queen Jenna—he had trouble thinking of them as his parents—dressed as if they were farmers and not the heroes of the damned Gender Wars.

Only his brother Corrine had any sense of style, though he dressed too much like an artist, his hair too long to fit beneath a proper wig. He also had an inch-long fingernail on his little finger, for playing the tembla, he insisted. But Corrine had not played any kind of instrument before Jemson went away, and he doubted that Corrine was musical in the least. It was more like an affectation. The very idea made Jemson ill.

As for that one-armed freak, she is the worst of the lot, Jemson thought. She had never been any great beauty before and the years had not treated her well. Now she had a swarthy complexion from being out in the sun like a peasant, and mouse-black hair. She was muscled as any soldier, too. *And worst of all*, he thought, *the stupid slut dresses to hide the missing arm which only emphasizes the loss*. He could not think of her without shuddering, the more so since she was still called heir to the throne.

Had he hated her so much when he had left as a hostage to the Garun court? He could not remember. What he did recall was how, right before he had gone, she'd nearly gotten Corrine killed and he had had to rescue them both with his bow and arrow. Jemson smiled. It was a story he had told over and over in the Garun court, one his hosts never tired of hearing. He was ever so much better now with the bow.

When he and Corrine had met again, he'd noticed right off the marks on Corrine's neck, still there after all the passing years, but he had refrained from mentioning them, not wanting to spend past coin too soon. As King Kras liked to say: *The anvil must be patient. Only the hammer can be strong*. He would be patient until he was in a position to be the Hammer of the Dales.

THE BALLAD:

Jemmie Over the Water

The oceans between are blue and black,
Sing Jemmie over the water,
Oh will ye come back? oh will ye come back?
Sing Jemmie over the sea.

He rode the wild waves to his land,
Sing Jemmie over the water,
They gave him but the back of the hand,
Oh, will ye come home to me.

He left in winter, back in spring,
Sing Jemmie over the water,
To find his sister crowned the king,
Sing Jemmie over the sea.

An' will ye take silver, will ye take gold,
Sing Jemmie over the water,
Or will ye take the throne to hold,
Oh will ye come home to me.

I neither gold nor silver make,
Sing Jemmie over the water,
But I the throne will surely take,
Sing Jemmie over the sea.

So, kill the girl upon the throne,
Sing Jemmie over the water,
And then, oh then, will I come home,
Oh I will come home to thee.

THE STORY:

Carum rallied after that dark night, and was now back in the council room if not back on the throne. Neither his infirmarer nor Jenna would let him sit in the cold, drafty hall where anyone might cough or sneeze on him, spreading further contagion to his already-weakened lungs.

Instead it was Jenna, with Scillia by her side, who held the long Realty Sessions where farmers and fishers and herdsmen and weavers alike could bring their complaints and sue for the Queen's justice.

It was a time the balladeers called "Anna's Court," but Jem referred to it in letters back to King Kras as "The Sluts' Assemblage."

"My All-Father," Jem wrote in one letter, "*if you could but see her making judgments, ruled not by her head or by the precedence of law, but making decisions on what she is told by her weak, womanly heart. It makes a mockery of justice as we know it, and I can see that the people are not pleased. And there next to the queen sits my stepsister—who owns no blood in common with any royal—squatting all the day like a toad on a log but without a jewel in her head. Or a notion either. And my mother—curse the day she won her war—lets the one-armed slut make fully half or more of the rulings.*"

And in another: "*I know you have cautioned me, All-Father, to patience. So I shall remain, smiling and playing the Dalian fool. I will try not to overpraise you in the presence of your enemies, but rather keep the Garunian counsel of the wolf who waits to tear at the meat till his packmates are by his side.*"

And in a third: "*My father, who had a bad turn when first I arrived, is well enough now, but the women rule him completely. I cannot stand to see a king so unmanned; he has no pride of himself and does not seem to care who knows it. He speaks in council chambers still, but that is all. When we have dinner together—in his bedchamber and not the dining hall—he will often ask me about my life on the Continent. They are never seriously probing questions, however, nor does he—I think—really listen to my answers. He is but a shadow of that great tree that once overspread this kingdom root and branch. The women are like rats gnawing at the oak's foot.*"

It did not occur to Jemson that his letters might be opened and read, that their contents might be reported to his increasingly angry mother. It did not occur to him that Jenna, after months of making excuses for her eldest son, might need to confront him.

A lot of things did not occur to Jemson. Or if they did occur to him, he always recast them in a pleasanter light.

Still, when his letters from the Continent carried no responses to his questions, no praise for his astute observations, he did worry that one or two of them might have gone astray. However, he did not allow that worry to go deep enough. He merely set up an alternate mail route, bribing a Garunian sailor on one of the smaller ships that brought pantiles from the Continent in weekly trips across the narrow sea.

And so he wrote twice a week instead of a single weekly letter. One he sent by way of the royal pouch and one by the sailor. He never suspected that half his mail was being read by strangers; his only suspicion lay at the feet of the Dale couriers whom he believed to be incompetent fools.

"I worry, All-Father, that you have not received all the letters that I have sent. Nothing here in the Dales runs as it should. They are a lazy, worthless folk, and I never stop thanking Lord Cres that I was delivered to you in time."

The contents of Jem's letters were not made known to many, but certain members of the council knew, Jenna knew, and Skada—of course—knew as well.

"Do not bother Carum with this," Jenna cautioned as she sat with her three oldest friends in the council chamber. It was a grey day and the tapers were lit, shadows dancing around the sconces.

"Bother him? A son plotting with our enemies and we should not bother him?" Piet pounded the table with a meaty fist. "This is not some child's scrape, some madcap moonlight escapade, Jenna, like stampeding the army's best herd of horses or . . ."

"Do not see plots where stupidity can prove the motive," Skada remarked. She flickered in and out of the conversation as she flickered in and out with the guttering candles.

"Pah!" Piet stood and turned his back to her, speaking to the far wall. "I mean no disrespect, Anna, but that boy of yours . . ." He was holding onto his beard as he spoke because he knew the beard tended to wobble when he was angry. And he was furious now.

Petra broke in, her voice soft but firm. "Jenna, you must see the seriousness of this. He is boy no longer. He is twenty-three years old."

"I cannot see him as such," Jenna said. "I did not watch him grow up."

"He has not grown up at all. That is the problem," Skada whispered.

"They are a tricksy sort, those Garuns," Piet went on. "And they have turned a Dales prince into a . . ."

"Shut up, Piet," Jareth said. "The dark sister has the right of it. Do not insist on evil where the evidence points to idiocy."

Piet turned. "I warned this council thirteen years ago that the boy would be molded by his Garun masters much to our despair, and you did not listen then."

"We heard you, dear friend," Jenna said.

"But you did not listen!" Piet spin on his heel and was about to exit the room.

"Piet, *please*," Jenna called to him. "Do not bother Carum with this."

Piet turned back and this time he spoke quietly. "He is dying, Anna. Of course I will not tax him with this. But you—and Queen Scillia that would be—*you* must deal quickly and sternly with young Prince Jemson. Or the land will suffer."

"I will. When the time is right," Jenna said.

"The time is already well past right," Piet said, walking out.

Jenna looked at Jareth. "Is it too late? Must I speak now? Now when there is so much else that needs doing?"

Jareth smiled sadly. "I do not think it needs to be just *now*, Jenna. We have Jemmie's letters and have sent our own forgeries in their stead. The letters we composed tell of a growing strength in the country, the folk united in their love of you and King Carum. There is no mention of Carum's illness and . . ."

"And must such news be forged?" Jenna asked. "Is the love of my people not true?"

"Who loves a king when the taxes have been collected?" Skada asked.

Petra glared at her across the long table but could not silence her.

"And don't we say: *Easier to love a dead hero than a live king?*"

Jenna looked down at her hands, now clasping and unclasping in her lap, as if they were being guided by some mind other than her own. "Oh," she sighed, "my poor people. My poor land." Then she stood, gathered up her papers, and walked out of the room where it was too dark for Skada to follow.

"Oh, my poor Jenna," whispered Petra, "you do not understand how well indeed you *are* loved."

"Or how you will be remembered in years to come," Jareth added, putting his head in his hands and trying hard not to weep.

"I need to get away for a bit, my love," Jenna said to Carum in the dark of their room. Only the embers of the hearthfire still glowed, rosy and comforting but shedding no great light. "I cannot think here in the close surround of the stone walls."

Carum was sitting up in the bed, one blanket around his shoulders and another over his legs. "You need the woods, Jenna. I do not begrudge you that. Have I ever?"

"But you are ill and Scillia . . ."

"Scillia has a solid head and the advice of Jareth and Petra and Piet. She will counsel well. Go. Go quickly. But do not be too long in your return."

She did not like the forced gaiety in his voice nor the look of terror she supposed she saw behind his eyes. *Or is it my own terror I see there?* she wondered. If she had hoped he would beg her to stay, he did not. And so to please him, to make him believe she was not worried, she left.

Corrie was reading a books of essays by the philosopher B'kana, when his brother entered the room. Jemson did not knock, but took the room as if he had some sort of siege machine.

"You're welcome," Corrie said, saving his place in the book with a tasseled silk marker. "Do you want some tea?"

"No. Yes. Damn."

"Is this the most recent Garunian mode of conversation? Or are you just not pleased to see me?"

"She's off again."

Corrie stood and began his tea-making ritual which gave him a moment before he had to answer. "Do you mean mother?"

"Yes. Of course I mean mother. Though she is a sorry excuse for one."

Corrie swished the hot water through the pot. "I did not hear that."

"I said . . ."

"I am not deaf, Jem. And you are not stupid. At least not as stupid as you have been acting."

"I don't know what you mean." Jemson sat down on his brother's bed. His face took on the kind of pout one might expect on a ten-year-old.

"*No one* could be as stupid as you have been acting," Corrie said. He was suddenly angry enough so that when he shook the leaves from the caddy a few floated down to the floor. "Damn. That's the last of the vervain mix."

Jemson stood, flushing. "I won't take that kind of accusation from anyone, not even one of royal blood." His hand went to his belt and fumbled there, as if expecting to find a knife that was suddenly not available.

"I am accusing you of nothing but acting stupid, dear brother," Corrie said, forcing himself to become calm. He poured the tea water into the pot. "You are not in the Garunian court now, but here in the Dales. You need to curb your natural tendency toward asininity and try to be one of us again."

"I am *not* one of you," Jemson said, "if it means bending the knee to that one-armed slut."

"Then you should probably book passage tomorrow for the Continent," Corrie said handing him the cup. "For it is my guess that mother will not outlive father by much."

"She is healthy as a horse. As two horses."

Corrie smiled at his brother sadly. "You never were able to see past your nose, Jem."

Jemson wrinkled his nose, took a sip of the tea, spat it out loudly. "What is this? Some sort of poison?"

"An herbal posset. For temper."

"I have no temper."

"You are all temper, brother. As I am all temperament. Scillia will make a fine queen. She has been studying for it since you left. Tutors galore!" He waved his hand about as if the tutors were all crowding in the room with them.

Jemson stood. He put down the cup carefully on the little table, though it was clear from his face that he wanted to fling it into the fire. "I came here to sound you out, brother, thinking that you could not possibly wish to live beneath a woman's hand. As I saved you once, so I wish to save you again."

"Save me? From what?"

"From cats, dear brother. From the feline race."

"Oh, by Alta's crown!" Corrie said, stopping himself from laughing just in time. His hand went to his neck and fingered the scars there. "The Cat Story as Jemson remembers it. Ah well, heroes are made by those who tell the stories, not by those who lived the life. Mother always said that and now I see it is true."

"What do you mean?" Jemson asked, squinting his eyes. "What *exactly* do you mean?"

"Just this—Scillia will eventually be queen, Jem. Bend the knee or board the ship."

"My All-Father has often enough said that where there are two answers, there are three."

"What on earth does that mean?" Now it was Corrie's turn to be puzzled.

"Use your *temperament* and figure it out." Jemson went out of Corrie's room the same way he had entered, leaving a large silence behind.

"Oh, sweet Alta!" Corrie said after a minute into the silence. "He plans to fight. The bloody fool plans to fight her for the crown." He put down his own cup and went at once to speak to his father.

THE FABLE:

The mice in the stable wanted a king and they asked one of their own to lead them.

King Mouse proved a good king. He found them warm places in the winter and cool burrows for the summer. He managed the grain supplies well. Still the mice were not happy, for they had to hide from hawks and owls. They had to run from weasels and wolves.

"We need a king who is not just like us: long tail, quivering disposition, and a passion for cheese," they said. . . . "We need someone bigger and stronger to lead us into the light."

So they held a great assembly and threw down King Mouse.

"Now who shall we get to lead us?" they cried.

"Why not Cat from the big house?" called out one young mouse in a loud voice. Loud, that is, for a mouse. "Cat is big and rough. No one troubles him. He will keep us safe."

"Safe from what?" asked one old mouse. "Safe for *what?" But he had been King Mouse's chief advisor and besides his voice was weak with his age. Even those who heard him did not listen.*

So the mice sent an emissary to ask Cat to be their king.

And a second.

And a third.

When the fourth emissary escaped Cat's claws by just a whisker, the mice understood at last what the old one had been trying to tell them. They rallied once again behind King Mouse, too late for some, but in time for most.

THE STORY:

Jenna was half a day down the eastern road before she had fully thought out which direction she meant to take. The white mare plodded dutifully along, unmindful of the familiar burden on her back, until Jenna reined her in sharply at a crossroads.

"I think," Jenna said to the horse as if expecting a conversation, "that we should go where we are not expected. By ourselves least of all. What do you think?"

The mare shook her head, an answer that had more to do with the sudden reining-in than Jenna's question.

"Everyone knows how I love the woods and the mountains," Jenna said. "But my son has brought with him a contagion from across the sea. Let us go to some lonely shingle and camp there on the sand. Perhaps if I stare across the water long enough, Alta will send me a sign and I will at last understand what it is I must do."

She urged the horse southward and the mare once again

shook her head. But Jenna did not notice, or at least did not take it as any kind of message, for she was already contemplating some interior notions of tides. And so it was in silence that the horse and Jenna continued down the grassy road that led, eventually, to the sea.

The first evening they camped off the path, close enough for access but far enough away to be hidden from prying eyes. Jenna was neither particularly hungry or tired, but she knew how quickly both could come upon the unprepared traveler so she forced herself to eat a creditable meal of journeycake and spring greens boiled in water from a nearby stream to which she added a touch of dried herbs and salt from her waist pouches. She was long past the days when she felt she had to be pure in her approach to camping, eating only what the fields or an evening's hunt provided. And she always carried tea leaves in a small separate pouch—hawthorn mixed with sage and balm for her traveling, and a smaller pouch of boneset sweetened with wild mint in case of the damp.

Skada ate with her while the fire was great enough to shed some light. They were both quite mellow with the evening and the hot tea, and Skada even recited one of Petra's old praises to the evening's drink:

When one's hands are idle,
And night sneaks in like an old friend,
Welcome him with a cup of agrimony,
Make him welcome with a cup of sweet balm tea.

"Unfortunately not only night might sneak in," Jenna said after a bit. "Our fire could signal to footpads and other night men. Good-bye, sweet sister."

Skada made no protest and disappeared as soon as Jenna damped the fire, for there was no moon to keep her in the camp.

Using a small log as a back rest, Jenna gazed up at the scattering of stars through the bare overhang of branches. It had been years since she had thought much about the priestess who had run Selden Hame, and how the women there had spoken of Great Alta hiding her glory in a single leaf. But that particular phrase came to her now.

"Hiding in a tea leaf as easily," Jenna murmured. She sipped the now cold tea, savoring its homey taste. The priestess had said something else as well. *What was it?* Jenna closed her eyes, trying to remember, tracking back to the day that she and Pynt and the other girls—how young they were then!—had been praying. For someone. For something. And the priestess had said . . .

"What?" Jenna whispered. "What had she said?"

And then suddenly it came to her: *Sometimes Great Alta, she who runs across the surface of the rivers, who hides her glory in a single leaf, sometimes she tests us and we are too small to see the pattern. All we feel is the pain. But there is a pattern, and that you must believe.*

Did she believe? Could she believe?

She burst into loud, hot tears, surprising herself and disturbing the mare who stamped her feet and houghed sharply through her nose. But Jenna could not stop herself from crying. She continued to weep until she thought her chest would burst with aching and her eyes would never see again. She was not someone used to tears.

It took a long time before she was cried out and lay, head on the log, squinting up through swollen eyes. The stars seemed to swim about in a blurry sea of sky.

Thank Alta no one saw that! she thought. Not even Skada. She threw out the remains of the cold tea with a wide sweep of her hand. Then she stood and stretched her cramped legs. At last she spread out her blanket and lay down to sleep. If she had dreams, she did not remember anything about them.

* * *

It took another full day of riding before they got to the sea. Jenna did not expect to cry again, thinking that in that one night she had cried enough for a lifetime. But as she sat on the silent beach gazing out across the lapping waves with dusk gathering its skirts around her, she began to weep once more. This time her sobs were loud enough that grey-coated seals rose up from the skerries to stare at her. Two even dove into the water to swim within a few feet of shore, their heads and shoulders high out of the sea, watching warily, curiously.

She did not see them through her clouded eyes, but her horse did and trembled while grazing on beach grass. When the mare whuffled at the seals, Jenna turned and looked at the horse. When she turned back to see what had so frightened her mare, the seals were gone.

But Duty's alarm recalled Jenna to herself. She felt she was a danger to both of them, giving in to such strong emotion. As beautiful as the shingle was in the growing dark, with the glow along the horizon line that separated sky from sea, it was not a safe place, and Jenna was a woman alone. A warrior—true. But she recalled Scillia's words spoken thirteen years earlier, a warrior no longer young. She needed to remain alert, to be ready, not to be disarmed by her own tears.

She wondered briefly if she dared light any kind of fire on the wide swath of beach, or even higher up on the peaty cliffs that sheered off into the sea. That way Skada could company her, and she would have a blanket companion, a partner in any fight. But she decided at last that the fire itself was more danger than it was worth. She fell asleep sitting up, the cliff at her back and her sword on her lap, lulled into dreams by the sound of the ebbing sea.

Morning showed her the long shallow paths of the low tide, a greater beach than any she had ever seen, even in Berick Harbor. She wandered out between the tidal pools, picking up fluted shells and creatures whorled into shell mazes. Berick never had such a great tide. The water lowered, of course, but it did not uncover such swatches of land. Why—she could almost walk the flats straight across to the land of the Garuns.

"And what would I say to King Kras when I got there?" she wondered aloud. "That he has changed my boy beyond all recognition?" She knew in her heart of hearts that was not true. In some awful way, Jemmie's years with the Garuns had only made him more of what he had been from the first. It was true. She had sent them a little boy. They had returned him a littler man. It was not Jem's fault. Or the Garuns. "Or even ours," she whispered. "He is what he is." But still, she knew he had to be stopped before he hurt himself, before he hurt the Dales. "Piet is right about that," Jenna told herself. "And who but I can stop him?"

She turned and, with the sun at her back, stared up at the peaty cliffs. There were ten horsemen ranged along the top gazing down at her.

I should have spoken to him before I left, she thought wearily. *I expect it is too late now.*

THE HISTORY:

Editor
Pasden University Press

Sir:

Pasden University Press has issued many monographs by the late and hardly lamented Dr. Magic Magon, most of them abusing Dalian historical subjects. I am sure you are aware that much of Dr. Magon's work has been seriously discredited in the last few years. His scholarly star is on the wane; my father's star is once more on the rise.

I have in my possession several articles of my father's, never published, that might well be expanded into monographs by myself.

I have followed in his footsteps, becoming a scholar in the field of archeohistography, studying Dalian history and iconography under Drs. Doyle and Macdonald at Colebrook College, and musicology under Dr. Eldridge. I received my doctorate at the University of Berike-on-Sea. A selected bibliography of my articles and my father's follows.

The piece I am most interested in enlarging into a monograph is the enclosed study of folk songs after the fall of the so-called Anna of the Dales. My father calls this time the Interregnum and explains that while this term usually refers to "the period between kings, in the case of the Dales it was more like a semicolon." (He was ever the aphorist.)

My one area of disagreement with my father—which I shall carefully limn in the monograph with complete documentation—is that I feel there really was an historical Anna (or Jenna or Janna or Jo-Hanna, all simple cognates) though I am certain she was but a minor tribal figure who fought alongside the others during the disastrous Gender Wars. A hazy shadow wraps about this real figure; bards remake history to please their own masters. Later tellers borrow what they need to craft a better story. This is not new to any folklorist or archeohistographer. But I plan to show in this monograph how history and story—a word which grows out of it like a child following a parent—can prove the heretofore unprovable: In the fall of a hero is the rise of a nation.

And I will be the child building upon the father's shoulders, thus lifting us both (and the monograph) to a higher plane.

I look forward to hearing from you and working with you—I hope—in the very near future.

THE STORY:

After a moment of fear Jenna recognized the horsemen, soldiers who patrolled the coast roads. She waved and one of them—the obvious leader—hailed her in return, urging his horse down the grassy cliffside slope.

"We do not wish to disturb you," he said, when he realized who it was, "but we check out all strangers on the shore."

"As you should, captain," Jenna replied. "Though the disturbances have been few."

"Even a few is too many," the captain replied. "I will leave you, my queen, to finish your . . ."

"My mood is over," Jenna replied easily. "And there is much troubling me at home. I would ride back quickly, and not alone. Can you spare me two of your soldiers?"

"I can spare all for you, Anna," he replied. "We are done with the patrol and are about to be relieved."

"Two will be plenty," Jenna said. "I need to move quickly and safely back to Berick. Three together will be an unassailable force on the road against which footpads and highwaymen will stand down."

"Especially if those three are armed and riding fast," the captain agreed.

"Especially then."

She saddled her horse speedily and rode easily up the slope after him to the spot where the soldiers were waiting. The captain chose two immediately: a well-muscled woman about thirty years old with corn-colored hair cropped short as an old man's, and a scarred veteran closer to fifty who sat his horse as if he no longer knew where his own legs ended and the horse's barreled body began.

"Sarana and Voss will make a fine escort, Anna," the captain told her.

"We will make fine companions," she countered. "Sarana, Voss." She nodded at them. "You will shorten the road for me."

Voss nodded back curtly, but Sarana gave her the goddess

sign and Jenna smiled at them both. Then she turned back to the captain. "My thanks, good captain. We will feed them well at Berick before sending them back to you. But now we must ride, and ride hard."

At first the road was empty of travelers and the three kept a steady pace, galloping for a while, then fast-walking the horses, then settling them to a trot. It was a pattern the horses could keep up for hours, but Jenna made sure they gave the beasts plenty of times to rest and graze.

"I am in a hurry," she explained, "but I will not kill a horse for it."

Voss grunted his approval and took advantage of each rest to lie down on the verge of the road and catnap. It seemed to matter little whether there were rocks beneath him or moss, he closed his eyes and was immediately asleep, his breathy snores sawing the air. But Sarana took the rest stops as a time to walk about, stretching her legs and simultaneously putting a hand to the small of her back.

"If you ache," Jenna said, "I could give you a rub."

"The queen's touch?" Sarana snorted. "I don't believe in that."

"Nor do I," Jenna said. "My touch will not—as some think—cure scurvy or bring down swellings in the neck. But I am a fair hand at rubbing out aches and I've a lotion my infirmarer makes me carry whenever I go for my long ride-abouts."

Sarana ran a hand through her stubbly hair. "That I wouldn't mind." Without a word more, she stripped off her guard's coat and shirt. She wore nothing—binding or vest—beneath and seemed to have no embarrassment at being naked before a stranger.

"Sit," Jenna commanded.

Sarana sat on a high, flat stone, her back to Jenna, and

Jenna was horrified to see that her back read like an old river valley, scars meandering like watercourses across it.

"Who did such a thing to you?" Jenna asked.

"My mam and pap," Sarana said evenly. "It's why I joined the guards as soon as they'd have me. I knew no one else would ever hurt me as much as my own kin. Don't you mind it, ma'am. I don't. Not any more."

Jenna got out the lotion and spread it gently across the scarred back. "I'll be careful."

"It don't hurt," Sarana told her. "Not for years."

Jenna put more strength in the rub-down then, pressing her fingers deep into the woman's taut flesh. She knew it was a silly notion, but she could feel every one of the scars rising up in protest against her fingertips.

After a long while Sarana gave a contented sigh. "It's been a time since I felt so good. You do have a fair hand, Anna."

They heard Voss starting to stir in the grass.

"I thank you, ma'am," Sarana said slipping quickly back into her shirt and coat. "I'll ride days on that rub, I will."

They rode on, sharing the last of Jenna's journeycake and a skin of raw wine Voss carried "for medicinal purposes." The trip—which had taken Jenna two nights and two long days in the going—was shortened greatly in the return. They came upon the towers of Berick Castle as a dark shadow under the brilliant predawn sky.

Jenna reined in her horse, calling to the others. "We must go more slowly now, or an alarm will be raised. Follow in my track."

They were riding one by one by one, Jenna's white horse almost gleaming as the sun rose behind them, when ahead the great gates of the shadowy castle opened and they could see twenty or so torches lighting the way. A single rider galloped out to meet them.

"Scillia!" Jenna breathed, for she knew her daughter's one-armed outline at once. Fearing the worst, she kicked her horse forward and it gave her full heart in its gallop.

"Quickly, Mother," Scillia cried out. "Thank Alta you have returned. It is Father. The infirmarer fears this time for his life. I was going this morning to trail you."

Jenna nodded, thinking: *Not too late then, but late enough.*

They raced back to the castle together, leaving Jenna's companions far behind.

The infirmarer had no encouraging words and the Altan healer was even more blunt.

"He worsens by the hour," the healer said, her own face greyer than Carum's from sitting up with him. "All of a sudden he took a turn. I would not put a time on it, but it will be soon. I am sorry, Anna. Though the ballads already have it he reigned fifty years, you and I know the truth of it. This is the end, and not half that time."

"My children all know? And the council?"

The healer smoothed down her hair which was almost as white as Jenna's. "Your daughter knows and understands. It is she who has been handling the duties these two days. As for the boys, the Garun prince has been all but unmanned by the thought. I have given him a sleeping draught for the nights, but these past two days he has been like a ravening beast. Prince Corrine seems to blame himself for his father's sickness, though what blame there is for in an illness of the lung, I do not know. He does not listen to me, though, and has sat up through both day and night at his father's bedside trying to lighten the king's waking moments. He will make himself ill if he does not get some rest. Then I will have two patients and not the one. As to the council, I have not spoken to them. It is not my place."

"I will see them anon," Jenna said. "Let me see my husband now."

She went into the chamber they had shared the past twenty-five years and drew the heavy drapes away from the window to let in both light and air. Then slowly she turned and stared at the figure on the bed. He was much too still. When she neared the bed, his eyelids fluttered open.

"You have come back in time," he whispered.

She wept and could not stop.

He patted the bed by his side and she sat down, perching as carefully as a wren on a branch.

"I am always in time," she whispered.

He smiled and for a moment looked well and young. But only for a moment. "*Ich crie thee merci*," he said in a cracked voice.

She smiled back at the memory. Those had been the very first words he had spoken to her. "I will give you *merci*, my love. At least what I have of it." She took his hand. When had that hand become an old man's? The veins were like the traceries of a map. She knew suddenly what must be done and, after a few moments of silence, told him.

He did not argue much. It was as if he knew he walked the knife's edge of life and too much wasted breath on one side or the other would cause him to slip off early.

She kissed his hands, then his brow as well. "It will be a short journey, Longbow, though I cannot promise it will be an easy one."

He smiled again, this time at the use of his old nickname, the one the soldiers had given him in the war.

"But you will go in as much comfort as we can supply," she added. "And now I must make the preparations."

* * *

She was as blunt as the healer with the council. "He has reached the end," she said. "A day, a week at best." She sat with her back straight, hands folded on the table before her. If any of them knew that she had ridden all day and night, they would not read it in her demeanor.

Scillia sat beside her, her mouth in a thin, straight line.

Jenna gazed around the table at her oldest friends. Petra wept openly. Jareth had tears shining in his eyes that would not fall. The rest looked shocked, uncomfortable, angry. They had all known Carum was ill, but they had not let themselves know *too* much. Kings may die; heroes do not.

Only Piet spoke. Standing, he walked over to the window and stared across the courtyard before starting, then said "We have had a good king and queen on the throne, Anna. If the king goes, the queen still reigns. We will follow where you lead, as we have always."

Jenna did not react immediately to his well-meant words. Instead she hesitated a long moment before saying what had to be said. When at last she spoke her voice was steel. "A queen on the throne will reign indeed. But that queen will be Scillia. She has been trained up to it as I never was. She has lived her entire life knowing that one day she would rule. The tutors tell me that she has been an an apt pupil and I have sat with her on councils and in sessions. She has a strong heart and a good mind. She will make a fine queen."

"But, Jenna—" Petra was the first to protest.

Jenna held up her hand for silence. "I will *not* be parted from Carum. We are one soul. You all know I was never meant to rule, except by his side. And side by side we will go together into the grove."

Piet spun around and stared at her. "Do you mean to immolate yourself like some queen of the Injs? We will not let you. We need you, Anna."

"I mean to take Carum into the Grenna's grove," Jenna said softly. "I have always meant to do it. Till the world shall need us again."

"Pah! A fairy tale. We need you now!" Piet was near shouting.

"The grove is no fairy tale," Jenna said softly.

Piet strode to the table and slammed his hand down on it, making the goblets rattle. "Do you dare tell me anyone—*anyone*—in this chamber believes such a story?"

Jareth stood. His voice raspy with emotion did not break, but it was a near thing. "I was there with the Anna in the grove before, old man. Believe me, it is no tale. If Jenna is returning, there are some of us who would be willing to go with her."

"*No one*," Jenna said, the steel once again in her voice, "*no one* goes with me into the grove but Carum. Great Alta said I could take but one back and he is the one I choose. And if we do not make the preparations at once, I will be going there alone." She turned to Scillia who was still stone-faced by her side. As if the steel had finally been broken by a greater force, Jenna cried out, "Help me, daughter, I can do no more by myself."

The plea, so unexpected, broke Scillia's heart. She gathered her mother to her and held her, saying over her shoulder, "Make a bed in a long cart with bedding enough for comfort. And fix a strong canopy over it to keep out sun and wind. Have the healer make a good dozen draughts of poppy liquor to soothe the king if he needs it. I want strong horses to draw the cart, and a dozen soldiers to accompany us. And . . ."

Piet nodded. "It will be done."

But Jenna pulled away abruptly shaking her head. "No soldiers."

Scillia brushed a lock of hair from her mother's brow. "Soldiers for as long as they are needed, mother. That at least you must grant. You are not the only mourner here."

Jenna nodded wearily.

Standing, Petra came over, holding out a hand. "What can I do to help, my dear friend?"

"Bring me my sons," Jenna said. "They must be told."

"I will be here when you tell them, mother," Scillia said. "Dark sister to your light."

"And queen to my queen," Jenna said.

No one in the council disagreed.

The boys were found and brought into the chamber and then, as if by agreement—though none had been spoken—the members of the council left. Jenna and Scillia sat together at one end of the long table and Corrie perched, birdlike, on the edge of a stool he had drawn up near them. He stared at his hands, tears silently coursing down his cheeks. He did not bother to wipe the tears away, but continued to weep without sound.

On the other hand, Jemson could not be still. He sat in one chair, stood, tried another, then stood again to pace back and forth by the window while Jenna spoke. Finally he turned his back on them all and stared out of the window east, over the water, as if he could actually see the Continent by looking hard enough.

Jenna's dirge-like voice rose and fell. She told them how sick Carum was, what the healer had said, and what she planned to do. As she spoke, though she did not realize it, her hands in her lap clasped one another so tightly, the fingers went as white as her hair.

When she had finished speaking, there was a long silence in the room till Jemson turned and, nearly shouting, cried "It is *not* the end. It cannot be."

Jenna's hands flew apart at his words. She wondered briefly if she were more shaken by his strange anger or his even stranger certainty. Forcing her hands back into her lap, she spoke more calmly than she felt. "My dears, it is."

Jemson strode angrily to the table, picked up one of the chairs he had recently vacated and suddenly threw it against the wall, breaking off two of its legs. He made an odd grunting sound and it took a moment for Jenna to realize that he was actually crying.

Scillia stood abruptly and as abruptly Jenna put out a hand and pulled her back down into the chair.

All the while Corrie continued to weep silently.

"I will have no more of this, Jemson," Jenna said softly. "Let the two of us go with some measure of dignity."

"Two of you?" Jemson shouted in a mocking voice. "Two? There are never just the *two* of you! A bit of moon, a shred of candlelight, a fire filled with meat drippings—and then there are three. It is unholy."

Jenna bit back her own anger and answered quietly, "This time there will be but two. That is the law of the grove."

"And what of us?" It was Corrie, his voice husky with tears. "How can you leave us alone?"

Jenna leaned over and put her hand on his. "You are not alone, Corrie dear. There are the three of you and the council and . . . and the entire kingdom. Why your family is as large as this land."

"Three cannot rule a land together," Jemson said bitterly, "no matter who they are." He did not seem to realize the irony in what he had just said.

"No, perhaps not," Jenna replied. "Though we have tried. But one surely can. And she *will*."

"You cannot really still mean to have . . . her . . . be queen." Jem had moved close to his sister, leaning menacingly toward her. "She has not the blood for it."

"If you mean the passion for it—that she surely has. If you

mean the mettle for it—that too she has. If you mean the breeding for it—what breeding did *I* have?"

"You married father and he was born to be king," Jemson said.

"Father was born to be a prince. War made him a king. And only because mother won the battles for him," Corrie reminded him. "It was a throne bought with the blood of many men."

"And many women," Scillia added.

Jenna's voice returned to steel. "We have had enough of that kind of blood."

Jemson turned and went back to the window, looking out once more toward the sea.

"The people expect Scillia to be queen," Jenna finished, "without the necessity of blood. And queen she shall be."

"Blood . . ." Jemson muttered, implying much. But his voice was lost to them, carried out the window to the east.

"Corrie, Scillia, you may go now. There is something that your brother and I must speak about. I know he would prefer to hear it alone."

At that Jemson turned around. "If it is more about blood, mother, let them stay. I would have them know my mind entirely. And *my* mind is bloody right now."

"It is about letters, Jemmie." Jenna's voice was hard. "Not blood. And I think you have lost what mind you once had."

Scillia looked puzzled and Corrie ill-at-ease. They had never heard that particular tone in their mother's voice before, as if she had drunk a bitter tincture of wormwood and rue.

"Go!" Jenna suddenly shouted at the two of them. "Go now! And do not listen like children at the door!"

They bolted for the door as if they were still youngsters, propelled by a sense of foreboding, Scillia ahead of Corrie. Jenna waited until they had slammed the door behind them, then reached into the leather pocket that hung from her waist. She pulled out a handful of letters.

"These speak treason, you know." She pushed them across the table at Jemson.

He reached out to touch them, then drew his hand back as if the letters had been nettles, but he did not deny the letters were his. Nor the treason. Instead he went on the attack. "How dare you, mother? How did you get those? They are my private . . ."

"Private?" Her voice was once again quiet. But it was not gentle. "Did you think that a prince who has been public in his condemnation of his country has a right to any privacy? Did you think that a boy who has been raised in the house of our enemies would be fully trusted? Did you . . . even . . . *think* at all?

"But those were not . . . They were to be . . . private." He bit his lip.

"Nothing a royal does is private," Jenna continued. "Why do you think I run off to the woods whenever I can? Why do you think I am taking your father away now? If you want privacy, child, do not seek a throne. Surely your Garun masters taught you that."

"I. Am. Not. A. Child." He glared at her and all at once Jenna felt cold. She did not recognize those eyes. They were angry, distant, mocking, sly. They were a Garun's eyes. They did not belong to any son of hers.

"What do you plan to do with those?" he asked, gesturing to the letters.

"Give them back to you," she said. "With a warning." She held the letters toward him.

"Blood to blood, mother?" he asked, snatching the letters up and cramming them down the neck of his shirt.

She did not answer. She did not answer his unasked question, either. Could he possibly suppose she was the only one who knew of the letters? Could he be so stupid? So careless? So selfish? So low?

Without another word, Jemson turned away from her and walked over to the door which he opened with such sudden violence, he surprised Scillia and Corrie who were waiting close enough to have overheard the entire exchange.

They lost no time in crowding past Jemson into the council room, but he paid them no heed, striding on down the long hall and out of sight.

"What did those letters say, mother?" Scillia demanded. "Were they treason indeed?"

"He is plotting with the king across the water for your throne," Jenna said, her voice like her face drawn and old.

Corrie said nothing, but there was no surprise written on his face, only a lingering sadness. Jenna noted it and wondered.

"Then why did you give him back the letters?" Scillia asked.

"Think," Jenna said. "Think like a queen, Scillia."

Scillia was silent. If she was thinking, it was not apparent. She just looked angry.

Corrie put his hand on his sister's shoulder. "She's made copies, of course. And shown the originals to the council."

"Hold your brother Corrine close, Scillia," said Jenna. "Dark sister to your light. He has the mind of a plotter and the soul of a saint." She stood. "I am tired. Alta alone knows how tired. But I have no time to sleep. Come with me to your father's room and give him your farewells."

"With all my heart, mother," Corrie said, bowing his head.

"But I am going with you to the grove," Scillia said. "Surely I can say my farewells there."

"Only as far as the grove, daughter. Not into it. And I have no guarantee your father will be able to speak to you there. Besides, it is not yet your time to come into the grove. This is your turning."

"What do you mean, mother?" Scillia asked, but she spoke to her mother's back. She turned to Corrie. "What does she mean?"

This time he had no answer for her.

Their goodbyes were short for Carum, already groggy from the healer's strong poppy decoction, could barely keep his eyes open.

Scillia knelt by the bed and held her father's hand. She marveled at how light it felt, as if dying were merely the loss of bone. Corrie stood at the bedfoot, his shoulders hunched, his right hand on the canopy's tester. He was so tall and silent a presence, he almost looked like the figure of Alta's Last Watcher that was embroidered on the main arras in the throne room: that dark-robed, vulture-headed character from the tales.

Jenna looked at the two of them rather than at Carum and sighed. *They will do!* she thought. Then for a moment she worried about Jemson, off somewhere in the bowels of the castle or perhaps down at the Berick docks bribing some poor Garunian sailor to take one last message for him. *That he should be such a sorry son . . .* She stopped herself. *He is what he is.*

She knew that Scillia and Corrine between them would serve the country well, and they could handle their treasonous brother with the help of the council. Jemson was sly and he was a braggart, but he had no real strength. Of that she was sure.

"For this turning," she whispered.

As if he heard her, Carum moved fitfully in the great bed. His eyes flickered open and his lips formed Jenna's name. "I need to tell . . ." he began. Then his eyes closed.

"I am here, my love," Jenna said, quickly shooing the others from the room. Before they quite got out the door, Jenna whispered, "Scillia, I count on you." Then she closed the door behind them with a quiet *snick*.

Jemson was neither in the bowels of the castle nor at the docks. He was high on the battlements, a tame dove in his hands. In a small pouch tied to the dove's right leg was a message.

This being a time of peace, there were no guards around to see what Jemson was about, but he moved stealthily anyway. When he was certain no one had seen him, he flung the bird into the air.

The bird flapped once, twice to get its balance. It flew east to the water's edge, then south along the coast, till it found its heart's compass. Then it headed straight east again across miles of open water toward its home.

The cart with Carum's bed was pulled along the King's Way by two broad Dales mares bred for placid dispositions and massive strength. The road was still broken and pocked by the long winter's upheavals, and the cart lurched along like a drunkard just come from the ale house. Carum was drugged much of the time and did not notice how long or how wretched the road was.

"Or else he would be sitting up and making lists for the repairs," Scillia said.

Jenna agreed, even smiling for a moment. Then she grew serious again. "Soon enough he will have to endure a harder route, and without the tincture at the end. For he must be awake to agree to the last. I will, myself, pull him through the woods to the grove. It will of course mean tying him to the sledge, but . . ."

"Two to pull will make things go more smoothly, mother,"

Scillia argued. "Two. Or more. We have the soldiers. Surely they can . . ."

"We have been over and over this, Scillia," Jenna said. "No one but your father and I are allowed to go all the way. Great Alta said I can bring one other into the grove."

"But you are already two in a single breast, mother," Scillia pointed out. "There is Skada."

"If I go by night. But if I go by day there will be just Carum and me."

Scillia shook her head. "How can you leave your dark sister behind?"

"As you say, she is here, within me. So in a way I do not leave her at all. The Book of Light says: *two sisters, two sides*. But there are no shadows in the grove. She could not come in bodily even if I wanted her to." She put up her hand as a signal to stop and the soldiers leading the two mares eased them to a gentle halt. "Here. Here is where we stay."

Scillia dismounted and checked her father who still slept heavily in the cart. Then she turned to Jenna. "You cannot mean *here*, mother." She pointed around them where the great trees crowded in toward the broken road. "There is nothing here but forest. You cannot mean to stop here."

"This is exactly where I mean to stop." Jenna turned from her. "Take the sledge down," she ordered.

"Then you cannot know what you are doing," Scillia said. "I forbid it."

Jenna turned to her and smoothed a lock of Scillia's hair that had come unbound on the ride. "You cannot forbid me anything," she said softly. "I am still queen. And your mother besides." If she meant to be comforting, her humor missed its mark.

Scillia took a step back, away from her mother's hand.

"Sil, you must trust me on this. You and Corrie. As for Jem . . ."

"Jem trusts no one and no one trusts Jem," Scillia said bitterly.

"That you shall have to sort through yourselves," Jenna said. "Do you know what the Berick fisherfolk say? *The skate and the eel do not swim the same, but they both live in the sea.* That is you and Corrie and Jem."

"We are not fish nor have we fins."

"You are not hearing me."

"I am not listening."

They glared at one another while around them the soldiers completed their tasks.

"When father is dead, then will you come home?"

Jenna took the step toward Scillia again, and put her arms around her daughter whose body remained rigid with anger. "*Listen* this time. He is not going to die. Nor am I. We will live on in the grove till you need us again."

"The grove or the Green Hall? Wasn't that what the M'dorans call it?" Scillia tore herself from her mother's arms. "Whatever its name, it is nothing but a nursery story. I will not be cozened at such a time with such tales. I am no child." This time she walked two steps away, her one hand balling into a fist.

Jenna smiled sadly. "Such stories hold their own truth, Scillia. And the truth is that your father and I were at the beginning of this circle, but it is your turning now."

"You intend to die with him!" Scillia cried. "I will never see you again."

Jenna went over to her and took the fist in both her hands, gently prising the fingers open. She kissed her daughter's palm. "When you look in the mirror, Scillia, when you speak to your own daughters and sons, you will see me and hear me. I will be with you when you need me most."

"I need you most now, mother. We all need you most

now." Scillia fought the tears that glittered in her eyes, willing them not to fall.

"The Dales need *you* now, not me," Jenna said. "My work is done. It was done twenty-six years ago but I stayed for love. Your work is just beginning. Take the soldiers and go. Do not make me weak now when I need strength for two." She embraced Scillia once again and this time Scillia returned it, her body shuddering with emotion.

They stood breast to breast for a long moment, before Jenna broke them apart. She turned and started lining the sledge with cushions from the cart. A single soldier helped her, a woman with hair like a newly threshed wheat field.

"I know you," Jenna said slowly. "You are Sarana! Did you not go back to your own captain?"

"No, I stayed on at the castle and sent Voss home."

"And have you been here, on the road, with us all the time? I did not recognize you till now."

"We notice what we must," Sarana said.

"And your back?"

"Better than his," Sarana said, nodding at Carum still dozing fitfully in the cart.

Sarana and Scillia helped Jenna lift Carum into the sledge where they tied him down with a soft belt across the chest and feet so that he would not slip out. Scillia leaned over and kissed his face, but he did not stir.

Then one by one the soldiers filed past to gaze down at their king. Sarana was the last of them.

"Now go," Jenna said to them and they started back down the road in a line more ragged than they were used to, but Scillia stubbornly stayed behind.

"You must go, too," Jenna said to her. "For your father. For me. Be a queen. Your people need you. *Now!*"

Reluctantly, then angrily, Scillia mounted her gelding and

rode after the soldiers. She did not look back to see Jenna, white braids atop her head like a crown, pick up the ends of the sledge in which Carum lay and start to pull it over the grass and into the nearest woods.

Sarana peeled off from the troop at their first rest and, putting the woods between her and her mates, raced back the way they had come. She found the mark of the cart and the sledge tracks going into the woods. Leading her horse, she followed carefully deep and deeper still.

After a while the trees opened out again onto a meadow where the grass was still winter brown. She puzzled over the muddled trail. Jenna's track and that of the sledge were clear. But all around them, sometimes going across and smudging the prints, were the signs of many small naked feet, as if a gang of barefooted children had gathered around the woman and her burden.

Sarana had heard stories of the Grenna, the Green Folk, the Little People, but she did not credit them. She had put her childhood—stark and terror-ridden—behind her along with childhood's stories. Still she could not imagine what a group of children would be doing in this high meadow, so far from any town, shoeless and tracking the queen. She did not like the look of that circle of small prints. In her experience, things that could not be explained were dangerous things.

Mounting her horse again, she galloped along the sledge trail to where the meadow ended once again in the woods. She had to dismount there to follow the trail along a crumbling ridge. In her heart she was all admiration for Jenna who must have been gifted with enormous strength to have come so far so fast dragging the sledge. But her head was full of warnings.

"Ain't natural," she whispered to herself. "Ain't right."

The ridge ended at a cliff's edge. So did the trail. It took her all the rest of the day to climb down that cliff, sliding at times on the rocky scree.

There was no sign of the sledge, the sick king, the queen.

A week's scouring on small rations and less sleep brought her no more answers. She gave up only when there were no more crumbs of journeycake and her stomach clenched at the thought of more boiled ferns. She rode her horse slowly back toward Berick Castle and the barracks she now called home.

Scillia and the soldiers had been four days going and three days coming back. Her mood was not helped by the weather: it was grey and foggy in the mornings, grey and rainy in the afternoons. Only at night, under a surprisingly clear sky where stars flickered like fireflies, did she find some measure of peace.

But she did not sleep.

And she did not weep.

The sergeant in charge of the guard tried to find her a place strewn with pine needles, soft and scented, since she would not rest in the cart.

But still she did not sleep.

And she would not eat.

"Please, princess," the sergeant begged, his homely face scrunched in concern. "If you do not sleep or eat, your mother will have my head."

He does not know, Scillia thought. *He does not understand that she is never going to return*. She did not try to enlighten him.

Only when they arrived back at the castle to find the gates closed to them and the watch inexplicably wearing the colors of Garun soldiery did she tell him what she knew.

"A queen three days and no longer," she said with a self-deprecating laugh.

"You will be queen for all time, ma'am," he replied. It was

all he said while he marshalled his few men and Scillia, leading them away from the castle and into the cover of the deep mazed woods before the Garuns within the stone walls had time or inclination to follow.

THE LEGEND:

Three days ride from Berick is a deep old-growth forest known as Gemma's Grove or Queen's Own. The woods there are thick with oak and blackthorn, rowan and ash; three species of squirrel live there and nowhere else in the Dales. In the deepest part of the woods is a strange meadow called The Green. Trackers and huntsmen will not willingly cross that lea. Men have fallen down sinkholes or otherwise disappeared. It is said that in the last century an entire troop of scouts wandered by mistake across that meadowscape, boys in their first training. Twenty boys went in, only five came out again, and they had no idea what had happened to their mates.

THE MYTH:

Then Great Alta took the girl child by the hair and turned her around ten times. "Now," quoth she, "you are a queen."

"I have no throne," said the girl.

"Make one. Or take one," quoth Great Alta. "Or do without."

"Can I do such a thing?" asked the girl.

"Can you not?" Great Alta replied.

four

Usurper King

THE MYTH:

Then Great Alta saw the girl on the ground and she was weeping.

"What ails you?" quoth Great *Alta.*

"I want my mam," cried the girl.

"You are too old for the nipple, too young for the grave. Mother yourself," quoth Great *Alta.*

THE LEGEND:

There is a story they tell of the hundred-day king that when he returned from over the sea he killed his mother and father, his sister and brother all on the same day. And when the soldiers came to take him to the judgment room, he cried them merci.

"For I am an orphan child," he said. "And the last of my line."

So they showed him merci *who had showed none to others. And from that day forth it is said in the Dales:* He is as merciful as a hundred-day king, *meaning someone who has absolutely no thought for others.*

THE STORY:

Jemson found the throne a hard seat.

He sent for pillows and tried them each in turn, pillows garnered from all the bedrooms and sitting couches in the castle.

Corrie heard of the search when a server came to his room and demanded his bed cushions, for he had been confined to the one room since the day the seven Garun ships had sailed into the harbor and taken the castle with scarcely a blow dealt.

"A hard seat indeed," Corrie said, and laughed. "And he will find it harder still in the days to come. Here—take them with my blessing. Jem will find no good in them."

Trying to curry favor with the new regime, and being somewhat of a toad, the server reported this conversation to the new council chief, a Garun, who in turn told Jemson.

At the news, Jemson's face turned a variety of colors, all shades of red, starting with a flush at the neck. He was finding his brother less of a help than he had hoped, than he had counted on. "Blood," he had warned the Garuns, "that is mine will not be spilled." By that he had meant Scillia was fair game, but not his mother or brother. But when his mother had not returned, nor Scillia, and when Corrie had proved intractable, Jemson had to change his plans. He did not make new plans easily.

"What . . ." he asked, thinking he was crafty in the doing and not realizing how transparent he was, "do you advise?"

The Garun was the same Sir Rodergo Malfas who had come across the sea thirteen years earlier to take up the young prince. He had molded him, child and man, with an ease that was laughable, though he was always careful not to laugh at Jemson to his face. Jemson did not take teasing well. And any laughter he counted as ridicule, whether it was meant or not.

"My King," Malfas said, making such a low obeisance it was almost an insult, "your brother will not change. He can only gather around him those malcontents and wishers-of-ill. Best you put him with the others in the dungeon."

"But he is my brother," Jemson said. He had half expected this advice from Malfas, indeed hoped for it. But faced with it in truth, he had a sudden qualm.

"He is therefore your chiefest enemy," Malfas explained. Sometimes he thought it would have been easier to work with the brother; he at least had brains and a sly wit. But it had been Jemson who had been gifted them, and Jemson they had trained. *Art is inborn, craft outborn*, the *Book of Battles* said. "We will not have him killed. Just . . . controlled."

"Good. I do not want him killed. He is of my . . ."

"Your blood is sacred to us all, my king," Malfas said, stroking his elegant moustache and smiling indulgently.

"Then dungeon him," Jemson said, glad to have had his mind made up for him. "And let's get on with the coronation. You may call me king all you like, but I am not yet so in the eyes of my people."

Malfas nodded. "I will be but a minute," he said, and went out into the hall to call the guard for that particular duty.

The guards who came to take Corrie to the dungeon were Garuns as well. Few of the Dale soldiery had come willing into the new army. Those who had not been killed or imprisoned on the day the Garuns sailed into Berick Harbor, were long since fled to the woods.

Corrie was not surprised by the sudden imprisonment. Indeed, in the weeks he had been confined to his bedroom, he had already managed to contact the two or three still-loyal servers in the castle—a cook, a scullery, and a girl whose father was one of the forest soldiers. He sent messages through them to his sister, though he did not expect to hear back from her. His comments on the guards and Malfas and Jemson were quite specific. He gave Scillia numbers and locations of the soldiers as best he could determine. He gave her his thoughts on the castle staff morale. While he did not consider himself Jemson's chief enemy, no matter what Malfas might think—for he too held sacred the bonds of blood—he considered himself Scillia's chief spy. Family, more than mere blood, and the safety of the Dales were first in his thoughts.

Corrie was not surprised, but he was annoyed. "I am a prince," he said to the Garuns, something he would never say to someone of the Dales. Still, he knew such things mattered deeply to the Garun men. "Do not dare put your hands on me."

They hesitated to touch him, and they let him put on a pair of heavy hose against the cold under his caftan as well as carry an extra cloak, but they chivvied him out the door, and down the stairs nonetheless. He walked before them, head held high, a bit of play-acting to impress upon them that he was Jemson's brother and not to be tampered with.

He supposed he could have tried to escape, but he was neither a hero nor a coward. He believed in time and in the Dales proverb: *An hour makes a difference between the wise man and the fool.* If it meant spending that hour in the wine cellar—for they had no real dungeon in Berick Castle—he would do it. He wrapped the cloak around him as if he suffered already from the cold. Actually it was to hide the short sword he had managed to take from his dressing room, hidden as it was against just such an eventuality under the very cloak he now wore.

The wine cellar was not a dungeon, but its heavy oak door made it an effective gaol. The Garun guards opened the door for Corrie and did not touch him, but it was clear that they *would* handle him if he did not go in on his own. So he walked in, muttering "Peasants!" as he passed them. He was pleased to see that one of them, at least, had the grace to redden at the slander. It was hardly much of an insult in Dale terms. Most Dale folk were proud of their peasant origins. But the guard had the last laugh for he was the one who got to slam the door behind Corrie and lock it with the wine steward's own great key.

At least there were torches alit in the cellar and Corrie wandered through the barrel-vaults of stacked wine, some dusty and old, most of newer vintage and brought over the water with Jemson's return. He came, at last, to a back room that was set up like a barracks. There were several dozen people sitting on pallets or playing cards in the flickering light: men, women, and several young boys as well.

"Petra," Corrie cried when he recognized her with the card players.

"Ah, Corrie," she said, looking up, "we wondered just how long it would be before Jemson put you in here, too." She stood and came over to embrace him.

"I am not sure it was Jem who did it."

Piet, who had been leaning against the wall, snorted. "Who else?" He joined the two of them.

Corrie shook his head. "You know as well as I that he is a poppet. The hand on his back is Malfas' own."

"And the hand on Malfas' back?" Jareth said. His voice was husky as always but lower than usual, and he had a brief coughing spasm after speaking.

"King Kras, of course."

"A long reach," remarked Petra.

"*Drink with Garuns, use a long straw,*" said Corrie. "Father says that all the time."

"Your father is dead by now," Petra said gently. "And your mother."

Corrie shrugged. "Speaking of him living is an old habit, Petra. I know he is gone. As for mother, who can say for certain? She has not come home these four weeks. Try as he might—even offering a reward for information that would make a prince of a farmhand—Jemson has had no real word of her."

A shadow peeled off from the wall, intruding into their conversation. "I have some word."

"From her?" Corrie asked.

"*Of* her."

"And have you told these good people?"

"I did not know who in this prison to trust so I have kept my own counsel till now. But as they have put you in here, Prince Corrine, you who are her son—and not the *other*—" here she spat expertly to the side "I shall say what I know."

"Who are you?" Piet asked.

"I am a soldier," the woman said, running a hand through her short hair. "My name is Sarana. I was with the queen when she took King Carum into the woods."

"I know all my guard," said Piet suspiciously. "You are none of them."

"Well, I was new come to them, and you raving about the king's illness. I doubt you ever saw me. Till I came here, I had been with the southern border patrols. I rode back with the Anna on her last Wanderings, from the south."

"And why are you not there now? Did you leave them? Did you . . . ?" Piet's questions tumbled one after another till Petra put a hand on his shoulder.

Sarana shrugged. "I am no Garun, sir. I am not the enemy. I came for love of the queen. I stayed for love of the queen. I volunteered to go with the cart and sledge. Would you have me prove more?"

"Pah! It would be just like Jemson to put a spy in our midst," Piet said, shrugging off Petra's hand and turning away.

"I . . . am . . . no . . . spy." Sarana's voice was like a honed knife.

"What else would a spy say?," Piet said.

"This is nonsense," Corrie put in. "He would not use a woman at any rate. Tell us, Sarana, what you know. We will decide if it is to the point and how to use it."

"You are her son, indeed," said Sarana. "I will speak to

you. As for the commander, I wonder that he has not lost the greater part of himself in the king's death."

"You saw the king die? It is true?" Corrie asked.

As Sarana started to explain just what she had seen, and what she had not seen on her search, the room grew quiet except for her voice. Every one of the prisoners came over to listen, and she wove them a story-spell.

THE TALE:

Whenever danger threatened the Dales, King Cronin went into the New Forest, to the very edge of the Great Grove, and said a special prayer to the Anna, the queen in waiting. And in this way danger was always averted.

But at last and finally King Cronin was gathered, and the new king, Jemin took the throne. Whenever danger threatened the Dales, he too went into the New Forest, to the very edge of the Great Grove. But he had never been taught the special prayer to the Anna. Still it was enough. The danger was averted.

But at last and finally King Jemin was gathered, and the new king Solon took the throne. Whenever danger threatened the Dales, he too went into the New Forest. But he did not know the way to the very edge of the Great Grove, for it had been destroyed. And he had never been taught the Anna's special prayer. Still it was enough, and the danger was averted.

But at last and finally King Solon was gathered, and a new and nameless king took the throne. Whenever danger threatened the Dales—well, he had never been taught the Anna's prayer and he did not know the way to the very edge of the Great Grove for it had been destroyed. And in fact the New Forest had been cut down and houses built up in its stead. All the nameless king knew how to do was to tell this story.

But it was enough.

THE STORY:

Of course none of them actually believed her, except Jareth.

"I have been to the grove," he said between coughs. "I have seen the Grenna."

"That was many years ago in the middle of battle. We all remember impossible things in the heat of a fight. War is, itself, an impossible thing. Men killing men." Piet turned away.

"And women," Petra added.

"Perhaps what you saw were the tracks of wolves," Corrie offered.

"Yes, wolves," said a man in a guard's uniform.

"A pack, circling them," said another.

Sarana drew herself up. "I know wolf tracks," she said huffily. "They are nothing like human . . ."

"*Human!*" Piet interrupted. "You see, she calls them *human*. Not little elves. Little green men. The Grenna. Which is something my old nurse used to talk about, when she wasn't telling me stories about fairies. And wings. And the water horse who steals away pretty women. And the crier at the water's edge who prophesies death."

"I do not know about those—the fairies, the water horse, the crier," Sarana said. "I only know what I saw."

"What you *didn't* see," Piet said.

"I saw the tracks. The footprints. Where the sledge prints ended."

"But," Corrie said, his voice soft and muzzy, "you didn't see my mother, the Anna. You didn't see my father. You didn't *see* them. . . ." He stopped suddenly.

Sarana put her hand on his arm, a gesture she would never have dared outside of the dungeon. "I didn't see them dead, Prince Corrine, no."

Corrie shook off the muzziness. "Then they are not dead."

"But are they alive?" Piet asked. "That is the more interesting question."

"Isn't it the same question?" Petra was clearly puzzled.

Corrie managed a smile. "For us, here in this dark hole? Not the same question at all."

A few of the listeners—the boys and some of the servers—moved away and one or two resumed their card game on a nearby pallet.

Furious that no one believed his memories, sacred as they were to him, Jareth left the barracks room and went through one of the archways into the red wine cellar where he brooded alone. But Corrie, Piet, Petra, and Sarana kept on talking with an audience of guardsmen and soldiers.

The conversation was desultory at first, rehearsing the days that had led them all to the dungeon: Jemson's casual usurpation of the throne "temporarily until the queen returns." The arrival of the Garun ships. The turncoats within the palace guard. Jemson's welcome to the army from the Continent. The mastery of Malfas.

"It sounds like a bad song cycle," Petra said. "I expect we will be singing of it anon."

"If we are alive to do any singing at all," one soldier grumbled. "We are corked up in here like bad wine."

Another added, "The air is impossible. It is cold and damp. Old Jareth's cough worsens. The rest of us will be coughing soon enow."

And a third added his plaint. "My old wound aches, young prince. My leg draws up in the damp. We will either die here or Jem-Over-the-Water will have us executed."

The first soldier came in again. "There is nothing we can do for we are weaponless and with no way out."

"That," Corrie whispered conspiratorially, "is not entirely true." He waited until the announcement had sunk in, then he reached under the cloak and produced the sword.

"But that's . . ." Piet said.

"My father's short sword," Corrie said. "From the Gender Wars. So we are not *entirely* weaponless. And as for a way out, there is a small oriel window behind the Basilion Red. My brother and I discovered it one day as children when we were playing hide-and-then-seek. The window is quite small. Child-size really. And it drops down to the rocks that sheer off into the sea. Father had the poor wine shifted over there after Jemson dared me to climb out and I got stuck halfway." He smiled and patted his ample stomach. "I was rather a pig in those days. Screamed bloody fratricide until the wine steward heard me. Jem had long since scampered off to his room. Declared he had nothing to do with the jape, not that anyone believed him. The window was too high up for me to have gotten to it alone."

"I remember that," Petra said. "I thought your father had the window walled up."

"What is walled can be unwalled," Piet said.

Sarana laughed aloud. "Especially now that we have something to dig with."

"Not the king's sword!" Petra was scandalized. "It's from the wars!"

"Of course his sword," Corrie said. He held it aloft. "We will do it now."

"Not yet," cautioned Sarana. "They will be feeding us soon. But after that they leave us alone for the rest of the night."

Corrie nodded and quickly disappeared the sword back under his cloak, but he could not disappear the lightened mood of the group. Jareth was persuaded to return from the wine room reluctantly, led by Petra. But when he heard the news, he smiled and joined in the chatter.

Things seemed suddenly so improved, the prisoners even sang songs and told stories till the food arrived, brought in by three servers under the watchful eye of the heavily armed Garun guard. If the guard thought the prisoners somewhat uplifted, they put it down to the new addition to their ranks. A prince, even an imprisoned one, could well charge the atmosphere.

However, one of the Garuns dutifully reported the change of mood to King Jemson who was alone in his chamber. The Garun particularly mentioned how the prisoners had been singing.

"They was going on and on with tunes about the Wars," the man said. "Not very melodic, sire, but they sung them with gusto. There were 'King Kalas and His Sons' and another were 'Well Before the Battle, Sister.' And others I didn't know. Never made it over the sea, I guess."

"Corrine has always been a fool," Jemson said. "He will go to his death joking and singing." And having thus made the pronouncement, he quickly forgot about it, neglecting even to mention the guard's report to Malfas, who might have put a different face on the news altogether.

The food given the prisoners was rough: porridge and goats' milk. The spoons were wooden as were the porringers. Clearly the Garuns were taking no chances that the gaoled soldiers might make weapons from their implements. In fact the bowls and spoons were counted out when they were distributed and again at their collection.

"I have had worse," Corrie said cheerfully.

"When?" Petra asked.

He winked at her.

"So have I," declared Sarana. "For most of my childhood." She dug into the porridge with an enthusiasm Corrie had to pretend.

As soon as they were all done eating, they piled the

spoons and bowls by the wooden door. Two servers, guarded by Garuns, collected them and the door was once again locked tight.

"They will come in the morning with new torches and food," said Piet. "We will have the long night to do what needs be done." He snatched up a bottle of red wine and brought it back to the barracks room. Hitting the neck against the stone wall, he broke it cleanly and raised the bottle high.

"To the queen," he said. "She who was and she who is." He did not name Jenna and Scillia, but they all knew who he meant. He took a deep draught and then passed the bottle to Corrie.

"Can't we arm ourselves with broken bottles?" Corrie asked.

"Against their long swords?" Piet answered. "It would be an awful slaughter. And to no end."

Sarana shook her head. "We have spoken of this before you came, my prince. I say we should rather die fighting than languishing in prison. But Piet—the head of the army, mind you—says no."

Piet glared at her. "The head of the army needs to know when to fight and when to wait. Drink, Corrie."

Corrie lifted the bottle and glanced at the label. He nodded approvingly. "*An hour makes a difference* . . . Piet is right. To the queens!" He drank and passed the bottle to Petra.

They drank the bottle to the end; even the boys had a sip. Then Piet took the empty bottle back, set it carefully on the ground, and turned to Corrie. "Now we must work. You and you," he said, pointing to two of the taller soldiers, "and you three," he added nodding at two burly men and Sarana, "come with us. And Corrie, show us where that window used to be."

In the end the seven were joined by Jareth and Petra. The rest of the prisoners were cautioned to stay in the barracks room. "Too much noise could sink us," Piet warned.

The Basilion wines had long been drunk up, but Corrie knew the wall nonetheless, for it was the western wall, the one alongside the sea.

"Here!" he said, pointing to a great floor-to-ceiling rack of mostly undistinguished northern reds. The rack on the eastern wall held the better vintages, some dry reds that were quite acceptable table wines and about a hundred bottles of a heavy, sweet red from vineyards from the area south and east of Berick. He was glad they did not have to move the drinkable wines.

Forming a single line, with the two tall soldiers at the rack, they passed the wines silently down the line till they reached Petra, who stood in the archway into the barracks room. She handed each bottle to one of the boys who then had the task of placing them upright against the walls.

"Silently," Petra reminded them again and again. "Do not let the bottles clink together," though she knew very well that the greatest danger was not there but in the wine room, so much closer to the door and to the ears of the Garun guards.

It took them a quarter of the night to remove the bottles and then the rack as well. But when they were done, Piet held up a torch to the wall. There was indeed a square patch boarded over with wood.

"Give me the sword," Piet said.

"No, 'tis my father's. I will do the damage," said Corrie. Then he laughed. "It is not so high now, this window. Look it comes barely to my shoulders. That Jem and I found it such a labor before!" He took the sword and using it as a pry, stuck it between two of the boards and levered one of them off with a single solid wrenching. The board clattered to the ground before anyone could catch it and the noise that it made on the stone floor was horrendous.

Everyone froze except Sarana who quickly crept through the archway into the next room, the room that was filled with the white wines. She stood for a long time in an attitude of listening, before returning to the still frozen group of prisoners.

"It is all right. No one seems to be stirring. My captain would have had our heads were we so lax. But we best not have any such noise again."

The next board was taken down with two sets of hands holding on. And a third board revealed the window itself, too dirty to see out but with a cold sea wind seeping in through some cracks.

"Better than we could have hoped," Piet said. "I expected it to be mortared."

"I am sure Father expected that the boards and the racks of wines were more than sufficient to keep us from attempting another sortie," said Corrie. "I was certainly not to be caught twice that way, and Jem only wanted someone else to try the escapade. He had no such courage on his own."

"But it is too small for one of us," Petra pointed out. "And we dare not send one of those boys." She nodded toward the barracks room.

"Why not?" asked Jareth. "I was a boy when I fought in the war. And surely we are at war again now."

"But they are small boys. Not near man's estate as you were," said Petra. "And what would I say to their mothers . . . ?"

"I believe I can fit," Sarana said. "Take out the glass and the casing and I can surely slither through. I have been in caves and tunnels. We've a lot of them on the coast. It's all a matter of knowing when to twist—and how. If my shoulders can get through, the rest will follow."

"It is a drop onto the rocks, and into the sea thereafter," warned Corrie. "I remember now why I was happy I had become stuck!"

"We can make a rope out of your cape and any extra clothing we can find," Sarana said. "I am a strong climber."

"But can you swim?" asked Petra.

"Like an oyster," Sarana said laughing.

"Meaning you will sink to the bottom?"

"And crawl along to the shore, if necessary," Sarana replied. "But I do not expect to go into the ocean at all. It is too cold for my taste. And too filled with salt."

So while the two tallest of the soldiers helped Corrie prize out the window, halting between attempts when things got too noisy, and bemoaning the ruination of a good weapon, Sarana and Petra organized a search for clothes to knot and plait together into a rope. It was necessarily a makeshift strand, but Sarana continually tested its strength and declared herself pleased at the end.

They wrapped one end of the line around the burliest of the men, once around his waist and once over his shoulder. "To serve as anchor," Piet said.

The other end Sarana tied around herself, up under her arms. Then, boosted up to the oriel window—but a hole in the rock wall now with a brisk wind blowing in—she twisted head and shoulders through first.

"What the shoulders go through, she said . . ." the tallest soldier commented.

"The rest will follow," said the rope handler.

"I surely hope so," Corrie whispered, "though that is not what happened the time I tried."

But clearly Sarana was more agile than the young Corrine had been. And not near as thick around at the waist. She shifted a bit, kicking her feet, and suddenly slipped through the hole and was gone, down faster than anyone could see out the window. But the rope grew taut around the soldier's waist and shoulder and his companions helped him hold on.

Suddenly the rope was loosened and Corrie whispered, "May the goddess speed you, Sarana; Great Alta at your heels."

They coiled the makeshift rope back up and spent the rest of the night setting up the wine rack again and reshelving the bottles. The broken glass and window casement, plus the boards, they put under the pallets. If it made sleeping thereafter uncomfortable, not a one of them complained.

Only Corrie worried about the missing window. But at dawn, when the wind died down, he forgot about the problem as they all laid bets on how soon Sarana might make her way out of Berick and find Scillia and her loyal troops.

THE BALLAD:

The Ballad of Corrine Lackland

Harken to me, gentlemen,
A ballad I shall tell,
Wherein two brothers royal born
In Berickshire did dwell.

The one of them was Jem the Bold
Who fought with either hand,
The younger was Prince Corrine
Who was left with little land.

As they were drinking ale and wine
Within his brother's hall,
Prince Corrine pointed to a port
That opened in the wall.

"That green gate is to Faerieland,
Where Mother dear does dwell."
"Nay, brother," quoth the bold Jemson,
"That is the gate to hell.

"But if you're sure, my brother dear,
Then you the path shall find.
And as I am king on the throne,
I shall remain behind."

He pushed his brother through the port,
Far down Lackland did fall.
His portion was six feet of earth
And death to bear his pall.

THE STORY:

The difficult part had not been wriggling through the window, though Sarana had cut her knee on a piece of broken glass that had somehow resisted the enlarging of the portal, and was sticking out at an angle beneath the outside edge.

Nor had the descent been a problem. The makeshift rope had held.

Held too well, actually. It had taken her precious moments getting the knots under her arms undone, and her increasingly cold fingers made the problem worse. But when she finally was able to shrug out of the harness, she gathered up the prince's cloak, which had been one of the end pieces, unknotted it, and put it on. It warmed her at once.

She looked to her left where the sea was muttering in its rocky bed.

Low tide.

At the turn, she would be long gone, and glad of it. She

had not told the other woman, but she was petrified of water. Her father used to half-drown her as a punishment, sticking her head down in the horse's trough until she was forced to breathe in the dirty water and rise spluttering, coughing, and vomiting up everything she had eaten for days. The very thought of falling into the sea had almost undone her. But she had known that of the few who could get through the small window, she was the only one who could find the queen. None of the boys would have had a chance. So when she had stuck her head and shoulders out and seen with the light of the full moon that the tide was low enough for her to wade around the rocks, she had twisted through the window without another bit of fear.

Sliding down the cliffside rocks, the cape billowing behind her, she landed ankle deep in the sea water. For the first time in days she smiled, kicking up water as she went.

First she knew she needed to get free of the town. *Too many Garuns for comfort here*, she thought. There would be fewer of them near the villages and farms. Seven ships might garrison a castle, but they were not enough to go warring and whoring too far into the countryside. She guessed King Kras would wait to see how well his hostage-son ran the port town before committing more Garun soldiers to another war.

Which gives me time, she thought. *But not a lot*.

Sarana stuck to the rocky shingle till dawn drove her into the trees where she paralleled the main road until the first farm house. There she waited in the trees until she could see the farmer off in his fields. When his wife came outside and started washing linens in a great tub by their well, Sarana left the trees, crossed the road, and began walking with a rolling gait as if she had no troubles in the world. But she was careful to keep the cloak tight around her so that her uniform, dirty and several weeks from seeing a washtub itself, would not be the first thing the woman noticed.

"Blessed be," she said when she knew she was close enough to be heard.

The farm wife, who had seen Sarana out of the corner of her eye, gave the blessing back, but tentatively, as if she were long out of practice.

"Could I trouble you for a drink of water?" Sarana asked.

"Sister to sister," the woman replied. Then she glanced over her shoulder toward the field, where the farmer was still walking his rows. Only when she was satisfied he had not noticed their visitor did she haul up a bucketful and offer it in a tin cup.

Sarana took a long draught before speaking. "My thanks, goodwife. I have come a long way," she said at last.

"From Berick-ward," the woman countered. "I seen you come down the road."

"Away from the king across the water," Sarana said with little affect in her voice.

"And where be the queen?"

"I go to find her," said Sarana. "But I must go slow." She pointed down at her feet and then at the torn trousers bloodied from the cut.

The woman glanced over her shoulder again, but the farmer was now behind his oxen and plow, the reins wrapped twice around his long waist. He was concentrating on the beasts and their furrows and did not look up.

"I will give you my horse," said the farm wife. "She is but an old mare, spindle-legged and not quick in her paces. But she is steady. It is all the Garuns left us."

"Will your man mind?"

"I will tell him the soldiers came for her as well. He will believe me. He is a steady man, but like the mare, slow."

"May Alta bless you."

"She already has."

"Then may she bless the queen."

"The one that is or the one that will be?"

"May Alta let me find them both."

They went into the tidy barn and the farm wife hauled out the saddle. It was feast-day tack, thankfully not a sidesaddle, but not for a long riding. Still Sarana dared not ask for any other. She simply fitted up the mare who took the bit willingly enough but blew out when the saddle was put on her. However, Sarana was ready for any such tricks and did not let the mare have her way, tightening the girth with grim authority but at the same time careful not to hurt the little horse. Then she led the mare from the barn.

"Go into the woods over there," the farm wife said, pointing in the direction Sarana had come from. "Do not let himself see you."

Sarana nodded. "And your name, goodwife, that I may count you in my blessings to Alta."

"I am Klarissa, wife of Bornas who owns five fields and the river rights as far as the second turning. I have two girls, but they are off in Berick at the market. And you?"

"Sarana, of the Border Patrol."

"Ah—with that cloak I thought you of higher rank."

"It was loaned me by Prince Corrine."

"Then you go on borrowed beast under the protection of the crown."

"The crown that was," Sarana said.

"The crown that will be," the woman countered. "The Garuns have forgot the last war." She looked back again at her husband who was even then turning the oxen to make another row. Leaning conspiratorially toward Sarana she said with great fire, "And some of our own men have forgot as well. It matters little to him who gets our taxes. *Blood is blood,* he says, *no matter who sucks it.* But I say those Garuns come for our money and our horses first, and next they come for our daughters. Then what will he say, who speaks too late?"

And with that last passionate declaration ringing in her ears, Sarana took off, first south into the woods and then north through them, riding the little mare as fast as she would go.

Scillia was lost. *Or*, she thought, *not so much lost as bothered*. It was something her mother had once said to her: "I have never been lost in the woods, but once I was bothered for three days in a row."

No, Scillia told herself, *better to be honest. Honesty may be all I have left to give these good soldiers*.

"We are lost," she said to the sergeant as she and the guards muddled together in a small clearing.

They had ridden quickly into the mazed woods without taking time to consider their path, just following Scillia's frantic lead. The underbrush had given way to first-growth forest, then old-growth trees, and finally to a small meadow that was humped with grassy mounds.

"No, ma'am," said one of the guards. "We are but in the Gammorlands, and if we ride north we will come out t'other side."

"How long a ride?" Scillia asked.

"Three days, no more," the man said. Then added sheepishly, "I believe."

"He believes," put in another. "But he does not know."

"Beyond that, half a day, is the place where the king and queen took their great stand against the Garuns," the first man added. "If we are indeed where I think we be."

"The king and queen that was," the sergeant said quickly.

Scillia gave him a half-smile for the effort. "Do you mean Bear's Run?"

The man grabbed off his helm and held it before him like an offering. "Aye, ma'am, that's it. Where the Bear fell. And the other bloody Garuns with him. And mind, they should have taken that Garun prince Jemson with them."

At this Scillia had to laugh. "Jemson was not even born yet at the Battle of Bear's Run. I was but a babe tied to my mother's back as she fought."

"Aye, well she's a fighter, Queen Jenna. That we know. Bless her."

Scillia did not even try to correct him. The loss of her mother—*and Jenna was my mother in truth*, Scillia realized with sudden sharp longing—was still an overriding pain in her chest.

"Well, my friends, three days is not impossible, if we are indeed where we think we are. We certainly all know how to live on a forest larder that long," said Scillia. She remembered her father saying *A good shepherd tells his sheep of green grass, not grey wolves*. That was not being dishonest with them, just circumspect. "And if we get to the old battlefield I will know my way. My mother and I spent some time there." She did not say how many years ago it had been.

A collective sigh ran around the guards then.

"Now tell me your names, my soldiers. I will endeavor to learn them all. For who knows how much time we will be forced to be strangers in our own land."

The farm wife's mare turned out to be sturdier than Sarana had first thought. Or perhaps she was just delighted to get out of the barn for a ride. She carried Sarana easily through the woods till they were well out of sight of the farmer's holdings. Only then did Sarana guide her back to the road.

There was little traffic, though the road was the main one, the King's Way. They met several wagons, two pulled by oxen and three by large Dales plough-horses. Sarana nodded, acting as if she had every right to be on the road. There were only one or two singleton riders, who passed her by, one dashing at breakneck speed toward Berick. He was not wearing a guardsman's uniform, but Sarana was suddenly greatly afraid that his fast pace meant he had news for the usurper king.

"Perhaps," she whispered to herself, "the queen has been found." She urged the mare with her heels and the little horse responded.

They rode through the long day and Sarana only let them rest a short part of the night near a small stream, rising again well before morning. The horse had grazed and drunk its fill and was more than happy to start off again. Sarana had found some wintered-over hickory nuts which she cracked open in the small campfire she allowed herself. And she dug with a stick beneath a saxafrax tree and boiled up some of the roots in the farm wife's tin cup which she had taken without leave. The tea's flavor was thin for she had no time to dry the roots in the sun. But though it was little enough, she had gone hungry before. The nuts and tea stayed the worst of her belly pains.

It took her another full day before she got back to the trail she knew, where the scumbled pattern of little feet had first led her along the cliff's edge. But the footprints and sledge tracks were now all gone. Several hard rains and something else—she did not know what—had made them disappear.

"Well," she said to the mare, "we have lost the one queen for good, I'm afraid. Now we must find the other before she is gone, too." She led the horse back along the ridge to the meadow which was fully green, a deeper spring than in the woods.

They galloped through the grass and at the far edge she found what she was looking for, a trail of sorts. It first led into the shelter of trees and then out again. Further along she was able to pick the trail up once more, though only when it was under the protection of the dense forest. She could read the signs, though barely: a cart and numbers of horses. She had to believe that it was Scillia's track, though weeks had gone by and it could have been anyone's leavings by this time. The trail, though, led back toward the city.

When did they discover that the throne had been taken? she wondered. *And where did they go from there?* She knew they could not have been captured. There was—so Corrie had assured them—only the one wine cellar. Nothing else in Berick would have done as a prison. And she was certain Jemson could never have kept from gloating if he had captured the queen.

Sarana was exhausted by her search and her lack of food. She was filthy. And she did not know where to go next.

The third full day in the dungeon—which he counted by means of their porridge morning and evening—Corrie was sent for. Two Garuns, fully armed, opened the heavy door and called his name, without his honorific. Just "Corrine, to the door!"

He let them cry his name five times in all before he strolled out to the front door. He knew he was not a brave man, but he had a great sense of drama. In some circumstances it could seem the same.

Forcing himself to stop ten strides from the guards, too far for their swords but close enough for conversation without shouting, he remarked, "*Prince* Corrine at your service." Then he sketched a Garunian bow, a very flamboyant bow, his hand making a great circle that started at his head and, with a variety of curlicues, finally touched his knee. The bow suggested an insult rather than a greeting. It was one of the first lessons Gadwess had ever taught him, and he had never forgotten it. His clothes, of course, were filthy from sleeping on the wine-cellar pallets and having been worn without change for three full days, though even thus he was far tidier than Piet or Petra or Jareth or the any of the others. But his bow's insult did not take the raggedness of his garments into account.

One of the two guards, an older Garun with a weak chin and watery eyes, understood the offense and flushed. The younger did not and he bowed back.

"Come, sir, the king wishes to see you," the younger guard said.

"Then I will come with you," Corrie drawled. "For he is someone who needs much counsel."

Again the older man flushed and his weak chin set determinedly. This time even the younger guard understood the contempt in Corrie's answer and he looked to his companion for guidance, but none was forthcoming. The older man was simply too angry to respond.

"Come, come," Corrie said, enjoying their confoundment. "Take me at once to my dear brother. We are of the same blood, though not—it is clear—of the same aroma. I shall give him what advice I can." He held out his hand.

They both drew their swords, as if his hand offered them some danger, and in this manner they marched Corrie between them up the stairs.

Oh dear Gadwess, Corrie thought, *if only you could have heard. The first blood to me, I believe*. And he smiled.

They walked quickly and without further conversation up the stairs and into Jemson's chambers, the room that had once been Carum and Jenna's. It was midday and warm, but there were torches lit on every wall and a fire roaring in the hearth.

Jemson lay propped up in the great bed, a dozen pillows behind him. A small table held a full tea—hyssop by the smell—with many little cakes, some iced and some plain.

Corrie refused to stare at the cakes, but he could feel his mouth fill with water. Porridge was not entirely satisfying for an only meal. Sketching another insulting bow, he said "Throne still too hard a seat, brother, that you must lie abed at noon?"

"You smell," Jemson answered.

"I could have bathed in wine, I suppose," Corrie remarked, less to Jemson than to the guards who hovered by his side. "There was plenty of it where I have been staying. Perhaps I could have found vinegar in the older bottles and used it as we do for the horses, to keep down the flies." He smiled at Jemson. There was no mirth in it.

"It is your own fault, you know," Jemson said. He sounded like a whiny child. "All your own fault. You should be my chief friend. We are brothers."

"*I* know we are brothers," said Corrie. "It was not *I* who put my brother in a dungeon."

"Well it was not *I* who refused to support my brother as king."

"As far as I know, mother is still queen and this is the Dales, not a possession of the Garunian royal family."

"Ah—mother." Jemson sat up in bed. "She's dead, you know."

"I know no such thing."

Jemson looked up slyly. It was a look Corrie remembered well enough from their childhood. "But what if she is?"

"Then," Corrie spoke slowly, knowing it had to be said if he were to remain true to himself, but knowing as well it could mean his death. "Then Scillia is queen after."

"But what of our blood?" Jemson asked, sitting straight up and turning as red as blood in his face. "And what of the times I have saved you?"

"What times are those?" Corrie asked back.

"Why, now—I have taken you from the dungeon where you would surely have died."

"Of too much wine? Or of too much dirt?"

Jemson shivered. "It is cold and damp down there. And not at all pleasant."

"That is true, Jemmie," Corrie said, smiling slowly. "But that is also true of ships where sailors labor and mines where men dig for gold. It is true of the flooded rows where rice is grown and of many a forest wherein the woodsmen labor. And they do not have access to all that vintage wine!"

"Must you always joke?"

"Must you always take offense where none is offered?" Corrine knew this was not actually true. He had already offered plenty of offense to Jemson.

"Well, perhaps you were not ready to die in the dungeon. But what of the time I saved you from the cat?"

"Scillia saved me from the cat. You stayed on shore and stained your pants." The minute he said it, Corrie was sorry. His mother had always warned: *A knife wound heals, a tongue wound festers*. He could have said the same thing without the hurt, especially in front of the guards who would—as guards always do—tell tales in the morning.

Jemson stood. He was shaking with anger. "Well I will not even attempt to save you a third time. The next we talk it will be with Sir Malfas by my side, and that conversation will not be anywhere near this pleasant for we mean to find out where Scillia and her toads are hiding. I am king now. I will remain king. All my life I have been trained to mount this throne. You had best make your peace with that if you wish to stay alive."

"*To take is not to keep*," Corrie reminded him.

"The Garuns say rather, *Small keys open big doors*."

"And small men," Corrie said, determined to outlast him, "need bigger men behind them."

But it was Jemson who had the last word. "Take him away."

* * *

They did not even let Corrine change clothes but brought him directly down to the wine cellar again. This time they rough-handled him as well. He was thrust not at all gently through the open door and when it was slammed behind him, he heard the younger guard cursing him with such originality that Corrie had to laugh.

"A man without a tongue cannot laugh," warned the young guard's voice through the door.

This time Corrie knew better than to answer back.

When he turned around, Piet, Jareth, and Petra, along with the two tall soldiers, Manger and Tollum, peered out at him from the first archway.

"Thank Alta, you are alive," Petra cried, running up to him and embracing him.

"Alive but not at all happy with what I have learned."

"And that is . . . ?" Jareth asked.

Corrie held a finger up to his lips and wordlessly led them all back into the barracks room for he feared listeners at the door. When they were as far from the door as possible, Corrie began to speak.

"My brother has now firmly claimed the throne, believing that mother is dead; he says not how he knows. He is entirely out of touch with what is real otherwise, so I do not entirely credit it. But he is far more dangerous than I could have guessed. I do not think any of us can count ourselves safe here in this musty cellar. I had hoped if we were out of his sight, we were out of his thoughts. Jemmie had never such a long memory. But he has Malfas to remind him of us every day and he has become a jackal's pup trying to please its master. He has even threatened my life, complaining all the while that our blood should be the greater binder. He is mad with this kingship. Quite mad. And he believes we all know where Scillia is hiding. With Malfas holding the sword, Jemmie will have us fall on it if we do not betray her to him."

"We could not even if we wanted to," Petra said. "None of us knows where she is save, perhaps, that girl Sarana and she is away from here."

"Sir, should we not try and escape, too?" It was Tollum, the taller of the two soldiers. He addressed his question to Piet. "At least send the boys and the smaller women through the window. We could widen it tonight and . . ."

"We will do it once the evening porridge bowls are collected," said Corrie, even before Piet could answer. "After having converse with Jemmie and knowing him to be mad, it is the only sane thing left for us to do."

"It will put us all in danger," Piet cautioned. "If they make noise; if they are seen; if one stumbles into the ocean and . . ."

"We are all in danger already, old friend," said Jareth. He began to cough again and the spasms this time were so bad, they had to break open another bottle of wine and get him to drink a good draught which served to soothe his throat enough that he was able to continue helping with the plans.

The night meal did not come quick enough for any of them. Then they waited quite some time more, till there was little noise beyond the door except a low snoring.

"I believe the guards are napping," Corrie said when he tiptoed back from the front room.

Having devised the unstacking of the bottles and the rack before, they worked with the ease of familiarity, though Petra found she had to caution the boys more and more often about being quiet. Everyone seemed to think the work a lark this time. They knew it was possible and therefore they lost what natural caution they had had the first time.

Because of this, they were not prepared for the sudden rush of wind through the opened portal when most of the bottles at the top of the rack had been taken away. The gust was cold and brisk and shuddered the rack, which was no longer firmly attached to the wall. Several of the bottles on the lower shelves began to rattle and one fell to the ground, breaking with a tremendous crash.

"Here!" came a shout from beyond the door. "What is going on in there?"

Piet grabbed Manger by the collar. "Quick, man—into the next room and take up a bottle of the white wine. I shall take another. I want you to hit me as hard as ever you can." He grabbed up the broken bottle of red and followed the soldier, shouting at him "You traitor. You gall-ridden cretinous boob!" He took a swing at Manger's back, missing him by a great deal.

Manger understood at once and raced into the room where the white wines were housed. He grabbed up two of the finer Garunian spring wines. One he dropped immediately on the floor, the other he held above his head, shouting back "You are no captain of mine. I say give him the bitch, and good riddance to her."

The door was opened and four guardsmen, swords drawn, came in.

"Put those bottles down," the leader of the guards said. "Now."

Manger put his bottle down at once, but Piet took his time, making a half-hearted lunge at Manger who shrugged back into the arms of the guards.

"He will kill me," Manger cried to them. "Take me with you."

"If he kills you, it is one less Dalite for us to worry about," said the leader. "But if I hear more in here, I will run you both through and sleep well after. Now old man, drop that bottle."

Piet let the bottle drop and it exploded on the floor, drenching him and the guard near him.

"You dog spittle!" the guard cried and raised his sword as if to strike Piet.

"Leave them," his leader warned. "He is probably the one who knows the most."

"And will tell the least," said the drenched guard.

"We do not know that for sure," said his leader. "Remember how it goes: A *hard head hides a soft tongue*. Now go back to your other room, old man. Away from this door. Leave this one . . ." he nodded at Manger "alone or it will go hard with you." Then he looked up and saw that the rest of the prisoners were crowded into the archway. "Go, all of you. This show is over."

Piet turned his back, shrugged extravagantly so that none of the guards could miss it, and winked at the prisoners in the doorway. Then he moved toward them and they made a small passageway to let him through.

The guards backed through the open door and slammed it shut. The sound of the key in the lock was all that could be heard.

Manger waited by the door, whimpering "Take me with you, please. . . ." until the guards all left. Then he walked back into the back room. "I am sorry for calling the queen such a name," he said to Corrie.

Corrie laughed. "I have called her worse for no such good cause," he said. "That was quite a performance. I have never seen its like."

"We must be gentler," said Petra.

"And quieter," Jareth said.

"And quicker," added Piet.

* * *

They got the boys out, having to add Petra's petticoat to the lowering line in place of the missing cape. One boy was to make his way back into the town roundabout, so as to let the loyal townsfolk know what was happening inside the castle. The other three were to go by the low road along the coast to the north.

"Do not take chances," Petra warned them.

And Corrie added, "The queen would not have you be martyrs. Nor would I."

The four boys had all nodded seriously, except for one, a ten-year-old, who had spoken up gallantly. "My father was killed in the first war," he said. "It is not wrong to die for what is right."

Corrie had put his hands on the boy's shoulders. "They say up north: *Both the hunter and the hunted pray to a god.*"

"But sir," the boy answered, "we pray to Alta and they to Lord Cres." At the Garunian god's name he spit expertly to the side.

"You cannot dispute that," said Piet, smiling.

"Nor shall I," Corrie said. "Go, my good boys, may Alta speed the soles of your feet." He stood at the window and helped lift the boys, one at a time through the window. The youngest went first.

But after they had all gone, and Petra after them, one of the servers—a smallish man with large shoulders—got stuck in the opening. It took much hauling and muffled moans on his part before they could bring him back in.

And by then it was too late.

The door was flung open, and in came two guards, three of the boys marched between them.

No one dared speak, to ask about the fourth boy, the ten-year-old who had spit at Lord Cres' name. Or about

Petra. And the guards did not leave, but were locked in with them.

There were to be no more attempts at escape.

THE HISTORY:

Editor

Nature and History

Dear Sir:

In my late father's notes are some interesting musings on forms of execution as portrayed in the folk songs of the Dales, particularly the so-called Interregnum. I am very interested in putting together an article using his notes as my starting place. The emphasis of the article will be the difference between the ideals of the Interregnum (a beginning democracy, an emphasis on jail as a retraining ground for uneducated felons, the freeing of political prisoners, the opening of the first public hospitals, the restructuring of the army, cf Cowan's seminal article "From Idea to Ideal: A First Look at the Time of Kings," Journal of the Isles, History VII, 9) *and the way prisoners were actually dispatched.*

My father's notes begin with

1. **Defenestration,** *as alluded to in the ever-popular "Ballad of Corrine Lackland."*

The notes then go on to detail nine more different methods of execution in total. They include:

2. **Hanging.** *("Three times around/the noose was wound/till Old Pit felt the rope. / Then up he's strung / and there he's hung / and gone was ev'ry hope." From "Old Pit's Gone.")*
3. **Disemboweling:** *The drinking song from Berick that goes back at least a thousand years, "So drink with the devil / A toast to the queen / Reach into his belly / Where guts are so green / And ups with the hamstrings /*

And off with his head / If you're in the navy / you're better off dead! / Drink it round!"

4. **Decapitation:** The humorous "Head Beneath Her Arm" from Lanard, with the chorus: "Her head well tucked / Beneath her arm / to keep herself / from further harm . . ."
5. **Garroting:** The little known Carreltown Hymn refers obliquely to this method, and of course Carreltown is on the seacoast. When the great Garun fleet washed ashore there and the Garun sailors were left to the mercy of the locals, many eventually married into the peasantry and brought their songs with them. We believe the Carreltown hymn can be traced back to them—and the Garun custom of garroting prisoners who were of the upper classes. "The thin red line" referred to in the chorus is clearly a silken garotte.
6. **Suffocation:** The only known reference to stoning, a rather obscure and gruesome method of execution, slow and painful, is found in the Lackland medley of songs. "Pile them on, lads / pile them on" is the chorus. Dr. Cat Eldridge argues rather forcefully (see his chapter "Sea Changes in Sea Chänties" in his book More Music of the Dales that this is rather an old capstan ballad badly and baldly borrowed, with a traveling chorus. But I rather agree with my father's position here that it points to yet another form of torture/execution and feel I can easily justify its use in my article.

The rest of the methods of execution include

7. **Drawing**
8. **Savaged by Bears**
9. **Pierced by Arrows**
10. **Drowning.**

I know this is a very unusual article idea—and for some of your readers possibly quite unsettling. However I feel very strongly that it has a place in a magazine such as yours which has always been on the very cutting edge of Dalian research.

THE STORY:

It was the horse that decided Sarana, for it went lame. Not badly lame, but needing tending. She led it down the road till they came upon another farmhouse, this one a poor place with but a back garden and no farm stock except for a few scrawny chickens that ran from her as if she were a butcher's knife.

An old woman came out to stare at her when she entered the yard.

"I have been many days on the road," Sarana began.

"Weeks, likely," the woman said in the clipped speech of the far northern Dales.

"Weeks likely," Sarana agreed. "My horse is lamed."

"Strange horse for a queen's guard," the woman commented, taking in her filthy uniform.

"Strange times for a queen's guard," Sarana answered.

"Get in afore yer seen."

"And the horse?"

"I'll tend to her. I know horses, though you wouldn't guess it from this patch." She nodded her head at the farm. "Come down but not brought down."

Sarana said nothing.

"Into the house then," the old woman said. "There's a tub."

Sarana did not wait to ask her if the tub was filled, but went in and gratefully took off her clothes, folded them by the metal tub and slipped in. There was water, though it was only lukewarm, but she didn't care. She lay back and slipped entirely under, grateful for the wetness. She could feel layers of dirt and dust and dungeon peel away. When she sat up again, the old woman was in the house and bringing her over a scrub brush and dark yellow soap.

"Got some of those mysel," the woman said, gesturing to Sarana's back where the scars glistered from the wetting like runes of a terrible tale. "Why I left."

"Left where?"

"My man. My home. My land. But it's an old tale. Done with."

Sarana nodded.

"So girl, do you want a meal?"

Sarana nodded again.

"Will you work for it?"

"I have little time. But I will come back and work double when the queen is on the throne again."

"A good answer."

"A good promise," Sarana said. "I do not make them lightly."

The old woman laid the soap and brush on the tub's edge. "Best scrub afore the water turns ice. I'll tend that mare."

It took two days, not three, to get through the woods for Scillia hardly let the guards rest. *Good shepherds must also be tough taskmasters*, she told herself, *when needs be*. The soldier had been right about where they were. It took half a day to Bear's Run after that.

Scillia scarcely recognized the battlefield site till they were on it. The field looked smaller than she remembered. And the stand of trees larger. But then, thirteen years can make a vast difference in the life of trees. *And the life of girl*, she thought. The two mounds were unmistakable.

"Make camp," she said to the sergeant. "And let me be for now. There is something I must do."

As if he knew her mind, the sergeant nodded, and turned

to the task of organizing the campsite. Scillia left them and went directly to Iluna's grave.

It was midday, but shadowed and cold between the mounds. She knelt beside the grave marked by the goddess sign. For a long moment she was still.

Above her some bird wheeled in the bleached sky. By her toes, a line of dark insects moved quickly through the winter grass. She felt herself between times. She did not like that feeling.

At last she rose. The truth was that she knew nothing of the woman in the grave beyond her name and the fact that she had been a warrior of M'dorah.

M'dorah!

"I am Jenna's daughter," she said to the grave. "But I will fly home to my throne from M'dorah.

The grave did not answer.

Sarana left the farmhouse before dawn, a pocket of journey-cake and a flask of wine tied to her waist. She had to leave the little horse behind. But the old woman had given her more than a gift of food and a long-needed bath. She actually had had an idea of where Queen Scillia and her followers might be heading.

"Her mam was from M'dorah," said the old woman.

"Her mam was Queen Jenna."

"Second mam."

"And how do you know that?"

"Everyone knows."

Sarana did not point out that *she* had not known.

"Besides, there's prophecy."

"What prophecy?"

The old woman put her head back, closed her eyes, and in an eerie, quavering voice sang: "*An eagle's girl shall gain the throne, but she'll not rule the land alone.*"

"How does that mean Queen Scillia's from M'dorah?" Sarana was puzzled. "There's nothing in the prophecy that says the name."

"M'dorah. High-towered. Where eagles dare not rest. Do ye not know history, girl?"

The connection had seemed thin in the evening when they first spoke of it. But by morning the logic seemed inescapable. Besides, Sarana had no other leads.

"Where is M'dorah?" she asked.

The old woman drew her a map in the yard, as scratchy as if one of her scrawny chickens had made it. But Sarana had read many such maps, drawn in mud and sand and snow.

"Take good care of that mare," Sarana had said in lieu of a parting.

"Like she was my own," the old woman said, smiling, because they both knew the mare *was* her own, now.

STREET RHYMES:

Eagle, eagle in the sky,
Watch the queen as she rides by.
How many soldiers has she now?
One . . . two . . . three . . . four

—*Counting out rhyme, Mador Plains*

Shoe the horse, shoe the mare,
Ride the long riding alone.
One comes east and one comes west
And one comes riding home.

—*Baby lap game, South Ridings*

Pick up stones and pile them on,
One, two, three until they're gone.

—*Circle game, Berike Harbor*

THE STORY:

"They tried to escape!" Jemson cried, his voice rising in anger and breaking on the last syllable. "They tried to escape!" His hands gripped the arms of the throne so hard his knuckles turned white.

"Well of course they tried to escape," Lord Malfas said calmly. "Though being Dalites they sent the women and children out first. Stupid, stupid! What good are women and children in a fight?"

"But we have them," Jemson said, his anger ebbing as he remembered the outcome. "The three boys, and old Petra." He smiled. "Can't you just see her skinning down that makeshift rope?" Then he laughed. "Her petticoat was part of it, so it was a make-shift indeed." He waited for Malfas to applaud his joke and when no applause was forthcoming, he sat back in the throne pouting.

"Your Majesty," Malfas said, making another of his almost-an-insult bows, "the boys, being boys, know nothing except that they were to head north."

"Away from the center of the fighting of course."

"Toward your sister's hold. *Of course*."

Jemson crossed his legs casually. "We don't know that. They did not tell us that."

"We can make a good guess at it, though. Think, boy, think! What does the *Book of Battles* tell us?"

Jemson's face screwed up in concentration. He had never been good at memory games, and he had positively hated all the drills in battle lore he'd had to endure in the Garunian court. Much better had been the action games—dog-fighting, bear-baiting, watching the duels. *What had the cursed* Book of Battles *said?* Then he had it. "*The spider sits in the center of its web and entices the fly to come to it.*"

"Good, good. That certainly comes from the *Book* and might even apply here. But I was thinking rather of the notion that, '*The further north, the greater noise.*' "

"I do not remember any such." Jemson began to study his fingernails with great concentration.

"And your father a scholar, your dam a fighter. How they ever threw you . . . still the *Book* knows that, too."

"What do you mean, man?" Jemson glared at him.

Malfas did not moderate the insult in this bow. "*A white ewe may have a black lamb,*" he said. His voice was strong and was meant to carry.

"Damn you!" Jemson stood, grabbed up the scepter which was resting against the throne, and flung it at Malfas' head.

Without glancing at it, Malfas reached up and plucked the scepter from the air, turned, and walked out of the room, his back offering his final insult to the young usurper king.

The broken window was boarded up by the guards, the wine rack restored and checked every hour. The men were all shackled, wrist to wrist, except for Corrie who, as the king's brother, still had certain privileges.

The three boys were not bound, but they had been so maltreated by the Garuns when they were caught, they did not even dare walk into the next room without asking permission. Instead they fell asleep on the dirty pallets without speaking, though one of them cried for an hour in his sleep, a sound so despairing that Corrie sat down on the bed by his side and rubbed the child's forehead. The boy's exhaustion was deep and the touch did not wake him, nor did it seem to salve him.

Corrie wanted desperately to ask about the fourth boy who had gone with them through the window and about Petra. But he feared alerting the guards who, in pairs, now stood at attention in the archway. Instead, he joined the card players. It was not an easy game, shackled as they were, but it was the only way to lighten the gloom in the wine cellar which now, truly, felt like a dungeon.

They whispered among themselves, but without any real information the talk went in circles until one soldier in a husky voice said, "We still have the king's sword."

"And what good is it, the blade ruined from sawing at that window?" said Piet. "And only the end man in our chain with a hand to swing it."

"There's Prince Corrine here," the man answered. "He's both hands free."

"He'd be no match for the two of them," Piet cautioned, gesturing with his head toward the doorway where the guards strained to hear them.

"Then let him distract them and we can . . ."

"*If you are an anvil . . .*" Piet said.

"*. . . be patient*," answered the soldier. "I know that one. My sergeant says that all the time. *And if you are a hammer, be strong*. It is time we all became hammers."

Corrie whispered to them. "I am more anvil than hammer it is true, but even I have lost what patience I had. There is something our poor land needs and only I can supply it." He stood slowly and walked over to the guards. They were instantly on the alert, but he held out his hands to them. "Take me to my brother, Jemson-Over-the-Water. He will want to speak to me."

Piet started to stand but he could not pull the others up in time. "No, Corrie," he cried.

But they were already gone.

"What is it?" asked the soldier, the one who had been speaking before. "What is it that he alone can supply?"

Piet looked down over the boys, now sleeping peacefully, the bruises on their faces and arms beginning to show in the flickering light of the torches.

"Blood," he said, loudly and with great feeling now that

the guards had left them alone. "Royal blood. And courage in its shedding. He means to be a martyr."

Corrie stood before the throne where his brother sat on three pillows, comfortable at last, his right leg crossed over the left. There was a guard standing at attention on either side of the throne and Sir Malfas waited on the left side of the dais.

"So you have something to say to me," Jemson said. He smiled and turned to Malfas. "I told you he would come round at last. He is my brother. Blood will tell."

Malfas stroked his moustache, as if the feel of it between his fingers lent him comfort or strength, but he did not respond.

"I do," Corrie said.

"Well out with it then, Corrie. No games. I am serious," Jemson said, uncrossing his legs and leaning forward in the great chair.

"No games? But I thought that Garuns loved games. And you are more than a match for any Garun at game-playing." Corrie smiled and cocked his head to one side. He suddenly thought about Gadwess and the games they used to indulge in. Jemmie would never admit to any of those.

"You know what I mean."

Malfas stirred, took a step closer to the king. "He toys with you, Majesty. There is nothing to tell."

The Garun's words made Jemson's face prune up.

"I know where Scillia is."

"See—he knows where Scillia is, that dough-faced slut." Jemson said. He grinned and spoke again to Corrie. "So . . . ?"

"Oh I know—but I will not say. *That* is what I have come to tell you." Corrie spoke slowly, carefully, as if speaking to a child.

Malfas went up the steps to the throne and whispered in

Jemson's ear. "He is merely playing you like a reed flute, Majesty. Do not sing to his tune."

Jemson shook his head violently, trying to rid himself of the Garun's voice. His hands made fists and they trembled as he spoke. "I can make you tell, you know."

"No, Jemmie, you cannot."

"*King* Jemson!"

"Mother always said: *You can call a rock a fish but it still cannot swim.*"

Jemson's whole body began to tremble. "You'll be sorry you spoke to me like that."

Corrie smiled again. "I expect I will."

"Take him away!" Jemson shouted. "Now! Out of my sight! But not down in the dungeon again with his friends. They will laugh there. They will laugh at me. And I will not have it. I will not. What I will have, though, is Prince Corrine whipped. Like a slave. Like a dog." He stood up partway, holding on to the arms of the throne. But his legs trembled so much, from anger, from humiliation, that he sat down again heavily. One of the three cushions skittered to the floor. "No! No! I will have him pressed. *Then* you will talk to me, Corrie. The stones will make you speak. Only *I* may not listen right away."

Three guards came and grabbed Corrie by the arm and they were no longer polite with him.

Malfas shook his head. "Do not do this, Jemson. Whatever he says to you in agony will avail us nothing."

"He will talk. I will make him talk. And you must call me king. King Jemson. Or I will crush you, too."

"You will only make him a martyr, Sire. A martyr could stir a somnolent countryside. King Kras will not be pleased."

"King Kras can go suffocate!" Jemson screamed. "I am all the king needed here." He looked up at the guards. "What do you wait for? I have given you your orders. Take him. Take him and guard him till the stones can be found. Then we shall see who will talk and who will not."

There was a note in the bottom of one of the evening porridge bowls and, as Alta's luck would have it, Piet found it. He turned his back to the guards, slipped the note out of its messy resting place, and stuck it down the front of his tunic. When he turned back he handed the bowl to one of the boys who had the task of gathering them up.

He waited.

He waited till the guards were distracted by the servers taking charge of the empty bowls. Then he leaned into the guttering torchlight and read.

Wet porridge had obscured some of the writing. But the message was still clear.

Mada_ Petr_ __ been k lled_ __hers captur__
I am __town. All __ __t lost. Praise Al__.

The boy had made it into town, so all was indeed not lost, as the note said. *But Petra.* He could not bear to think on it. Tucking the note back into his shirt, he turned away from the light.

Shackled three down from Piet, Jareth's eyes were closed but he was not asleep. He was still coughing badly and the spasmodic jerking kept the men on either side of him from sleeping. Still no one complained. Jareth was a good man, a hero of the wars. *Imprisonment,* Piet thought, *has made brothers of us, more than freedom ever did.*

He wondered briefly if anything would be served by telling Jareth of Petra's death, then decided it would not.

"My friends," he said at last, "it is time we were hammers indeed."

Jareth eyes fluttered open. "Then Petra is dead," he said. It was not a question but Piet was forced to nod anyway.

The men stood as one, though the last stooped and reached under the pallet, pulling out the king's battered sword. Then, without further consultation, they snaked quickly through the archways, and caught the Garuns off guard as they were closing the door.

The man with the king's sword sliced down heavily, using his left hand, the only hand he had free, his anger and hatred lending strength to it. He managed to gut one of the Garuns badly, and the man began to scream. Jareth and the others used their chains to choke off the sound. But the other Garun guard started out the door for help.

He was hauled back roughly by Piet who grabbed him one-handed by the neck, pulling him off his feet.

"Kill him," one of the boys cried. "Kill him!"

Piet brought his shackled hand up and gave a vicious twist to the man's head. The snap as the Garun's neck broke was as loud as a hammer on stone. Piet caught the man's sword as he fell away.

"For Alta!" Piet shouted. "For the queen!"

They had three swords now, but no time to try and hack off the shackles, for the Garuns were on them. Still they managed to kill a dozen Garuns on the way up the stairs before their own losses—dead weight to be hauled along—so slowed them that they could gain only the first landing. There, back to the curving wall of the stairs, they made their final stand.

The best part of a Garun troop was loosed on them, man after man charging down the stone steps.

The fighting was fierce, but the ending, everyone knew, was predetermined by the numbers. Not a one of the Dales men still standing thought he would come out of the battle alive. Still they fought on to the end.

Blow after bloody blow was delivered, was taken. In desperation, they used their fallen comrades as shields and those poor bodies were pierced till they had no more blood to bleed.

Piet's head was almost severed from his body but he managed a final thrust even then that took a captain down. Jareth, his cough miraculously cleared, bent over to get the sword Piet dropped, and was cut down just as his hand touched the hilt. He sighed Petra's name at the last.

Two of the boys were the only prisoners left alive of the fighting force and they were taken off to be hung at first light.

The third boy had stayed behind in the cellar. Because of the noise of battle no one heard him shove the wine rack over. When it crashed to the ground it was simply one more sound, and too far from the main fighting to be counted.

He drank several great gulps of red wine from a shattered bottle for courage. It was a red heat down his throat. *Like blood,* he thought, and shivered. He managed to open the boards over the window by standing on the overturned rack and using some of the slats from the rack as a prise. Then he shimmed through the open window, cutting himself on the same glass that had caught Sarana's knee. He had no line to let himself down, but it was a full tide. So he flung himself out as far as he could, barely clearing the rocks. His right hand broke upon a stone outcropping, the three fingers furthest from the thumb and the bones in the palm, but he made it into the sea and it was hours later before he felt the pain of it.

He swam along the shoreline till he was exhausted. Being from a fisherman's family, the water held no fear for him, especially not this close to the sandy shore. When the tide drifted him onto the shingle, he headed north. He wanted to be as far from Berick as he could go. He never wanted to see a Garun again.

* * *

Scillia's guard had managed to round up several dozen more men from the farms and villages between Bear's Run and M'dorah. Or rather they had gone to the farms and inns to see if they could beg for supplies and found eager farmers and innkeepers, often veterans of the last war, ready to fight for their queen.

"The queen that was and the queen that will be," became the rallying cry.

Scillia was pleased to see the new recruits. She told them so, greeting each with a handshake and a request for a name. She rarely forgot a name after.

But at night, sitting alone and away from the rest of the camp, she held a troubled conversation with herself. Speaking aloud, as if she were arguing with a dark sister, she set out her awful burden. She did not know that her sergeant set a watch over her, too far to hear what it was she said, but close enough to keep her from harm.

The soldiers believed she spoke to her dead mother. And in years to come, someone who talked to herself was said to be "speaking with the Anna."

The burden of the conversation was the same night after night.

How can I ask these good people to follow me?

How can I ask them to kill for me?

How can I not?

They brought Corrie to the castle courtyard and forced him to lie down on his back. He was then spread-eagled, his hands and feet bound to stakes.

Squinting in the sun, he said "It is a fine day on which to die, brother." He did not know if Jemson were near enough to hear him, but he did not care. The news of how he died would last as long as the Dales. History was all story, after all. A martyr must die with courage. He would spin the tale out bravely to its end. Afterwards—and there would be an afterwards—would come the tears. But not his.

The first stones were put on his hands and feet. They were uncomfortable, and they made his ankles hurt. But he only smiled. He knew that would infuriate them all.

"Do you have aught to say?" asked one of the guards.

"I say that you should set sail back to your own land and leave us ours." He said it loudly, boldly, before closing his eyes against the pain and the sun.

The next stones were placed on his chest, large enough to make breathing hard and speaking close to impossible. But still he managed by husbanding each shallow breath.

"Where is the king's stepsister?" asked the guard.

"Do you mean the *queen*?" Corrie forced each word out. He thought he heard a few muffled cheers, but it might have only been the roaring in his ears.

The guard did not ask him again.

When they put the heavy stones on his hips and thighs and groin, he groaned.

"Speak," said a different guard. At least his voice was different. Corrie could not open his eyes to check. It was all he could do to figure out how to breathe.

"Sire, he cannot make a sound," the man called out, which was when Corrie knew, as he concentrated on his breathing, that Jemmie had to be close by.

"A prince . . . killing a prince," Corrie managed. "It will not sing well." He tried to laugh but it sounded a great deal like a groan.

"No royal blood is being spilled." The speaker was Jem himself, and he was clearly close by.

The guards moved forward and set another large rock on Corrie's chest, on top of the others.

"You . . ." Corrie said. Then he took another, shallower breath beneath the heavy stones. "You never understood."

Jem leaned over and Corrie felt his shadow blot out the sun. "I never understood what?"

"The spirit . . . of the law. Only the . . ." He must have passed out for someone was suddenly pouring water on his face. It felt wonderfully cool. *Drowning*, he thought, *would have been preferable*. He wondered if it were too late to suggest it.

"Will you tell me?" Jem was shouting at him. "Why won't you tell me?"

"Tell . . . what?"

"Where Scillia is. Then I can have them remove the stones."

"Too . . . late," Corrie said. "Find her yourself."

"By the eyes of Lord Cres!" Jem cried. "You are *making* me kill you." And when his brother did not answer, Jem called out to the guard, "Pile them on!"

Then he turned and left before the biggest stones, held between two large guards, were settled onto Corrie's chest. But even as far away as the doorway he could hear the cracking of the breastbone as the last stone was placed. He snuffled into his embroidered sleeve and went up the stairs to be alone.

As Jemson sat alone in the throne room, Lord Malfas walked in carrying a short sword. "The prisoners are all dead, Sire. They had this." He placed the sword in Jemson's hand.

"But that is my father's short sword. The one he had in the Wars. See, here, at the hilt. This dragon carved with the bat wings. I always loved that. What awful use has it been put to? Why is it so broken and so . . ." he shuddered ". . . so bloody?"

"It served as a prise to open the windows for their attempt at escape. And then it killed seven of my soldiers."

"Not *your* soldiers, Lord Rodergo. *Mine*." Jemson hefted the sword in both hands, marvelling at how light it was to have done so much.

"We must get your brother to talk, Sire. He must tell us

where your sister is. Now. Time is precious. King Kras will only be patient so long."

"My father always said "*An anvil must be patient. Not a hammer*. Is the king across the water anvil or hammer?"

Malfas stroked his moustache rather than return a remark. When he spoke, it was to a different part of the conversation. "I know ways to make men speak, Majesty, even when they will not."

"You may not spill a prince's blood," Jemson said. "It is the law."

"The law here, perhaps. But not the law across the sea."

"It matters not—here or there. Prince Corrine is beyond your scheming."

Malfas glared at him, suddenly understanding. "You little fool, what have you done?" Without waiting to hear an answer, he turned and started toward the door. "Guards!" he shouted.

"Guard yourself!" Jemson screamed at him. "No man calls me a fool, little or big. No man sets his back to me." He threw the sword at Malfas.

At the scream, Lord Malfas turned and the sword—which should have given him only a glancing blow to the back of the head—rotated over and the ragged edge sawed across his neck. It was not a hard knock, but it hit him right above the bone and a jagged piece of steel tore through the skin, puncturing the artery. Blood spurted out, fountaining into the air. He had no time to cry out, simply dropping like a slaughtered pig. As he lay on the ground, the blood stained his lace collar red. His right leg twitched for a moment, as if it were dancing. Then it stopped.

Only then did three guards run in, responding to Jemson's scream.

"He forced me to kill the prince," Jemson declared. "No man may force the king and live. Take him away." He shuddered. "Take the sword away as well. It is too . . . ragged for royal use now." He walked to the throne where he stood with his back to the guards and did not turn again to sit in the great chair until he was certain they were gone, and the corpse with them.

Corrie did not die at once, but he did not regain consciousness. He lay in the courtyard, scarcely breathing, till three guards at Jemson's best took away the stones and carried him into the king's chamber. There they laid him on the bed.

Jemson sat the rest of the day with him, alternately sobbing and cursing. Servers came with food and took it away, uneaten, as the king refused to touched a thing.

"I will not eat again till you are restored to us," Jemson cried. He took up Corrie's cooling hand in his. "It was Malfas did it, you know. It was his idea. He said he knew how to make a man talk. But not a man like you, Corrie. I saved you, though, from his awful tortures. I have saved you three times, you know. It was Malfas. He will not hurt you now."

Corrie's hand grew colder still.

When the evening torches were lit, the infirmarer came in and pronounced Prince Corrine dead. The king did not allow them to take the body away, though he promised them a royal funeral three days hence.

"Where is my dinner?" he demanded then. "I am fair starving." When the meal was brought, he ate enough for two and went to bed beside the corpse to sleep without dreams.

THE HISTORY:

There are three great chairs here in the Museum at Berike. It is said that one of these was the throne of Jemson-Over-the-Water.

Each chair is oversized and uncomfortable to sit on without the aid of large cushions. The arms are carved with lion's heads and the face of two women—one maiden, one crone, both possibly representations of Alta—adorn the spool-turned back frames.

The chairs differ in this way: one is of oak and has lion claws on the forward legs. (Figure 17) One is of ash and has a crown carved into the seat back. (Figure 18) One is of ebony with a wooden canopy cantilevered from the high back. (Figure 19)

It is certain that each of these belonged to a king, but which king and which reign, no one knows for sure.

—*from* Treasures of the Berike Museum, *page 27.*

THE MYTH:

Then Great Alta took the boy and dangled him far over the throne.

"Can you stand?" asked Great Alta.

"My legs are too short," quoth the boy.

"Rather say your heart is too small," she replied and dropped him from a great height till he shattered on the wooden chair.

five

War

THE MYTH:

Then Great Alta took the shattered boy in one hand, the girl with one arm in the other and set them side by side in the grass.

"Do ye love each the other?" asked Great Alta.

They did not answer but only glared.

"There is blood between you then," quoth Great Alta. "What cannot be ended, must be done." And she took her presence away that she might not see how things were settled.

THE LEGEND:

In the town of New-Melting-by-the-Sea is a great house, sometimes called Journey's End and sometimes Aldenshame. On the wall, in the entrance hall, hung up like a banner, is a tattered remnant of cloth. Under the cloth is the following legend:

"Alta's Blanket, said to belong to the legendary one-armed Queen Scillia. She brought it here at the end of the War of Succession, broken in health but not in spirit. She came on foot and alone, her great horse Shadow having been slain under her by her own brother, the tyrant Jemson. It was at the end of her thousand-mile Journey of Redemption around her kingdom, and this cloth was all that was between her and the cold. To show their respect, no one along the last quarter of her route looked at her, for to see her in nothing but a bit of stranger's weave, and it all tattered and torn through, would have shamed her, and that her people would not do.

When she came at last to Journey's End, the three sisters who owned the house let her in, and she lived with them till her death, seven years later. When she died, the sisters hung the cloth on the wall and such was its power, cloth and wall have remained intact though the rest of the building has been much rebuilt in the years since."

THE STORY:

By the time Sarana finally found them, Scillia and her troops were encamped on the M'doran plain. It was like a small city, with lean-tos and tents tucked in against the towering rocks. Sarana had never before seen M'dorah though she had heard about it, both in song and story. But nothing had really prepared her for the huge teeth of stone that looked as if they were biting into the sky.

She was stopped early by guards, then vouched for by her captain who greeted her with a great whoop and a hug.

"We heard you were dead," he said. "Voss has been in mourning."

"They exaggerated who said that." Sarana smiled crookedly. "So the old man has been drunk again?"

"Morning and night. But we considered it in good cause. In fact when first we heard it, I got soused with him."

"And the queen?"

"The old one or the new?"

"I was with Queen Jenna when she . . . took her leave of us. I found her tracks. I did not find her."

"Nor shall you, so I hear." The captain looked suddenly grim. "They say she is with the Green Men in the grove. And she will not return till we have need of her."

For a moment Sarana said nothing. Then she drawled: "Do you believe that?"

He laughed without mirth. "I am not certain. But should

it be true, I wish her here. We need her now. The new queen is but a girl."

"Queen Jenna was half her age when she led us to victory."

"Scillia is no Jenna. Nor—to give her credit—does she think she is."

"She is who she is. I have been her brother's guest. Trust me, you do not want to have him remain on the throne."

"His *guest?*"

"In the wine cellar. It is a long story. I will tell it to you while you take me to the queen."

The queen's tent was at the other end of the plain against a broad, crowned rock. Sarana stared up to the top of the stone, her right hand shading her eyes.

"Was that where . . . ?"

"M'dorah Hame sat? Yes. There was a wooden building on the top, so Queen Scillia says. In fact when we first got here, she had been two days already trying to figure out how to make a fortress up there. Even flew someone up to the top on a mammoth kite we made of sticks and cloth. But while defending such a place would have been easy, provisioning it in case of siege would have been impossible. She gave up the idea, but reluctantly." He hesitated, rubbed two fingers across his bushy eyebrows till they stuck up like feathers. It was something he always did when he was deciding how much to say.

"Out with it, Jano," Sarana said. She had been second in command in his troop, and in private never stood on much ceremony with him.

"She seems . . . distracted. At night she goes to the camp's edge and speaks with herself. Aloud. The men say she is communicating with her mam. But there is no one there."

"Perhaps she is not really alone," Sarana said.

"What I do not see, I do not believe."

"Then how can you believe in those little footprints I saw?"

"You have never been one to be guiled by what is *not* there. I know you, Sarana," Jano said. "We may not have the answer to what made those prints, but I believe they exist."

"A small distinction, captain."

"But an important one. And this queen, while she is ready enough to talk with an unseen spirit, is not ready for a fight. Not willing to command either. We sit here and she learns the names of the men and women in the troops. But she does not tell them what to do. Nor does she tell her captains. She is, I believe, preparing for a siege here at M'dorah rather than planning a raid there at Berick. She does not have . . ." His fingers went back up to his eyebrows as if he plucking at them further would be preferable to saying what he knew had to be said.

"That is her brother back there, Jano. *Both* of her brothers back there." Sarana spoke softly, making sure her remarks traveled no further than the captain's ears. "They grew up together."

"*Both?* They are both against her?" The feathered eyebrows raised up a notch.

"Na, na . . ." For a moment Sarana reverted to the dialect of her childhood. "Prince Corrine was in the prison with me. He is for Queen Scillia wholeheartedly. He is for the Dales. But that bloody Jemson drank too deep of Garun waters. They should never have sent him over the sea."

And that very moment, the tent flap opened and Scillia herself appeared. She looked at Sarana for a moment, almost as if she could not place her, then as if she were seeing a ghost. Finally she nodded. "You," she said.

Sarana bowed her head slightly.

"You were with us when mother left. But you did not . . . we could not find . . . where *did* you go? Guards!"

Sarana waited till the guards came and stood on either side of her. She had not expected this to be easy, but even so she remained with her back straight and her head high.

"You disappeared," Scillia said once the guards were in place. It sounded more like a complaint than a statement.

"I left to track your mother," Sarana said.

"And did you?"

Sarana nodded. "But only as far as a ridge." She explained about the footprints and the cliff's edge. "And when I made it back to the castle it was night and I had no warning."

"Ah," Scillia said. "We at least saw the closed gates and the colors on the guards. Did they take you?"

"As easy as a cat catches a mouse." Sarana's mouth felt sour at the admission. But she could not tell a lie to the queen. "Your brother Jemson has made a prison of the wine cellar."

At that Scillia smiled. "We do not do dungeons well in the Dales. Mother and Father had had a surfeit of them before the wars." She paused. "And during."

"I escaped but your brother Prince Corrine, and Commander Piet, and members of the council . . ."

"Not Jareth. Not Petra." Scillia's voice broke on the last syllable.

"I am afraid so. They are all in the dungeon in low condition. I did not like the sound of Councillor Jareth's cough. But Petra will not break easily, I think. And Piet . . ."

"Guards, please leave us," Scillia said. "You too, Jano. I would talk with this . . ."

"Sarana, Your Majesty."

". . . Sarana alone."

Scillia escorted her into the tent and dropped the flap to emphasize that they were not to be disturbed. She gestured to a profusion of dark pillows plumped up on an otherwise severe pile of soldier's bedding. Sarana sat down on the blankets but would not let herself sink back against the cushions.

"Tell me all."

"It has been a long riding, ma'am, and I am famished." She was not so hungry that she could not report, but she wanted to see how the queen would respond.

Scillia nodded. "You talk, and I will fix us both some tea."

"And something to eat?"

Scillia nodded her head. "Where are my manners? War makes monsters of us all. I will give you what I have."

"Anything but journeycake, Majesty."

"Here, in the tent, when we are alone, you must call me Scillia. I will not answer otherwise."

"Scillia," Sarana said, and sighed. She saw at once what Jano had meant. Scillia had neither Queen Jenna's innate power nor King Carum's born class. She did not seem intent on moving against an enemy who even now sat on her throne. But still there was something Sarana liked about the one-armed queen, a quiet intensity, a human-ness. That was something she liked very much. And those green eyes, dark, like a wood in shadow. She had not really noticed Scillia before, so intent had she been on the old queen and the dying king. Scillia had only been an annoyance then. But now, in the shadow of M'dorah's towering rock, Sarana suddenly saw her differently.

It will not do to fall in love, she warned herself. *Not here. Not now. Not with the queen.* So instead she gave herself up to the tea and to the cakes when they came—butter cakes no less, though a bit old and crumbly.

"The cakes came with one of the farm wives," Scillia said, as if embarrassed by the extra rations. "She insisted I have them. In fact, I have had them for some time. As you can probably tell."

Sarana did not mind. She ate and drank as if she were starving. But it was a different kind of hunger that she was trying to stave off.

In between bites Sarana told Scillia all she knew of Jemson's rule. "Malfas' rule, actually," she told the young queen. "Jemson—begging your pardon that he is your brother and all—has not the brains for kingship. No one in that poor gaol thought so. He has neither the patience nor the compassion. All he craves is the power."

"He is as he was as a boy," Scillia said. Then she sighed, a sound that nearly broke Sarana's heart. "He has no thought except for himself. The Garuns did not make him different. They just applauded his bad performances, which made him act the fool all the more."

"Majesty . . ."

"Scillia," the young queen scolded.

"In this I must address you as Majesty," Sarana said, standing and brushing off the crumbs from her shirt. "There are but seven ships worth of soldiers in and around the castle at Berick. But it may be that others are on their way. With just the soldiers you have here we can certainly stand against the few in the castle. However, should the Garuns send more . . ."

"I have thought long on that," Scillia said. "And my captains and I have discussed it well into the nights. Indeed, there is not much else to do here at the foot of M'dorah." She smiled to soften the statement. It was a lovely smile. "Have you intelligence for us?"

"I may have more, Your Majesty. I may in fact have a plan."

At the word *plan*, Scillia's entire face brightened and Sarana wondered that all the captains and all their conversations with her had not come up with something before. "It may not be anything new," she ventured.

"My mother used to quote *The Book of Light*, saying *A*

rabbit cannot put its paws on the deer's horns. She meant, I believe, that some things are beyond even our best intentions. All our previous plans have been flawed because they were too difficult for our capabilities. Though you think us enough, we are in fact few. We are relatively weaponless, and scarcely trained, and we are . . ."

"We have the entire Dales at our disposal, my queen. And if we can cork the Garuns up in that castle without hope of further ships coming to save them, we will have them beat."

"Are you forgetting something, Sarana?"

Sarana shook her head. "I do not think so."

"The heart of the queen."

"The heart of the queen?"

"You see, I am not sure that I even *want* the throne if it means killing my brother for it. He is a stupid young man, but not a beast to be slaughtered. If it means having people die in my cause, I do not want to fight. The heart of this queen is a deer's, not a lion's."

"You cannot stop people wanting to give their lives for you, Majesty."

"I can, however, refuse to lead them in the fight."

"Some leaders lead," Sarana said softly. "And some follow."

Scillia turned her back and whispered, but Sarana heard her nonetheless. "And some go away and do not return."

So, Sarana thought, *that is what this is about*. *Queen Jenna, you will have much to answer for in the days to come*. But what she said aloud was, "People have already died for you, Majesty." It was a guess, but she had been many days on the road already. The Garuns—and here she thought of Sir Malfas, not Jemson—were known to have short tempers instead of a long patience. "The least you can do is go to the rescue of those who still live."

"Rescue?" Scillia turned back and Sarana could see tears

welling in her eyes, tears that never quite fell. Sarana approved of that.

"Your brother Corrine, and the councillors, and the children in the wine cellar," Sarana said.

Scillia drew herself up, as if shaking off weakness. As if coming to a decision. Then she went to the tent flap and lifted it. "Guard!" she said, "call the council of captains." When she turned back, Sarana was holding out her hand. Scillia took it and Sarana wondered that the touch did not sear them both, though palm to palm their hands were both cold.

"You shall be my missing arm," Scillia said. "Dark sister to my light."

And your blanket companion, Sarana thought, *if only in my dreams*.

THE HISTORY:

From a letter to the editor, Nature and History, *Vol. 45*

Furthermore, I have been closely examining the stories of the Blanket Companions and have come to a conclusion that it is strong evidence of a sapphic society and not, as scholars Cowan and Doyle would have it, simple warmth on a cold night among the foot soldiery.

These "Friends of the Bosom" as they are often called in late songs (cf especially the famous Blanket Song: "Oh friend of my bosom, / oh warm by my side, / my shoulder, my gauntlet, / my armor, my bride . . .") would surely explain the stories of Light and Dark Sisters. Not magical replicants as Magon would have them, called up from another world, but inhabitants of very real group homes where single-sex marriages and rampant unnatural practices were not only condoned but actually encouraged by the older women called alternately altas and femmas. That these practices extended into the army ("gauntlet" and "armor" being more than mere metaphor) should not be surprising.

In fact, until the Garunian so-called invasion, such places—while abhorrent to the general public—were tolerated because of the perceived magical nature of the sisters of the Hames. My father had only begun to sniff out the depth of this sexual scam going back several thousand years, when he died.

How much clearer can it be? From the moment of the dissolution of the Hames, after the Gender Wars, when these women—and especially the young girls—were brought back into the main body of society, sapphic practices all but disappeared in the Dales.

THE STORY:

The plan was simple enough, though execution would be difficult. There were two parts to it.

Those with them at M'dorah who knew boats would make their way southward until the marshes at Catmara, cross through the fens by the secret passageways, come up the coast around the horn of land east of Berick. They would commandeer what great ships remained in the harbor towns of Josteen and Southport, sail them by night to the Skellies, that double line of dangerous rocks cupping Berick Harbor entrance. There they would scuttle the boats, between the two lines of rocks, sealing the harbor to any more Garun ships. Jano was to lead that force.

The second group, under Scillia's guidance, would march up to Berick from the west, making enough noise when they reached the castle foot to keep the guards from noticing what Jano's sailors would be doing. They were not to try to take the castle—half a force would have no chance against that fortress—but they might possibly tempt some portion of the Garuns out.

"Which," Jano said, "would then put us on an equal footing. Man to man we can beat them. We did it before. And not so long ago at that."

"Woman to man we can beat them as well," said Sarana. She grinned over at Jano. It was a long-standing joke between them. "And if you are not too tired from swimming to shore, you might just get what we leave alive." She did not see Scillia's mouth, already set in a hard line, twist downward at her comment.

And so it was decided. About a third of the assembled troops admitted to some knowledge of sailing and they gathered together to finalize their plans. The others listened to Scillia and Sarana.

"This is not a battle for a throne," Scillia told them. "Who sits on that hard seat is not the matter here. The matter is that the Garuns have taken what is ours, imprisoned our sisters and brothers, and threaten our way of life. If we stop more Garuns from coming in by sea to add their forces to those in Berick Castle, if we cork up those inside, even the Garuns will have to admit that they must leave us alone."

"And what of the king over the water?" someone cried out.

Someone else added, "That pimple! That pustule!"

"That pimple is mine to squeeze," Scillia said. "No one but me is to touch him." She smiled when she said it that no one there should know her heart.

But Sarana did. And while the others raised a great cheer, she alone sighed.

Jano's troops left at dawn. At his right hand was a young fenmaster, a man named Goff whose family had lived for centuries in and around the great marsh that extended between the Mandrop and the Killdown hills. Only those who understood the hidden causeways could travel across the fens, those lands which lay under brackish water. It was a family secret, passed father to son, or mother to daughter. They would need Goff to lead them over the flooded lands.

When Scillia had asked Goff how his people could live in

such a place, he had smiled slowly. "We drive the big tree down," he replied. "And we-ums live atop." He seemed to think that explained it all.

There were few horses among Jano's crew. Only his own soldiers and another twenty guardsmen rode good steeds. The rest—fisherfolk and farmers and a few townsmen who had joined the ragtag army when they processioned to M'dorah—were horseless or rode plow mares. Those on foot would make for slow progress but the horsemen did not dare outrun them, especially since Goff had no horse nor did he know how to ride one.

Seven days at best with such a troop, Sarana had guessed, if one was to go due south along the King's Way. But cutting through the great swamp and around the heel of the Dales would add another three at least.

"Our troops should have a quicker time of it," she told the captains. There were no good roads on the western route, but except for a few scattered peat bogs—which they would have to be careful to avoid for the peat-hags could haul down even a great Dales mare—the way led through second-growth forest and farmland carved out of the old King's Wood.

So Jano and his followers left first. They did not go quietly. Instead they were lustily singing the old war songs, marching songs like "King Kalas" and "The Long Riding" and "When Jen Came Home." Their voices held hope and promise and Sarana almost wished she were going with them until she turned and saw Scillia's face. Her lips were drawn together in a thin line and another thin line furrowed her brow. But her eyes were clear and the color was more like meadow grass than shadowed woods now.

"My queen?" Sarana asked.

"I want to memorize their faces," Scillia said. "I need to remember their names."

Sarana understood. They might never see any of those spirited singers again.

When the strains of "Langbrow's Battle Hymn" had faded, they were past the last of the M'doran rocks. The plain ended there and the forest's edge began. Holding his hand up, Jano turned his horse around to face the marchers. They quieted at once.

"It is good to sing, comrades. It quickens the heart, it shortens the way. But it also gives notice. Best we go now as quiet as we can." *Though how a hundred can go quietly, who are not trained up to it, I know not*, he thought.

He had little hope for their bedraggled army. All they had was heart. What weapons they carried were old—swords or pikes that had not been used since the Gender Wars, almost thirty years before. The swords were pitted with rust as they had, for the most part, simply hung on farmhouse walls or over an inn's bar as a memento of the Great Fight. In fact, the first days at M'dorah he and his soldiers had to show the new recruits how to grind and polish their old blades to bring them back to some measure of usefulness. One man had even arrived with a Wirgilder ax and shield, which put his weapons at over a hundred years old since the Wirgilders had not come raiding the Dale shores for at least that long. The broad, crescent-shaped ax head had been fine, but the handle had had to be replaced. Jano took on that job himself as he wanted to feel the weight and heft of the axe, never having held one before. It had felt powerful and he almost thought he could hear the blood singing to him from the ax blade. He wondered, idly, if it were singing a victory song or one of ignoble defeat.

But odder victories had happened in wars before this, and it would never do to let the troops know his secret fears.

He said, with more confidence than he felt, "I will send scouts ahead on horse back and, at the hump of the day, hunters will be dispatched to each side to find meat for our evening meal. There is a trained soldier to lead each twenty-person unit, but should there be any complaints of that leadership, bring them direct to me. We have much to do and far to go, but we fight together under Alta's eye and cannot fail of our purpose."

"How far do we march this first day?" called out one of the farmers. Jano tried to remember his name and could not.

"We will not go on till some few of you drop. Every one of you is needed in this fight. But still we must get to the edge of the fens in three days. And we must be there together for we have but one fenmaster to show us the way across."

"What if there are stragglers?" asked a woman whose shoulders were as broad and powerful as any two men of the company.

A butcher's wife, Jano thought. *Or the butcher herself*. He answered her seriously. "If you cannot keep up, turn back. Do not dare the fens on your own. The queen will be glad of your company."

"Or find another fenmaster," added Goff, with that same slow smile. This time there was a kind of challenge in it.

It took four days, not three, to reach the marshy tidal river that marked the edge of the swamp. Jano suspected he had over-reached when counting on three days. But he was not discontented with four.

There was an unsettling mist over the river's grey water, obscuring all.. The men and women of the company spread out along the shore, trying to peer through to the other side. They whispered to one other, as occasionally a dark smudge of land seemed to appear and then disappear before them.

Goff startled them all by pulling a reed pipe from his

leather pocket and blowing three shrill, ululating cries. The sound seemed to stop at the river's edge, swallowed up by the dense fog.

"How long will this mist last?" Jano asked Goff.

"Oh—always and e'er." The fenmaster smiled again. "'Tis Alta's own cloak. It be our best defense."

"When can we go across?"

"Whenever thou wishes." Goff cocked his head. "We of the fens be nowt fuddled by the grey shroud. It be our blanket from the cradle. Hear the boats?"

Jano listened. He could hear nothing but an odd creaking as if the trees along the shoreline were stretching.

A hush had fallen over the company at Goff's first notes but as the creaking sounds grew louder, first the men, then the women clustered together with an uneasiness born part of fear and part of wonder. Only Jano and Goff remained separate from them, Goff because he knew what to expect, and Jano because he was always ready to expect the worst.

And then a dozen dark shapes plowed through the mist to hump onto the shore where they were revealed as coracles, skin boats. Their masters leaped out and pulled the little boats the rest of the way onto land.

"Who be calling?" a woman of the fen folk asked. She was small but well-muscled, her dark skirt kirtled above her knees and a band of bright material binding her hair. At first glance she was young, at second old. "Who be blowing the signal pipe?"

"Auntie, I be," Goff said, stepping forward.

"So thee be coming home, a bad son, a worse nephew, and expect a welcome for it." For a moment her face was like a cloud and Jano feared they would be turned away. Then the woman laughed and opened her arms to him. "Thee mun nowt be expecting thy mum to be treating thee so."

Goff gave her a hug that lifted her off her feet.

"And who be this great company?" the woman asked.

"Soldiers for the queen, auntie," Goff replied.

"We be caring nowt for queens nor kings, Goffie," she said. "We be fen folk. We commerce the causeways. We be nowt bending our knee to woman nor man."

"Nay, auntie, if we be nowt for the queen, then the men across the sea will be the worse."

Jano got off his horse and came over to them. "The men across the sea are here already, mistress. If they stay, they will drain these swamps and build their fortresses on the river shore. They will commerce without you."

"They do nowt be knowing the fens. The glassy water will eat them. The river will have its way." The fen woman folded her arms across her chest.

"Auntie, listen," Goff said, his face dark and serious. "I be seeing them at the Great Harbor where I be working the boats. They be taking and they be nowt giving back."

"Alta be protecting her own."

"Aye—as we be protecting the river."

"Aye."

"So will you be taking this company over the causeway."

Jano intruded once again. "We will pay, mistress."

"Ah—that be different." She held out her hand.

"We will pay when the devils are back on their own shores."

The fen mistress withdrew her hand. "Now or nowt."

Goff shrugged and turned to Jano. "It is the fen way."

Jano nodded. He was not surprised. "Hold, mistress. I will see what can be found." He returned to his horse and reached into the saddle pack, pulling out a velvet bag. For a moment he held it against his heart. Then he walked back, handing it to the woman and saying loud enough that all could hear: "My father was named Sandor, one of the five who rode with the Anna into the Grenna's grove. Some said he was a tale spinner and no such thing ever happened. But he would not retract his life. So he was most of his life without friends, but for me. He had brought back nothing to prove his tale but a single gold coin from the Grove which he never spent. All his life he worked hard as a ferryman though he had a fortune in his pocket. When he died, he left the coin to me. What better way for a ferryman's son to use that coin than this? Mistress, carry us over the fens."

She took the bag, emptied the coin into her hand, held it up to the grey light, then bit it. "Five in a boat, then, till ye be over." She put the coin back in the bag, and tucked the bag into her belt. "We swim the horses behind."

It was, Jano thought, *like a dream of floating. Like the dreams he had of home, the little cottage by the side of the ferry slip. The bad dreams. Where house and ferry were devoured slowly by some sort of inexorable grey tide.*

What he had not told them was that his father had died of drowning, falling drunk off the ferry on one homeward trip. Jano had long blamed himself for his father's death, though he understood now that he had been much too young to pull the sodden man back into the boat, had in fact been asleep on a pallet aboard the ferry when it had happened. He had not awakened until his father's final desperate cry for help. If anyone was to blame, surely it was his mother who had deserted them when Jano was a baby. Or the blame lay on the shoulders of those who did not believe Sandor's stories of the wars. Or perhaps the blame lay on the man himself. He did not have to drink. He did not have to die. *Still—what did it matter now?*

The fog was, if anything, thicker than before and Jano could scarcely see the boat he sat in, even though it was crowded with five people plus the boatman. He could not see the three horses swimming along behind, guided by reins which were looped through an iron ring fastened to the boat's side. However, he could hear the creaking of the leather, the slight splash of oars, a muffled cough. There was a sensation of movement if he closed his eyes.

How long? he wondered briefly. *How long till we get there?* Then he simply closed his eyes and gave himself up, like an ardent lover, to sleep.

When the boat ground onto another shore and the horses, now happily on dry land, started snorting their pleasure, Jano woke with a start, his hand automatically reaching for the hilt of his sword.

"We be putting you at this place," said the fenmistress. "We be going back for the others."

"How many this time?" Jano asked, though he had already counted and knew.

"We be getting the rest," Goff answered.

"You be setting a camp for the night," added the fenmistress. "Fire and all. There be nowt here to sight it."

He believed her. Even a great blaze would not be seen where they were. Wherever they were. On an island or on a hidden shore.

THE BALLAD:

Fen Love Song

(Chorus) *Speed the boat, pull the oar*
Off to the isles;
Speed the boat to the shore
Over the miles.
Speed the boat, pull the oar
Off to the isles,
Speed the bonnie boat o'er.

Little skin boat, so tough and so tight,
Speed the boat o'er, speed the boat o'er,
Carry my lover this festival night,
Speed the bonnie boat o'er.

Little skin boat, so rough and so new,
Speed the boat o'er, speed the boat o'er,
Tell him I love him and that I be true.
Speed the bonnie boat o'er.

Little skin boat, so taut and so trim,
Speed the boat o'er, speed the boat o'er,
Take this my token, be bringing it him,
Speed the bonnie boat o'er.

If he refuses, I'll jump in my boat,
Speed the boat o'er, speed the boat o'er,
Over the fenway to sink or to float,
Speed the bonnie boat o'er.

(Chorus)

THE STORY:

It had been ten days and still Prince Corrine was not buried. He lay on Jemson's bed and though the hearth fire was no longer being lit—for none of the servers dared do more than leave a tray of food outside the door for the king—the room was hot enough by spring's standard. The windows stood open day and night and still the room stayed warm.

The smell was awful and daily Corrine's body grew bloated, and his skin began to streak red, yellow, and black. But Jemson seemed oblivious to any changes. During the day he sat by the bed conversing with his brother as if Corrie could hear. Mostly Jemson told him about what life had been like on the Continent, how the first days had been difficult, so far from home, but that soon gave way to a pleasurable stay when he had found that Garun ways were more palatable to him than those of the Dales.

"I thought to stay there forever," he said companionably to the corpse. "Yet here I am. Once again at home. And king. As I should have been all along. And since you have remained here beside me, you must agree."

If he noticed that Corrie did not answer, Jemson did not remark on it, but went on instead to tell of his prowess at Garunian games. The boar hunt and his first kill, a bloody romp that took two days. Bear-baiting and how he won enough money on one bet to buy himself an Andanavian horse, a white stallion who could do the "airs" without a misstep. Pigeon-fletching where feathers for arrows were taken from a still live bird and the winner of the contest was the one whose pigeon lived longest and yet lost the most feathers. He boasted about his vast skill at cards. "I am good at skittle and fair at le mont, but I am best in the court at three-card royale." Corrie had no response to any of this, though a faint buzzing of flies arose from his body which Jemson ignored.

The king ate but little of what was left outside the door—a few spring berries, a plate of mushrooms broiled in butter, slices of goat cheese. He hardly ate but he drank great quantities of wine, whole bottles of the heavy, sweet red from Berick. At night he slept by the side of his dead brother, so sodden he might as well have been dead himself.

The Garuns had buried Sir Malfas days before, and having no one else to direct their lives—two of their captains having been slain in the fighting on the dungeon stairs and the rest either drunk on the Garunian wines, or incompetent—they slowly began to desert the castle, by ones and twos and threes.

A few sought to buy their way aboard ships to sail home. They were filleted by the very sailors they offered money to. The canny Dale fisherfolk, while not used to fighting pitched battles, were quite adept at seizing what chances they were given. They rowed the dead and dying Garuns out in their boats well past the Skellies and dropped them over, weighted down with old anchors or chains.

Others of the Garuns, however, took to the countryside and, in troops of seven or ten or fifteen, began careers of rapine and pillage that the nearby farmhouses and small country towns could not stand against. These were well-organized groups of soldiers and they made lightning-fast raids, escaping with what prizes they could find—a girl, cellars full of cheese and wine, even gold rings, some cut from the fingers of fainting women. As one of them said "We have made more each night than in all the days of soldiering here together."

Only a small ship's company worth—some seventy-three men—stayed loyal to the Dales king, if loyalty to a madman could be prized. They sent off messages using Jemson's carrier pigeons with little hope that King Kras would send ships for them. He was not a monarch who took defeat well and had never been one to support losers or deserters. Spread thin around the castle, the remaining Garuns guarded Jemson's shrunken domain with a fierce kind of pride well mixed with anger and despair. They held the servers hostage to that pride and only one—a wine steward who knew about the window in the cellar—escaped to alert the rest of Berick town about what was going on inside. The townsfolk already had some notion of it, from the farmers and foresters who had fled to the city in the hope that the king might call back his troops. They had some notion of the deserters, but not of how few remained to guard the castle. So they did not try to besiege it. Instead they sent delegations to try and talk to the usurper king, the "king from across the water."

But the king would not see the Dales folk.

He would not see anyone.

He spoke to no one but the dead man.

And after a while, the dead man spoke back.

Scillia had led her own company, some two hundred strong, away from M'dorah the hour after Jano's troops had gone. Sarana rode by her side. Scillia never glanced back at the plain and the rocks that reached jagged fingers toward the sky but kept her face grimly set on the path before them.

"Once I thought I might find my mother there, in M'dorah," she said suddenly to Sarana.

"She is gone over the ridge and into the realm of story," Sarana replied.

Scillia did not explain that it had been a different mother and a different story she had been seeking. She liked Sarana well enough, trusted her more than anyone else in their small army. But there were some things a queen could not share.

And, Scillia thought, *now I am forced to be a queen indeed.*

That thought bothered her greatly, that what she once longed for was now a burden. But there was no one she dared tell this to. Except in her conversations with herself late into the night.

They had made a good start on their march home that first day, camping in a small meadow that lay deep in the woods.

Exhausted, the troops lay on their pallets, most already deeply asleep. But Scillia could not sleep at all. Instead she went from campfire to campfire, speaking softly with the few men and women who were still awake. They thought she did it for them, to give them heart. She knew she did it because she did not want to dream.

Her wanderings that night took her to the far edge of the encampment which was lit only by half a moon, and then a foot more into the woods. The dark folded around her. An owl cried out from within the deeper forest, a sound much like a child crying. Scillia shuddered and pulled her cloak strings together, tying them with a quick one-handed movement that was both awkward and efficient.

A bit of movement beyond the shadows, in the deepest dark, put her on alert. There were pinpricks of light moving toward her, but they moved without any sound. Not a snap of twig or a rustle of leaves or a scuffling of ground. It was as if the forest itself had stopped breathing.

She turned to shout a warning to the others, and suddenly found herself surrounded by a circle of some thirty mannikins each half the size of a man, dressed all in green, with a skin that had a translucent green glaze over fine bones.

The shout died in her throat.

"Grenna!" she breathed. She had thought them but a story. Her mother's story about them, she had never credited. She had thought the tale only some sort of parable she had never quite understood. "Green Folk."

One of the mannikins moved forward, breaking the circle. He came close enough to her that she could have reached out and touched his head but she did not dare such familiarity even though she was queen. He raised his hand in greeting, speaking in a strange, lilting tongue.

"*Av, Scillia, fila e soror. Av Scillia, regens circulor.*"

Scillia thought she understood him, for it was like—and not like—the Old Tongue that her mother had insisted they be taught as children. The Grenna was hailing her as a daughter, a sister, and queen of the circle. She managed to hail him back, though it had been years since her last lessons. "*Av, magister circulor.*"

The little man nodded. "Your mother taught you well," he said speaking plainly, his voice only slightly accented.

Scillia nodded back. "I did not always listen."

"That is the way of the Tall Folk," he said. "But a few learn."

"My mother is well?" Scillia's voice broke in the middle of the question.

"She is *quonda e futura*."

"Well, *quonda*—now—is when she is needed."

"She is not needed here. *You* are the One. She sends this message: Every path has a turning. Every turning is a path."

Scillia houghed through her nose like an impatient horse. "I *hate* that kind of talk!" She took a step closer to the little man. "Tell her that . . ."

But whatever Scillia was going to say, there was no one left to say it to. For the moment she took the step toward him, the little man and the entire circle of Grenna were gone as if they had never been. Scillia spun around in place once, then again. But she was quite alone.

When she turned to go back to the camp that, too, was gone. Or at least the troops were gone. Her horse grazed alone. The fires that had been burning steadily at her back moments before were now ashes.

Cold ashes.

The conversation with the Grenna that had been but a few sentences long had taken days. Or weeks. She could not tell which. There was no one to ask. She sank to the ground and, for the first time in years, she wept like a child, those deep, horrible, shuddering cries that went on and on and on until the dawn.

Sarana lay on her blanket alone. She felt every inch a solitary. If she could have wept she would have. She had given up weeping when she was a little girl, knowing that it changed nothing. When Scillia had disappeared, they had spent precious days searching the woods for her. But the scumble of footprints—the circle of tiny naked feet—was exactly the same as Sarana had seen on the ridge when Queen Jenna had gone. At the end of two days, she had called a halt to the search, though she left Scillia's horse—just in case.

"We must go on or all indeed will be lost," she said. "Jano and the others cannot move without our protection."

"But who will be our king? Who will rule the Dales?" asked one of the farmers, a man named Flag, whose mouth often flapped like a banner in the wind.

"Scillia will return," Sarana told him.

"You do not know that," Flag replied.

"You do not know otherwise," she said.

She thought it a strong rejoinder. But that day and the next, several of the farmers and villagers slipped away in the night, back to their holdings, melting away into the forest as efficiently and mysteriously as Scillia had.

Do not think, Sarana promised them in her mind, *that I will forget your desertion*. She had learned all their names with the queen. But she put the deserters out of mind as she pushed the others to move more quickly the next day, through the forest and then out of it onto the narrow western road on their way toward Berick.

They moved too fast for care, without scouts to give them a measure of safety, for speed was uppermost in all their minds. Therefore they were totally unprepared for the slaughter at the West Road's turning.

Five bands of the renegade Garun soldiers, a tight-knit force of sixty-three men, had been shadowing them for a day without their knowing it. The Garuns had waited above a narrow cut through two cliffs and when the main body of Sarana's marchers were caught below them, the Garuns fired off arrows and rained down boulders on the trapped Dales folk, then scrambled down the cliffside to finish them.

Only Sarana and ten men at the front on horseback, and a half a dozen at the rear, also mounted, escaped injury. The rest were slaughtered where they lay. Sarana, stone-faced and shaking, watched from afar, held back from adding her own body and those of the few survivors to the defeat by dint of her army training.

"We are still enough," she told the men, "to create a diversion for Jano's sailors. There is nothing we can do here but die. We must ride. Ride for Berick. Ride for the good of the Dales. But never forget what you saw here today."

And they rode as if the Garuns were chasing them. But the Garuns, looking for more easy prey, went north instead.

"My brother and I," King Jemson announced to a startled server on the morning of the fifteenth day, "want to invite the lords of the Dales and their good ladies to a dinner this night. Full dress is required. See to it."

The server, a girl of fifteen with a pronounced limp, nodded, unable to speak.

"Send me my dresser. And a cook for I wish to plan the menu. This will be a great feast. I will show the Dales how the Garuns give a party."

Shaking, the girl took away the breakfast tray which had scarcely been touched and went as fast as she could below stairs to the kitchen where she dropped the tray on the floor and proceeded to have a shrieking fit until the undercook was able to calm her with a draught of berry wine.

"He wants . . . a feast!" she cried.

"Who does?" asked the cook.

"Him. And his dead brother that was the good prince."

"Nonsense, girl," said the cook who was as sensible a man as a cook could be. "The dead do not eat."

"Nor less the living," pointed out the undercook and nodded at the scattered breakfast things on the floor.

"Nonetheless, they want it. A big feast, too. With lords and ladies."

"Have we any?" asked the steward's lad who doubled as sauce cook when needed.

"We have the council," said the undercook.

"We *had* the council," put in the scullery maid. "That bloody king has killed them all."

"What will we do then?" asked the server.

"You will round up whoever is not actually serving and find them clothes from the queen's summer things. And the good king's store. Bless them in Alta's memory. And I will go up to the mad Jem and work out a menu. Else he'll kill the rest of us. And have *our* corpses at a fancy-dress ball no doubt." And saying that, the cook dusted his hands of the bread flour and went up the stairs. He kept his apron on, thinking even a mad king would know him for a cook and not ask more of him than the menu, though he left his white chef's hat behind.

Jemson was actually waiting for him at the door. "I want seven courses," he began without any other sort of greeting.

The cook was happy enough to hold the conversation outside the room. Even in the hall he could smell the corpse. It was worse, much worse, than hanged grouse. He nodded at the appropriate pauses in the king's dinner orders, though all the while he was wondering if there were some way he might poison the man without harming others at the party or getting executed himself. *But he is the Anna's son*, he thought suddenly. The cook had been in the army that had liberated Berick Castle, had been cook at the castle from before Jemson was born. *Such a small baby. Such big lungs*. And with that, all thoughts of regicide fled the cook's mind.

"At dark, when the candles are lit, we will come down the stairs, brother light and brother dark," Jemson said and then giggled. "Won't Skada be jealous, silly shadow bitch. And see you that the dinner is served promptly. And with the appropriate wines."

"You can trust me," the cook said.

"You can trust me *what?*" There was an awful look on Jemson's face.

The cook was momentarily confused.

"You can trust me, *Majesty!*" Jemson said. "Do not forget." He put his finger to the side of his nose and smiled. "Wouldn't want to whip you for forgetting." He shook his head. "I was whipped for that, you know. But only once. I am a quick learner. King Kras himself said so."

The cook nodded and took his leave, feeling lucky to have escaped. But as he went down the stairs—two at a time despite a bad back—a voice came floating down after him. "Send me my dresser!"

"You can count on me, *Majesty*," the cook called back, feeling both foolish and treasonous at the same time.

Scillia found the first burned-out farm house before she had gone very far. The second was a field away. From the state of the ashes, she knew the homes had not been on fire long ago. That there were two of them was very suspicious.

When she came upon the third along the same road, she began to suspect the worst. "The Garuns have been here," she said aloud to her horse, not expecting any reply. But she was feeling incredibly alone and even hearing her own voice was better than the silence.

"If the Garuns are no longer corked up in Berick Castle, then they have deserted and taken to raiding, or else they have been resupplied from the Continent. Either way, our situation is worsened." She did not dare think about Sarana and Jano and their troops or try and guess how long they had been gone. "One problem at a time," she whispered.

The horse shook its head. Not at her voice, as she first suspected, but at a shadow that suddenly crossed the road. Scillia saw it from the corner of her eye, began to draw her sword, then stopped when she realized it was a girl, not more than ten, with coppery hair as short as a boy's and a smudged nose. She was dressed in a brown shift, or else the material was muddy. It was difficult to tell.

Scillia reined in the horse, but did not dismount.

"Madame," the girl said, "can you help us? You have a sword and we have none. My pa has been killed. My ma has only me, and she so tore up by the Garuns. . . ."

Scillia dismounted then and held out her hand to the girl. "Take me to your mother," she said.

The girl took the hand, and lead her into the trees. There, some fifty yards from the road, was a rough lean-to and under it lay a woman. *Tore up* was a bit of an understatement. Scillia gasped when she saw how cruelly the woman's face had been slashed, the untreated wounds still gaping, the new flesh trying unsuccessfully to patchwork across the damaged cheeks, the red line on her neck from a garrotting, the broken nose. What was not slashed was bruised. Scillia did not doubt the woman was hurt the same way all over her body. It was a wonder she was still alive. She had no clothing on but a blanket that was loosely draped over her.

"How did *you* escape the same fate?" Scillia asked the child.

"I was in the fields," the girl said. "I lay down in the rows, between the new timothy. They did not see me."

"We said . . ." the woman croaked, "we were alone and they believed us. Bless Alta who saved my girl."

"But who did not save you," Scillia said, trying to pull away the blanket to see the wounds. The blanket was stuck to the bloody flesh and the woman screamed softly at each attempt. "I wonder why."

"I will ask her when I see her," the woman said. "Which will be very soon. Take my girl. My Sarai. Pledge me that." She held her hand up to Scillia and when Scillia reached over to take the hand in hers, the woman gasped. "One arm. You have but one arm. Be you the queen's child?"

Scillia nodded. "Now I am the queen," she said.

The woman closed her eyes, clearly understanding. When she opened them again she spoke to her daughter, "Go with the new queen. Do not mourn. It is the turning. That is all."

"The turning?" Scillia asked. But with a deep sigh, the woman was dead.

Sarai knelt by her mother's side and covered her face with the blanket. Then she stood. "I be yours," she said to Scillia, and bowed her head.

"Then our first task together," said Scillia, "is to bury your mother." She patted the child on the head. "I did not get to bury mine."

When the woman was buried, and Sarai's father as well—though that was pretty ghastly, for the foxes and buzzards had been at his bones—Scillia helped her on to the horse and then mounted behind.

"Where do we go?" asked Sarai. "Do we go to your castle?

"Not for a while yet," Scillia answered. "First we must get us an army."

"An army?" the child asked.

"To get my kingdom back," Scillia told her.

"How do we do that?"

"Farmhouse by farmhouse, lane by lane," Scillia said. She spoke with more enthusiasm than she had, but she did not want to tell Sarai how small their chances were. After all, a child who had already lost so much did not need the promise of more loss to come.

Scillia and the girl rode for three days, past more smouldering farmhouses, seeking out those who were still alive. She learned then that she was not weeks or months late, but had lost only two days to the Grenna.

"Thank you, Alta," she whispered when she first heard that news. Still, even two days put her at a great disadvantage. She had no way to catch up with either Jano or Sarana, or to know how they might fare. She could only do what she had told Sarai she would do: collect an army.

With an army she could march on Berick Castle herself.

So by ones and by twos she and the child collected promises at farm houses. In the villages—often no more than a house or inn left standing—they collected more. Scillia did not care who she asked: men, women, children. The aged. The infirm.

"Come with me to Berick," she said. "Help me take back our land. It was done once by my mother and father, by your mothers and fathers, by your sisters and brothers. Now we must do it again."

She never raised her voice when she spoke; she was all the more compelling for it. What the Garuns had begun with their savagery, Scillia completed with her quiet compassion and strength.

Men and women and children. The aged. The infirm. They all pledged her their support. And she gave them the same message: They were to meet at several crossroads on a particular day hence. *At the Turnings*, Scillia called them. The older folk approved the name, though Sarai did not.

The child ran a grubby hand through her coppery hair. "That is not what my ma meant by a turning," she said.

"If it gathers an army, I will call it a tumbling. Or a tossing. Or a tussling." And when Sarai laughed at that, the high trilling sent the first bit of pleasure into Scillia's heart since she had left the castle to take her dying father into the woods.

On the appointed day, a group of some thirty women stood at one turning, waiting. The moon hung by a thread of cloud overhead and the women spoke in uneasy whispers. Their distress showed in the shadows beneath their eyes, in the angular hunch of their shoulders.

"Where is she?" a middle-aged woman asked, the moon writing runes across her forehead in deep groves. "How can she be late in coming? The night is cold, and passion turns cold, too, with each hour. And what of the Garuns? We would make easy pickings standing out here in the night."

"Hush, Manya," the woman by her side cautioned. They could have been twins, though one was dark-haired with streaks of grey, the other light. "She will come. She promised. And isn't it said, *Better late in the pan than never in the pot?*"

Two younger women, hardly more than girls, stood arm in arm, gazing up at the moon, one of them with braids as light as that wintry moon, the other with plaits blue-black as the sky. The cloud had become a fringe over the upper half of the moon, so that it looked like a broken coin.

"Look!" the light-haired girl cried, pointing. Her sister pointed as well.

"If the clouds completely . . ." Manya's warning began. She did not have to say more. They all knew that once the moon disappeared, the dark sisters would go as well, back to their shadow world and their part of the mission for at least this night would be that much more difficult.

"Where is she?" Now it was Manya's twin who gave the complaint.

"Hush, Sonya," Manya cautioned, and they both gave a single laugh at the reversal, a mirthless laugh, more like a sigh.

"I do not understand," another woman said. "Why does she dally with the men of Suldan Village? Men are the enemy."

A mutter of agreement ran around the ragged circle.

"Not all." It was the girl with the light-colored braids. "Not all men." She spoke with feeling, but without proof. She was that kind of girl.

"All," said Manya. "Even the ones we like."

"Liked," corrected Sonya. They lived in a small village made up mostly of women who were the remnants of one of the Hames that had been broken up after the Gender Wars. A group of thirty Garun renegades had fired their houses but a week before, driving the women before them like cattle. Only a few had escaped in the night. The village men had not come to their rescue, instead turning over their coins to the Garuns, begging for their lives. It had not worked. They had not been spared.

The two girls, too, had been in the drive. But with their young legs they had sprinted to safety early on and had not seen how brutally the Garuns had used their mothers. They remembered the village men with a good deal more affection and were still mourning their deaths. They walked away from the circle and towards the woods, as if that were their answer.

The moon's fringe, like a curtain, had lowered even more, and the whisperings from the circle of women grew even more frantic. Then suddenly a drumming of hoof beats signaled them. The girls turned back and called to the circle: "She is here? She is come?"

The moon disappeared into the cloud completely and a single horse, black as the solid center of an eye, emerged from the woods as if the forest had spit it out. There were two riders, one large, one small and when the horse got closer, the women could see that one rider was a grown-up, the other a thin little girl with red hair.

The horse was covered with sweat from the run, but when the grown rider got down she was not sweating at all. In fact she was shivering violently for she was wearing only a thin shirt, the one empty sleeve tied up with a bedraggled ribband to her shoulder, a pair of leather trousers, and high soft leather boots run down at the heels. The child was swaddled in what was surely the woman's cloak.

Manya shrugged out of her own cloak and offered it. "Here, my queen," she said.

"Scillia. Until I am on my throne again, that is my name."

"I cannot call you that, my . . ." Manya said.

"You *will* call me that," Scillia ordered. Her voice was tired but full of authority. It was a new voice for her and she used it sparingly. The voice told them what she would not—that she was the queen. Still, she tired of the same argument whenever she met with her recruits. The men were willing soon enough to call her by name. But the women . . . *I am getting perilously tired of women*, she decided.

"Still, my . . . Scillia," Manya stumbled a moment over the name so plainly spoken, "take my cloak. You have none."

"The child needed it more than I," Scillia said, but she accepted the proffered cloak. She thought she knew the difference between courage and foolhardiness. A cloak against the cold was not the difference between a hero and knave. "Tell me your name, now that I have what is yours."

"Manya," the woman said. "Of Craigton Village, and before that Nill's Hame."

"That is a name I have heard from my mother," Scillia said, nodding, though what her mother had said of it, or when, she had no clue. Still it was best not to admit that now. "Manya," she said again, thus committing the name to memory.

"What news then of our army?" the girl with the braids cried out, grabbing hold of Scillia's reins.

Scillia turned toward her. "News? There is much to tell, but first give me your name."

The girl was suddenly shy. "Seven, madame." She stuttered on the name and handed the reins back to Scillia.

Scillia smiled to put her at her ease. "Was that because you were the seventh in your family?"

Seven giggled at that. "No. Seven because it took them

seven years to get me. And then when they got me, and I was only a girl, my father said: 'A girl is less than no child at all.' My mother was so hurt by this, she took me in her arms, still bleeding birth blood, and walked to the old Selden Hame where she left me."

"And did not stay herself?" Scillia asked gently.

Seven shook her head. "Na, na. Stayed only long enough to be cleaned up by the sisters and to give me a name. Then she walked back to her man. But it is better so. We say in Selden, *Many mothers are best*. Besides, without them I would not have my dark sister. None my age know how 'tis done. But I do. I was the last at Selden, though." She smiled shyly up at Scillia.

"Well, then you are beyond me, for I have no shadow but the one that follows me on the ground. Though my mother's dark sister, Skada—blessed be—helped raise me up. And once I visited your Hame, though you would have been a little child."

"I do not remember you," Seven said.

"Nor I you," Scillia said. "But I have you now."

A moment later the cloud moved away from the moon and Seven's sister appeared by her side. Scillia smiled.

"And you are?"

"Tween, Your Majesty," the girl said.

"Scillia," Seven said, poking her in the side, getting poked in return.

"And I am Sonya," said Manya's sister. "Do you wish to name us one by one, or should we be about our business? There is more than chattery to be done this night."

"It never hurts to be named," Scillia said gently, pulling Manya's cloak tighter around her. "If we are to die, best not to go unnamed into the dark."

"We will not die. We will win this fight," Manya said. The

other woman echoed her, all but Seven and Tween who were silent and the girl Sarai who was still napping atop the horse.

"We all die sometime, my good Manya. Only Alta is forever." Scillia's voice was low, but nonetheless full of steel. "And some of us will die in this fight. It is best that we understand that from the start. If you cannot go into it content with that knowledge, best not to go into it at all." She dropped the reins and, whipping off the cloak, handed it back. Her horse, as if made of stone, did not move. Nor did the child on its back.

THE HISTORY:

Editor, History and Nature:

Sirs:

Female infanticide, so common before the reign of King Carum, has been long held to have disappeared completely with his ascendancy. But new evidence disagrees with these old assumptions. According to old population records discovered recently by Sir Elric Hanger and his wife, Lady Nan, in the ruins of the Northern Palace Grounds at Berike, a lingering misogyny in rural villages still led to an underground trade in girl babies. (See "Farm Babies and Baby Farming in the Midlands" by S. Cowan. Demographics Annual, *Pasden University Press, #79.)*

So convincing are these records that they make clear the patterns of abandonment changed only in subtle ways, slowly being incorporated into the so-called fostering laws, those laws that concerned the rearing of children away from their natural homes. (See "Forgotten Fosters" by A. S. Carpenter-Ross, Psychological Abstracts, Conference on Daleian Research, *1978.)*

Of course a foundling must needs first be lost! This simple fact has been overlooked for years in the studies done on the many fostering relationships, such as apprenticeships, oblation, parental death by suicide, or even godparenting. And while there have been many scholarly studies done on fostering in the higher levels of society—for example, King Carum's own son was sent abroad to live as a royal hostage/fosterling at the palace of the Garunian king till he was sixteen and married to his foster-sister who was known as Mad Jinger—foundlings at the low end of society's scale have been lost a second time by the historians. With my father's notes and my own research I hope to write an important essay on this subject.

What is the difference between fostering and abandonment?

Ask the child.

THE STORY:

Scillia turned to the girls. "I was a foundling myself."

"I did not know, Majesty," Seven said.

"Scillia."

"I did not know, Scillia," the girl repeated.

"Queen Jenna was not your mother?" Tween asked.

"White Jenna was certainly my mother in truth, but she did not give birth to me," Scillia told her. "She rescued me when my first foster mother, a warrior of M'dorah Hame, died. I had been left on a hillside by my birth mother and found by the M'dorans. The women of the South Dales may say *All history begins between a woman's legs*, but I am no longer convinced."

She smiled at them. "But we must now talk not of birth but of war. Manya has the right of it."

"A man's war," added Manya.

Scillia stared over at her. "It is a woman's war as surely," she said. "It is my war. The one who thrust me off my throne was a man, yes. But not all men are cruel."

"I have no proof of any other," Manya said, and her dark sister echoed her, adding "And doesn't it say in the texts that *Man is wood, woman water?*"

"*Water weights wood*. That is also written in the texts. In

The Book of Light, as surely you must know," Scillia said. She had grown up hearing her mother and Skáda argue from texts. It did not impress her, but she could do it if she had to. "And if you want proof, I shall give it you. My brother Corrie is proof. A sweeter man you will not find. Honest, generous, funny, dear. He supports my claim against the Garun king." She found she could not say Jemmie's name, as if by naming him he had some kind of hold on her. "My father Carum, too, was always kind and generous and loving." She thought a minute. "My friends on the council—old Jareth and Piet. I have never had less than good faith from them. And the man who commands half my army now—Jano, of the Southern Guard. No, I cannot say all men are this, all men are that. Men are neither all good nor bad."

"And the man who raped me?" asked a young woman standing to one side. "I was neither handfasted nor married to him, but still he had me. And my own father called him 'brother' and told him to ride me the harder."

"And the man who cut my own mother's throat in front of me," added Manya, "as if she were no more than a pig for the butchering. It was then I ran off to Nill's Hame."

Scillia shook her head. "We cannot waste time here countering man for man, tale for tale. We will never convince one another. History begins in the heart, I think. I cannot deny there is cruelty in the world. Certainly we have all born the Garunian yoke. But in this one thing you must trust me. There are good men here in the Dales and they will be fighting with us side by side. The throne will be won back only when we bind ourselves by friendship, not separate ourselves by history. Sisters, give me your hands on this." She thrust her one hand forward.

Seven and Tween grabbed her first, then the others. Manya and Sonya were near the last. But finally they too were carried, if not by Scillia's oratory, at least by the fact that they were afraid to stand alone.

"Sisters, if I had a second hand I would use it to hold you all fast. But I have only the one. Still I have a heart—and that you have entire."

Manya and Sonya did not look completely convinced, but Scillia ignored them and kept on speaking. "You must all ride on to Greener's Hollow. We gather there tomorrow eve. Collect what weapons you can. Surely even in the ashes of your homes there can be found a sword, a pike, a knife, a bow. A simple cudgel from a stout tree will serve. If the Garuns think this a man's war, we will prove them mistaken. If women think they cannot fight, then in this they are wrong. But I must ride now. There are several more Turnings I have to visit, bringing them news of the meeting place and time. You are the seventh. I will get no sleep this night."

She walked back to her horse, placed her foot in the stirrup, and pulled herself up one-handed. There was nothing awkward in the movement.

"We will come with you this night, Scillia!" Seven and Tween cried out together.

Scillia looked down at them, her arm around Sarai who still slept wrapped in her cloak. "I have promised one mother to take care of her child. I cannot watch after more." Then kicking the horse into a sudden canter, which served to wake Sarai for a moment, horse and riders were quickly gone into the dark woods.

Above the clearing the moon was a full, bright promise. Seven cocked her head to one side. "She has no dark sister and only one hand. She needs us."

"Do not fancy yourself, girl," Manya said. "She has been one-handed from the first. And perhaps a queen needs time to be alone."

"She is not alone," Tween pointed out. "There is the child. . . ."

Seven nudged her to be quiet and Tween shut up. But the nudge was as much promise as warning. They walked away from the other women as if they no longer cared.

THE LEGEND:

About two hundred years ago, in Cannor's Crossing, the wife of the town cobbler gave birth to twin girls who were joined at the hip and shoulder. The midwife took such a fright at the devilish sight, she left before the birthing was done, making her way across the ford in a shallow boat and leaving the poor mother to die in a pool of her own blood.

What was the cobbler to do, never having seen such a thing before? He took his leather-cutting knife and severed the girls, sewing up their wounds at hip and shoulder with heavy black boot thread. Only the misfortune was that the babes had just three arms between them, so one girl got two arms, the other just one.

The one-arm girl got married, and lived to a ripe old age, the other didn't. No accounting for a man's taste, I suppose. The two-armed girl stayed with her father and learned his trade. But when the old man died, she died, too, as if he—and not her sister—had been the twin and they joined together.

My grandmother told me this story, and as she was born herself in Cannor's Crossing, I have no reason to disbelieve it.

THE STORY:

Sarana and her ten fellow soldiers rode through day and night toward Berick. The horror they had seen, the bodies left unburied, haunted them and they did not dare sleep. They also did not know that a few at the rear of the marchers had escaped back into the deep woods. Only one thing was on their minds—to get to Berick and do what they could for a diversion so that Jano and his sailors might block the harbor unseen.

When they got to the coast it was almost day, and but a quarter of that day's journey by foot more to Berick. Sarana halted their headlong flight. The horses were near exhaustion, the riders likewise. She knew that they would have to rest before the last part of their exercise. Besides, they did not dare let themselves be seen so close to the city. There were certain to be patrols ahead of them, though they seemed to have outrun any Garuns at their back.

"We will travel no more through the day," she said. "We will go the rest of the way tonight."

"Why waste time?" asked Malwen, a short man with a notoriously short temper that had not been improved by his lack of sleep. "It is tomorrow's morning when we should be making our noise."

"The time will not be wasted. We have to build ourselves a withy ladder," Sarana said.

"A ladder? A single ladder to scale a castle held by hundreds of Garuns?" He spit expertly to one side. "Pah! Woman, you may have had Jano and the young queen fooled, but I think you have broth for brains."

"We are not going to scale the castle where we will be seen. We are going around the water's edge. It will be a low tide at the night's middle. There is the window into the wine cellar that I wiggled out of. What goes out can go in. With luck . . ."

"We have had no luck so far," another man pointed out.

"With luck," Sarana continued, "the window will still be open. Without luck, we shall have to bash the boards away which will likely give away any element of surprise. But if the

Garuns are still using the place as a dungeon—and I cannot see why they should have changed their plans—we will be helped by the prisoners themselves."

"Hah!" Malwen said. "And become prisoners *our*selves. If we can squeeze through, that is." He patted his stomach which was rather girthy.

"Those of us who can get through will. The rest will guard the ladders down below. But if we become prisoners, it will not be to the Garuns' pleasure, for we will be well-armed prisoners," Sarana reminded them. "And trained fighters. There were but a few such in the dungeon when I left. My guess is that, with luck, there will be more by now."

"With luck, with luck, with luck," Malwen said. Some of the others were nodding with him and it looked as if his sourness was going to carry the day.

"Have you a better plan?" Sarana asked pointedly.

He had not. He was a masterful complainer, but he never had any better ideas. Complaint was his one tune, though he played many variations on it. But because he was silenced by Sarana's question, whatever support he might have had was quickly leached away.

"Then we will go with my plan for now. Back there, before the last turning, we passed a stand of alder and willow, by the river's edge, close to where the river opens out into the sea. We'll retreat there. It will make good cover for the day and we can work on the ladder. We've no nails so we will need to bind the rungs with leather. That will mean stripping reins, belts, whatever, then wetting it down and letting things dry tight in the sun."

"And with *luck*," Malwen added, his mouth still puckered with bile, "there will be sun."

Someone slapped him, not at all jocularly, on the side of the head. It was the last thing anyone said until they were back in the copse of alder and willow, cutting what they needed for the making of the withy ladder. So Malwen's sentiment did not change what they did but it set a sour mood.

The man designated as the king's dresser, a middle-aged Berikian named Halles, had come to Jemson's bedroom reluctantly. The smell in the hallway was still overpowering, worse than the run-offs in the streets after a great celebration when men and women alike thought nothing of spewing their entire night's drink on the ground. Halles wanted to put a cloth to his nose, but the cook had forewarned him.

"Do not let the king think there is something wrong," Cook had said. "Just humor him and get out as quick as ever you can."

But it was not that easy. Jemson wanted not only to be fully dressed himself, but that his brother be dressed as well.

Halles had not always been at the court. As a young man he had fought alongside the old king—not Carum but his elder brother—had held the king's head as he lay dying in the field. He had seen what a week or two did to an unburied corpse. There had been many such in the Gender Wars. And this body, he knew, had lain at least a fortnight on the king's bed. *Will there still be flesh?* he wondered. *Will there still be eyes? Will the maggot worms have burst through the clothing, through the skin?* He shivered. He was not yet an old man and he had hoped to grow gracefully into his age without any more bad dreams.

"Your Highness, Gracious Majesty," Halles said, "I can see that you will want to be dressed in the very height of fashion for this feast. But may I point out that your brother, the good Prince Corrine . . ." and here he nodded vaguely in the corpse's direction, "is already beautifully attired. His caftans are his signature and he has always worn one to the royal parties." It was only a slight exaggeration. The caftan that Corrine had on was of painted silk, brought over from the Continent, but he knew it was now filthy from the prince's days in the dungeon, and the stones that were his death. It would also have been wet and dry and wet again from those effusions that come with dying. Halles understood the king was mad; he hoped that the king was mad enough. "You have no way of knowing this, of course, having been so long at the Garunian court."

"Ah, I see," Jemson said, as if he really understood. "Well I will not impose my will upon my brother. We are both princes together. He may wear what he has on if that is his pleasure. But come, good dresser, you must help me chose what I should wear. As you do, you must remember—I am as much Garun now as Dales. We are more fashionable on the far shores. Perhaps . . ." and here he giggled ". . . perhaps I will teach you rather more than you teach me."

"I am always keen to learn, Your Majesty," said Halles. Which was true. But what was truer was that he was relieved not to have to handle the corpse. "Show me what you will."

Jano and his troops reached the coast in less time than they expected. The crossing of the fens had been accomplished in one long morning after their night on the isle. The horn of land that led around the coast to Berick had been empty of Garuns and they had managed to get to Josteen a full two days ahead of schedule. A few of the men were from the town and wanted to see their wives and mothers. But Jano would not let them go.

"When we are done with what we have come to do, you can stay in Josteen forever for all I care," he said. "But we need everyone to stay here. And we need not put your loved ones in danger by letting them know what we plan."

The last part of his argument settled them and they waited the two days in a small forested area east of the road till the night that had been settled upon. Then they waited some hours more, till half past the midnight low tide, when the waters were already high enough to sail out into the bay. At that point, Jano split his hundred into two groups.

"You into Josteen," he said, putting a Josteen man in charge. "And we will go on the extra to Southport." It was the sister town and only one cove away. "Set five men to the oars of five skiffs."

"He means a sculler," called out a Southport man.

"Skiff or sculler," Jano said quickly.

"We 'uns call 'em skelleries," said the Josteen man he had set in charge.

"Never you mind, captain," the Southport man put in laughing. "The Josteen lads never did know how to talk. Bottom feeders every one!"

"We'll show you what bottom . . ." called the Josteen men.

The Southporters turned, bent over at the waist, sticking their bums toward the Josteeners. "These bottoms!" someone shouted.

Jano growled at them. "Leave these town quarrels alone. We have work here. Save your fighting for the Garun soldiery."

The Southport man straighted up, turned and laughed. "Just a bit of funning, captain. To get our blood up on a cold night. Trust us. We fisher folk will not let you down."

Jano nodded, not certain of the townies but knowing they had no time to waste. "We must trust that Sarana's crew will make the diversion we need so no one of the Garuns in the castle is aware of what we do. You know the plan."

"Aye," came a dozen voices.

"But I will repeat it now to be sure."

A Southporters laughed and one said, "True—the Josteen lads need reminding."

Jano ignored him. "Take the largest ships you can find and sail them to the Skellies. Once nestled between the stone hands, scuttle those ships. Stay with them till they go down to be sure. The skiffs and scullers and skelleries or whatever other bloody name you want to call them will be out there to pick you up from the sea."

"And make it fast!" a Josteen man said. "That water is as cold as Lord Cres' cock-a-doo."

"And the fish won't mind picking at our bones," a Southporter added.

"I do not like that she rides alone, with only that child with her," Seven whispered to her dark sister. "Queen or not, she could use a bodyguard, someone who knows the roads, the woods, the ways."

"Then," Tween said slowly, "we must go after her."

Without a word to any of the older women, they mounted their grey gelding, kicking him into a trot. It was his fastest gait because he was too old for anything else, especially with two of them riding. Once into the cover of the trees, however, Tween disappeared and, lightened, the grey went faster.

Even in the dark it was easy enough to follow where the queen had gone. There was only one path through this part of the woods. But Seven could have found her trail off the path as well. She had learned well the art of tracking at Selden Hame under the guidance of the old singleton Marget.

"What we learn here is for hunting game," Marget had often said. "It is not for war. Never for war."

It was well then, Seven thought, *that Tween and I left the Hame*. She had loved the old woman and would not have wanted to disappoint her. But the training got there would serve for war as well as game, and she said a small prayer to Alta that the women at Selden remain safe during any fighting.

Seven had no idea how long she rode in the woods because the grey slowed to a ground-eating walk that swayed so continually, she fell asleep in the saddle and did not wake again until morning was already creeping though the lacings of leaves. Still, she trusted her horse. It had been trained at the same time she had been and, besides, they were still on the one track.

The path ahead was brilliant with sudden sunlight and opened onto a meadow dappled with early spring flowers, the place known as Greener's Hollow. There was the queen's own black and the queen herself—*Scillia*, Seven reminded herself—lying under the horse's belly curled around the child.

Fallen or asleep? Not knowing which, Seven rode over and dismounted even as the grey was stopping. But before she could reach the black horse, the one-armed queen was awake and on her feet on the far side of the horse, her sword in hand, the child cowering behind her.

"Not dead then," Seven said.

"Not even close," came the reply and then a laugh. "I do not know who is more frightened, girl. You or me."

"I am not frightened," Seven said. "Now." It was clear from her voice that this was no idle boast.

"Alta's hairs! You should be," Scillia said, sheathing the sword. "I might have spitted you, had it been night and not day with the sun shining on your innocent face." She sheathed the sword and stroked her horse's neck. "See how Shade's flesh crawls with fright. My heart is racing still."

"Mine, too," said Sarai.

"Truly, I did not mean to fright you."

Scillia came around the front of her horse. "Then, young Seven, why are you here before time? I said evening at Greener's Hollow. We had hoped to sleep till all arrived."

"To serve you," Seven said.

"There will be plenty of time for that."

"And Tween thought you should not be left alone."

"Sarai is with me."

Seven looked down at her feet. "Nevertheless," she said, "we are here."

"Indeed you are," Scillia said, taking pity on the girl. "And in a way I am glad of it. You and Sarai can take the horses down to the stream over there." She motioned with her head toward the north end of the meadow. "I will find us something to eat."

"I have journeycake," Seven said. "We could share it."

"So have I. And I am mightily tired of it. Besides, we should save what we have for those times when nothing else can be found. We have many miles still to go to get to Berick, and the Garun forces will be difficult to overcome once we are there." She was careful not to mention what they might meet along the way. "Journeycake will not shorten the road, no matter what the songs say."

THE SONG:

Journeycake Ho!

Into the meadow and out of the woods,
Carrying nothing but bartering goods,
Running so fast, there is nothing to take
But a skin full of wine and a good journeycake.
Journeycake ho! Journeycake ho!
Make it and take it wherever you go.
Traveling swiftly or traveling slow,
It will keep you filled up in the morning.

This wasn't a trip I was planning to make
As I fled through the door with some good journeycake.
But my horse was all saddled, so off I did ride
Thankful I still had my head and my hide.
Journeycake ho! Journeycake ho!
Make it and take it wherever you go.
Travel on water, on ice, or on snow,
It will keep you filled up till the morning.

The master was after me, likewise the noose,
I had to go quickly and lightly and loose.
So I grabbed what I could and I let the rest be;
I didn't have much—but at least I had me.
Journeycake ho! Journeycake ho!
Make it and take it wherever you go.
And if you've no money, you'll still have the dough
To keep you filled up in the morning.

THE STORY:

Seven took up the reins of her horse, Sarai led the big black, and together they walked across the meadow toward the stream. Scillia let out a deep relieved sigh. A sound answered her, and she listened for a moment before realizing it was just a song thrush. She forced herself to relax, but at the same time she listened a moment more. Just because the sun was out did not mean they were safe. Sarai's mother's face came back to her. *That* had all been done in the daylight.

She glanced around the meadow. It was awfully quiet, except for a lone squirrel busy at the near end of the field. *Squirrels*, she thought, *could mean buried nuts. And nuts would be a wonderful change from journeycake*. She went over and scraped about with her foot, but either the squirrel had already found his wintered-over nuts, or he was as hungry as she. All she found was an owl pellet, old and brittle, with a shrew's skull inside. She made a face. Not much eating in shrews, even if she *could* catch one. They were not worth the effort. *This wood*, she told herself, *is but a meager larder*.

There were a few new ferns, but she did not want to start a fire to boil them. The less attention she brought to the Hollow before nightfall the better. But on a mossy path, she found three different kinds of mushrooms and that—at least—was promising. One kind had an inky top and she knew it was especially good eating. The others were chancy this time of year. Still there were enough of the blackcaps for Sarai and Seven to have a meal. And perhaps further along some for herself as well. She was bending over to collect them and heard a muffled yell and then the high scream of a girl.

Without stopping to think, she straightened up and was running across the field in a single fluid motion, unsheathing her sword as she ran. When she came to the crest of the hillside leading to the stream, she saw there were two men in leather face masks—Garuns—more intent on having their way with Seven than killing her.

Anger rather than fear steadied Scillia, and she gripped her sword hilt tightly.

The men did not notice her, for Seven's screaming masked other sounds. And, since there was no sign of the black horse, it might mean the men didn't know there was more than one girl at the stream. The one man atop Seven was holding both her hands over her head with one massive paw, loosening the leather string on his pants with the other.

Scillia knew which one to tackle first. The more dangerous one was on his feet still; the other would be too busy for the moment, and with his pants around his ankles would be effectively bound. She half ran, half slid down the grassy slope and came up silently behind the standing man. At the last minute she coughed and, when he turned at the sound, spitted him expertly. His face as he died was full of surprise as much—she was sure—that he had been killed by a woman as that he was dead.

When he fell, she braced her foot against his chest and pulled out her sword. She made a face at the sound. Suddenly she was a girl again and the sword slicing through the man's chest felt like a knife through venison. She shook head, then turned, throwing herself atop the second man.

"Wait your turn, Brun—" he cried, thinking it his friend. He was dead before he could finish the name. Scillia pushed him off Seven who was still screaming.

Throwing her sword to one side, Scillia gathered Seven to her, saying, "There, hush, girl. They are both dead and can no longer hurt you." But Seven continued to scream, pushing Scillia away, and it took a minute to understand.

"Three," the girl was screaming. "Three. One finished and went after your horse."

The sword was too far for her to reach and besides, it was already too late. Someone had caught her hair up from behind, jerking her backward.

"*Carnes!*" came a man's voice, straining through the leather mask. It was the Garunian word for a female jackal.

Scillia let herself go slack against him, a trick her mother had shown her. She was ready to fling herself forward and catch him off guard, when the man cursed and dropped his hold on her hair, for a thrown rock had caught him in the back of the head. Scillia seized the opportunity and pitched forward.

Seven screamed again, a cry this time of fury not terror. She stood and picked up the sword, then flung it at the man's head. It struck point first between the eyes of the mask. It did not sink in terribly deep; the mask's leather was too stiff for that. But it was deep enough to kill him. He tumbled backward slowly, like a mountain falling, his head resting finally on Sarai's feet. She had a second rock ready to fling. When she saw he did not move she dropped the rock and threw herself onto Scillia's chest.

"I did not save my ma," she sobbed "I could not let him take you, too."

Scillia hugged Sarai, then looked up at Seven. "Alta's hairs!" she said. "You could have killed *me* with that sword."

"No chance of that," Seven said. "He was much too big to miss." Her words were brave, but the tremor in her voice and the tears running down her cheeks gave them the lie.

"Did you learn that at Selden Hame?" Scillia whispered, rocking the weeping child as she spoke.

"It's the Game," Seven said, finally.

"Game?"

"The Game of Wands." She tried to smile and failed. "The mothers taught us. 'Round the circle, round the ring,' " she began in a breathy voice.

"I know, child," Scillia said, gathering her in as well. "I once called it a silly sport. How was I to know?" And she thought how her own mother had taught her only games of peace. *Well, it will be the children who are my teachers now.*

THE RHYMES:

Trot trot to Selden,
Trot o'er the lea,
They caught seven children,
But they never caught me.

—*Ball-bouncing rhyme, South Dales*

Ride a black horse,
Ride a grey mare,
Follow the lady
If only you dare.

—*Toe-and-finger-count game, South Dales*

The number of the beast
Is three times seven.
All good children
Go to Heaven.

—*Counting out rhyme, North Dales*

THE STORY:

Well before the lowest tide, Sarana led the men along the shore, leaving their horses in the willow copse. Three of them carried the withy ladder and they slipped through the dark, being silent a shadows.

This time luck *was* with them. They were not seen.

The wind off the ocean was cold and they were all shivering by the time they got to the rocks below the castle, but it did not slow them down. They set the ladder against the wall, sighting on the single dark window above them, then anchored the bottom of the ladder between two boulders, with a man on each side. The ladder was within a hand's span of the window and Sarana let out a sigh of relief.

"I'll go first," she whispered. "I know what to expect. Or at least I knew better than anyone else. If I scream, scatter and find some other way to divert them from looking out toward the sea."

"We should have gone the other side, then," muttered Malwen and several of the men grunted their agreement.

"We no longer have the numbers for that sort of thing," Sarana reminded them, though in truth she half believed him right. Without another word, she began to scramble up the ladder, pleased that the rungs held.

Near the top, she slowed and felt cautiously with her right hand over the sill, something biting deeply into her palm.

"Alta's braid!" she cursed quietly. How could she have forgotten the broken glass? She inched up two more rungs, keeping her head and body to the side of the window, and carefully peered in.

The window was not boarded up but inside the wine cellar it was pitch black. Not a single torch lit the rooms. *That is odd*, she thought, remembering the flickering light of the prison. She listened carefully for a moment longer, than scrambled down the ladder.

"What is it?" someone asked. "Were you seen?"

"There is no one there," she said.

"What do you mean?" Malwen asked sourly.

"Just that. The rooms are dark, empty. Can we make a torch before I go back?"

"I can," someone whispered, and was gone back up the beach, returning shortly with a stick of driftwood wound round with dry grasses. "It won't last long."

"I just need it for a short while to see what is wrong up there." She felt in her leather pocket for her flints. "Give it me. I'll signal as soon as I know."

"A scream will do," Malwen said. He hadn't meant it to relieve the tension but everyone laughed.

Sarana scrambled back up the ladder, with less caution this time, though made awkward by the driftwood torch. She balanced for a moment on the sill, and leaned the torch against the side of the window. Then she got out her flints, struck a spark, and lit the torch. She held it in front of her into the cavernous dark and the light flowed like water over the wall and floor. She could see nothing that might be a danger, so she jumped down, slipped on a wine bottle, and stifled a yell. But her head hit the floor hard and she not only saw the torch, but repeating stars as well.

When the stars finally cleared and there was only a nasty throbbing at the back of her head, she got up and carefully looked around in the torch's flickering light. The rooms were empty of prisoners and the door out into the hall gaped wide open. Torches in the hall lit the passageway. She was not sure what that meant—whether it was a trap or simple abandonment—but she was about to go back to the window and call the others up when she heard footsteps coming down the stone stairs toward her. Quickly she guttered her torch and faded back into the second room, standing by the door where she could see but not be seen.

Two men with torches—Garun guards as far as she could tell—entered the wine cellar and after them came two other men, probably servers. One was saying something about the king and his feast. She could not hear it all. Silently she drew her sword and then reached as well to the knife on her belt.

She waited a long awful moment until the guards were nicely silhouetted in the doorway. Then she stepped full into the doorway of the second room which was still in the dark. Flinging her knife at the one guard's head, she followed its path before either man realized there was only one of her. She cut the second guard crosswise from neck to underarm, then swung around and thrust the first guard through as well, though he was already falling, the knife through his left eye.

Immediately she stood up with her sword raised, but the servers were both on their knees before her.

"Is it the queen?" one asked, unable to raise his head to be sure.

"I *serve* the queen," she said, horrified at how squeaky her voice sounded.

"Then we serve you," said the other man. "The usurper is quite mad."

She let them stand, but slowly, and had them pull the two dead Garuns out of the light. Then, still sighting them with her raised sword, she had them carry the torches to the open window.

Leaning out the window, she called down. "Come on up. Even Malwen, I think, will be able to make it through with our help."

By the evening hundreds were gathered at Greener's Hollow, mostly women, all armed. Scillia was one of the few on horseback. Her arm around young Sarai, she addressed her troops under a moon that had a blackened side.

"I have heard of the Garuns who daily rape and kill. I have seen their handiwork. They have turned our green woods and hillsides, our valleys and farmyards, into slaughteries. We have been their cattle too many days. Now they will become ours."

She paused and let them cheer her because it would make them warm while the message she brought them could only bring them chill.

"We will fight hill by hill if we must, blade of grass by gold of grain. Green and gold then are our colors. Theirs will be the red of blood, the brown of the earth where they shall lie." Again another cheer, and she waited.

"But know this—though I was born a warrior, I was not bred up to it. My mother and father wanted me to know only peace."

"Alta bless them!" shouted someone from the crowd.

"My mother said she would wait in the Grenna's Grove till the Dales should need her again. We need her now," Scillia said. "But we have only me."

Sarai twisted in the saddle and looked up at her. "We want *you*, Scillia!" she cried. Her little voice managed to be heard by those in the front who picked up the cry.

"We want you, Scillia! Scillia! Scillia!" The chant continued till it had gone out to those furthest from her.

With that cry still ringing, Scillia led them out of the Hollow and down the long road toward Berick Castle where the enemy waited.

The feast was laid out for a party of twenty. More "lords and ladies" than that Cook had not been able to find. He hoped, with Alta's blessing, that the king would not be displeased.

Several maids and one of the assistant gardeners had been

conscripted to wear the old queen's clothes, though the fit was poor. And Scillia's wardrobe was all one-sleeved and too obvious for them to dare. The king might be mad, but he was not stupid.

Every man from the kitchen, with the exception of the cook himself, was dressed in King Carum's clothes. Cook was too fat to fit and, besides, someone had to make the meal. Three gardeners and the boy who had delivered flour from the mill were dressed for the feast as well.

They all waited silently in the great dining hall, the room that had not been used since well before King Carum's illness. All the torches were ablaze and five of the seven-branched candelabra lit the table so that not a shadow was seen. The king had been explicit on that point.

"I want light," he had said, not once but many times as he was being dressed.

Old Halles had been practically apoplectic on the matter.

There were silver platters on side tables piled high with rabbit and venison, cress salads, fresh mushrooms, and goblets ready for the wine. Cook looked uneasily out into the hall. He had sent the wine steward and his assistant down to the cellar long ago and they had not yet returned. The assistant had to be threatened in order to make him go down into the wine cellar. There was a story—no more than that, Cook was sure—that the cellar was haunted now. That the spirits of the dead prisoners—Jareth and Petra and old Piet and the rest—were waiting to be released and were smashing bottles in their frustration. The problem was, the servers could often hear the sound of those smashing bottles and the story had taken on a life of its own.

Rats, the cook thought. *Or Garun soldiers getting drunk. That is all it is*. Then he smiled. *Perhaps they are the same thing*.

He glanced once again out the hall and this time saw an odd parade coming toward the room. The king was in the front and right beside him came two Garun soldiers carrying the dead prince in a chair, four other guards behind them. The body was slumped over and when they turned into the brightly lit dining hall, Cook could see how grey the corpse's skin was, how ruled with red and yellow and black lines. *His face*, Cook thought, *looks more like a pudding than a person*. It took him a minute to see that what was sitting in Corrine's lap was a slipper with a part of his foot and leg. The poor corpse was starting to fall to pieces.

The soldiers carrying the chair were almost as grey-faced as the dead man. Only the king showed any kind of animation.

"Set my dear brother at the foot, two pretty ladies on either side," he said. "And I shall be at the head, of course."

Cook prayed to Alta that the two ladies chosen—one a scullery maid and the other a gardener—would not have hysterics any time soon. He signalled to the servers to begin bringing the food to the dining table.

The corpse's chair was put in place and the two guards remained close by. The other four Garuns stood at attention on either side of the door to the hall.

And where, Cook wondered a bit crankily, *is the wine?*

At that very moment, the wine steward, his assistant, and three men Cook did not immediately recognize, entered carrying bottles. The three were dressed in shirt sleeves and leather pants, and one had a red smear of what might have been blood soaking his sleeve. Cook certainly had his suspicions. But the entire evening being already so strange, he did not voice them and left by the side door back to the kitchen to finish preparing the rest of the meal.

King Jemson clapped his hands with delight. "Wine now for my guests. And the special bottle of Salubrian Red for my brother." He gestured grandly to the foot of the table where the corpse had further collapsed against the chair.

The wine steward nodded but his assistant suddenly, and without apparent reason, dropped one of the bottles he was carrying. It crashed on the floor, soaking into the rushes and spraying both the king and the guests seated by his right side.

Jemson screamed, a sound like a woman in labor. Two of the Garun guards rushed over to help him, kneeling down to mop up the spill with table napkins. At that same moment, one of the new servers—the girthy man with the bloody sleeve—lifted the wine bottles he was carrying by the necks and brought them down, simultaneously, on the heads of the kneeling guards. Meanwhile his companions flung their bottles at the two guards by the door. The guards tried to catch the bottles and missed, cursing wildly as the bottles exploded in front of them.

The door burst open then, and Sarana with the rest of her men rushed in, swords drawn. Three of them carried an extra sword each which they tossed to the steward's new helpers.

The two Garuns at the door were killed quickly, the two by the corpse's chair wounded so badly that they swooned from the pain. And the two who had been crowned by Malwen's bottles were tied up and a watch set over them by the gardener's girl who was armed with a carving knife. The surprise had been so complete, not a one of Sarana's crew was even slightly injured, except for Malwen who had a long gash on the underside of his right arm, got not in the fight but when he had been hauled through the wine cellar window.

"This is an outrage!" screamed the king who had not moved from his chair during the fight. "An insult to me and to my dear brother, Corinne."

Sarana cast an awful glance at the dead man at the end of the table. Prince Corrine. *Scillia's favorite*, she thought suddenly. He was entirely slumped over now, the stench of death overpowering even the smell of Cook's hearty food.

"Tell her, Corrie!" Jemson cried. "Tell her whose fault this is."

"He is dead, Jem," Sarana said, walking over to the blubbering king. Raising her sword over her head with both hands, she added, "And so are you, my prince." She brought the sword down on him with all her might, thinking that with this single cut she was severing herself from Scillia forever. Pity might have stayed her hand. But the mad Jem commanded no pity from her. Only anger and disgust. Alive he would always be at best a distraction, at worst a rallying point for malcontents. She had to do what Scillia could not.

"And so are you," she repeated as the sword sliced through him, crown, bones, and all.

Scillia's army, which she and Sarai had gathered by ones and by twos, was now so many and so noisy—singing battle songs as they went—they met no resistance at all. The better fighters, the men and women who had served thirty years earlier in the Gender Wars or who were professional soldiers in the Dales guards, rode on the outside of the ever-swelling troops.

They came upon no Garuns on their march. Whoever had been raiding the lonely farmyards and small villages was too smart or too wary to tackle a mob almost five hundred strong.

The second day, near evening, six men, who had been waiting in the shadows of the oak forest till they were certain of the noisy troops, came out onto the road. Leading their horses, they held their hands up in supplication.

Riding at the forefront of her people, Scillia stopped her horse about thirty feet from them. "Who are you? Garun or Dales?" she called.

"Great queen," said one, "I am called Voss."

"I know you. You were with Sarana," Scillia said. "But why are you here? Have you deserted her?"

"We are all that is left of Sarana's troops. The rest lie slaughtered between two cliffs. You must not go this way."

"There is no other way to Berick," Scillia said.

"There is only death here."

"We know," Scillia said. "And we are ready to meet it." She got down from her horse, then, and went to them, embracing the man and his companions, calling them by name.

They camped for the night, the watch set hourly that all might be refreshed for the duties of the awful morn. Scillia sat up with the six men till she knew their story by heart, as if she had been there at the cliff's slaughter herself.

"If Sarana is dead," she said to them, "then surely Jano's part in the plan has miscarried as well for there would have been no one to provide a diversion. We have only ourselves to rely on now. I am not such a fool as to think sheer numbers will stand against a trained force. Few in my ragged army know how to fight. You men must take on more than your share of the burden. I ask you to do this not for me, but for the Dales."

"Our Queen, we will," the men said. They did not see that at each mention of her station, she shuddered. Or if they noticed, they assumed its origin was the coldness of the night.

She left them to their sleep and went back to her own fire, not daring to stir from it lest she risk another encounter with the Grenna. But she thought about their terrible adventure as she sat by her dying embers, the girls asleep at her feet. She thought about her mother as well. She remembered how often Jenna had gone off into the woods on her own, claiming that the crown was a cruel burden, the throne an uncomforting seat.

"Oh, mother," she whispered, "how I understand you now." She covered Sarai with her own blanket and stroked the child's head, but softly so as not to wake her. By the fire Seven and Tween slept fitfully, their sleep punctuated by moist little hiccuping snores.

* * *

In the morning Scillia sent several dozen outriders ahead to secure the cliff tops and the rest, led by Scillia, marched the long road. When they rounded the bend and came to the cliffs, they were not as prepared as they had thought. The hundred dead lay right where they had been slain days before, their ravaged faces and hands and legs testimony to the efficiency of the local scavengers.

Scillia forced herself to look at them, to commit them to memory. *This*, she thought, *is the result of kingship*. As if in refutation, a sudden memory her father's face, kind and concerned, came to her.

For a long time she looked for Sarana's body, but was not surprised when she could not identify it. The faces were too damaged for that.

"We will bury them here and do them honor," Scillia said, kneeling by the side of one guardswoman whose breast had been pierced by an arrow and whose face was but shards of bone. "We cannot leave them shriven by buzzards alone."

"But it will take time, Scillia," Seven said to her.

She looked up at the girl, tears in her eyes. "I would hope that you give me such time when mine is all gone. Besides, what is another half day to the Garuns who squat like great toads in our castle?" Standing she said, "Let this place be known from now on as 'The Hundreds' in honor of the slain."

She wondered how many would come, as she had to the mound at Bear's Run, to remember their kin who had died so awfully here. She wept inwardly that anyone should have such a duty.

They did not depart from that place till past dinner, but none wanted to camp the night there. The ghosts of the slain would be loud enough in their dreams.

* * *

Arming the people in the dining room with table knives and the captured Garun swords, Sarana ordered them to barricade the doors. There were seven doors in all. It was not going to be an easy room to defend.

The servers—and especially the gardener's assistant—were quick to follow Sarana's orders. She wondered that the castle folk had not revolted before, or at least run off, leaving the usurper prince to serve himself. But, something her father had always said—her mouth turned sour remembering him and his leather belt—*Many will show you the way once your cart is turned over*. She would not blame the Berick folk aloud, though her thoughts might rub black thinking of them.

"The table—put it there," she said, pointing to the main door. And when she realized the great banquet table was actually not a single piece but broke into five even sections, she ordered each section against five of the other doors.

"And that carvery to hold the back door."

Which left one door still open.

"We can pile chairs against it, and the wine tub as well," the gardener's assistant volunteered, kirtling up her skirts and starting in on the job.

"Not yet," Sarana said. "We will use that door for ourselves. One small door can be defended easily. The pass phrase will be 'The queen lives.' "

She knew they could hold out for a couple of days in the room if beseiged. There was enough food for that. But how they would ever get out again without losing most of their party, was another problem altogether.

One foot at a time, one step after another, she told herself. The first thing she needed to do was to give Jano a signal that the diversion was well under way.

"Malwen," she said, "Check these windows. They look out on the water. See if you can manage to light some kind of signal fire. One that will be seen out to the Skellies and beyond. Perhaps the tablecloth will burn. There are certainly enough candles."

"Me?" He was taken aback. "You want me to do that?"

"Either that, or serve me some wine," she said. "You were splendid as a steward, handling that bottle as well as you do a sword." It was the closest she could come to a compliment, but he took it as such and grinned. She had never seen him smile before. *It is not*, she thought, *a very pretty sight.*

The men picked up in the skiffs shivered with cold, but when they saw the fire burning from the castle window, they cheered loudly. They did not know how Sarana and her troops had gotten in, for they supposed the place heavily guarded. But she had had the majority of their own people, and perhaps they had outnumbered the Garuns in the end.

"Numbers always tell," said a Josteen sailor to his companions.

"Not when they are bottom eaters," called a Southporter from the stern of the boat. As he was the only Southport lad there he was pushed into the water for his sass. He nearly drowned before the next skiff pulled him in, but if he learned any lesson from it, it was to knock in the head of the next Josteen fisherman he met.

THE HISTORY:

From a letter to the Editor, Nature and History:

Sirs:

As I have not yet heard from you about my several ideas for articles for your magazine, I am enclosing a chapter that I wrote for a children's book to give you an idea of the range of styles I possess and so that you will understand the manner in which I can—with the proper editorial guidance—manipulate the Matter of the Dales. I hope that the enclosed will be of interest:

The War of Deeds and Succession is a rather large title for a very small period in our history. After the death—or rather the disappearance—of the aged and ill King Carum and his warrior queen, the country was split by three rival claimants to the throne: their son, their daughter, and the G'runian prince Jemson who, being the youngest of a family of seven brothers, had no hope of inheriting the throne of G'run.

The G'run prince, called popularly Jemson-Over-the-Water, had certainly been trained for kingship as were all princes on the Continent. He spoke the Dales language with a heavy accent and was more conversant with the brutal G'run sports of bear and bull-baiting than the songs and play-parties of the Dales, an affinity that some say carried over to his relationship with people. However, in his short time as king he did manage to put the army on a professional basis, close the last of the Hames, and introduced both hunting dogs and warm ale into the country.

Carum's own son, Corrine Lackland—so named because it was his older sister who was to have ruled the Dales—remained loyal to the crown, if not the particular crowned head. He was a young man of thought but not action. As a king of the Dales he would probably have been a disaster, but as a hero and a martyr he has no peer in Dalian history.

Indeed much of what we know of this period comes from songs and stories about him. For example, the "Ballad of Corrie Lackland" which ends this chapter, as well as the song cycle "St. Corwin of the Stones" at the back of the book. There are hundreds of other poems and songs from the South Dales especially where St. Corwin is one of the more popular saints. Badly corrupted by time and the passage of mouth and ear, these poems and songs are still recognizably about the War of Deeds and Succession. For example, the children's game-rhyme: "Stoneman, stoneman, say your prayers/Brother Jemmy's on the stairs."

The real favorite among the people, of course, was Ancillia Virginia, the virgin queen, who ascended to the throne not once but twice. The first time was on her parents' disappearance and once again after her brother's death and the death of the G'run prince. She was known as the One-Armed Queen because she lost her right arm at the ten-day Battle of Green Hollow where—so the stories tell us—the rivers ran red for a year after.

The problem was that Ancillia Virginia was a queen at the time the land needed a king; gender still being an issue in the Dales. Furthermore she refused to marry or to bear a child and thereby guarantee the succession. Her death ten years later ushered in nearly thirty years of commoner kings until the Dalian Circle of Seven was finally established, a method of rule by council which—in somewhat modified form—still runs the country to this day.

(See the Meacham Award winner for children's fiction, "Year King" by Giles Tappan which details the life of one of the first of these rulers. Though heavily fictionalized, it is still one of the most readable accounts of life at that time.)

from A Short History of the Dales, Grade Level sixth form

THE STORY:

On the third day, Scillia's army came into Berick, marching along the coast road. As they neared the castle, someone pointed out to the Skellies, sparkling in the spring sun. It was nearing noon, the tide turning, and there was something odd about the formation in the harbor.

"Look!"

Scillia looked. It was a scene she knew well for her entire life had been lived in Berick. And yet—yet the scene was subtly changed.

And then she knew. There, between the stone hands of

the Skellies, were the remains of sunken ships. *At least one mast, and the hump of a stern,* she thought. Jano had done it. Even without Sarana and her troops.

With that she began to weep, for Sarana and all the dead men and women left at The Hundreds, for Sarai's mother, for her own. "I am *nowt* a queen," she whispered into Sarai's hair, "nor do I want to be if it means I must not weep for my people." She could not remember ever seeing White Jenna cry.

Then, getting control of herself, she turned in the saddle, stood upright in the stirrups, and shouted "The harbor is blocked. The Garuns will not easily send more men to our shores. Now we must take the castle, my friends."

The cheer they sent up surrounded her, filled her up. It was still ringing in her ears when she lead them to the castle gates.

She stared for a long time at the gate, so familiar to her and yet totally alien as well. How many times had she walked through them, and yet never noticed the carvings on the doors? The signs of Alta so cleverly worked in wood, the relief of the goddess dancing on a flower, her hands above her head.

She looked up and saw a Garun guard on the battlements staring down at them. He began to shout.

"My queen," said Voss, "what is your plan?"

Plan? she thought. *I have no plan.* She had not expected to come this far, or get this close, without great losses. But she did not say that to him. Thinking quickly, she said, "Sarana spoke of the wine cellar dungeon. Take one man with you, around the water side, and see if you can spot an open window about one floor up."

As Voss and his chosen man raced around the side, several more Garunian guards began to gather on the battlements. They were pointing down and waving their hands.

"Scillia," Manya said, "surely we should get out of arrow range."

"Indeed," Scillia agreed, and called her troops back from the gate.

The dining room was quiet. So were the halls outside.

Too quiet, Sarana thought. *Time to stir things up*. "I want two volunteers to come with me," she said. "One soldier and one server who knows the castle well."

"I will come," Malwen said. "Since luck seems on our side."

"And I," said the gardener's assistant.

"Then tell me your name, girl," Sarana said. "The queen always asks. And so should I."

"Allema," the girl said. "I was born in this castle. I know every hidden room."

"Then Allema, show us the fastest, easiest way back down to the cellar."

"Not that window again!" complained Malwen.

"Only the girl will go out," Serana said. "To go into the town. If they know the usurper is dead, perhaps the townsfolk will help us. We are only along to make sure *she* gets through."

Malwen put the crossbar of his sword to his lips. "I hear and obey." Then he laughed. Unlike his smile, the sound was ripe and comforting.

"Remember the pass phrase," Sarana said to her men. "*The queen lives*. Let no one else in but us."

And then they were gone, snaking along the hall and into a servant's passage that led down the back stairs. They met no one along the way.

Voss and his man found the withy ladder against the wall and, seeing the open window, got up, in and through. They were just feeling their way through the first of the dark rooms—for the window shed but little light past a square patch on the floor—when they heard the sounds of steps and some whispered confidences ahead of them.

"Back to me," Voss growled and immediately felt his companion's back against his. They stood that way, swords raised, waiting for the enemy to find them. The surprise, they knew, was theirs.

A sudden torchlight blinded them both.

"Hit for the torch hand!" Voss shouted, slashing out.

A girl screamed.

And then a voice he knew well cried out as well. "Voss, you fool. You utter fool!"

"Sarana? But you're dead!"

"Not I, but you will be if you have injured that girl permanently." Sarana picked up the guttering torch from the floor and held it over Allema.

The girl was crying, but from shock, not injury. It was the end part of the torch that had taken the brunt of the blow.

"Alta's crown, but you have gotten slow in your dotage," Sarana said. "In the old days, that arm would have been clean off. She was smaller than expected, I guess. And quicker."

"Lucky for the girl," Voss said.

"Lucky for you," Sarana replied.

Malwen brought them all to their senses. "If we are not quieter, we will have the entire Garun guard down here."

"Right you are," Sarana said. "But Voss . . ." and she spoke more quietly, "what are you doing here?"

"The queen stands without the gates," he said.

"Which queen?" Sarana could scarcely breathe.

"The queen that is."

"And that is?"

"Scillia, of course, you silly cow," Malwen said. "Who else would it be?"

"Is is the truth?" Sarana asked, her head swimming as if she were suddenly drunk.

"Aye. She's rounded up some five hundred to fight for her, but half are children or dotards. How many do you have here?"

"A handful. The rest . . ."

"Gone. I know. We saw them die. Ran for the trees when it was clear we could not help."

"Buried them, too," his man put in. "Thought for sure we'd buried you. Old Voss here weeping like a . . ."

"Shut up, mind you," Voss said. "I'll not miss an arm a second time. Even in the full dark."

Sarana hushed them both. "If the girl goes out with your man, you can tell the queen we are quartered in the dining room. With the dead king."

"The usurper is dead?" Voss sounded impressed.

"By my hand. Do not tell the queen that. It should come from me."

"I'll get this child and Nohm here out the window and down the ladder before you can say Alta's Hame. And then I'll accompany you back up to that room. Dead, eh?" said Voss. "I want to see it before I believe it so."

"It is quite so," said Allema. "And her other brother even more so."

"A bundle of news, and not all of it good, I see. Well, up you go, lass. And you Nohm after. Tell the queen to storm the gates and we will take them Garuns by surprise from within."

Sarana, Malwen, and Voss had made it only to the second landing when they ran into a quartet of Garun soldiers making their rounds.

"Only four," Voss called. "I'll have two."

Sarana dispatched her man by the simple expediency of kicking him in the crotch while he set himself for a sword fight. Then she chopped down with her blade and cut his neck half through.

Quickly turning, she went to help Malwen who was having a tough time with his man, who was ten years younger and half Malwen's weight. Malwen was down on the floor, his left leg buckled beneath him.

Sarana got the Garun from behind right before he brought his sword down on Malwen's right leg. The sword fell from his hand, its downward path still true enough that it took a slice of Malwen's trouser and ran a bloody line up along his thigh.

"Voss?" Sarana called.

"Do you need help?' Voss called back.

Sarana turned and Voss was wiping his sword on the back of the guard's shirt. Another Garun was underneath, equally dead.

"We had better get back to the dining room and regroup," she said.

"I thought our group was doing fine already," Voss said.

"I forgive you," Sarana told him. "For frightening the girl."

Nohm and Allema got down the ladder and around the castle wall to the queen's troops as fast as they could.

Scillia was stunned by the news. "Sarana alive?" She could hardly credit it.

"Very alive, ma'am," said Allema. "And gone back to the dining room which is barricaded except for one door."

"Which door?"

Allema told her. "There's words that must be said to get in."

"And those are?"

"The queen lives."

"I do indeed," Scillia said. She turned to her troops. "I want the men and women who have battle experience or training up front. Children are to go into the town. Knock on every door and tell them what it is we do. Tell them: *The queen is here and where are they?*"

"And what if we meet any Garuns in town?" asked Seven sensibly.

"Run like stink," advised Sarai. "I will."

In the dining room, Sarana's instructions were brief. "Do not fight if you have neither the nerve nor the heart for it. No blame will attach to that. You have done your part already," she said to them all. "But I and my men will be out in the halls harassing what Garuns we find. You stay here and keep the barricades up."

Five maids plus the oldest of the gardeners, Halles, and several of the younger pot boys elected to remain behind, but the assistant head gardener and the miller's boy, plus three of the cooks, all of whom were still dressed in their borrowed finery, chose to go with Sarana. They were armed with Garun swords.

"Stay behind the soldiers and follow our lead," Sarana said. And like the mice in the story, they went nose to tail down one long hall after another.

It was when they heard shouting from below that Sarana glanced through the nearest window. She turned to her men, laughing. "Here we have been creeping about floor after floor, and all of our foe are hand-fighting at the gates. Come on, lads! Let's get down the stairs and give them a big surprise!"

As they raced down the great winding staircase, one of the young cooks tripped on his long robe, and almost threatening to bowl them all over. Voss picked the boy up and skinned him out of the bulky garment. He was wearing only a shirt over hose beneath.

"A fine figure of a fighting man," Voss said to him. "Stay to the rear, lad. You've scant protection in that."

But the boy did not mind him and charged after Sarana with Voss having to follow after.

They got out into the courtyard without being noticed for the Garuns—about sixty men in all—were busy trying to hold back a tidal wave of Dales folk who were pushing at the great wooden doors. The Garuns, frantically trying to shore up the gates, all had their backs to the castle.

"With me!" shouted Sarana to her men, and a few of the Garuns turned at her voice.

Just then the right hand gate fell inward and the rush of Scillia's followers came in like the flooding tide.

What Garuns were not killed in that first onslaught, were quickly captured. Sarana was everywhere, her shirt stained bright red, then black with blood.

Scillia proved able enough in the battle, but after the first minutes her heart was not in it. She knew at once that they had won and she could not bring herself to strike just for the killing. So she stood to one side and watched as the Dale folk—women even more than men—put fleeing Garuns to the sword. Tears rained down her cheeks.

This is not what I want, she thought. *This is not the way I would rule*. But she could not think how to stop them, what word would recall them to their senses. The slaughter went on till over half the Garuns were dead.

By then it was clear even to the bloodthirstiest of the Dalites that the Garuns who were left proved no threat. The killings eased to an end, and the rest of the Garuns were bound with leather ties—arms, wrists, knees, and ankles.

The infirmarers spent their time first working on the few Dales folk who had been hurt, Voss and the cook's boy among them, before they turned their attention to the Garuns.

Sarana found Scillia and kneeled before her. "My queen," she said.

Scillia shook her head, and bending down, raised Sarana

up. "Do not call me that," she whispered hoarsely. "How can I be queen now? I cannot rule over such a bloody place. I would have my brother Corrine be king."

She does not know, Sarana thought. *Someone must inform her*. And then she knew that she alone was the only one who could tell the queen.

"You must come with me, Scillia," Sarana said. "There is something you must see."

They stood in the dining room together, side by side, but not touching. Scillia no longer wept but she was rigid with sorrow. Sarana did not dare to climb the mountain of that grief.

Earlier she had sent everyone else away so that the queen might mourn by herself. She had meant to leave as well. But then Sarana could not go. Not when the queen was so very much alone.

Scillia had surprised her by weeping as much for Jemson as for Corrine.

"He died a boy still," was Scillia's only explanation. "He never had a chance to grow up."

He was a man, with a man's capacity for evil, Sarana thought. She did not say it aloud.

"But Corrie died a hero," Scillia added. Then she turned to Sarana and, quite surprisingly, smiled. "Songs will be written about him. And stories told. He will like that." She turned and said over her shoulder, "I will like that, too."

Then she walked out of the room.

The two princes were buried side by side, Jemson in his dinner finery and Corrine sewn up in a golden bag made from his favorite caftan. It was the only way to keep his parts all together. Scillia was right. There were songs made about him almost at once. Two were sung at the funeral: "Pile Them On, Boys!" and "The Death of Prince Corrine."

The dead Garuns were burned in a pyre that flamed late into the night. The Garun prisoners were long debated about, for Scillia knew they could not very well be kept in the wine cellar for long. There were simply too many of them.

"And while we could stone and mortar the window, they would always be a dangerous presence," Sarana added.

In the end their fates were decided by a council made up of Sarana, Jano, the fenmaster Goff, old Halles—Cook having declined—the harbor master of Berick, the headman of Josteen, and the boat mistress of Southport. Chained together seven in a line, the remaining Garuns were rowed out in small boats from the tiny harbor in Southport. Behind the boats large masted rafts were towed. Halfway across the water, but long before the Garun shore was in sight, the prisoners were transferred to the rafts with a flask of fresh water each and one journeycake.

"Tides and wind helping," the boat mistress said, "they can make it to shore. But chained like that—only if they work together." She smiled. "I do not know if they will manage. A Dales crew might."

Jano laughed. "Not if half were from Southport and half from Josteen."

She cocked her head at him, then broke into laughter. "Been troubled by bottom feeders, have you?" she said. She did not expect an answer.

How did it all end? How does any story end? They lived happily, they lived long, they lived ever after. And then they died. The saga of the Dales is not so different.

Scillia refused the crown. Supposedly she said, "The land has had enough blood shed in the Anna's name. It is time to take a different path."

Instead, she turned the ruling of the kingdom over to a circle of councillors. *So none is higher, none is lower*, goes the story. She was not to know it, but in this she echoed the Greena. In her own way, Scillia changed the Dales more than ever her mother had done. She returned to Selden Hame with the girls—Sarai and Seven and Tween—where she learned the Game of Wands from old Marget. In the end she played it better than any of the two-handed sisters at the Hame. None of the girls stayed on at the Hame, but when Scillia died of a lump in her breast they all returned with their own children to do her honor as their mother. And to weep at her grave.

Gadwess outlived his childless brother, becoming king of the Garuns when he was quite old. It took him five years of careful politics, but he managed a treaty with the Dales that has lasted—with only one or two minor disturbances—till this day.

Seven and Tween married a Josteen fisherman and had five children, all girls. Sarai went to Berick as a councillor for the women of the South, and lived there till she was seventy-five. She adopted three children with her blanket companion, Allema, who had once worked as as assistant gardener in the castle. They named the children Carum, Jenna, and Sil.

Sarana captained her own Riding in the north after serving a month as a farm worker for an old lady she said she owed a promise to. Voss and Malwen became her unlikely lieutenants in the Riding. They harried the remaining Garuns unmercifully till the last of them was dead, some seven years later. Voss was killed in one of the encounters. Malwen took a blow meant for Sarana during another, and though he lived, he was never quite the same after. Sarana retired from the guard to care for him till he died, cursing her heartily, though she never took that as mean-spirited. She knew how to read his eyes and they had spoken a blessing at the end. But she lived on alone after that to a ripe old age in a little house that faced the sea, tending a small cottage garden and spending hours staring across the water, as if keeping a watch out for Garun ships. She never saw Scillia again.

Jano gave up his captaincy and went to dwell in the fens where he learned enough to become a fenmaster, which surprised all the fen folk except Goff. Jano spent quiet days fishing the silvery waters, or piloting people over the hidden causeways. At last he married Goff's sister, and they had a son who went to Berick as a member of the council for a year. But he so hated the city he came back before his term was over to live the rest of his life in the fens in his parents' home.

Old Halles died the year after the princes, of a shock it was said. Cook took to drinking and frequented the wine cellar more than the kitchen. And the laughing man, who had helped rescue the young Prince Corrine from the cat—well he made a living telling stories about the family of White Jenna, some of them true and some of them false and all of them told with great good humor.

As for Jenna and Carum, it is said they are waiting in the Grove till the Dales needs them again. But if they did not come at Scillia's call, I am not sure they will come at ours.

THE MYTH:

Then Great Alta took three children and set them next to the One-Armed Queen.

"One of you is for war," quoth she. "And one is for peace. And one is for the time that is in-between."

"But which is which?" asked the children.

Great Alta smiled. "The question is never which," she said. "But why."

The Wisdoms of the Dales

A snake sheds an old skin but still he does not go skinless.
Before you make a friend, eat dirt with him.
A woman's mouth is like a spring flood. (From the Garunian)
The King should be servant to the State.
One can never repay one's debts to one's mother.
A girl is never too young for the Game.
Do not roll up your trousers before you get to the stream.
The sharper the thorn, the sweeter the rose.
Do not speak to a man's girlchild lest you come bearing a
wedding ring.
Dogs bark, but the caravan goes on.
Help first, chat later.
If you cannot swim, do not go near the water.
Never trust a cat to do a dog's job. (Garunian adage)
Sorry puts no coins in the purse.
What you give away with love, you keep.
Better a calf of one's own than a cow owned by another.
If your mouth turns into a knife, it will cut off your lips.
Let a new wind blow through an old place.
Storm in Berick, sun in Bewick.
To speak is to sow and to listen is to reap.
Do not measure a shroud before there is a corpse.
Kill once, mourn ever.
Stretch your feet according to your blanket.
Even a highest tree has an axe at its foot.

The anvil must be patient. Only the hammer can be strong. (From the Garunian)

Easier to love a dead hero than a live king.

Two sisters, two sides.

The skate and the eel do not swim the same, but they both live in the sea.

Art is inborn, craft outborn.

An hour makes a difference between the wise man and the fool.

Drink with Garuns, use a long straw.

Blood is blood no matter who sucks it.

A good shepherd tells his sheep of green grass, not grey wolves.

A knife wound heals, a tongue wound festers.

To take is not to keep.

Small keys open big doors. (From the Garunian)

A hard head hides a soft tongue. (From the Garunian)

Both the hunter and the hunted pray to a god.

The spider sits in the center of its web and entices the fly to come to it. (From the Garunian)

The further north, the greater noise. (From the Garunian)

A white ewe may have a black lamb. (From the Garunian)

You can call a rock a fish but it still cannot swim.

A rabbit cannot put its paws on the deer's horns.

Better late in the pan than never in the pot.

Many mothers are best.

All history begins between a woman's legs.

Man is wood, woman water.

Water weights wood.

Many will show you the way once your cart is turned over.

The Music of the Dales

The Two Kings

Stolidly

The one ruled East, the one ruled West,
Lonely, oh lonely, the queen rides down.
The one ruled East, the one ruled West,
And neither ruled the kingdom best,
The queen rides in the valley-o.

Ill fares the land where two are king,
Lonely, oh lonely, the queen rides down.
Ill fares the land where two are king,
For names and swords and bells do ring,
And blood flows down the valley-o.

Pynt's Lullay

Achingly

Sleep, my child, for the past is a dream,
And women do weep that it's gone.
But we shall not weep anymore for the past
For after each sleep comes the dawn.

Sleep, my child, into dawn's eager light
And wake to the song of the dove.
Forget all the dreams of the past, for the past
Is present in all of my love.

Song of the Three Mothers

With passion

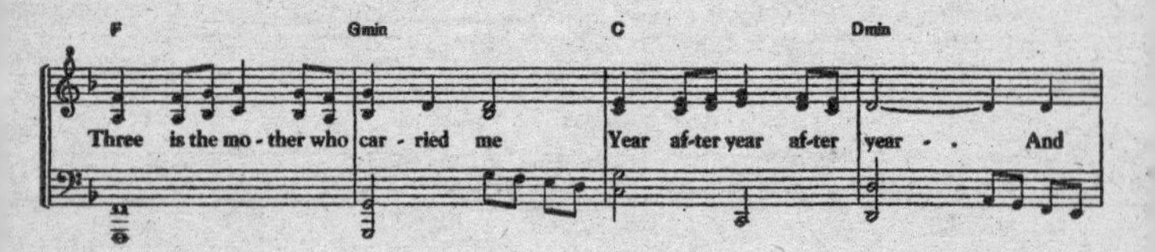

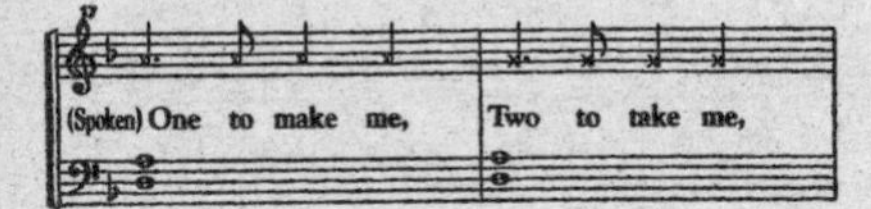

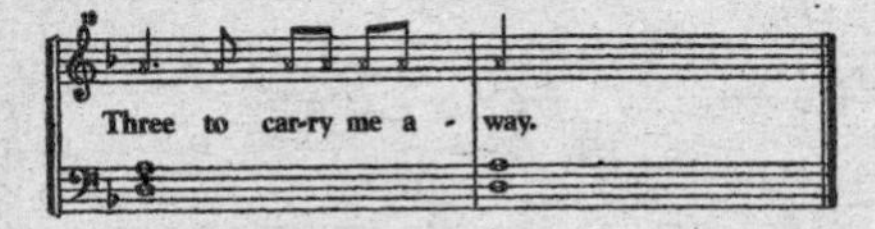

One is the mother who bred me,
A moment of passion and heat.
Two is the mother who fed me
Her blood and milk and meat.

Three is the mother who led me
Through love and pain and war.
She is the mother who's wed me
To all that is worth living for.

(Chorus) One to make me,
Two to take me,
Three to carry me away.

The Feast Song

With Spirit

Bring in the black breads, the brown breads, the gold,
Bring in the honey-sweet beer.
Bring in the onions and garlic and cloves,
Bring in the cup of good cheer.

Bring in the berries, red, purple, and black,
Bring in the caramelized candy.
Bring in the fruit pies, the cakes, and the tarts,
Bring in the possets and brandy.

(Chorus) Fast day to feast day to fast day again,
We feed down from castle to cottage.
One week we're ample with courses to spare,
Dining on venison, wild pig, and bear,
Finishing off with both apple and pear.
Next week we dine upon pottage.

The Dark Sister's Lullaby

With sweet passion

Come to me, sister, the night will be deep,
And sleep comes not easily soon.
I'll cradle you closely, my promises keep,
My night for the light of your moon.

Come to me, sister, the stars all take flight,
Come kiss me this once ere I go.
I'll cradle you carefully night after night
As I did in the dark long ago.

The Warrior's Song

In a gallop

Swords are now red that were shiny and new,
Arms that were white are now blackened and blue;
Still we are sisters and always are true,
And we will win through to the morning.

You kill the man who is fast on our track.
I kill the man who has you on your back.
We parry and thrust and we sever and hack,
We always win through to the morning.

But when we grow old and our hands lose their guile,
And we cannot kill with a casual smile,
Pray turn on me straight with your usual style
And I'll run you through, too, in the morning.

Jemmie Over the Water

With longing

He rode the wild waves to his land,
Sing Jemmie over the water,
They gave him but the back of the hand,
Oh, will ye come home to me.

He left in winter, back in spring,
Sing Jemmie over the water;
To find his sister crowned the king,
Sing Jemmie over the sea.

An' will ye take silver, will ye take gold,
Sing Jemmie over the water,
Or will ye take the throne to hold,
Oh will ye come home to me.

I neither gold nor silver make,
Sing Jemmie over the water,
But I the throne will surely take,
Sing Jemmie over the sea.

So, kill the girl upon the throne,
Sing Jemmie over the water,
And then, oh then, will I come home,
Oh I will come home to thee.

The Ballad of Corrine Lackland

Plainly

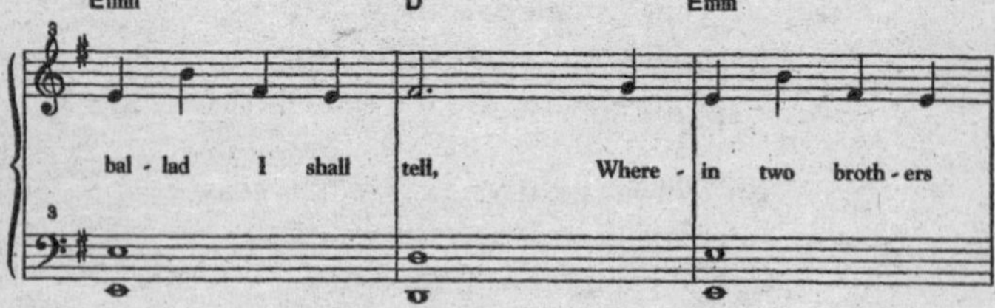

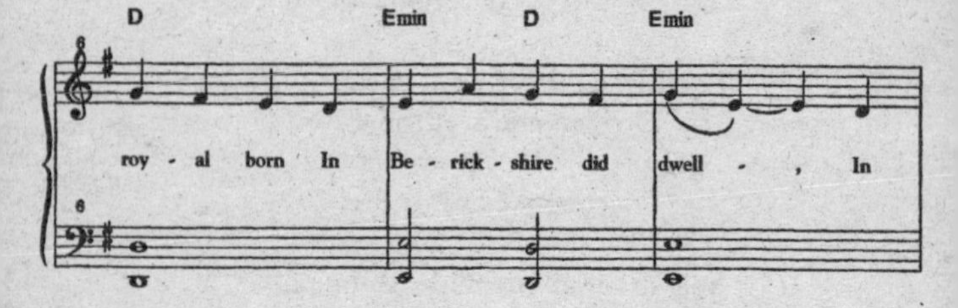

The one of them was Jem the Bold
Who fought with either hand,
The younger was Prince Corrine
Who was left with little land.

As they were drinking ale and wine
Within his brother's hall,
Prince Corrine pointed to a port
That opened in the wall.

"That green gate is to Faerieland,
Where Mother dear does dwell."
"Nay, brother," quoth the bold Jemson,
"That is the gate to hell.

"But if you're sure, my brother dear,
Then you the path shall find.
And as I am king on the throne,
I shall remain behind."

He pushed his brother through the port,
Far down Lackland did fall.
His portion was six feet of earth
And death to bear his pall.

Fen Love Song

With sweet joy

Little skin boat, so rough and so new,
Speed the boat o'er, speed the boat o'er,
Tell him I love him and that I be true.
Speed the bonnie boat o'er.

(Chorus)

Little skin boat, so taut and so trim,
Speed the boat o'er, speed the boat o'er,
Take this my token, be bringing it him,
Speed the bonnie boat o'er.

(Chorus)

If he refuses, I'll jump in my boat,
Speed the boat o'er, speed the boat o'er,
Over the fenway to sink or to float,
Speed the bonnie boat o'er.

(Chorus)

Journeycake Ho!

With a bounce

This wasn't a trip I was planning to make
As I fled through the door with some good journeycake.
But my horse was all saddled, so off I did ride
Thankful I still had my head and my hide.
Journeycake ho! Journeycake ho!
Make it and take it wherever you go.
Travel on water, on ice, or on snow,
It will keep you filled up till the morning.

The master was after me, likewise the noose,
I had to go quickly and lightly and loose.
So I grabbed what I could and I let the rest be;
I didn't have much—but at least I had me.
Journeycake ho! Journeycake ho!
Make it and take it wherever you go.
And if you've no money, you'll still have the dough
To keep you filled up in the morning.